CHRISTOPHER KENNER

Codename: Marvel

Nazec Chronicles: Book One

First edition

This book was professionally typeset on Reedsy.
Find out more at reedsy.com

To my beautiful Bee. None of this would have ever come to fruition if it wasn't for your love, support, and your never-ending faith in me.

Prologue:

orbin Kent could still remember the day as if it were yesterday. September 11th, 2001 had started off like any other day for him as a sophomore in high school. Not long into his first-period class, one of his classmates came up to him and, completely out of the blue, pointed out matter-of-factly that a plane had crashed into the World Trade Center. Corbin, who was much less than a fan of this particular class member, and who didn't immediately realize what the World Trade Center was, somewhat coldly responded, "Who cares?" As far as he could imagine, someone had made a navigational error and smashed their single-engine Cessna into the side of a building and broke a few windows. It wasn't until shortly after this exchange, that he came to the full realization of the gravity of the situation.

His teacher scrambled into the room from his office, which was attached off to the left of the large main part of the classroom. Without saying a word, he turned on the television at the front of the room and Corbin felt his heart stop. The image he saw wasn't anything what he had expected! The World Trade Center...that was the "Twin Towers!" He was far more familiar with the latter term, and it wasn't until the news coverage had come up that he connected the dots and immediately felt sheepish to the fact that he had reacted in a far underwhelming manner when his peer had spoken to him earlier. Corbin watched in horror as a gigantic plume of smoke billowed from the north tower and news feeds followed the chaos of civilians and emergency responders scrambling to and from Ground Zero.

This...this couldn't be happening. It was all surreal. Corbin couldn't wrap his head completely around what was unfolding before him and could only begin to reason that maybe this all was some sort of accident. Maybe there was something wrong with the instrumentation on the airliner and the pilots couldn't correct their flight path in time to avoid the collision. It was a stretch, but it was the only sort of potentially logical thought that his mind could grasp at the time. He tried to hold onto that thought, that minuscule thread of optimism, per se, until there was a sudden exclamation from one of the news anchors. A quick pan of a camera was able to catch the split second before a *second* airliner plowed into the side of the south tower, erupting into a colossal fireball. Any other explanation instantly left his mind at this point, and he knew that this was all planned. His suspicions were confirmed soon after this conclusion when reports came flooding in that another aircraft had struck the Pentagon as well as a fourth was brought down in a field in Pennsylvania, its intended target: The White House.

Whatever had been happening that fateful day, or whatever had been planned for that day, was put on indefinite hold as Corbin, his entire school, and the nation, sat fixated on any television close by and watched in terror as the damaged skyscrapers burned, groaned, and eventually fell in a crescendo of chaos, wreckage, death, and complete disarray. He could still recall one of his teachers relaying the fact that nearby cars to the World Trade Center were exploding because of the catastrophic concussion from those collapsing towers, and that these car explosions had first led some to believe that they were just another facet to an even bigger coordinated terror attack. As each second ticked by during the day, Corbin could feel his fear being replaced with a new emotion: fury. He felt pure, unadulterated anger and hatred towards those who were responsible for the deaths of all those innocent people, in the planes, in the towers, the first responders, and even those who were bystanders too close to the towers to be able to get away.

In the blink of an eye, Corbin had made a resolution that would forever change him. He was going to enlist in the military and make these murderous dogs pay! The United States would surely respond to this attack in kind, especially knowing who was responsible for all of this as al-Qaeda messages soon followed in news reports, taking credit for the mass murder with an almost gloating fashion. That was the last straw. There was no other solution. Just as these murderers were responsible for so much death and terror, he was going to be the bringer of death and terror to them. As soon as he was out of high school, he was going to enlist in the Marine Corps, they being the first and foremost branch that caught his eye amongst all the recruiters to show up at his school. He was going to be one of, "The few, the proud," kicking down doors and putting bullets in the faces of al-Qaeda members and, if he could have it his way, taking Bin Laden's head clean off his shoulders bare-handed.

The following months after the attacks were filled with essays, poems, journal entries, and any other literary outlet Corbin could utilize, to illustrate how he was dead set on ensuring he was going to be responsible for making any and all terrorists pay for hurting the country he felt so much more patriotism for. It was, in fact, one of these essays that he figured was the reason for him being called to the counseling office one morning during his English class. His English teacher had always been a fan of his writing; however, when he was summoned from his class, he feared that maybe one of his recent essays had been a little too over-the-top with patriotism or violence, or whatever the case may be. Standing up from his desk, he quietly packed his books into his backpack and walked, embarrassed and with is head down, out of the classroom and shuffled his way to the counselor's office, his mind weaving all sorts of potential scenarios, most of which ended with him getting expelled. He hadn't anticipated, nor could he have ever anticipated what—-or rather who—waited for him.

Stepping into the waiting area of the counseling office, one of the several school counselors slipped out of her office and greeted Corbin warmly. To his suspicion, she didn't seem to be greeting him in a patronizing way as he had expected— like she was trying to keep a friendly demeanor while escorting him into her office so he could be put in a straitjacket and hauled off to the loony bin or something. (Which was one of the more prominent imagined scenarios he had). Taking slow and incredulous steps, he followed her to her office and stepped inside. The counselor stayed outside of the doorway and said, "I'll let you two get acquainted, just let me know if you

3

need anything." '*Oh crap,*' Corbin thought, '*I'm in for it now if even* **she** *doesn't want to be here for whatever is about to happen.*' What made him worry more was her comment as she shut the door quietly behind him. Was the invitation for him, or for whomever sat at the desk behind him? Corbin didn't turn around right away; rather, he stood and stared at the closed office door for what felt like a few hours of silence but was probably only a minute or two.

He didn't turn around until he heard a man clear his throat politely. Well, there wasn't any escaping it now, he might as well just turn around and face whatever fate awaited him in the swivel desk chair behind him. Corbin noticed immediately as he turned that the visitor was most definitely NOT who he had expected. As he turned, he first noticed a digital camouflage pattern in his peripherals. It was one that he didn't recognize. There were Velcro patches on the shoulder pockets on the sleeves of the man's uniform. On the left sleeve, it was a patch depicting an eagle, wings spread, holding a missile in one foot, and an olive branch in the other. On the right sleeve, there was an American flag, (that looked like it was facing backwards), and a patch that depicted two crossed swords and a smaller patch above it that read, "Mountain." The patches on his chest read, "Easton," on his right breast, "U.S. Army," on his left breast, and a square patch in the middle of his chest had two subdued black stars in a vertical configuration. His hair was cropped short, military-style, and graying at his temples. He was smiling kindly as Corbin gawked at him for a moment, trying to fathom what was going on. Corbin could feel his heart racing as he looked the man in the eye, his blue eyes glimmering behind his square glasses. At this very moment, he was looking at a two-star general from the United States Army! What was going on?!

In that moment of elation, Corbin also felt a little bit of disappointment. All this time, he had planned on enlisting in the Marines, and had imagined himself as a Marine so much that it sometimes felt more like a memory rather than a dream. It was a bit of a letdown to him that General Easton wasn't a Marine general here for him. In fact, he was one hundred percent certain that he had said in practically all of his English essays that he was going to be a Marine, a "Leatherneck," a "Jarhead," and if his teacher had anything to do with referring a military leader to him, she would have had to be completely dense not to get that. Corbin's brow furrowed a little as he continued to eye the general who just sat patiently and quietly, his hands folded, fingers interlocked, on the desktop.

"In the interest of your legs getting fatigued, you're more than welcome to sit down as you size me up, Corbin," General Easton said.

Corbin was taken aback that not only had this man addressed him but spoke to him by name. Okay, sure, he most definitely got that info from the counselor. Corbin slid into one of the seats that stood across from the desk, setting his backpack on the ground next to him and not taking his eyes off this man, his mind reeling with questions. Easton seemed to know what he was thinking, which was also very off-putting to Corbin.

"Now, you're probably wondering what's going on here," General Easton started.

"Well, yeah," Corbin responded sarcastically. He didn't mean to sound discourteous, but his confusion and intrigue were overpowering his diplomacy. Nevertheless, it didn't seem to affect the general, who continued without skipping a beat.

"My name is General James Easton. I am the state commander for the Special Warfare Operations and Response Division, or SWORD."

Corbin's face contorted again into disbelief and confusion as he looked over Easton's uniform once again, "...but your uniform says 'U.S. Army,' so what's the truth?"

General Easton smirked and chuckled a little bit at Corbin's perception, "Ah, yes, well, the military branch I work for likes to maintain a particular level of," he paused for a second, as if to carefully choose his next words, "anonymity. As such, we must assume the appearance of a branch of the military that this nation, and the world, are familiar with."

It didn't seem to make a whole lot of sense at first, but it piqued Corbin's interest. He sat forward in his seat, elbows on his knees, and did his best to sound like he wasn't as nervous as he was. "I'm listening."

Easton smiled at his response, "Well, due to growing terrorist concerns over the years, the United States and her Allies began a counter-terror organization that is both multi-national, as well as multi-organizational. The Special Warfare Operations and Response Division is a clandestine military organization that has been in the development and testing stages for some time now, however, in response to the 9/11 attacks, the Division has been put into full effect and is currently needing recruits. Your English teacher seemed to be quite impressed with your literary rhetoric, most especially regarding your patriotism as well as determination to bring retribution to those responsible for the attacks."

Now it was seeming a little far-fetched to Corbin, and, uncharacteristic to him at that time, he called this general out on what he assumed was a bunch of BS. "Right, so you're telling me that some secret counter-terror organization was contacted by a high school English teacher in regard to me, some insignificant sophomore?"

The general seemed bemused by Corbin's rebuttal. "Well, insignificant or not, SWORD has its ways of gathering information, particularly regarding individuals we feel might be a good addition to our ranks. To say that your English teacher, or even your school counselor, know about us, let alone contacted us, is very inaccurate and, truthfully, laughable. However, your patriotic and military fervor came up on our radar quite some time ago." He smirked a little at his analogy, as if what he said had a bit of truth regarding it. Corbin imagined for a split second like there was really some giant radar that somehow tracked people by their resolve to join the military, but it sounded fantastic and impossible, just like SWORD.

"You're telling me that this, SWORD, has been keeping an eye on me and thinks that I would be a good match for them? What kind of 'Big Brother,' crap is all this? I mean, I know people are paranoid that the government is watching them and stuff like that, but this takes the tinfoil hat-wearing to a whole new level. What are you going to tell me next, that you also need my help guarding the gates at Area 51 because the aliens are threatening to get out?"

Easton smirked thoughtfully without ever taking his eyes off Corbin. He tilted his head to the side slightly as he watched the sarcastic high schooler. "Well, if you'd like to guard aliens, you're more than welcome to choose that after Basic, however you seem to be more interested in a career of killing terrorists," General Easton answered calmly, still eyeing Corbin.

Corbin was taken off guard. Did his sarcasm just get met with sarcasm? It's not like it didn't ever happen, but it didn't seem to happen with adults, especially ones who were as old as General Easton, however old he was. Nevertheless, there he was with a graying general who just met his quip with a bit of his own sarcasm and left him feeling defenseless. At this point, what was he supposed to do, meet Easton with some more sarcasm and see just how long he could get this "battle," to keep going? To his better judgement, he let the comment go and chuckled a little.

"Are you serious?"

General Easton smiled and nodded slightly, "About killing terrorists, at least. Last time I checked, Area 51 is an Air Force installation, so if you are still interested in guarding aliens, I can have you in touch with one of their recruiters."

Corbin raised his eyebrow. He felt as if Easton had bested him in a game of wits, and he was the one known in a lot of his classes as the one with the edge on humor or wit. Nevertheless, the prospect of serving in the military was far beyond compelling. As far as he was concerned, if there were some way to leave school at this very moment and enlist, he would have done it. The difficult part of that was, as many times as he had spoken to the Marine recruiters that had come to his school, it was unavoidably evident that they didn't take guys his age, and even if they did, Corbin would have the insurmountable task of convincing his parents to sign the consent form that was needed to permit someone under the age of eighteen to enter a government contract. They already were pretty skeptical about letting him join the Marines, which he had talked to them about on more than one occasion. It wasn't anything about his parents not liking the military or being any degree unpatriotic, it was that they *really* didn't like the prospect of their son joining the military in such a tumultuous time, let alone joining a branch that would practically guarantee that he would deploy to a combat zone the minute he finished Basic Training.

Once again, General Easton seemed to be aware of his thoughts. "I am

7

aware that enlisting in the military is a bit more difficult for someone at your age, however, under the circumstances of the formation and mobilization of SWORD, certain legal requirements are, how shall I say... bypassed? When it comes to your being too young to enlist without your parents' approval, we can circumvent those legalities and have you on the next shipment of recruits to Basic Combat Training. I'll have you know, that despite your departure from high school, the Division will make sure that you complete your schooling and obtain your diploma. We don't want any dummies in our ranks." Easton smirked a little at the last remark.

Corbin's heart had sped up to the point that it felt like it was going to burst out of his chest. What was once fear that had gripped him was now excitement, almost too much for him to contain. He stood on the threshold of his life's dream, all he needed to do was take the first step towards the rest of his life. Nevertheless, there was still a great deal of doubt and fear mixed in with all his emotions. Sure, SWORD may have the means to go around some legal hurdles that would normally keep him from getting into the military, however, what sort of means did they have regarding convincing his parents that what he was doing was a good idea? Well, not even that it was a good idea, but rather, something like convincing them not to be so angry with him that they disowned him, or something? At this point, Corbin had already made up his mind as to what he was going to do, but his brain was still addressing legitimate concerns that were still in play. The biggest one was his parents.

"General, I don't want to sound like I am just diving into this without thinking, but I'm in, one hundred percent. But" for some reason, he felt like he needed to choose his next words wisely, "what about my parents? They aren't too big of fans of my infatuation with the military, and I'm sure they aren't going to be all right with me just coming in and saying to them, 'Hey, joining a secret military group and there isn't anything you can do about it, Bye!' My dad would probably just kill me just to make sure I didn't do anything that he would think was stupid."

Once again, Corbin's mind wandered in imagined outcomes, one of which was General Easton simply assuring that his parent's wouldn't be an issue, and then black-clad, Special Operations-esque soldiers kicking down the door to his house and offing his mom and dad and making it look like some kind of accident or something. Corbin loved his parents, and got along with them well, generally, it was just the subject of military service that was a sensitive subject to them and had been the cause of quite a few bitter arguments between them. There had been, in fact, a period when Corbin had refused to even speak to his parents when they had refused to give consent to his enlisting before he was eighteen. Probably not the best way to handle rejection and promote their support of his decision, but his stubborn, teenage mind had decided that that was the best course of action for that situation.

General Easton let out a soft sigh, slight smirk still on his face. "Well, I can come with you to speak with them, however, I need you to understand, that the circumstances of SWORD's secrecy, we would be telling your parents a much different story compared to what I have told you here. I don't know how keen you are about lying to your parents, but- "

"I don't think that will be a problem, sir," Corbin quickly answered. After all, he was a high school kid. How many times had he already "bent" the truth to his parents in some way?

"All right, I'm in," he said resolutely, "Whatever you can manage with my parents, which would have to be nothing short of a miracle, I would appreciate it."

"Let me guess, your parents aren't against military service, but they are more against the timing of your desire to enlist as well as reluctant to sign any sort of consent form for you?"

Corbin was a little confused now. He didn't remember sharing anything specific about his parents and what their stand was on the whole subject, but Easton had just spoken about it as if he had sat in on the countless conversations he had gone through with his mom and dad. Just as he had started to feel like this all wasn't some sort of dream; Corbin began to get that suspicion once again. He subtly pinched his leg to make sure he could feel it. He didn't know if that was actually something that one did when in a dream, and if it certifiably confirmed or denied if someone was dreaming, but he figured he would give it a shot. Yes, it hurt, so, based on anything he had seen or heard on TV, he wasn't dreaming. How in the world did Easton seem to know so much about him?

"To say that your parents were the first to have concerns regarding SWORD would be a lie," Easton started with a slight smirk, "so I'm sure there's something I can do to make sure you can take your first steps in the military with us."

Corbin felt his heart flutter in his chest. If what he said was true, then that meant it was as good as done when it came to him enlisting. He clenched his fists with excitement in his lap and bounced his legs with a shared enthusiasm. General Easton simply looked at him with a quiet smile for a moment before he spoke once again.

"How about you leave your home address with me, and I will give your parents a visit? Perhaps we can talk this evening?"

"Definitely!" Corbin produced a pen from his pocket quickly and scribbled his address on a sticky note he took from the desk. Handing it to General Easton, he did his best to keep his hand from shaking with the emotions he felt.

General Easton took the note and folded it once, slipping it into his breast pocket, "Thank you, Corbin. Between now and when we meet again, let's just keep this all on the down-low, if you don't mind? You know, the whole concept of anonymity and such?"

"Yes sir," Corbin responded quickly.

"Excellent. Dismissed."

Corbin stood up resolutely and left the office without saying another word. He was so lost in his elation and the thoughts running through his mind that he wasn't sure if anyone said anything to him as he headed back to his class. As a matter of fact, he couldn't really remember the rest of the school day, he was so distracted by what was ahead of him. He hoped that General Easton was to be the key between himself and the foreboding and proverbial gate that was his parents.

Well, to say the initial introduction of General Easton to his parents was awkward would be a gross understatement. His father, (Randall), was less than thrilled to see a soldier at his door, and even less entertained when he found out that Corbin had been speaking with General Easton before he had ever shown up at their home. His demeanor was one of distrust and disgust, as if Corbin had been plotting something behind his back for years that had finally come to the surface. His mother, (Regina), wore mostly an expression of worry and concern, one that said she doubted her son had any idea what sort of trouble he was getting into. Despite the obvious signs of animosity in his father's face, Randall let Easton in, and even offered to have him stay for dinner as they discussed the elephant in the room.

When dinner had first started, his dad hadn't said much, if anything at all, to General Easton directly, but something had changed just enough to seemingly permit him to treat their visitor as if he were a human being and not some foreign threat come to take their eldest son to inevitably die.

"So, tell me what you are all about, General," Randall said, in a somewhat interrogatory manner.

General Easton, who had seen far more terrifying things in his experience in the military, was completely unfazed by how Corbin's parents were reacting to him and spoke with confidence and poise as if they had already accepted whatever it was that he was going to present to them. He calmly ate his food, keeping most of his answers short and to the point, showing he was aware that using too many words would make him less credible to Mr. and Mrs. Kent. He set his fork down, clearing his throat at this question.

"Yes, sir. I am a general of the United States Army and currently the dean of a military academy based out of Fort Benning, Georgia. We were recently established in 1998 to provide an introductory course of training for those interested in enlisting in the military. Generally, our cadets begin training in their sophomore year of high school and continue each summer until they graduate from the academy by the age of eighteen. At that point, they can decide whether a commitment to the armed forces is something they would like to pursue."

"So, he wouldn't be enlisting in any sort of military contract before he was eighteen, right?" Corbin's dad still seemed incredulous about it all, like there was something he wasn't being told, which was true.

"No, sir, not at all. The entire program is like a," Easton paused for a second, as if to choose an accurate term, "military summer camp for teenagers. We provide uniforms, room and board, transportation, the whole experience. Seeing as Corbin here has such a fascination with military service, it seems that something like my program would be right up his alley for the time being. He could get a feel for what the military would be like, without any of the commitment or risk of life, and you would have the peace of mind that he isn't off gallivanting somewhere mischievous all summer. Then, before the start of the new school year, we will bring him home and he can continue his studies until the next summer, and so on until he graduates."

From one of the chest pockets on his uniform, Easton produced a pair of pamphlets that he handed to Randall and Regina. They looked so professional and legitimate that Corbin was almost convinced that he was going to the *School for Warfare, Operations, Reconnaissance, and Defense* rather than enlisting in the Special Warfare Operations and Response Division. Ah, they even recycled the SWORD acronym. Nice! The reading material seemed to have enough information to soften Randall's demeanor a little the longer he looked through the pamphlet. After a moment, he looked at Corbin over the top of the paper.

"How long have you known about this?"

"Just earlier today, Dad," Corbin said, which was true, he had only met General Easton this morning at school.

"And how did you know about it, Corbin?"

"Well, I didn't really until today."

"We have been networking with high schools all around the country, suggesting to counselors and other faculty that they keep an eye out for students they think would enjoy and benefit from the program. At least until we can establish a solid marketing plan and execute it to the general public. Corbin had written a few essays in his English class that got the attention of his teacher, in a good way, and his work was submitted to us as, in essence, an essay for admissions. Corbin is quite the literary and has a very strong conviction for serving his country. Now, considering his age, it isn't very advisable to get him all worked up over something like a military commitment and have him dive into something he may not even like. Military contracts are quite impossible to get out of once your name is on the dotted line, and it would be very unfortunate for him if he ended up hating everything in military service then getting deployed overseas to a very dangerous combat zone, which the probability of deployment is almost guaranteed with the current situation in the Middle East."

Corbin's mom shifted in her seat as if uncomfortable. She knew that her son was impulsive when it came to things he was excited about, and he would be the prime candidate for a recruiter to rope him into a contract with little to no effort. She looked at Corbin and then back to Easton. "Would we be able to see him while he is gone?"

"As part of the experience, which is geared towards being as accurate to the real thing, he wouldn't be able to have visitors during most of his time there, however there are graduation ceremonies where family members are invited, and the usual forms of communication are open to our cadets just like they are for recruits going through Basic Training."

What his mom and dad weren't quite aware of was that recruits could write letters, just like in Basic. Not particularly the fastest form of communication, but a nuance, really. Corbin was sure that, if his parents bought off on this whole thing, there were going to be some details they found out that were really going to piss them off, but it would be too late for them to do anything. Subversive as it may be, he felt like this was the only way he was going to be able to be a soldier without having to wait until he was no longer under the guardianship of his parents. He was only fourteen right now, having started school in a different state and then moving to their current home, which had different start times, so he was a year younger than everyone in his grade, meaning that he would have had to wait an entire year after graduating high school to be old enough to enlist on his own, and he sure didn't want to wait that long.

Randall glanced at his wife as if he were a little more comfortable with the idea being presented, and for a moment, Corbin felt like the thing was in the bag. However, he felt like the air was leaking out of his lungs slowly and painfully as his father spoke.

"We will need a little bit of time to think this over. Is there a way that we can get in touch with you once we have had some time to talk about it?"

Easton smiled a half smile as if he completely expected this to be the response he'd receive. Generally speaking, parents would use this as a deflection tactic to push the entire subject aside as if to entertain the possibility of accepting but already having decided against it. Corbin was aware of this ploy, as he had seen it many times with other propositions that he had put towards his parents, like the competitive off-road tour he had been invited to be a spotter for a contestant, or the several different occasions he had told them that he wanted to join the military. However, there was a sense of knowing in General Easton's eyes that suggested that Corbin may, in fact, get what he was hoping for. Corbin prayed that was the case. Otherwise, this opportunity to fulfill his dream would come and go in the same fashion as others, with a passive word to think about it, and then fading into oblivion when it was no longer discussed. Corbin knew that whenever this happened, it was no use trying to bring it back up, because it would be dismissed just as easily as it had been originally, and that would only frustrate him more and make him resent his parents further than he did whenever they did this.

"I have a card that I can give you, and the contact information for the school, as well as my office, is on the literature there, " Easton responded, nodding towards the pamphlet that Randall still held, "May I ask, is there a time frame I can give you before following up? I'd prefer not to be a bother; however, I do need to make sure I am pursuing only potential leads. As you are in the sales business, Mr. Kent, I'm sure that you understand."

Once again, the general seemed privy of information that Corbin couldn't remember having provided, or in this case, having been discussed during dinner. Yes, it was true, his father was a sales representative for a major pharmaceutical company but, when did they ever talk about that? Or did they? Was that information someone could just look up on the internet? He would have to do a little personal research on that later.

Though, on the surface, Randall didn't seem phased by the knowledge this general had about his employment, something flickered behind his eyes, and a slight lump formed in his throat. It seemed highly unlikely that the dean of a military school would have the means, or even need them, to know the occupation of individuals, specifically the parents of those whom he sought to enlist, but it did add an edge for him. Randall felt taken aback, as if someone had just found out a secret he had been hiding for years. Granted, what he did for a living wasn't some big secret, however, he didn't go around broadcasting to anyone who could hear what he did for work. Nevertheless, here was someone who he had never met, and with whom he was, at least, pretty sure he hadn't told about his career, pointing that very fact out to him in casual conversation.

'He is a government employee,' Randall thought to himself, 'and the government has access to practically everything they feel they have business to know.' However, then came up the question of, "need to know," if that was even really a thing. That term was tossed around so easily by non-government personnel that it was difficult to know if that was even a reality or not, and if it was, what it meant. Randall felt, at least in this situation, someone in General Easton's position didn't really have an actual need to know what he did for a living, if any of that made sense, which it did in his mind. Then again, maybe the government had a much more in-depth reach than he could imagine, or that they let on.

Still, unnerved by the moment, Randall nodded cordially and forced a smile. "Of course. I would say, if you don't hear back from us in," he looked to his wife, "three days, you can give us a call."

Corbin did his best not to roll his eyes. He had seen this act so many times now that he knew all too well that his parents didn't have any intention of discussing this matter, let alone even getting back to Easton to tell him no. To add insult to injury, did his parents really think that their son was going to forget about this all within three days? He had never been so close to enlistment in his life; he could practically taste it. Yet here his mom and dad were, setting the stage to ghost Easton and move on as if Corbin didn't have the attention span to remember something like this a mere seventy-two hours later. The more he thought about that, the more he wanted to throw his plate at his dad's face. Also, did they not think that General James Easton of the United States Army, (as far as they knew), wasn't going to follow up with them after those three days if he didn't hear from them? The problem Corbin could see with this all was that his dad was a salesman as well, so he was sure to be aware of most, if not all, of the "counter-sales" tactics and be bound to employ any and all of them to make this situation go away. Randall and Regina Kent had never been interested in letting their son enlist in the military, and were bound to show their disapproval even if he were to enlist when he was of legal age to do so on his own, so why would they even bother to entertain the possibility of SWORD, the "school?"

There was an awkward moment of silence before Randall spoke, "If Corbin were to go to this school, what would be the cost of tuition?"

'Oh sure, dad,' Corbin thought impatiently, 'make it about money so you can shoot it down even faster than waiting around for three days.' He didn't know if it was audible or not, but Corbin heard himself grumble. Randall didn't acknowledge it, so it might not have been.

Corbin looked to Easton, realizing that this might be the nail in the coffin of this proposal. If it wasn't already dead, it certainly would be the moment any answer other than, "completely free," came as the answer. If they already didn't like this whole military school idea, they definitely weren't going to like **paying** to have their son do it.

The general sat for only a moment, as if to ponder the possibility of a better answer than what the actual tuition would cost. Despite the short pause, he didn't seem to miss a beat at all as he spoke. "I can't imagine that the matter of money is anything that you would need to be worried about, Mr. Kent. However, I am certain that I could have a full-ride scholarship awarded to Corbin based off his school essays alone. He has a very deep desire to serve in the armed forces and to exact retribution to those responsible for the recent September 11th attacks. I honestly haven't seen a candidate more suited to this program as your son is."

There was a sincerity to the answer that surprised Randall. He knew that flattery and compliments that were well-placed in a conversation could tip the scales of a sales pitch, but the way this Easton said the last sentence, it seemed even **he** was convinced that his son would do well and wasn't just trying to blow smoke up his . . . well, you know. Generally speaking, a good sales pitch has some truth, as well as some flattery and little white lies, so to speak, to sway someone the way you intended them to. However, this General Easton character seemed to just put things as straightforward as he could, and didn't waste time on needless conversation, coercion, or flowery presentation. That was what put Randall off guard; the fact that there didn't seem to be some sort of ulterior motive to this whole "SWORD" recruitment. Everything seemed to be in order, and nothing about it seemed too good to be true to the point that it was obvious truths were being omitted.

Corbin wasn't sure if his dad was trying to make the long, awkward silence even longer and more awkward with the way he just sat there, a blank look on his face, as if someone had just pressed pause on him. He was certain that it hadn't been all but a few seconds of silence, but it sure felt like it was drawing out to be hours long. He didn't want to seem too urgent, or intent toward anything, especially enlistment, so he kept quiet, hoping that his not contributing to the uncomfortable tone of the conversation was doing more good than harm, or at the very least, just not making things worse. He resolved mentally that he shouldn't say something stupid, as he tended to do whenever he was nervous, or excited about something. He was never a good verbal communicator, preferring written correspondence over anything else. It was much easier to be rejected when the person wasn't standing right in front of you to make or break the whole situation and see you feel dejected and embarrassed if the answer was in the negative.

Corbin looked to General Easton to see how he was handling what felt like a hostage negotiation, rather than a discussion about future career options. As uncomfortable as the entire experience felt for him, Easton didn't seem to be affected by it one bit. The general sat calmly, eating casually during pauses and keeping a somewhat expressionless, partially smirking demeanor like he was confident that he was keeping the upper hand in the situation as well as giving the non-verbal message of, "You don't scare me." Corbin glanced back and forth between his dad and General Easton, feeling like he was watching the effects of an unstoppable force slamming head-on into an immovable object. At this point, he had no idea how this was going to play out. To ease the tension that he felt, he took a sip of his water and made it look like he was maybe sort of interested in his dinner.

It was Randall who finally spoke, a small hint of annoyance in his voice. "As good as it all sounds, I think we are still going to need a few days to talk things over, General." Randall didn't even really know why he felt bugged about this all. Maybe it was because this general was making it excruciatingly difficult to just reject him and make him go away. He was like a little kid selling cookies who just didn't seem to understand the subtleties of being told "no," without actually hearing the word. Truthfully, that was what he was trying to do the entire evening, but General Easton had a legitimate solution or rebuttal to everything that he tried to throw at him. He could see from the expression on Corbin's face that this was something he was very, VERY, interested in, probably more so than anything he had ever tried to convince him of previously. He didn't want to smash his son's dreams in one painful act by just flat out telling this man that they weren't interested, but he also tried to think of how else he would get this recruiter out of his home. When he couldn't think of any other "diplomatic" way to do it, he just opted to close the door on the subject once and for all. It was definitely going to burst Corbin's bubble, to say the least, but he would get over it. He could obsess over girls or something more age-appropriate in Randall's mind, rather than trying to focus on possible post-high school career options.

Randall sat back in his chair with a sigh, gently tossing the pamphlet onto the tabletop, it landing on his fork with a soft, "clink." Regina appeared to know what was coming up, judging from her husband's body language, and felt a wave of relief come over her, as well as a pang of regret and guilt for not really entertaining an idea that her son seemed to be very genuinely interested in. She looked to Corbin, who was glancing at his food, then back up to General Easton, waiting for her husband's inevitable response.

"I apologize, General, sir," Randall started, "but this doesn't seem like something that we would be interested in having our son participate in."

Forget feeling like someone had sucked the wind out of his sails, it felt like someone had blasted the masts off, riddled him full of holes, sunk him, raised him back up, and sunk him again. Of course, he didn't **really** think that his parents were going to buy into this all, but at the same time, there was a shred of hope that maybe they would be okay to entertain the idea, and he was pretty certain that he had held onto that shred of hope a lot harder than he should have, knowing the snowball's chance in Hell that his whole proposition had. He felt immediate resentment towards his father and wanted to jump across the table and stab him in the eye with his fork. The level of betrayal he felt at that moment was far beyond words could describe, and he could feel tears beginning to build behind his eyes, but he clenched his jaw and held them back, not wanting to look emotional in front of a soldier.

Evidently, General Easton wasn't swayed by what Randall Kent just said. He smiled and tilted his head to the side as he spoke. "With all due respect, sir, you did originally state that you would think about this for the next three days before contacting me with a decision. Seeing as it has been only a minute or so, I will keep the timer running and allow the remaining seventy-one hours and..." he glanced at his watch as if to gauge the remaining time, "let's say fifty-eight minutes, to elapse before I am able to accept any final decision. With that being said, I hope that it is okay to contact you on your mobile phone at the end of that time to confirm what you have decided?"

Corbin was flabbergasted. He had heard of not taking "no" for an answer, but Easton seemed to take that to an entirely new level he had never seen before. Of course, he didn't share his father's sales abilities, so this all could have been well within whatever normal parameters for a sales pitch were, but he was astonished that General Easton had just taken his father's "no," and returned it with a "no." He couldn't imagine that would make his dad very happy, so all he could do was turn and watch how his father would react to it all.

Randall was blown away. Immediately, his mind began to rush through all the assumed, unwritten laws of sales, trying to cross-reference something in his mind that could prove Easton had violated some rule of engagement. Unfortunately, there wasn't anything that came to mind other than Easton having not accepted his attempt to shoot down this whole military school idea. Once again, he buried his emotions so as not to show any signs of all the annoyance he felt, before replying, aiming to go with a diplomatic rejection.

He was about to speak when Easton interjected.

"Now, I don't expect an answer from you right away, I think three days is more than reasonable to consider something like this, and I appreciate your time and this meal together; however, I believe it is time for me to go. I look forward to hearing from you. Thank you, Mr. and Mrs. Kent."

As General Easton stood, he shook both Randall's and Regina's hands, took his dishes to the sink, and then turned towards the door. He only took a couple of steps before pausing and turning back to face the three Kents, who were still sitting at the table. "If you don't mind, may Corbin see me to the door?"

Randall looked somewhat bewildered at first at the request, but then nodded his consent to Corbin, who reluctantly stood up and accompanied Easton to the front door. It almost felt like some sort of torture having to do it, like his dad was making him prolong the inevitable leaving of General Easton and his never coming back again, as well as the idea of ever getting into the military. It stung especially hard this time because of how close he seemed to have gotten, in his mind, to being on the first plane out of town to fulfill his dream. Now, with this, he wondered if it was even worth having the dream at all, when his parents were there to stymie his ambitions. Whatever, just another lost opportunity thanks to his friggin' parents.

As they reached the front door, General Easton turned back to Corbin before stepping out. "Would you mind walking me to my vehicle?"

Corbin had hoped that maybe there was some "Hail Mary," sort of tactic that Easton was keeping until the end of this evening. He had envisioned some kind of response or argument the general would use in some sort of come-from-behind movie style victory over his parents and win them over to the whole idea of SWORD. So, hearing him make this request just made his heart sink to his feet. He nodded wordlessly and stepped out of the door, shutting it behind them. The slow shuffle towards the dark, government-issued sedan was one of staggering defeat, in Corbin's mind, and each step felt like it was even heavier than the last. By the time they had gotten to the car, Easton opened the car door and started to get in, before pausing for a moment.

"I will follow up with your parents in seventy-two hours. Understood?"

"Yes, sir," Corbin answered in a dejected tone.

General Easton looked around as if to make sure they were the only ones within hearing distance, and then leaned a little closer to Corbin, "You think you can be ready to go in forty-eight?"

Chapter One

The September 11th attacks had changed a lot more than just the New York City skyline and the patriotism and morale of the American people. It had also prompted many legislative changes; many that were known by the public, at one time or another, and others that managed to stay hidden from mainstream media, such as facets of the 2001 USA Patriot Defense Act. Its focus was to increase the effective nature of both law enforcement and military organizations regarding counter-terrorism responses and prevention. Anyone with a television or a radio was almost immediately aware of the enactment of this legislation and its aim to keep another 9/11 from happening as well as to track down terrorists and their cells in places one wouldn't have previously thought was possible, such as in their own country or even neighborhood. Of course, as there are objections to legislative actions from either side of the aisle, there was already growing unease and upheaval considering some of its allowances, such as surveillance of American citizens in the pursuit of greater national security.

Also, a truth about these legislative actions: there are far more unseen paragraphs to their ledgers than there are the parts televised by the media. The USA Patriot Act was no exception to this. Under some of its provisions, it reserved the right for certain military organizations to draw recruits from age brackets that would normally be considered underage. Specifically speaking, that addendum to the Act was passed unanimously at the formation of SWORD. With the upswing in enlistments across the entire board, this new anti-terror organization was going to need to be able to pull recruits from wherever they could get them, within reason. One fear that the Joint Chiefs of Staff had regarding a new branch of the military was that it was going to take Soldiers, Marines, Seaman, and Airmen from the existing branches, specifically the picks of the litter, and leave them in need of finding and training replacements for all their top players. As such, Congress had put a limit on the amount of existing military members SWORD could pull from, and General Easton and his staff used that limit to pull the very best of all five branches of the military to fill many of their leadership and cadre positions. If SWORD soldiers were going to be some of, if not the best group of soldiers out there, they were going to need to be trained and led by the best.

Once they had filled many of their initial positions with the limited quantities they could have, SWORD also faced another challenge; populating their ranks with military-aged men and women would come with limitations as well. Recruiters from the Army, Navy, Air Force, Coast Guard and Marines didn't want to miss out on this absolute gold mine of opportunity to get butts into seats on flights to their respective training installations, and when you have existed hundreds of years longer than a newcomer "black" organization, like SWORD, you tend to have a much bigger sway with the leaders and politicians who make the rules. As such, SWORD couldn't recruit within the normal military-aged population beyond a certain quota. However, an up-and-coming organization was still going to need staff. As such, the Patriot's Defense Act included a clause stating that recruitment of individuals could meander outside the regular age of consent, or adulthood, to include minors as young as fourteen. Granted, there would be an immensely more rigorous screening process to make sure that those who were underage who were acquired would be able to stand up to the difficulties of military training and life. Under the Act, it would also legalize the entering into government contracts to those individuals recruited who were under the age of eighteen.

So, shady as it sounded to have Corbin literally run away from his family to join the military, thanks to the 2001 Patriot Defense Act, it was one hundred percent legal. Despite that fact, Corbin felt more excited over the detail that what he was doing was COMPLETELY against what his parents wanted him to do.

As he rolled out of bed two mornings later, he had a level of excitement that he had never felt before in his life. He quickly and surreptitiously packed his school backpack with the few essentials he would need, as outlined by General Easton, and quietly slid his stack of schoolbooks and folders underneath his bed. His mom and dad would probably never find them, and if they did, by that time, he would already be well on his way to Basic Training, if not already there. There would be a lot of paperwork and stuff that still needed to happen, but Corbin had already been assured that all the entry "red tape" would be complete, and he would be on a plane to Georgia before he would be expected to be home from school.

'Man,' Corbin thought to himself, 'when the government wants someone, they sure as heck make sure they can get them.' He was a little familiar with the entrance processing for the military, and he was certain that it would take more than a day, let alone the seven hours someone was going to be at school. Then again, this was some super-duper SpecOps whatevertheheck he was joining, so maybe a group like that had some sort of express pass.

It was hard to sit still on the bus to school, knowing that just after his first class, he would walk out the side doors of his high school, hop in the car with General Easton, and go to the MEPS, Military Entrance Processing Station, that was near the downtown area of the city. Corbin would have preferred to go straight there, but Easton had pointed out that if he didn't show up to school at all, there was a greater likelihood that the whole plan would get blown out in the open if he didn't at least *start* his day like normal. It would also give him a chance to, in some way that he hadn't figured out yet, say good-bye to his friends.

That was what almost got him second-guessing his decision as he stepped into his first period class. *Almost.* He hadn't ever been one of the popular kids, but he had developed a close gathering of friends that he had kept all through most of grade school, middle school, and now the introductory year of high school. On top of that, he had also become increasingly aware of girls he found attractive and had thoughts of maybe even trying to ask them out. In his mind, though, he was far out of the perceived lofty league of practically any girl he had a crush on, so who was he really kidding? Perhaps, he pondered, he could show up to the high school sometime after he got back from Basic, wearing his uniform, and even the meathead football players would be invisible to all the girls compared to him. That almost seemed like the perfect "revenge" plot, in his mind. Granted, it wasn't like he was picked on or anything, even by the football jocks, but he did feel like it was unfair that all those muscly half-wits had to do was wear their football jersey, then girls practically threw themselves at them. Hell, they weren't even good. Their best season, so far, had been three wins TOTAL. It was evident to pretty much everyone in the school that this particular high school had much more proficiency in the arts, not sports, but it didn't keep the jocks from getting girls.

Whatever. In just a few months, even high school wouldn't matter, because Corbin was going to be a mean, green, killing machine, and he was certain that even fickle high school girls would pale in comparison to whatever kind of women were probably going to be throwing themselves at him. All right, he wasn't joining SWORD for the chicks, but man it was a fun prospect to daydream about as he sat in his first period class and tried not to look too distracted. Apparently, it wasn't working very well, because his teacher had called on him on several occasions to answer a question, which was something he generally only did when he thought someone wasn't listening. Thankfully, Corbin had a good enough memory of the class content that he could regurgitate whatever answer he needed to, even if he did stumble for a second, letting his mind shift gears between daydream and reality.

At one point, his best friend, Drew, leaned over to him and nudged him, "Yo Bro, what are you up to after school today?"

Corbin just shrugged. Even if he told the truth, it's not like it sounded real enough for Drew to take him seriously.

"I dunno, might go off and join the Army or something. What do you think," he whispered.

"Yeah right, dude. Even if you could, your parents would freak out."

"Well, if I could, I would. I don't give a crap what they think anyway," Corbin hissed back. It was true, even the hint of bitterness that was in his voice. After that lousy display by his parents that night at dinner, he hadn't even thought much, if at all, about what his parents were going to do once they found out where he had really gone, or even the panic and worry they were for sure going to experience when they first learned that he was gone.

"Wow, tell me how you really feel," Drew said with a smirk.

"I'm serious, man," Corbin insisted, "they keep being such douches about the whole idea of joining the Marines, that if someone came along and said that I could enlist today, I'd do it just to give my parents the middle finger."

Drew was starting to sound a little genuinely concerned, "Yeah...but the Marines? Those are the front lines, middle-of-all-the-action guys, and things have really been heating up over there since 9/11."

"I wouldn't want it any other way. I'd want to be the guy kicking down the doors and putting bullets in the faces of those terrorists. I wouldn't ever want to go unless I was right in the thick of it all."

"Man, just when I think you sound crazy," Drew scoffed quietly, gently shaking his head, "you go and outdo yourself by saying something like that."

Corbin just laughed and threw his shoulder into his friend. They both sat up straight and alert as the teacher turned in their direction, whether because he could hear them or not, they couldn't say. When he turned away, continuing his lecture, the two friends shared knowing glances and stifled quiet chuckles. It was going to be tough to leave Drew, most of all. They had been practically inseparable since they met in the third grade. They regularly thought the same on everything, except when it came to girls. Thankfully, they hadn't ever liked the same one, as that assuredly would be about the only subject that could cause disagreement between the two of them.

As the bell rang to end the class, Corbin stood up and suddenly felt flushed. His heart was thudding in his chest as he picked up his backpack and slung it over his shoulders. He was literally on the threshold to the rest of his life and uprooting and tossing away his current life. As he stepped out into the hallway, he started to look more meaningfully at his surroundings. Suddenly, the annoying, loud shrieks and conversations in the hallway didn't bother him. Actually, he was already feeling like he missed them. Each step towards the door that led outside made him feel almost like he was marching off to pending doom. It was the only time that he truly began to second guess what he had been so resolved to do. Each cute girl that passed by, especially the ones he had a crush on, he wanted to just grab by the shoulders and, in some "chick flick," dramatic and theatrical way, kiss them full on the lips before smiling and walking out the door before they could say something or, at the very least, slap the daylights out of him. Was he really going through with this?

The door that he and General Easton had agreed upon was one that led out of the building via the recently constructed stairwell that served as an additional fire escape that was needed due to an updated building fire code. As the stairwell was so recent, the school hadn't taken the opportunity yet to install CCTV cameras at the door or on that corner of the building, even though it was a new thoroughfare for students as they made their way between classes or outside during lunch break. So, it wouldn't be out of the ordinary to use the door, but there would be no video evidence to show where Corbin had gone once it had been discovered that he was "missing." Even though there wasn't anything that anyone could do regarding his enlistment, both Corbin and General Easton agreed that they needed to stay as many steps ahead of his parents to make his entry transition as smooth as possible.

Corbin almost felt like he was going to throw up the closer he got to the door. When he pushed outside, the cool, crisp air of the fall season met his nostrils, filling them with the scent of fresh air and decaying leaves. It helped a little with his nausea until Corbin saw the now familiar dark sedan he knew had Easton sitting behind the wheel. Even though he recognized it, he double-checked the license number of the government-issued tags against his memory, which checked out. He didn't know why he did, but he had a random habit of memorizing the license plate numbers of vehicles, as if he were some secret agent or something who would need to recall that important information later. Maybe it would prove useful in his new profession, or maybe it wouldn't, but it helped his nerves a little bit in this situation, nonetheless. The closer he got to the car, he could hear that the engine was running, idling quietly and almost noiseless against the loud din of high school students.

Glancing back and forth quickly, Corbin checked to make sure no one was looking, or at least someone who would recognize him didn't see him hop into a "stranger's" car. However, as he was on the side of the school that he habitually wasn't on at this time of the morning, none of his friends, nor even distant acquaintances were in the vicinity to spot him as he opened the door and ducked into the passenger's seat of the sedan, closing the door quickly and placing his backpack over his shoulder into the backseat. General Easton wore his uniform and his glasses, which had those automatically tinting lenses, were darker to compensate for the sunlight peering through the windshield. Despite his fairly daunting appearance, he smiled his familiar smile.

"Good morning, Mr. Kent. Are you ready to go?"

Corbin's heart still pounded against his ribs, thudded in his throat, and thumped in his ears almost to the point that it muffled the sound around him. Disregarding his nerves and his deafening pulse, he nodded and spoke as confidently as he could, "Let's do this."

General Easton simply nodded, shifted the vehicle into gear, and steered out of the school's parking lot, and Corbin never even looked back. It took a lot of willpower not to, but he figured that if he was really going to go through with this and not chicken out, he needed to make sure that he didn't give himself any reason to. Plus, looking back was probably going to make him do that, and he had come way too far, in his mind, to wuss out now. If he really wanted to be a soldier, he needed to act now, because who knew if or when he would ever get another chance at this?

The ride to the MEPS was shorter than Corbin would have anticipated. Did General Easton have a lead foot, or was the distance between the school and their destination really that short? Part of him wished that the ride had been just a little bit longer because there was something soothing about sitting in the front passenger seat in silence and watching the world pass by outside as if time were paused, waiting to start up again once he had stepped out onto the curb. It also probably would have helped to have a little more time to ride to really convince himself that he was ready to do this, because as ready as he had felt before to take this plunge, there was a little voice at the back of his mind that told him, "Maaaaayyyybe I could use a few more years to think this over...."

As General Easton parked and shut off the engine of the car, he looked over to Corbin, whom he could tell was struggling a little internally. He knew what to say in this setting, and it wasn't something that was going to introduce any more doubt into the young boy's mind. Sure, he could say something like, "So, ready to do this," or something like that, but that was just the thing to say to completely break the confidence of a young man who may have even the slightest of second thoughts. So, instead, he waited for a moment in the silence before taking a deep breath through his nose.

"You know, I have a quote that I like to repeat to myself that helps me any time I feel a little insecure about something."

Corbin looked at Easton suddenly, as if he couldn't even fathom a time when this seasoned-looking general had ever felt insecure about anything in his whole life. However, it did help his nerves knowing that someone like this man had second-guessed himself before, and now, he felt more interested and curious than he did nervous.

Easton saw the subtle change on Corbin's face and knew that his opening statement had worked. He sat back in his seat, looking towards the plain-looking brick building in front of them.

"Every normal man must be tempted, at times, to spit upon his hands, hoist the black flag, and begin slitting throats," General Easton quoted, a gentle smile spreading across his lips.

The moment of silence following the quote was enough to let the words sink in for Corbin to start to think. How badass did that sound? He really *was* tempted, at times, to "start slitting throats." Okay, maybe not literally, in some cases, but he did get that feeling where he just wanted to throw caution to the wind and just do what he wanted, despite what others thought. Come to think of it, wasn't that what he was doing now? Wasn't he just giving in to that "temptation" that he had felt? The itch that he had been dying to scratch for so long, and that he couldn't viably scratch until now? Wasn't he just a "normal man," being tempted by the urge to spit on his hands and take matters into those hands? A smile crept across Corbin's face that affirmed his feelings.

"Yo-ho, General," was his response.

General Easton smiled in return and opened his door, getting out of the car, Corbin following his lead and grabbing his backpack as he exited. The two of them stepped inside the entrance to the unassuming building and approached a front desk that was behind a pane of glass like a ticket booth at a theater. There was a young, stern-looking man in dress blues that Corbin wasn't sure which branch of the military they belonged to. The man was busily typing on his computer until he noticed their presence out of his periphery. His eyes widened when he noticed the pair of stars on Easton's chest. He stood up quickly, snapping to attention.

"General, what can I do for you sir?" said the young soldier in a loud, crisp manner.

"At ease, son," said Easton, "this young man is here to go through the entrance processing, and his file needs to go PMEP."

General Easton handed a thick-filled manila folder through the opening in the glass to the soldier, who took it quickly. He thumbed through the contents swiftly and eyed the patch on Easton's left shoulder sleeve before nodding quickly. "Yes sir, we will have him processed on Priority Status."

"Excellent, Sergeant, I appreciate the attention to detail. Also, make sure this young recruit gets whatever he needs or asks for, he is a high score on the ASVAB."

"Yes, General, sir!"

As far as this young Sergeant, or any other member of the MEPS staff was aware, "PMEP" was a term that stood for "Priority Military Entrance Processing," and that "High score on the ASVAB" was some sort of code term that was follow up to confirm that the recruit referred to as PMEP was to be processed as soon as possible and should be treated like a VIP. This particular Sergeant noticed that any time that this code term was mentioned, it was by someone who had that same unit patch that this general did, the one with the eagle, missile, and olive branch.

The Sergeant stepped around his chair and marched to a small panel to the left of his desk and pressed a button. There was a subdued buzzing noise and a door on the wall opposite where Corbin and General Easton were standing popped ajar with a click. Easton stepped toward the door and opened it, gesturing for Corbin to step through. Corbin tentatively stepped forward, looking to Easton as if to make sure that it was safe to do so. As he moved through the doorway, General Easton didn't react. Corbin could feel himself panic a little bit when he noticed that. Once again, General Easton seemed to be able to know what he was thinking.

"This is where we part ways," General Easton said resolutely, "However, it isn't the last time that I see you, I can assure you that. The good Sergeant here will take good care of you, and if he doesn't, I will hear about it."

The Sergeant swallowed a little, looking at Corbin, then back at General Easton, "Yes sir, he will get the VIP treatment sir."

"Excellent. And make sure his flight arrangements are this evening, I'm sure you have some other recruits who are outbound today?"

"Yes sir."

"Perfect. Your CO has my information should there be any questions or concerns. I want to make sure that our man here gets started on the very best foot."

"Yes sir, understood."

General James Easton looked at the somewhat scared, but resolute-looking young Corbin Kent and gave him one last reassuring smile before simply nodding and letting the reflective glass door shut. Corbin stood for a moment and tried to make sure that this was what he really wanted to do and then, remembering the quote, nodded to himself and turned to the Sergeant.

"Lead the way."

To say that the entire MEPS experience was, well peculiar at best, was an understatement. Sure, there were things that Corbin expected, like medical records, criminal records, background checks, stuff like that, but then there were some REALLY strange things that he didn't ever think he could have prepared for, like sitting in a room full of other military recruits in his underwear and being told to "duck walk" from one end of the room to the other with everyone else. What that had to do with anything, he didn't know, and probably never would. Everyone else in the room, (also in their underwear), looked and reacted like it was the strangest thing they had done as well, so at least they were all in good company in that regard.

Another interesting detail that Corbin noticed was how many times the "PMEP" term seemed to detour him from the other recruits along the entrance processing, and how that "codename" appeared to keep anyone and everyone from pointing out how young Corbin was. As far as he was concerned, he looked old for his age, and had been told that on many occasions, but he looked like a veritable baby compared to some of these guys being processed in the group. However, no one said anything, and every so often, as he followed the line of recruits to the next step in processing, a staff member would look at his file and say, "No, this one is PMEP, he goes this way," and then separate Corbin from the group. After his little "detour," he would end up in a room where the rest of the group would inevitably end up, but long after he had gotten there, and he was sure that there were several rooms or steps that he had skipped passed completely.

By the time Corbin was being ushered out of the building and into a late-model minivan being driven by a pock-faced seaman, the rest of the group he had been processing with was still inside going through whatever rigmarole that still awaited them. Everything had been a whirl to this point that Corbin hadn't even taken a moment to look at his watch, or any clock in the building, if there had even been one. When he finally did see the time, he had been in MEPS for almost six hours. He would be getting out of school within the next few minutes or so. Easton wasn't kidding when he had mentioned how long, or not so long, it was going to take to get through that processing. As he climbed into the minivan, the driver began to look a little confused until "PMEP," was mentioned, and then he nodded knowingly and started up the vehicle.

The driver steered off toward the interstate, following the signs that indicated the direction of the airport. Corbin was somewhat familiar with the route and knew that he had about half an hour or so until they reached their destination. He felt exhausted; however his mind was still racing as if trying to catch up with all the goings-on happening. His nervousness had subsided considerably, probably because his brain was still trying to register everything that had happened from the point that General Easton had left until now. In and of it all, he kept that quote in his mind to keep him feeling pumped and hopeful for whatever awaited him next. He clutched tightly to the manila envelope that General Easton had originally held. Apparently, according to just about every single staff member in MEPS, it was of the utmost importance and losing track of it was just about a fate worse than death. Corbin couldn't really see how that was true, nevertheless, the constant badgering and threatening about the folder and the documents inside was effective enough to cause him to hold onto it until his knuckles were white.

He recognized the area they were driving through as they neared the airport. Sitting up in his seat, he focused on where the van was heading. Rather than follow the rest of the traffic flow, the driver steered the van off to the right, off a little exit-ramp-sort-of-road that ended at a gate with a security booth. Slowing to a stop, the rough-faced seaman at the wheel rolled his window down as the security guard approached. The guard, an overweight, middle-aged man, looked a bit annoyed as if their approach had interrupted something more important, in his opinion. Corbin tried not to look incredulously at this man because, what could *anyone* be doing in a tiny security booth like that that warranted any amount of import?

'*Sorry to interrupt your movie,*' Corbin said sarcastically in his head.

"Can I help you?" the guard asked in a bored tone.

"MEPS personnel. Have a recruit going on the flight leaving in twenty minutes, Hangar two."

None of that seemed of any importance to Corbin, but it did to the security guard, who produced what looked like a garage door opener from his pocket and pressed it, which raised the gate in front of them. The driver and the security guard said nothing to each other as the van rolled forward, the gate closing behind them. Corbin wanted to ask questions, but he didn't know if his escort was the talkative type, and he didn't feel like he wanted to find out. Besides, the questions were more out of curiosity, rather than necessity.

They drove between two rows of hangars that looked like they were reserved for private jets. They were massive, but nowhere near the size needed to house something as big as a commercial airliner. After a right turn towards the end of the hangars, the van turned right once more and into one of these hangars, through the enormous front door, that stood open. Inside was a matte-gray C-130 Hercules cargo plane, its crew shuffling about around it, performing pre-flight checks. Just to the right of the side door leading into the cargo area of the plane stood a handful of young men, all holding backpacks or small duffle bags, and manila envelopes. They were flanked by two men in uniforms, arms folded across their chests and stern looks on their faces. Most of the young men in the group looked nervous, whether because of the uniformed men, or just the situation in general, it was hard to tell.

The van slowed to a stop a few feet from the group and Corbin stepped out tentatively, as if he wasn't sure whether he should be following the lead of the driver, or if he was missing some sort of cue that he should have been aware of. When no one said anything, he figured to himself that he must not have screwed anything up too badly and made his way over to the rest of the group. Some of the others in the gathering looked up when Corbin approached, but most appeared too lost in their thoughts to react to his arrival. Corbin could feel his nerves starting to get the best of him, and he felt a perpetual chill down his spine and a tremendous feeling of uncertainty wash over him. Judging by the appearance of everyone else, he was the youngest in this group of recruits. At this moment, he was glad that most of them were staring down at their shoes, or the bags they held in their hands, otherwise, he feared they would have lots of questions about him specifically. It wasn't that Corbin thought himself any different or more special than the others there, he just had that incessant sense of self-consciousness that made him feel like he was always the odd or peculiar one in the room.

Even the two soldiers who appeared as if they were guarding the group failed to react to the newcomer to the scene. They were probably indifferent to everyone around them, or so accustomed to this sort of thing, or a little of both. Corbin, for the time being, thought it best if he just kept quiet and followed instructions as they came. Speaking of which, he thought that the guy who drove him here would have something helpful to say. However, when he looked around, he was dumbstruck to find that the driver and the van were already gone.

"Well, thanks for nothing, I guess," was all Corbin could think. He shuffled as inconspicuously as possible to the approximate center of the group of young men waiting and did his best to look as if he considered this all normal.

As he waited, the thought struck him that he should probably do something to buy himself a little bit of time, when it came to his parents. Not coming straight home from school was no big deal, but at some point, they were going to start calling him and his friends if they didn't have some sort of cover story given them. He quickly slipped his phone from his pocket and fabricated a quick message that he sent off to his mom, something about being out with friends and left it at that. It was genuine enough to pass as a nonchalant teen like himself, but vague enough that, as soon as they had suspicions, his mom and dad weren't going to have a specific friend of his that they would know to call first to ask of his whereabouts. At least that way, there was the chance of them making a few calls before really getting worried. Though Drew didn't know what he was up to, he knew that his best friend wouldn't make any speculation to make the situation worse. He would just tell the truth, which was when he last saw Corbin, and that would be that. Still, Corbin felt like he had inadvertently made his buddy an accessory to a crime, or something like that. Whatever happened after all of this, he would owe him an apology.

The others around him had obviously begun to feel a little more comfortable, as a low murmur of conversations began to rise. Corbin looked around tentatively, as if feeling like an outcast, fearing that those around him had shown up with someone that they knew, like a buddy or something, which made him feel even more alone in his mind. He had almost abandoned himself to his self-inflicted sense of solitude. Thankfully, someone was standing next to him who looked as if he felt just as alone as him. He was just a couple of inches taller than Corbin; and thin, with very short dark hair and blue eyes. He adjusted the glasses on his face to either assist their position; or simply as a nervous tic. He looked in Corbin's direction and gave him a sort of half-hearted, upward nod.

"Crazy stuff, huh," Corbin asked, trying to break the ice.

"Yeah," the boy answered, looking a little bewildered,

"Well, I mean, did you ever think you would be standing here, in a hangar, waiting to load up on a military cargo plane to go," Corbin hadn't even thought about where they were headed, and no one had bothered to tell him, nor he to ask, "wherever they are sending us?"

The boy laughed lightly in agreement, "Yeah, totally. I mean, the military had always been something that I had considered, but I never thought that I would ever get myself into something like *this*."

"Seriously. You think everyone who enlists feels a little uneasy at first? I kind of feel like I'm about to freak out, to be honest," Corbin felt a little better after admitting his feelings, while at the same time hoping that he hadn't made a fool of himself by saying it. With his luck, this guy was going to answer in the opposite manner, saying something like he wasn't nervous, but as ready as he could ever be.

"You have no idea," responded the boy, "Part of me is seriously considering running out the door. Of course, I bet that wouldn't blow over all that great."

The two of them chuckled a little at the thought. It helped ease the tension they were both struggling with, and with that, they introduced themselves to each other. Corbin was in the company of Alex McMann, a resident of the same city that he lived in, and who was only about eighteen months older than him. The longer they stood in the crowd, chatting quietly, the more they seemed to get along. It was comforting for Corbin to know that, at the very least, he now had a familiar face, an acquaintance, he could speak to, and, even if it felt a little early to say so, consider as a friend. They were a lot alike, Corbin and Alex, and it took almost no time to develop what felt like a friendship that was years older than the few minutes they had shared. Whatever happened from here on out, Corbin made a mental goal to make sure he and Alex stayed in touch.

Around thirty minutes later, the two soldiers moved to the side of the aircraft, next to the open door, and were joined by a tall man in a pilot's jumpsuit, his rank pins showing he was a major. His gait was very stiff and precise, almost as if he were a machine. He stood in the center of the doorway leading into the aircraft and cleared his throat loudly, causing the low hum in the room to quell.

"Gentlemen," he began, "how many of you here have ever flown on a plane before?"

As odd of a question as it seemed, and as taken off guard as most of the people were, about a third of the group slowly raised their hands, including Corbin and Alex. The major smiled and shrugged his shoulders in an off-handed sort of way and replied, "Oh good, that's one more time than I have."

Corbin was sure that was an icebreaker, a joke to put them all at ease, but at the same time, part of him worried that this man was serious. Well, if there was any way to go out of this world, next to being killed in some military firefight, might as well be in a military aircraft on the way to being KIA in a firefight, or something like that. Not that the joke wasn't funny, it made Corbin laugh a little, but there weren't a lot of favorable reactions to the pilot's humor, and that was assuredly because of everyone's nerves. It didn't seem to affect the major in the slightest, and he simply shrugged and moved on.

"Flying on one of these will be a little different than what you guys may be used to. It'll be a little rough, a little louder, and the flight attendants are uglier than sin." (Again, very little response) "Unfortunately, you will become well acquainted with the fact that the military makes its vehicles based more off function, rather than comfort. Board the aircraft, single file, and fill the seats from the front of the seating area to the back. Buckle up, sit tight, and wait for further instruction. Our flight time today will be just a hair under four hours. In case anyone hasn't told you, we are headed to Georgia. Once we get to the airport in Atlanta, there will be a charter bus waiting for you to take you to Fort Benning. Congratulations, gentlemen, and good luck."

As the pilot turned and entered the plane through the open door, everyone started to shuffle into a single-file line. Alex and Corbin ended up getting shifted more towards the back, which wasn't of any consequence to them. Corbin glanced around occasionally as the queue slowly made its way into the aircraft, and it wasn't long until he stepped through the door to see their flight accommodations for the first time. The cargo area of the C-130 was empty, save a cluster of seats arranged neatly in the middle, looking as if someone had bolted about twenty rows of commercial airliner seats to the floor in the center of the cargo bay. The line of men was filing neatly into the seats, from the front rows, as directed. The two uniformed guards had positioned themselves at the front and rear of the rows of seats, looking no less stern than they had when they were outside.

When everyone had sat down in a seat and situated their bag, either on their lap or under their seat, another member of the flight crew appeared from the front of the aircraft. He wore a jumpsuit that matched the pilot; however this man's rank showed that he was a lieutenant. His brown hair was neatly parted and combed to the side, showing a slight indentation on the top of his head where a flight headset would normally rest. The lieutenant cleared his throat and then immediately began to speak.

"All right, guys, we are going to be taxiing out to the runway soon, and I'm just gonna give you a quick rundown of the aircraft and exits. There is a latrine on board, it is to the rear of the aircraft. As the major mentioned earlier, this aircraft is built for function, not necessarily luxury. The toilet is no exception."

Mostly everyone turned to look in the direction that the lieutenant pointed towards the left and rear of the plane, near the ramp. Bolted to the wall was what looked like a toilet that had been taken from a porta-potty and repurposed here. There was a curtain beside it hanging from a thin track on the ceiling, identical to a privacy curtain in a hospital room. Corbin grimaced a little, seeing the almost blatant lack of privacy in the setup. He decided that if he ended up having to use the bathroom, he was going to just wait until they got to their destination. Judging by the looks on the faces of some of the others sitting around him, Corbin could tell that they were making the same internal resolution as well.

The lieutenant continued, "The props on this thing are very noisy. As such, everyone will need to wear ear protection. We will hand out ear plugs for everyone to use. Please keep them in at all times until the engines stop.

Believe me, you don't want to endure the noise any longer than you have to. If we get into any sort of emergency, follow the direction of the pilot, me, or either of the soldiers here. Other than that, please stay in your seats and welcome aboard."

Corbin immediately buckled his seatbelt and sat back in his seat, head against the rest. Alex followed his lead. The pair of soldiers retrieved containers from drawers that extended out of the wall behind them and began to make their way up the rows of seats, handing out small packages of orange foam earplugs to everyone. When the two got their earplugs, they wasted no time opening the plastic packaging then rolling and inserting the earplugs into place. Corbin noticed that the engines of the plane began to sputter to life as the foam plugs expanded in his ears. Though muffled, as the engines to the massive props along the wings began to speed up, the noise was still pretty uncomfortable. Corbin was especially grateful for the earplugs now. The aircraft began to roll forward as the pilot directed it towards the runway and Corbin could feel his stomach lurch. Up until this point, his decision to be a part of SWORD felt more surreal than reality. Now, at the literal point of no return, Corbin began to realize the gravity of the situation as the Hercules accelerated and then rose into the sky.

Chapter Two

Corbin never really had much trouble sleeping, and it was no exception when he flew. He wasn't sure what it was, but for some reason, he never stood a chance whenever he was in the air. Granted, a normal passenger jet has a very subdued humming sound attributed to its engines, and it was most likely what lulled him off into a slumber. Considering that, it was no wonder he had fallen asleep so fast on this C-130. The props were loud, muffled by earplugs, droning on and on, and adding a subtle vibration to the entire aircraft, which felt kind of like one of those massaging lounge chairs you could sample for free at the mall. The constant sound and vibration made quick work of his consciousness.

Corbin couldn't even remember where they were, or what they were doing at first until his awareness warmed up enough for him to think back on the day and "remember." That was why he felt so taken off guard and panicked when Alex nudged him awake, and he noticed that people were gathering their things and making their way off the aircraft. Where were they and why? Oh, right, he remembered now. As soon as he came to the realization to where he was, the minute sense of panic set in again as he came to consider what he had done. He swallowed hard and tried to calm his nerves as he stood up and gathered his backpack and his manila folder. Just as when everyone got onto the plane, it was the same, with everyone disembarking the aircraft in a single-file line starting from the front row.

Everyone stepped out of the same door they had entered through, and out onto the runway of the Atlanta airport, just outside the main terminal.

The first thing that Corbin noticed was how the air seemed to punch him in the face and feel like it stuck to the inside of his lungs. Up until this point in his life, he hadn't really ever experienced humidity as he had grown up most of his life in a dry, mountain-filled state. The sensation was a bit oppressive, but he kind of liked it at the same time. He didn't have time to dwell too much on the weather conditions because the group was moving quickly inside the terminal, led by the pair of guards who had accompanied them for the duration of the trip. As he hustled to keep up with the group, he pulled out his phone and quickly glanced at it. No messages or calls yet. Good. That at least helped Corbin's nerves a little, knowing that he wasn't going to have to add misdirection to his "to-do list" just yet, and that meant that he could keep focusing on what was going on, and he wanted to make sure that he made a good impression as he felt a sense of obligation, if not loyalty, to General Easton.

The group clamored through the terminal, passing through the food court area on the way out the front doors. He hadn't been thinking much about it yet, but Corbin couldn't remember the last time he had eaten something, and the smell of food suddenly made his stomach growl, and his mind get distracted, if for just a moment. It wasn't like he, or anyone else glancing longingly at the food stands, had even a moment's chance to do anything about it, because their escorts simply barreled on by, not even slowing their pace. Maybe they had some sort of food arrangements somewhere else, Corbin considered, or maybe he and the rest of the group were in for a long, arduous evening of hunger pangs. He didn't want to get himself too distracted by it, so he shook his head as if to physically rattle the thought of food from his mind.

As they all pushed through the front doors of the airport, they could see a large, dark gray charter bus waiting at the curb, its engine chugging loudly as it idled. The two escort soldiers gestured for everyone to get onto the bus, and the group did, quickly and silently lining up and beginning to climb onto the bus one by one. Corbin and Alex climbed on and found a pair of seats as near to the back of the bus as they could get to, what with most of those seats already taken by those who had embarked before they had. The general feeling of the group was hushed, somewhat insecure, as everyone waited for the next set of instructions, or additional information. The two soldiers who had accompanied them for the duration of the trip so far didn't get onto the bus. Rather, once the last person was aboard, they simply walked away, disappearing into the bustle of the airport crowd. Corbin found that somewhat peculiar, only because he considered it natural for individuals to give some kind of farewell in any given situation, even if neither of them had spoken much, if at all, the entire time. It almost seemed rude that they left so abruptly; however, he thought it a bit silly that he was looking so much into these two strangers.

The bus driver stepped up to the top of the steps at the front of the bus and everyone quieted themselves as he cleared his throat. "Good evening, gentlemen, we are headed to Fort Benning, which is about an hour and a half drive from here. If you would like, I can play a movie for you guys to pass the time, however, considering the circumstances, and personal experience, I would highly suggest that you guys get some rest."

The advice seemed almost ominous to Corbin, and he furrowed his brow as he listened. What kind of personal experience was he speaking from? Was he a member of SWORD? Was he a veteran of one of the branches of the Armed Forces? What would they need rest for? He had at least fallen asleep on the plane, so he had already got some rest, but as he thought of it, he could probably use some more sleep. Alex already looked a bit droopy and was probably going to pass out soon anyway, so, no use in staying awake and enduring a long bus ride with no one to talk to.

"If you happen to have any questions for me, I am happy to answer them for you, provided I know the answers. Otherwise, please stay seated, try not to get too loud, and enjoy the ride."

The driver turned to his seat and sat down, double-checking over his shoulder as if to make sure everyone was present and sitting down. Frankly, with everything that had happened so far today, it looked like no one on the bus wanted to do anything except keep quiet and probably sleep or rethink their life choices now that they were thousands of miles away from home and had some time to really think about things. When there was no response, movement, or any real sign of life, the driver turned forward, shut the door, and shifted the bus into gear, smoothly pulling out into the flow of traffic.

Alex looked around the bus quietly before leaning over to Corbin, "You hungry, Bro?"

Corbin looked at him, puzzled. "What, you pocket a cheeseburger on the way out the door from the airport?"

Alex chuckled a little and pulled a box of Teddy Grahams out of his backpack. Corbin raised an eyebrow at him. "Dude, what are you, like seven?"

"No, I figured I'd need something to snack on, so I threw these in my bag before I left this morning," he responded with a slight laugh, which he stifled, realizing that his choice of snack did seem pretty childish.

As silly as it seemed, Corbin was glad that it was at least something. He never really liked feeling hungry, and right now, he felt almost ravenous. Gratefully, he nodded to Alex and the two of them did their best to share the food without attracting attention. They really didn't feel like sharing, and they both felt that there were pretty good odds that everyone else on the bus would probably solicit some of their treasured treats if they knew the two of them were eating something. It didn't take long for the two of them to finish the whole box, which they quietly hid back in Alex's backpack.

"So, what made you want to go and do something like this?" Alex questioned as he sat back in his seat.

Corbin felt a little sheepish at his explanation. Sure, when he talked about wanting to be in the military, and his reasons why, to adults, people he felt he wanted to impress or have be proud of him, talking about his sense of patriotism seemed a proper place to do it. However, thinking about it in the context of telling someone his age, a peer, he feared that it would draw more criticism than support. True, someone older than him might think that he was pursuing a noble cause, something that any parent would be proud to see their son do, except his parents, apparently. On the other hand, when he thought about it from the perspective of a classmate, or someone near or at his same age, he thought they would probably think him crazy the same way people saw religious or political zealots.

"You first," Corbin deflected.

"My dad owns a security contracting company and has been a regular on the Air Force base for as long as I can remember. I even looked into working for him once I got out of high school."

Corbin could feel his excitement grow, "Whoa, like Blackwater sort of security contractor?"

"Nah, nothing that exciting. It's all, like, computer stuff. Mainframes and whatever. Anyway, I was up on base with my dad a lot during the summer, and I got interested in maybe joining the military. I had mentioned it to him one day, and the next thing I know, this General guy is at my house," Alex narrated with a nonchalant shrug.

"Was it General Easton?"

"Yeah, that's the guy. I don't know how he figured out that I was thinking of maybe enlisting, and I don't think my dad told him, because he looked as surprised as me when we saw the General. Plus, whatever this SWORD group really is, I'm pretty sure that it is just as secret, if not more, as General Easton said it is."

"He told you that too, huh?"

"Yep, and I believe it."

"What makes you say that?" Corbin questioned, intrigued.

"Well, to be able to handle the security contracts that my dad's company does, most everyone, if not everyone who works for his company, needs to have at *least* a Top-Secret security clearance. Of course, my dad is supposed to have all that clearance too, and probably even more, and he said that he had never heard of SWORD before and he had never even seen mention of anything like it."

Corbin thought back to his dinner with his parents and General Easton. As far as his parents were concerned, SWORD was just a military school for teenagers. Had Alex and his mom and dad been told more of the truth than his parents were? If so, Corbin figured, while not trying to feel oddly jealous, (not that the truth would have changed anything for his parents anyway), that if Alex's dad had such high-security clearances, maybe Easton could trust him more with the truth than with someone who didn't have any sort of government responsibility. Thinking of it that way, Corbin felt like he understood more than he felt envious about the situation. Again, not like his parents would have handled it any better. They evidently couldn't even stomach the thought of it all being some sort of summer military school. In the end, it wasn't like that even mattered anyway, seeing as it was all going to hit the fan big time when the truth finally came out.

Corbin was silent for a moment, looking out the window of the bus and admiring the number of trees that there were in Georgia. He lived in a mountainous and desert state where, to see any concentration of trees near to what there were here even just on the side of the highway, someone would have to trek into the mountains and pretty far, at that. However, it seemed like if there wasn't a road or a building here, then there were trees, sometimes so thick that you couldn't see even a few feet into the foliage. As he admired the scenery, his mind began to wander to what sorts of things someone could find in those deep, thick woods. Naturally, his imagination began to formulate scenarios and daydreams of everything from dead bodies to Sasquatch, because when his mind wandered, it went all over the place.

He wasn't sure how long he had been lost in the deep corners of his imagination, but it must have been most of the trip, because the next thing he noticed was what looked like an ornate bridge spanning the road into the base. Illuminated across the side of the bridge were the words, "Fort Benning" on one side of the median, and "Georgia," on the other side. It seemed that most of the others on the bus noticed where they were now as the hum of conversations subsided considerably, Corbin noticed handfuls of the other guys pressing their faces against the bus windows as they passed under the bridge. A little distance farther, the bus slowed as it approached a security checkpoint, and a uniformed soldier, clad in a full armor vest and M4 assault rifle, stepped out and stood firmly on the curb. As he noticed the bus driver and subtle marking on the side panel beneath the driver's window, he waved the bus forward without requiring a stop. The bus driver waved cordially and nodded his head as he accelerated deeper into the base.

* * *

The guard, a young Specialist and recent transfer from Fort Hood, Texas, stepped back into his confined guard booth with a shrug and sat down in his very old, very used, office chair. He had only been assigned to this post a couple of months ago, and he had seen countless vehicles go through this very checkpoint. It was mainly uneventful, until there was some sort of drill that involved testing response times to emergency codes or live roleplays of situations, and the occasional inebriated soldier trying to get on base before he needed to report for duty. Generally, there wasn't a single vehicle that ever caught his eye or even threatened to stick in his memory. However, these buses, like the one that just entered, were *always* memorable. When he was receiving training for his assignment, he was given one particularly interesting, and somewhat baffling bit of information. Naturally, every vehicle that came to the post was subject to being stopped, identification checked, and even being searched, if he felt that was necessary. However, when it came to these particular charter buses, always matte gray, always unmarked, save for a small insignia under the driver window, (an eagle with a missile and olive branch), he was to let these vehicles through every time without question. From what he saw, it just looked like a bus full of new recruits coming in for Basic, however, it was strange because the usual charter buses that came through with recruits were commercially marked buses, and they had a standard schedule of when they arrived. Also, he still had to stop those buses and check the I.D. of the driver, even though he was aware of who they were and what they were there for. These gray buses, however, tended to show up at different times of the day, and with no real normalcy or pattern.

It would have all been inconsequential to him if there appeared to be rhyme or reason to these arrivals, or even if there were some sort of explanation from one of his superiors as to the reason why there was a completely different protocol, or even, dare he say, lack of protocol altogether. However, he had found out already that attempting to inquire about the situation directly was usually met with a stern response somewhere to the effect of, "Mind your own business," or the classic Army answer, "You're not paid to think." Fine, he understood that there were plenty of things that were, as they say, "above his pay grade," but even some of those types of subjects still had enough speculation or rumor about them to provide even a plausible explanation, whether it be accurate or not. Heck, even items that were Classified or Top-Secret still made a lap or two around the rumor mill. Not this though. Anytime the Specialist brought it up in casual conversation amongst squad mates or others within his unit, their reactions were nothing more than just a shrug and a common phrase of, "That's just how it is."

As peculiar as it all was, it was still completely harmless. He had never seen anything negative happen in direct relation to these buses. It wasn't like some terror cell had managed to weasel its way on base and was secretly releasing sleeper agents amongst their ranks. Really, it seemed that all that happened, as far as he could see, was that these buses would show up, leave, and...well, that was it. Whatever. As dismissive as it may sound, it didn't affect him in any way, so it made no difference to him. Nevertheless, his curiosity was always piqued whenever these vehicles arrived, and he wondered what would happen if he were to ever stop one, even just to check the driver's identification. With his luck, it would get him in a heap of trouble, and most likely demoted, reassigned, or both.

* * *

As silent as the bus ride through the base was, it was about to drastically change. By the time Corbin had noticed that their transport had stopped, and the door opened, there was a pair of drill sergeants already on board. The one in the rear was who Corbin would have expected a drill sergeant to look like: probably six and a half feet tall, broad in the shoulders and chest, thick in the arms, strong jaw, and look on his face as if he would gladly tear your head off your shoulders just for entertainment. As he shouted for everyone to "Stand up," and "Get off my bus," his deep voice boomed and felt like it shook the walls.

As commanding as his presence was, the drill sergeant in front of him exuded a completely different bearing.

She stood no taller than about five feet. Corbin, admittedly, was average height, about five foot nine, and this drill sergeant looked short to him. To say she was hideous would have been a compliment, and her braces, despite looking about in her thirties, didn't help her situation in the slightest. Her voice was shrill and piercing, practically causing physical pain to anyone whose ears were assailed by it. If that wasn't enough to get you moving, it was the almost maniacal look in her eye that communicated a sadistic pleasure to the situation. She maintained a slight smirk the entire time, as if she anticipated there to be a lot of suffering at her hand. Corbin could only think of one word when he saw her and heard her strident voice...psychotic.

There wasn't a single person who hesitated the moment the two drill sergeants started barking orders. Corbin bolted up from his seat, Alex beside him in almost perfect unison. In somewhat organized chaos, everyone grabbed their bags and their manilla envelopes and shuffled off the bus as best they could and into the muggy, Georgia air. They were organized into several ranks, and then marched off, line by line, into a large, dull brown, brick building. Once entering the two sets of double glass doors, they were directed to an atrium area directly in front of them. The large, square area had a vaulted ceiling and arranged in the center were rows of wooden benches positioned in front of a large screen, one generally used for presentations. Everything seemed so chaotic and confusing, people tripping over themselves and others, scrambling to follow the shouted commands of the drill sergeants, but Corbin did his best to focus his attention on what was being demanded of him and following those instructions with laser precision. In classic military fashion, if someone didn't follow orders exactly, or was too slow to react, or for no perceivable reason at all, the offender would be subjected to push-ups. One of the drill sergeants was always close at hand to shout at and berate whoever was performing the punitive action.

Once everyone was seated, they were instructed to take out their cell phones and a prompt appeared on the large screen. It read:

I have arrived safely at Fort Benning, Georgia.
Please, do not send any food or bulky items.
I will contact you in 7 to 10 days with my new mailing address.
Thank you for your support.

Goodbye for now.

Everybody was instructed to call home and, regardless of what was said by their family on the other end, they were to read this scripted message and then hang up. To Corbin, it seemed excessively succinct, and practically anyone who received a phone call like this was bound to think that it was a prank. Slowly, tentatively, the young men began to extract their cell phones from their pockets, some who didn't have their own phones, either waited to borrow someone else's, or were guided to a row of telephones mounted to the wall to their left. Corbin hesitated for a moment, thinking for a second about what would happen once he made this phone call. Until this moment, no one, except for General Easton, was aware of where he had gone, and now he was supposed to call home and let the cat out of the bag. At least, Corbin considered, he was thousands of miles away from home, so no matter what the reaction was, he was nowhere near his parents for them to even do anything. Additionally, even if they wanted to do something, he felt certain that it would be nearly impossible for them to get to, and then onto base, let alone find him amongst the entire population here.

He also thought back to the night he and his parents had dinner with General Easton. He remembered how frustrated and annoyed he felt at his mom and dad for being so dismissive towards everything. He recalled how he wanted to jump over the table and beat his father silly with his dinner plate because he wasn't even going to entertain the idea of him enlisting, not even if he were to have waited until he was eighteen and didn't even need parental approval. Well, this was his chance at exacting some pretty sweet revenge. What better way to announce his rebellion than to call his parents from the threshold of Basic Training, and give them the extremely limited information the phone call script provided? He imagined it having almost the same effect on his dad as if he were actually in the same room to slap him in the face. Corbin hurriedly dialed the number for his home, heart thudding in his throat. He wasn't sure if it was exhilaration, or terror that made him feel the way he did, but it got more intense with every ring of the telephone line.

He knew from experience that the phone would ring four times before the voicemail would pick up, and if that were to happen, what then? Would he get another chance to call, or would that be the only opportunity he would get, and then his parents would be filling out a missing person's report? Every ring felt almost painful in his ear. One ring...two...three...

"Hello?" It was Corbin's dad. Perfect.

Corbin read the script word-for-word and then moved to end the call on his phone. As he pulled the phone away from his ear, he could hear his father say something to the effect of, "Corbin? What the f-," before he hastily pressed the "End Call" button.

Well, that was that. Much to Corbin's relief, the next set of instructions they were given was to shut off their phones, fill out a yellow card with their personal information, and put both the card and their phone into a resealable plastic bag they had been given. As he held the power button on his phone, Corbin felt it start to vibrate from an incoming call, stopped short as the power cut off. With a shaky hand, he filled out the card, placed all the required items into the plastic bag, and then put the bag into the large, plastic gray tote that was being carried around to each recruit by the male drill sergeant.

The rest of the evening went by in quite a blur. They were given a quick briefing regarding "Reception," the phase of Basic Training they were beginning, being assigned to the 30th AG Battalion. There was an amnesty period where they were instructed about items that were considered contraband and allowed to step into a small booth to discard any illicit items without risk of reprimand or penalty. A large pegboard stood in front of them with examples of prohibited items attached to it. Corbin could understand some of the things, such as weapons, drugs, alcohol, cigarettes, et cetera, but he found it peculiar that other items, such as playing cards and dirty magazines were considered on the same plane as the aforementioned items. What did it matter if someone wanted to kill some free time with a game of poker or a look at their favorite centerfold? No one in the group of recruits had anything that they needed to fess up to, so under the incredulous eye of the large, brutish drill sergeant and his ugly female counterpart, everyone was led through lines where their heads were shaved, then given a pair of black shorts and a gray T-shirt, each having the words "Army" printed on them, and then corralled through more and more lines until Corbin had completely lost track of time.

By the time they were being directed to their barracks area, Corbin remembered that he had a watch and checked it quickly as they were being assigned bunks. It was almost three in the morning! Each person was assigned to a bunk, either top or bottom, with an engraved number on the metal bed frame corresponding to a locker with the same number. For every pair of beds, there were a pair of lockers, one located at the head and foot of each bunk. Corbin was assigned to the bottom bunk, his bunkmate a young man by the last name of Kelly. Corbin watched his bunkmate for a time, considering how old he could be. From just the looks of it, Kelly looked like he could be the same age, maybe younger, even though that couldn't have been possible.

He looked around the open area, packed with bunks and recruits milling around, getting dressed into their shorts and shirt, or "PT's," as the drill sergeants had called them. He saw Alex climbing up onto the top bed just a few bunks away from where he was, and he shuffled over to him, pulling his PT shirt on over his head as he moved. The general demeanor of the group in the room was pretty somber, with very few conversations happening, and those who were talking did so in a hushed tone, as if they were nervous that the drill sergeants, who had left several minutes ago, would hear them and bring their military wrath down upon them.

"Hey, how goes it, man?" Corbin asked as he leaned against the bunk where Alex lay.

"I'm really nervous, dude."

"Yeah, me too, for sure. At least we know that we got each other's backs through all this, right?" Corbin said it in a way as if to offer comfort but also ask for reassurance for himself.

"Totally, man."

Corbin wanted to say something else but wasn't certain what he wanted to say. Alex took the moment of silence as a cue to roll over and start to doze off. It was right at this moment that a stern voice came over a PA speaker, stating that it was "Lights out," and all the lights in the room promptly shut off, leaving Corbin to feel his way through the darkness to his bed. He made a mental note of the location of his bunk, second row from the wall, dead center between the latrines and the door. He slid under the thin, practically useless blanket and extra starched sheets, grimacing a little at the inadequacy of the covers. Thankfully, the room temperature wasn't an issue, so the fact that his blanket couldn't keep a lizard warm in the Sahara was irrelevant.

Corbin felt like he had only begun to fall asleep when the lights suddenly turned on and the same stern voice from before announced over the PA that it was time to get up and get ready for chow. Rolling off his bed, he looked at his watch and discovered that the elapsed time between when they had lights out until now was only fifteen minutes! If their first night here was indicative of what their sleep schedule was going to be like the entire time, it was going to be one very **LONG** Basic Training cycle. Most, if not all the other recruits looked just as dazed and confused as Corbin felt as they stumbled from their bunks and tried to ascertain through their sleepy haze what was going on. Alex shuffled towards the latrines, toiletry bag in hand, aiming to do something to try to wake himself up a little more, such as brush his teeth. Corbin took a moment longer to try to wrap his head around the situation before he began to rummage through his locker for something to put onto his feet. The cold linoleum floor had begun to bother the bottoms of his feet, which were currently bare. Much to his dismay, he realized that, in the whirl of information and movement when they had first arrived, they weren't issued any kind of footwear, and they were under strict instructions not to wear anything that they had worn when they got there. Those items were stored in whatever backpack or bag they had brought with them, tucked into the locker of their assigned bunk.

Alex had returned from the latrine, and the two of them discussed what course of action they were to take when it came to what to wear on their feet. They deduced that there were only two options: one, assume that they needed to wear something on their feet, other than socks, and put on their shoes that they had worn here. However, they had been told specifically to pack everything up and keep it in their bags. Two, they adhere to the directions they were given and wear just their socks, because they were not given any other choice. They both agreed that it would be better to stick as closely to whatever command they were given, and assume any omitted details, and just hope for the best. At least that way they knew they were not *disobeying* any direct order, even if it meant kind of using their imagination as to what to do instead, which could also have ended up wrong.

They had made up their minds just in time, because at that moment, the two drill sergeants came bursting into the room, shouting, swearing, and barking orders, getting everyone to line up against the wall, shoulder to shoulder. Corbin noticed that there were mixed results when it came to who had decided to stick to their orders, and who opted to assume that they needed to put on some sort of footwear and retrieve their "civilian" shoes from their bags. Thankfully, Corbin and Alex had guessed correctly, because all those who were wearing shoes were immediately pointed out by the drill sergeants, ordered to step forward, and drop down and then begin doing push-ups until directed otherwise. The ugly female drill sergeant, whose name Corbin hadn't taken the opportunity to find on her uniform, looked particularly pleased each time she found another offender whom she could "correct" in any number of ways, such as push-ups, squats, wall-sits, or any other physically uncomfortable way that she saw fit. The drill sergeants referred to it as "smoking." Corbin made sure to make a mental note regarding following orders and that even if they lacked information, he'd make sure not to go against whatever it was that they *did* receive. If even something as simple as this situation was a sign of what the rest of Basic Training was going to be, he was going to make sure that he wouldn't muck it up.

After the offenders of the shoe instructions were "smoked" enough to satisfy the ugly female drill sergeant, who seemed to be more and more sadistic with each passing minute, she decided that everyone needed to join in on the "fun," as she called it. With a shrill command, everyone dropped down into a push-up position, or "front leaning rest," and was told to do push-ups until she decided that she was tired. It wasn't pleasant, but Corbin found it beneficial to just concentrate on doing what he was told and not thinking about when the smoking was going to end. It seemed like, whenever he did that, the smoking sessions ended almost as soon as they started, whether they did, or whether his perception of the endurance of the session was skewed, he didn't know, nor did he care.

Breakfast, or as Corbin learned was the term for every mealtime, "chow" was an eye-opening experience itself. Naturally, everyone was rushed through the line to get their food and sit down. They were only allowed to get and use a spoon, even though there were forks and knives available. When getting drinks, they were instructed to get two cups, fill them, then hold them close to their chests, elbows straight out to their sides like wings. No matter how strange or outlandish the order or instruction, Corbin and Alex made sure that they responded exactly to specification, just to make sure they avoided getting smoked. Along with being told what to get and how quickly to get it, they were told how to sit, (straight back, feet flat on the floor, heels together), where to look, (straight forward), and even how quickly to eat. Any infraction, no matter how big or little, was met with punishment. Corbin even witnessed one recruit attempt to shovel another spoonful of eggs into his mouth after the big drill sergeant shouted that he was done and was forced to spit out the food before being smoked.

In stark contrast to the chaos that erupted when they were woken up and during chow, the next leg of the journey was nothing more than waiting quietly in lines. They were ushered through lines to do paperwork, lines to get equipment, and uniforms, and even lines to receive vaccinations. All the while, they were not to speak to one another, maintaining almost complete silence, which made it extremely difficult to stay awake, another crucial demand from the drill sergeants. Corbin was grateful that any time he felt like he was about to doze off, he was startled back to reality as a shrill screech, or a booming shout would erupt from the silence as the drill sergeants spotted someone else falling asleep. That individual, as per the very quickly accepted norm, was then subjected to some sort of corrective punishment. On varied occasion, everyone in the group would be "smoked," just because the drill sergeants felt like it.

Exhausted at the end of another day of sensory assault and overload, Corbin practically fell asleep the very moment he sprawled out on his bunk. Alex shuffled by, looking just as out of gas, and a bit distressed as well. He wobbled a little on his feet as he stopped and stood next to Corbin's bunk. Corbin had started to doze and was somewhat unintentionally alarmed when he noticed someone near him out of the haze of his half-closed eyes. Sitting up with a start, he cleared his throat as Alex glanced at him without saying a word.

"Dude, you look like crap," Corbin pointed out.

"I feel about the same way too. How are you holding up?"

"So far, so good, I guess," Corbin responded with a shrug. It was, for the most part, true. He had spent so much time learning about the military when he was at home; he had even watched limited-time documentaries about Basic Training and had developed a pretty good idea about the general goings-on during a training cycle. He didn't know everything, but he did know that all the yelling and "smoking" and stressful situations they were subjected to were all for a purpose. Granted, he didn't know all the events that occurred during ten weeks of Basic, but he did know that almost everything had a purpose, generally to train each recruit to think and act like a soldier, rather than a civilian, and a moody, unruly teenager at that.

"You really aren't getting worn out by all of this?" Alex questioned incredulously.

"Well, I mean, it *does* wear on me, for sure, but I know that there's plenty of reason for treating us the way that they do." Corbin yawned, unable to fight the fatigue that was taking its toll on him.

"Yeah, they just like to mess around with us and see us suffer, that's why," Alex complained cynically. "I mean, what kind of psycho likes to torture someone constantly like these guys do?"

"It's all just to train us, man," Corbin started. "We have to be able to just take orders without question, no matter how weird it is, or how sucky it is, like getting smoked. I just try to do whatever they say, even when they are smoking us, and focus on doing whatever it is, until the next order, then doing that. It's crazy, it's like any time it happens, it's as over as soon as it starts, because I'm not just wondering in my head if or when it will stop."

Alex's demeanor softened a bit, evidence that he was realizing how

Corbin's words could help. A slight smile came across his lips as he looked off into the distance for a moment. "Yeah, I bet you're right, huh?"

"Of course! Just assume that I'm always right," Corbin joked, punching Alex in the arm in jest.

"Well, I wouldn't be so sure of *that*," Alex kidded in return.

The two of them laughed together for a moment, thankful to have even just the short times between getting into their barracks and lights out to feel like normal human beings. It was most assuredly a very eye-opening experience, getting into the military, and it sure made them feel like they had to grow up in no time at all. So, it was very relaxing to get even just a tiny sliver of the day to feel like they were teens once again and not have to do push-ups or sit-ups as a result.

Chapter Three

Reception seemed to drag on for an eternity, day after painful day, but also felt like it went by in a flash. Before Corbin could think, there they were, lined up in ranks and files, in full digital camouflage uniforms and two duffle bags at each recruit's feet. They waited silently, standing at attention in the Georgia heat, sheltered at least from the sun by the pavilion structure they were formed up beneath. That, however, didn't do anything to spare them from the suffocating humidity. Their two drill sergeants paced quietly around the group, watching like hawks waiting to divebomb their unsuspecting prey. It was nearly impossible for Corbin to keep from watching them circle; he felt like he needed to keep aware of where they were, as if his life depended on it. He knew he couldn't move his head, and it was a risk to even move his eyes as he was in the second rank, easily seen by either of the instructors. So, he did his best to focus his attention on them, while keeping his eyes forward, standing rigid in the position of attention, and then listening to their movement whenever they stepped out of his peripheral vision.

"Listen up, you little pukes," the ugly, short drill sergeant shouted. Corbin had never bothered to even look at the name tag on her uniform to discover her last name, he disliked her that much. "You may have gotten through Reception, but that doesn't mean dick when it comes to where you are headed. If you thought the last two weeks were tough, you better just pack now and go home. Believe it or not, we have been nice to you... soft on you this entire time."

Corbin had to catch himself from instinctively contorting his face into an expression of, "Are you freaking kidding me?" He hoped that she wasn't serious, because she was particularly sadistic at times. He thought back to one incident where she had come into the hallway where they were waiting, carrying a large cupcake in her hand, and an evil smile on her face. She had announced that it was her birthday, and that she was going to celebrate with the dessert and offered to share it with anyone interested, all they had to do was raise their hand. Naturally, most everyone stayed silent, feeling the ominous sensation that this whole thing was a trap. She hadn't bothered to try to be even remotely cordial with them the entire time they had been here, so what was this, other than a trick?

Unfortunately, someone within their company hadn't caught on to the *real* reason for her veiled intent and immediately raised his hand. The drill sergeant hadn't been looking in his direction at first, and Corbin prayed desperately in his mind for this idiot to put his hand down. Of course, he didn't, and when he was finally spotted, everyone's suspicions were confirmed as this hideous woman's face twisted into an evil grin. Dammit, he was in for it now. They all were in for it, because after this dummy was smoked for raising his hand, everyone else was smoked with him for not doing anything to stop him from raising his hand. If *this* was being nice, what could be considered unkind?

After some considerable time, a trio of white-washed school buses pulled up in front of the formation, stopping neatly and evenly spaced along the curb. The moment the doors to the buses were ajar, the two drill sergeants began barking and shouting orders, herding everyone onto the buses and into their seats in an organized yet chaotic mess. Their instructions to everybody were to sit in their seat silently, with one duffle bag sitting horizontally on their lap and the other standing vertically on top of that bag, with their faces right up against this duffle bag. Also, they were not to speak, look or turn their heads in any direction and, as per usual, told not to fall asleep. Of course, this would be the most difficult task of all, seeing as they all suffered from two weeks of sleep deprivation and exhaustion, both physical and mental. In the madness of loading onto the buses, Corbin wasn't able to get a chance to see where Alex had gone. He was originally in the second rank, the same as him, while in formation, however, the entire company of recruits scattered and clambered towards a bus when the shouting commenced. He hoped that he was okay.

The drive to wherever they were headed was silent and excruciating. Trying to stay awake was certifiably the most difficult task. Though no one knew how they would get caught if they dozed off, (there was no one else on board except them and the bus driver), nobody dared to even blink a millisecond longer than was considered normal. Corbin was so nervous about any infraction that he painfully held back the urge to clear his throat though it felt more and more parched with each passing minute. It also felt like his duffle bags were getting heavier, as if some unseen force was periodically dropping a new brick onto his lap. He was starting to worry that he wasn't even going to be able to pick up his bags to get off the bus, whenever that was supposed to happen. The bus continued onward, taking turns and stops every so often, confusing everyone on board to the point that they had no idea whether they were even on base anymore. Corbin started to wonder what the hell was going on. There was no way that wherever they were headed was so far out that it was taking this long to get there. He started to suspect that the bus was just taking a "scenic" route, and their orders to keep their faces against their bags were intended to disorient them.

Corbin wasn't sure if it was ten minutes or ten hours from when they had first boarded the buses until the point he felt the vehicle slow to a stop, the hiss of the parking brake signaling the end of their travel. He didn't have much time to think about it, though, because as soon as the bus stopped, the doors opened and everyone on board was assailed with an explosion of shouting, cursing, and deafening orders. He moved as quickly as possible to gather his duffle bags and scurry off the bus at the insistence of the quartet of drill sergeants that had so suddenly invaded the formerly quiet space. The occupants of all the buses were being chased, in many cases literally, by drill sergeants and herded off toward a large, dome-covered area about one hundred yards from the road. Clamoring through the large opening in the massive white dome, the recruits stumbled about as they were organized into a large formation of ranks and files, each person standing several arm lengths apart.

Corbin quickly remembered what this part of the Basic Training experience was called; "Shark Attack." The name was very fitting, considering the situation. All the recruits, like a school of unsuspecting fish, were led into an area they didn't know was potentially dangerous and, before they knew it, they were blindsided by a group of "sharks" streaming in for the kill. The drill sergeants were just like those aquatic predators as well wherein they would immediately swarm a recruit who showed any sign of weakness or intent to quit, just as a weakened or injured fish would meet a very similar, dismal end. During a particularly lengthy stretch of push-ups, Corbin began to struggle to keep going and showed signs of slowing down. Before he could even figure out what was happening, he was immediately surrounded by a quartet of drill sergeants who shouted, screamed, and berated him, insisting that he quit and just go home. Corbin could feel their hot breath on his face, despite the heat and humidity, as he set to continue to do push-ups, even though his arms were shaking and threatening to buckle underneath him. When the drill sergeants saw that he wasn't going to quit so easily, they swooped away in search of another individual to terrorize. Corbin sighed in relief but continued to exert all the energy he could in each workout to ensure he didn't subject himself to that particular situation again.

He couldn't even remember how long this interminable smoke session had been going on, but he was relieved when the company of recruits was ordered to stand at attention, and no further orders were given. With the rigors of the exercises, the weather conditions, and his heightened stress levels, Corbin's uniform was so soaked with sweat that it looked like he had jumped into a pool fully clothed. Everyone around him was sweating profusely as well and panting heavily from all the physicality. Corbin did his best to keep his labored breathing as quiet as possible, fearing that breathing too loud would subject him to further punishment. Doing so made it feel like he might pass out at any moment which also made him worry about further discipline.

At the front of the domed structure, referred to as "The Bubble," now stood eight drill sergeants. There were six male and two female drill sergeants and though they were both small in stature by comparison to their male colleagues, the two females looked far more fearsome and menacing. In the blur that had been the past however long it had been since they got off the bus, Corbin had almost forgotten that one of the female drill sergeants, who looked Hispanic, her name tape reading "Rodriguez," was the most aggressive and relentless antagonist towards him when his push-ups started to slow down. She had made that whole interaction the most intense thing he had ever experienced, and he hoped to keep himself in line enough to **never** have to endure something like that at her hands again. Beside the drill sergeant standing in the center of the row of foreboding figures was a black box that looked like a speaker with a microphone sitting atop. The centermost drill sergeant picked up the microphone and began to speak.

"My name is Drill Sergeant Leonard," he began, his voice booming over the speaker. "Welcome to Echo Company, Second Battalion, Twenty-Ninth Infantry Regiment of the 198th Infantry Brigade! Mustangs lead the way!"

There was a collective shout of, "Hooah," from all the Drill Sergeants.

Drill Sergeant Leonard was the senior drill sergeant of Fourth Platoon. He wasn't of commanding height, about 5' 5", however he was built like a silverback gorilla, and his overall presence was extremely intimidating. His shoulders were broad, his neck thick and, even though his uniform wasn't form-fitting, it was simple to see that he was very muscular and had the general demeanor of a soldier who had seen and experienced the rigors and chaos of war. Corbin had a feeling that Drill Sergeant Leonard had, for lack of a better term in his mind, "been there and done that." He was the shortest of the male drill sergeants, and looked dwarfed next to the tall, African American drill sergeant standing next to him; however, Drill Sergeant Leonard looked to Corbin as the one anyone would least likely want to cross in any way.

"You will now be separated into one of the four platoons within Echo Company. This will be your home for the duration of Basic Combat Training. The other members of your platoon will be your family. They will be your brothers and sisters, so you better get along, or this will be one very long ten weeks."

It didn't sound much like a suggestion to get along, and Corbin and Alex sure didn't take it that way. After a short pause, as if to make sure his words settled in, Drill Sergeant Leonard began to speak again and the rest of the drill sergeants began to split up, separating and dispersing amongst the recruits, again looking like sharks awaiting to strike the weakest member of a school of helpless fish. Corbin swallowed hard and did his best to look forward and maintain a stoic appearance in hopes of reducing the likelihood of looking like an easy target.

"You will notice that your duffle bags have been collected and had a tag with a number attached to each one. That number represents the platoon you will be a part of. Once you've collected your bags, return to your position and await further instructions. Understood?"

There was a collective hesitation from the crowd. No one was particularly sure how to reply. Corbin was sure that most everyone had at least seen a clip of some portrayal of Basic Training. Were the movies, television episodes, or whatever accurate? Did anyone even dare venture a guess? It wasn't until an unseen recruit shouted, "Sir, yes Sir," that they received their answer. The other drill sergeants had apparently seen who had called out and were immediately surrounding the unfortunate individual, screaming and swearing incessantly as Drill Sergeant Leonard boomed over the speaker.

"Absolutely NOT! Don't you DARE come at me with that 'Sir' garbage! I'm not some worthless Officer, I WORK for a living!"

At this point, the recruit was scrambling between push-ups, sit-ups, and several other exercises that Corbin wasn't familiar with as he tried, but mostly failed, to keep up with the torrent of shouts that engulfed him like a tidal wave. Corbin was a little confused, to say the least. As far as he knew, "sir" and "ma'am" were terms used to address someone respectfully. His father, who had grown up in the South, had always taught him that he was to always address individuals that way as a sign of respect. He supposed that Drill Sergeant Leonard was aware of this; however, his reaction to being called "sir" was almost the equivalent of him being insulted in some personal manner. Corbin furrowed his brow and glanced quickly over to Alex, who simply shrugged.

"You will address this cadre as 'Drill Sergeant,' and answer accordingly. 'Yes, Drill Sergeant,' or 'No, Drill Sergeant,' and let those words be the last thing that comes out of your filthy pie holes. Do you understand?!"

"YES, DRILL SERGEANT!" came the booming response from the recruits.

"Go get your shit!!"

Everyone broke into a sprint towards the mountainous pile of duffle bags stacked in the back corner of the dome. With no regard to anyone else, each recruit feverishly dug through the pile of bags, throwing out any duffle that wasn't their own. It was everything Alex and Corbin could do to find their own bags, let alone try not to get wiped out by a flying piece of luggage. As they were some who were furthest from the pile to begin with, and with all the pandemonium that ensued, Alex and Corbin were some of the last few to find their bags and scramble back to their original positions in the formation. As they were stragglers compared to others, they were subject to a little more "attention" from the drill sergeants who chased them, bellowing and snapping at them like rabid wolves.

Once everyone was back in position, the drill sergeants dispersed, giving Corbin a very cautious sense of relief, for the time being, anyway. He kept his gaze forward but allowed his attention to focus on his periphery in order to try to keep track of any cadre nearby who may be in an ideal position to barrage him with expletives in the blink of an eye. The general sense of unease had diminished a little as a hush fell over the entire company of recruits, all anxiously waiting for the next set of instructions. It may have only been a few seconds, but the silence made it feel like it was an eternity, which was why Corbin jumped a little as Drill Sergeant Leonard's voice boomed over the speaker again.

"Now! Look at the tag on your duffle. Whatever number it is, you will get your sorry self over to the truck with the matching number and form up behind it!"

Corbin looked down at his bags to find a tag with a blue number four attached to each of them. He looked up to find a quartet of large six-wheeled trucks backed up to the dome, each having a numbered plaque hanging from it, a number and color that corresponded with the numbers on the tags each recruit had. He almost lurched into action in order to sprint towards the truck with the number four on it; however, something inside him told him to stop, and he held still, despite his natural intention to follow what Leonard had commanded.

He was glad that he had held off, because almost as soon as he had resolved to stay put, he saw a scattered group of recruits begin to move towards the trucks. As soon as they began to move, they were met by the drill sergeants and their punitive commands and exercises. Corbin let out a subdued sigh and looked sideways at Alex, who looked a little pale, but determined. He noticed that other recruits around him looked just as pallid, but also somewhat relieved that they hadn't made themselves subject to further consequences.

"Did I say that you could move yet?!" roared Leonard's voice over the speaker. "If there is anything that you learn, it is that you do absolutely NOTHING unless you are told to do so! You do not eat, you do not sleep, you do not even utilize the latrine unless we say for you to do so. IS THAT UNDERSTOOD?!"

"YES, DRILL SERGEANT!"

"GOOD! Now MOVE!"

It was a little confusing to Corbin, to say the least, how each and every action was dictated by Drill Sergeant Leonard, even when he didn't really even need to say anything, in his mind at least. It was almost like an older sibling asserting some sort of ill-conceived dominance over a younger sibling by commanding them to do every little thing. *He had given instructions to get behind the truck with the matching number, so the recruits who had started to follow those instructions weren't in the wrong*, Corbin thought. So, why was it necessary to add an additional, unnecessary command when people were already going to follow what he had said? Maybe that was just the way of a Drill Sergeant, to be some overbearing, demanding, condescending prick who got their rocks off by being a sadistic dickwad to any recruit who rolled through. Then again, he did already know that everything was done for a reason, especially when it came to following orders, and getting rid of the civilian in every recruit there. Nevertheless, it was impossible for his young mind to avoid thinking this way.

Another leg of the journey ended, and another began as everyone scrambled toward the trucks, forming up behind the vehicle that matched their number. Corbin was pleased to see Alex get into formation with him behind the number four truck. Once everyone was in position, they were instructed to load their bags into the beds of the massive trucks and then follow them, in formation, to their barracks. It wasn't as long as it was, only a block or two away from where the large white dome was. The barracks appeared to be large, four-storied buildings constructed of tan brick with flat, white roofs.

Corbin glanced at the building through sweat-stung eyes and thought to himself how this was going to be his home for the next couple of months. He wondered what they were going to look like inside, and whether media portrayals of barracks were accurate or not. He pondered whether he and Alex would be assigned to bunks close to each other, and what they could all expect next. His fatigued and clammy body was aching for rest, and Corbin even allowed himself a moment to daydream about getting assigned a bunk and being able to take a nap, but the more aware part of his mind knew that there was absolutely no way that they were going to get a break now. His body throbbed, his muscles seeming to complain, almost audibly to his mind, regarding all the recent overexertion and strain they had endured. It was definitely the first time in his life that he had ever experienced sensory overload.

He wasn't quite sure how to process it all and didn't have time to as they were herded into the building, each group being moved to the floor that corresponded to the number that they had been assigned. As if his fatigue wasn't enough, Corbin felt like his heart was going to explode as he dragged his duffle bags up four flights of stairs and all but fell on his face as he pushed through the heavy steel door marked by a large, black number four. As part of the middle of the group that had made it to their floor, Corbin had to quickly shuffle himself and his bags to one side of the doorway as the remainder of their crowd thundered through into the common area where they all now stood, panting, sweating, and some even cursing repeatedly under their breath. It wasn't more than a split second later that they heard the pounding footsteps of Drill Sergeants Leonard and his partner, (a steely African American man named Drill Sergeant Melendez), coming up the stairs rapidly. Everyone moved away from the doorway as if to avoid being in the kill radius of an explosive.

The door swung open and slammed into the wall behind it with a deafening **bang**, which startled Corbin enough to make it feel like his heart jumped up into the back of his throat. In the cavernous common area where they stood, all linoleum and brick, the drill sergeants' voices echoed and discombobulated everyone as they shouted, "TOE THE LINE," and "THE KILL ZONE, THE KILL ZONE!" Naturally, as had already occurred several times now, the entire collection of recruits just fumbled about stupidly until they were directed pointedly to stand at the position of attention, their toes on a solid blue line that bordered what was referred to as The Kill Zone. This was a long, rectangular area in the center of the common area, a solitary desk in the center of it and a large painting of a three-headed pit bull emblazoned on the floor in front of it. Everyone stood shoulder-to-shoulder, toes on the line, facing inward towards this area as Leonard and Melendez paced the length of the zone.

Apparently, it was The Kill Zone because you might as well be dead if you ever set foot in that area without explicit instruction from a drill sergeant. It was where they were to receive instruction as a group each day, where they were to be corrected if, or rather when, occasion arose to do so. Corbin figured it was kind of their central hub for their...platoon, yeah, that's what they were called. He found out that they were Fourth Platoon, nicknamed the "Devil Dogs." It seemed a little strange to him that they, an Army platoon, would be called that because that nickname was for a Marine. However, the question was answered almost immediately as it was explained that Drill Sergeant Melendez was formerly a Marine. Additionally, in no uncertain terms, it was revealed that Drill Sergeant Leonard had served on multiple overseas deployments and had been involved in operations that had terminated very high-ranking members of al-Qaeda and other terrorist groups. It was easy to see that these two meant business, and Corbin felt like they had the most hardcore Drill Sergeants of the whole company.

Next was a shakedown, where everyone had to empty the contents of their duffle bags onto the floor and toss any contraband into the kill zone to be disposed of. Corbin didn't think that there was any way to get anything considered contraband, seeing as they had just spent their last two weeks in reception, in extremely controlled conditions, where obtaining anything against the rules seemed near impossible. Rather than dirty magazines or cigarettes, recruits were forced to get rid of things that seemed more innocuous, such as liquid body wash, cologne, even certain types of deodorant. They were assured that there would be a time that they would be allowed to obtain the "legal" types of hygiene items that they would need. He sure hoped so, because he had to get rid of his body wash. He was feeling particularly sweaty and grimy, and he knew it wasn't going to get any better.

After the shakedown, they were all assigned a "Battle Buddy," who was going to be their continual partner in everything that they would do for the duration of Basic. Everyone was paired off as Drill Sergeant Leonard read alphabetically by last name down the list of the recruits in Fourth Platoon. Much to Corbin's surprise and delight, there were no other recruits between Kent and McMann, so he and Alex were assigned as battle buddies. Then, the members of the platoon were ushered down one of four long hallways that branched off from the main common area, each hallway looking like a sterile dormitory hall with doorways that had no doors on them. Inside each room there was a pair of identical twin-sized beds with tall locker-like closets beside them, facing each other. Everyone was commanded to put their duffle bags into their lockers and then immediately, "Toe the line."

From that point, it was just a big blur to Corbin. From what he could remember, and in no particular order, they had "indoctrination," chow, were issued bedding and instructed on how to organize their lockers, had more indoctrination, got hygiene items, and got smoked on a regular basis, and even trained on Drill and Ceremony. It was exhilarating to already be doing things that he had always admired and hoped to participate in, such as marching and standing and moving in formation with his platoon. At the end of a day that felt like it had lasted more like three, Corbin collapsed into his bed, or "rack" as it was referred to, and didn't have much time to even formulate a thought before he fell asleep. The last thing he could remember going through his mind was a booming voice shouting, "Mustangs lead the way!"

Chapter Four

It's amazing what a human can grow accustomed to, and in a short amount of time. Anyone, even not in their right mind, would find practically everything about Basic Training strange, or even downright unnecessary. For instance, getting woken up by someone screaming at the top of their lungs, "Get out of the rack," or by an empty metal garbage can being thrown down the hallway would normally cause a lot of complaint. There was even one time where 4th Platoon's "alarm" in the morning was a few CS gas canisters being tossed into the barracks. Normally, someone *for sure* would be writing in some sort of letter of litigation or complaint regarding such treatment, but for Corbin and his comrades in the platoon, it was just business as usual and they would roll out of bed and get on with their morning routine, even with protective masks on in the instance of the gas. Corbin even thought back to times when he remembered some entitled brat in school completely blowing a gasket for getting their cell phone taken away during class and how they would be an ever-flowing fountain of whining and complaining for what they endured on a regular basis here in Fort Benning. Truthfully, even **he** would have had some things to whine about if he didn't already understand that everything they did was to get rid of his old, civilian self, and get him ready to be a soldier. Naturally, there were some within 4th Platoon, as well as the other platoons in the company, who did have childish things to say about their "poor treatment," but they either changed their attitude quickly, or ended up quitting. All he or the others could think when that happened was, *"Good riddance."*

It was interesting to notice the transformation in himself as the weeks passed. At first, he would naturally react to the things that happened in a way where he would think, "Hey, that's not fair," or "Well that's a bunch of BS," but nowadays, his initial reaction was more akin to, "Good, we didn't need him as dead weight anyway," or, "This is just another something to make us stronger." It was interesting for him to recognize the shift in his mindset, and his feeling of camaraderie towards those within his platoon, as well as the company as a whole. He and Alex had gotten off to a good start, and it only got better each passing day as they pushed through each trial as battle buddies. Corbin had noticed that there were plenty of guys who didn't seem to get along so well with their assigned companions, other than to placate the drill sergeants with only a superficial coalition.

Not Corbin and Alex, however. No, the two of them had grown to be like brothers, even better brothers than he was with his own biological siblings. The two of them were practically inseparable, and by choice, not just because the Army told them to stick to each other like glue. It made a lot of things more bearable, especially the hard things, and there were plenty of those. It was particularly helpful during their training where they were exposed to CS gas in what they simply referred to as "the gas chamber." It was emboldening to know that he had a brother by his side when the unseen gas stung his skin like a sunburn and burned his eyes and nostrils as if he had just been sprayed in the face with liquified cinnamon gummy bear.

The next challenge on the docket was what was called the Night Infiltration Course, or "NIC." The entirety of Echo Company was assigned to navigate through a stretch of three hundred yards of obstacles until they reached and assaulted a mock village where they were to clear hostiles from buildings and consolidate on the far end. 1st and 3rd Platoons were tasked with flanking and assaulting the village from the sides while 2nd and 4th Platoons were to hit it from the front. All of this, as most deduced from the name of the exercise, was to be done at night. It felt a bit daunting and exciting to Corbin as the Company reviewed the objectives and mapped platoon movements on a whiteboard just outside of the exercise area. Once the overall operation was reviewed, each platoon was separated into squads and fire teams, which were then separated into different areas of an opening in trees that resembled a large picnic area.

Corbin sat with his squad, a group of six, including himself and Alex. The assigned squad leader separated them into two fire teams, which he named each team and individual a highly inappropriate name, partially as a joke, but also as a way to keep their callsigns unique so they wouldn't easily lose each other in whatever was to come. They all leaned forward towards the center of their picnic table, which was old, weathered, and splintered. Corbin did his best not to let any bare skin touch the tabletop in hopes of preventing any slivers. Their assignment was part of the main assault group that was going to make their way through the course first, arriving at the edge of the mock village ahead of the rest of the platoon in order to provide cover for the other advancing teams. Once everyone had reached the rally point and was accounted for, they were to push to the village and systematically clear the buildings of hostiles, which were other members of Echo Company who the drill sergeants had already selected and taken off to brief them on their duties as Opposing Forces, or OPFOR.

As the sun set quickly, Corbin tried to look around and get a glimpse of the course they were to be traversing, but with how thick the Georgia pines were around them, combined with the sun being level with his eyes, all he could see was tree trunks and blinding orange light. When he realized there was no way he was going to get an advanced view of their objectives, he went back to listening closely to his squad discussing their movements as well as check their gear. There was a low din from the surrounding area as all the other squads and fire teams did the same.

When their prep time ended, the drill sergeants rounded everyone up and had them all get in a single-file line. Corbin and his squad were the second in line, putting him about the tenth man back from the front of the line. They were marched through the trees along a thin trail of sand, which was in stark contrast to the lush, green forest floor that it cut through. Everyone was silent as they marched, the tension amongst them almost painfully tangible. Corbin focused on his breathing and keeping it quiet as he looked over his issued weapon, an M16A2, adjusting the telescoping stock to a comfortable length and double-checking the magazine, filled with thirty blanks. In the pouches mounted to the front of his plate carrier vest were three more magazines, also filled with blanks. He could hear the hushed rattle of rifles and magazines as others did the same.

As they neared the course, the sun had almost completely set, leaving a dull glow along the horizon and leaving Echo Company in the cool and dim of twilight. Ahead of them was a wooden wall, roughly eight feet tall, punctuated by ladders positioned sporadically down its length. From a distance, Corbin could see that atop the wall there was sand, as if there were some raised sand box awaiting them over the wall. The first squads were positioned at the ladders, his squad being placed at one of them near the center. Drill Sergeant Leonard and a Drill Sergeant Poulson, (from 1st Platoon), moved up and down the length of the wall, shouting.

"Everyone in position! When we tell you to get over the wall, you move over the wall and keep moving! Stay low, don't stop, and whatever you do, do NOT stand up!"

They had been briefed during the safety portion of the brief that part of this exercise was going to include live ammunition being fired over their heads, tracer rounds. Not that it sounded like a fun time to begin with, but Corbin started to feel pangs of unease in his gut as the order of "don't stand up," was mentioned. They weren't particularly clear about how far above them the live rounds would be fired, but if they were told not to stand up during this exercise, he had a feeling those rounds would be a lot closer than he had previously imagined. Oh goody...

Over the repeated instructions from the drill sergeants, he also noticed a new sound. Somewhere above them and around them was the sound of loud Arabic-sounding music, gunfire, and screams of pain and pleading for help. He spotted a speaker mounted high in a tree that was emitting this cacophony of chaos. Hopefully this was all that was going to be used to help disorient them and immerse them in the simulated combat experience. His heart thudded in his throat as he clutched his rifle and waited, pressed closely together with the rest of his squad. Before he felt like he was ready, if he ever was going to feel like he was ready, Drill Sergeants Leonard and

Poulson were barking at everyone to get over the wall. His squad sprang into action, scampering up the ladder in front of them and rolling into the sand above.

The entire area was a raised course, three hundred yards long and at least one hundred wide. The ground was a rough, gritty sand, littered with anti-tank obstacles, razor wire, mock tanks with pneumatic guns that simulated machine gun fire, and open concrete-lined pits that spurted fire from them like some Hollywood special effect. As soon as they cleared the wall and began to low crawl through the unforgiving sand, the sound effect track in the speakers was accompanied by the "ratatatatat" of the pneumatic guns, the occasional "bang" of the fire pits erupting, and the staccato sound of two machine gun nests at the far end of the course, firing live tracer rounds above them that looked like lasers from a sci-fi movie blazing above them. To Corbin, the whole thing looked and sounded like an approach on Omaha Beach in Normandy.

As if the absolute insanity of everything going on around and above them wasn't enough, the drill sergeants threw in another little obstacle that they intentionally didn't preface. Aside from the group of recruits they assigned to be OPFOR, they had secretly pulled others aside to use as simulated casualties within the course. All of these participants were those who were taller, or more heavy-set, adding to the difficulty of aiding and moving them. No one knew about any of this until they had cleared the first row of obstacles and wire and the drill sergeants started shouting that there were casualties in the field that they not only needed to treat them but also needed to move them to the end of the course where their rally point was. Over the discord of the battlefield around them, Corbin could make out the strained voices of the simulated casualties, strewn about like driftwood on a beach.

Alex was quick to link up with Corbin and the two of them snaked their way through the course, occasionally having to duck their head down so low that they were blindly pulling themselves along the ground, their faces dragging through the sand as they did. They had made it about another fifty yards before they came across a body that lay still next to a Czech hedgehog anti-tank obstacle. Corbin almost considered leaving them there, as trying to assist them would only hinder their advance, and he rationalized that there would be plenty of others behind them who could help the downed soldier. However, that thought was quickly displaced from his mind as he was overcome with the undeniable drive to help a fallen brother. He looked to Alex, who seemed to understand his thoughts, and the two of them nodded to each other and hastily made their way to the casualty. When they got next to the body, they found it to be someone who was at least 6' 3" and slender. Thankfully not heavy, but their height was going to make movement difficult. He had a laminated red index card tucked into his belt that listed his condition. His card showed that he had been wounded in the abdomen by a gunshot and was losing blood quickly but was conscious. Alex quickly got to putting pressure on the imaginary wound while Corbin got his head close to the head of his fallen brother.

"Private First-Class Corbin Kent, 4th Platoon," he announced, screaming over the commotion.

"Private Brent Rice, 2nd Platoon," was the soldier's reply.

"Hey, my buddy Alex and I are gonna get you out of here! Can you put pressure on your wound while we move you?!"

"Yeah, I think so," answered Rice.

"Cool. Give me your other hand!"

Brent reached up with one hand and grabbed Corbin's hand, holding his invisible wound with the other. Corbin and Alex alternated pulling their comrade forward, Corbin by his hand and Alex by his belt. The sand piled behind Brent's body with each pull, making every tug that much more difficult and covering even less ground. Occasionally, they would have to roll him sideways to get him away from the sand that had accumulated so they could pull him a bit further and repeat the process. Every inch they covered felt more like a mile, and Corbin began to wonder if they were even going in the right direction because it felt like it was taking longer than he thought it should be taking to get to the rally point. All the while, the machine gun fire and explosions didn't let up, and the sand felt more and more like sandpaper being dragged on bare skin as they crawled even though their sleeves covered their arms completely. Despite it all, Corbin had a deep-seated drive not to let his brother down. Until just moments ago, he had never met Private Brent Rice from 2nd Platoon, but he felt an obligation to get him to safety even at the peril of his own well-being. He couldn't let him down, and he sure wasn't going to.

The three of them finally reached the end of the sand, Corbin and Alex pulling Brent across the cold grass, which felt like a balm to their burning knees and elbows. They tugged him down the length of the raised berm in front of them until they got Brent to the pre-assigned casualty collection point. They then called out the callsign of their squad leader, as well as their personal callsigns to triangulate their position and get to the rest of their squad. Once they had rallied with their squad, they coordinated with the rest of their platoon to assault the village and clear it of hostiles. Thankfully, they didn't take on any other casualties in their assault, letting them push through the village until it was cleared, and the cadre signaled the end of the exercise by bellowing, "ENDEX!" The madness that had so quickly erupted around them silenced just as fast. Everyone began to mill about, regrouping with their platoons at the instruction of their drill sergeants.

Corbin felt like all the skin on his elbows and knees had been sanded off. His flesh felt hot and sticky under his uniform and it hurt any time the fabric brushed against him as he walked. He was sweaty, exhausted, and starving. Thank goodness it was time for some chow, even if it was just an MRE. Carefully he sat down on the ground and began to unpackage his meal. Spaghetti and meat sauce, one of the better MREs, hallelujah. He laid his rifle across his lap, making sure it didn't touch the ground. It was definitely on the brink of jamming; thanks to all the sand they had crawled through. He had been able to use it just fine during their assault on the village, but he could tell just by the grinding sensation every time he pulled the charging handle that his weapon was going to need an astronomical amount of cleaning and maintenance. He didn't worry too much, however, because he found cleaning his rifle to be therapeutic, probably because he was a bit OCD, and it always felt satisfying to clean something. Alex took a seat next to him, followed closely behind by Brent, the guy they had rescued. They were all silent for a little while, taking the time to quickly consume their meals just in case a surprise order or something interrupted them. When it was evident to each of them that they had time to enjoy their chow, Private Rice was the first to say something.

"Thanks for bailing me out in there," he mentioned with a slight shrug.

"No problem," Alex responded, not looking up from his food.

"Not that there was much of a choice," Corbin added, "we couldn't leave you behind. I mean, drill sergeants aside, it would have been a dick move in a lot of ways if we just went on past you."

"Well, it was just an exercise, doesn't mean I was really in trouble or anything. What's the worst that could have happened?"

"Drill sergeants would have smoked the daylights out of us," Alex said, sounding a little annoyed.

"No, not even that," Corbin started, "Come on, you're one of us. You're part of the team. We don't just leave our team members behind; we bring everyone home."

"You're not going to go into some long, mushy speech, are you?" Alex joked.

"No, but I'm serious, dude. Whether it's an exercise or not, we don't leave each other behind. We gotta look out for each other, even if we are in different platoons. We are all still on the same team."

"Thanks, Captain America."

"Shut up, Alex," Corbin laughed.

The three of them laughed together for a moment before falling silent, somewhat fearful that a drill sergeant would accuse them of "having too much fun" or something like that. After a quiet pause, Corbin spoke again.

"So what got you into all this, Rice?"

"Truthfully? I wasn't too sure of what I wanted to do once I had graduated high school. I didn't want to end up going to college for something I wasn't interested in or end up in some crappy job I went to years of school for only to hate it and feel like I was trapped in it. I dunno, the military seemed like a decent option, considering, and it wouldn't end up being a waste of time *and* money if it ended up being something I wasn't all that into."

"So...just potentially a waste of time?" Corbin raised an eyebrow.

"Well, yeah, but I wouldn't be paying my own money in tuition to waste it. Might as well get paid to waste the time if it ended up being a bust."

As silly as his logic sounded, Corbin thought that he did have a point. If you were going to end up hating a job, you might as well hate one that you didn't build up a truckload of student debt to get. Hopefully Private Rice had some pretty solid contingency plans if things didn't pan out with SWORD, because a commitment like this seemed a bit more involved than even a "regular" military contract. Then again, he also felt like enlisting because it was just something to do sounded a bit ludicrous. Nevertheless, he respected his newly introduced brother-in-arms for even deciding to enlist. It was pointed out, on many occasions throughout every day, that those who enlisted in the military were among one percent of the population within the United States to ever do so, and as such, made them an elite group of individuals, regardless of their choices afterwards. It was this constant reminder from the drill sergeants that fueled Corbin's patriotism and easily adopted love and respect for those around him.

Corbin shifted his sitting position on the ground, so he was a little more comfortable. He had completed eating the main part of the MRE, the spaghetti, and was working on the smaller items that would be more easily stowed in his uniform cargo pockets should an impromptu order to move happened. Still, no surprise orders, so no problem. Even though the MRE crackers, which looked like two massive soda crackers, had very little taste and could suck all of the moisture out of your mouth the moment they got close, Corbin liked them, especially with a little squirt of steak sauce with each bite. It was a little bit of a crapshoot, because not every MRE came with steak sauce, but if he happened to find someone who did have it, it was usually an easy trade for a packet of peanut butter, or a promise of a breakfast bar from the chow hall the next time they had a meal there. Sometimes, the other person just didn't want it, and would give it to him "free of charge."

He marveled for a moment at what was adopted as currency among the recruits in their company barter system. The breakfast bars, usually NutriGrain bars, that were offered at each meal in the chow hall, they were only permitted to have one, were the most significant currency. The different flavors of those bars were like different denominations themselves, some flavors being valued more than others. Barters were usually transacted in exchange for MRE items, swapping out fire watch or cleaning duties, or any number of things. Then, the food items in each individual MRE were exchanged as the next tier of barter pieces. Since every MRE varied slightly in its contents, there were constant exchanges amongst recruits every time their chow was one of these. The cheese packets, peanut butter packets, and "Ranger Bars," (a sort of sweet, gritty energy bar) were the highest denominations for the MRE currency. The candy in each meal was immediately surrendered to the drill sergeants, but Corbin knew that if anyone was ever able to successfully smuggle one of those items, they would be a god among men when it came to trade. Thankfully, the Private who Corbin had obtained the steak sauce from didn't want it, so it didn't cost him his peanut butter package for the exchange. He hadn't much enjoyed eating peanut butter straight out of the container when he was at home, but he came to almost crave it here in Basic Training. It was crazy how effective eating a little sealed tube of peanut butter was for his energy in a pinch where he needed a little boost. On top of that, considering the absence of candy, the very low likelihood of a "Ranger Bar" in an MRE, and the impossibility that anyone would ever give one up if they got one, peanut butter was like candy to Corbin. Therefore, it was like a little treat to him, and one that would give him a quick shot of caloric fuel to push through particularly draining times.

It was about half an hour before the command to move was shouted and echoed by the recruits through Echo Company. Everyone hastily cleaned up the wrappers from their MREs and disposed of them accordingly. Afterwards, they were separated into their Platoons and ushered onto charter buses, which were a huge upgrade to them compared to their usual form of transportation, which was being stuffed into literal cattle trailers pulled behind outdated semi-trucks. Corbin sat down with a satisfied sigh, Alex next to him, and they dozed off almost instantly. Thankfully, this far into Basic, and due to the ungodly hour of this training exercise, it was actually *encouraged* by the leadership that they sleep whenever they had the opportunity to do so. It had become an obtained skill to be able to power nap at a moment's notice while also maintaining enough presence in the environment to be able to react quickly to whatever happened. Drill Sergeant Leonard referred to it as "combat napping," and that it was something that proved very useful in deployment situations. Corbin had quickly learned the value of sleep, and that should there be any moment that he could, it was requisite. Otherwise, he would have had to hoard all the peanut butter packets he could just to refuel in a pinch.

A few weeks later, Corbin, Alex, and Brent would add to their brotherhood as they faced another training obstacle; FTX Three. An FTX stood for Field Training eXercise, and Echo Company had already completed two prior exercises. The first was a three-mile ruck march to an open area where the recruits had a kind of "round robin" training where everyone was separated into groups and took turns rotating through training sessions regarding certain field crafts such as building makeshift defenses, squad movements, and constructing "hooches" out of a couple of ponchos, paracord, and some sticks. The second FTX was a little more difficult, employing the field crafts they learned in the first FTX in an overnight "campout." They were first separated into their platoons, taken to separate, undisclosed locations in the forest, and then left to construct an FOB, (Forward Operating Base). Next, they established leadership and patrols, and conducted twenty-four-hour operations, which included keeping watch and mounting "attacks" against the other platoons. Instead of carrying empty rifles like they did in the first FTX, they were given blanks to use during combat. This second FTX concluded with a six-mile ruck march back to their barracks. This was the next major instance where Corbin's camaraderie with his fellow platoon members flourished as they had to work together to govern themselves, protect their FOB, and conduct movement and combat drills against ambushes from the Drill Sergeants and opposing platoons. He savored the rush of adrenaline and the shift in his focus to one of laser precision as he hurried into the fray to return fire towards a simulated enemy, lay suppression to allow his brothers to move into better firing positions, or whatever the situation may be. He was impressed at his ability to automatically shift into "combat mode," and use what he had learned in training in an, "as real as real life" situation that Basic allowed.

This final FTX was going to be an accumulation of everything that they had learned in Basic Training up to this point, plus whatever else they were going to learn. At the end of this training, which would take an entire week, they would conclude with a twelve-mile ruck march back to their barracks. It sounded like it was going to be a huge kick in the ass, and that was just how Corbin wanted it. There was a sweet, almost masochistic satisfaction to him anytime the training was difficult and painful, knowing that he would come out the other side a better soldier for it. This last FTX sounded like it was going to be pure hell, just from the ruck march alone...excellent.

Just the drive out to the site of the exercise was hell. Once again, they were stuffed into a cattle car, literally baking in full uniform, armor vest, helmet, rucksack, and over one hundred degree temperatures in the oppressive summer heat. Corbin already felt like he was melting, and they hadn't even gotten to work. Alex stood nearby, sweat glistening on his face. Brent was also within sight, facing away, but sweat was still very evident as it trickled down the back of his neck. Whatever the temperature was outside, it was amplified tenfold due to the metal walls of the container, the weight of all their gear, and the fact that they were packed in like sardines into their oversized microwave of a transport. That wasn't even factoring in the humidity of Georgia wrapping around them like a heated, damp comforter that was progressively getting tightened around them. Despite the transport having holes milled in the sides of it, it felt like everyone's breath was getting trapped inside and augmenting the humidity even more.

Corbin could see some of the other recruits getting a little wobbly, and he would remind them, along with those around him, to hydrate. They all carried a hydration pack on them; however some seemed disinclined to drink the water in them, seeing as it was nothing more than water from the sink in their latrine, dispensed hurriedly before they left their barracks that morning. The unforgiving heat and humidity then warmed that water up to about the same temperature as their own body, making it seem like they were drinking their own sweat, rather than water. Nevertheless, no one wanted to become a "heat casualty," and end up under the increased watchful eyes of every drill sergeant in the Company. Just thinking that all made Corbin remember that it had been a little while since he had taken a swig of his water, and he did so, sipping from the rubber straw that lay clipped to his left shoulder. The water was very warm and resembled drinking from a water bottle that had been left in a hot car. He grimaced as he swallowed the tepid liquid. What he would give for even just one ice cube...

The truck came to an abrupt stop, and everyone struggled to keep from falling over. As the door, that doubled as the ramp to disembark the truck opened, Corbin could see where they would be staying for the next week. It was a mock FOB, complete with a razor wire perimeter, small huts to serve as barracks, and a guard tower looming over each corner of the rectangular area. A manually actuated gate served as the only entry and exit point to the base, flanked by a pair of guard booths. At the instruction of the drill sergeants, everyone separated into their platoons, took their rucksacks to a hut that they were assigned to and then were ordered to return to the large, main area between the rows of huts and what was going to serve as their dining facility. They received instructions on which platoons were going to be assuming what assignments which were going to be rotated throughout the exercise. First Platoon was assigned to play civilians and were whisked away to be given further orders and clothing to play their part. Second Platoon was going to be playing the OPFOR, also being led away to be supplied with further equipment and information. Third and Fourth Platoons were left and were briefed on their duties as the Coalition force occupying the FOB, and how to establish patrols, guards in the towers, and a QRF, (Quick Reaction Force), in case a surprise attack occurred, and they needed additional forces.

Once roles were established and operational plans set forth, the members of 3rd and 4th Platoons went to work setting up their FOB, dining facility, (or DFAC), and settled into their sleeping quarters. Corbin had been assigned with Alex and two members of 3rd Platoon to be a roving patrol where they would walk a predetermined route around the FOB and report or respond to whatever they might find. Their first patrol rotation wasn't for a couple of hours, so it was now their responsibility to establish their sleeping areas within their determined hut. Each hut was nothing more than a wood structure with a concrete floor, a window on each wall, and a door at each end. With their sleeping arrangements being nothing more than each recruit lying on their sleeping bag on a thin pad on the floor, each hut could easily fit approximately twenty-five people in it. Even with the windows open, the huts were stifling hot, and each private had removed their outer uniform blouse and wore just their tan under shirt as they unrolled their sleeping pad and bags in the spot on the floor that they picked. Corbin got situated and, not having a pillow, rolled up his towel, placed it behind his head, and rested his rifle on his chest as he laid flat on his sleeping bag.

"Have you met either of these guys we are gonna be on patrol with," Alex questioned.

"No, I haven't. Have you?"

"Nope, but hopefully they aren't lazy pieces of trash like a lot of guys from Third."

Corbin chuckled in agreement. Each platoon had taken on a collective "personality," per se, and when it came to 3rd Platoon, they seemed to have the laxest cadre, which resulted in them being a bit lazier when it came to regulations in general. They had already had some trouble getting some of the members of 3rd to commit to guard rotations when all they wanted to do was just lie down in their hut and sleep the whole FTX. Corbin had a feeling that he and the other members of 4th were going to be picking up a lot of the slack that 3rd was for sure going to leave about.

"Well, if they are useless to us, we will just link up with some more guys from 4th and make sure we have a solid group for our guard shifts," Corbin suggested.

"Deal. Now, let's try to get a little sleep; we've got the second watch, it's gonna go late."

Corbin nodded, arms tucked behind his head. Before he drifted off, he made sure to set an alarm on his digital watch, just to make sure that they would be up and ready to go when the time came to rotate the roving guards. Despite the inhumane heat, it didn't take long for him to doze off, hands still propped behind his head and his rifle on his chest.

Corbin awoke to the sound of the beeping from the alarm on his watch. He had set it early enough to allow himself and Alex ample time to get their gear on and meet the other half of their group at their predetermined meeting spot just outside the TOC, (Tactical Operation Center), a large hut located in the geographical center of the base. Corbin gave Alex a firm nudge with his boot as he got up, donned his uniform blouse, and began to strap on his armor vest and helmet. The two of them equipped themselves with their armor, helmets, four total magazines loaded with blanks, and their night vision monocles mounted to the front of their helmets. They locked them up in their disengaged position for the time being, and both stepped out of their hut into the evening. The sun had begun to dip, leaving the base in an evening glow. The temperature had gone down, maybe a couple of degrees, but it was at least noticeable enough to feel better than a few hours ago. The two of them hustled to their meeting point, weaving between other recruits as they set about their duties, whether guarding, cleaning, or supporting other roles around the FOB. As they reached the TOC, they noticed a box of MREs lying open at the corner of the building. They immediately understood that this was their dinner chow, and each took one and quickly stowed it away in their backpacks.

As they were putting their packs back on, two similar-looking Privates came up to Alex and Corbin and nodded. They both looked a little sweaty and out of breath as if they had hustled to get there in hopes of not being tardy. Well, that was a good sign, considering they were from 3rd. It meant that they weren't lazy like a lot of that platoon. When Corbin thought that they looked similar, he thought that they could be brothers. They had the exact color of hair, a dusty brown, and hazel eyes, and their overall face structure looked the same. One of them was about the same height as Corbin, broad shoulders and trim build, while the other was about a head shorter and overall slender build. Alex and Corbin nodded in response and then the two spoke.

"Private Randy Hunt, 3rd Platoon," the older Private introduced.

"Private Jason Hunt, also 3rd Platoon," added the younger, shorter one.

"Brothers?" Corbin asked, raising an eyebrow. He thought it a peculiar situation where brothers served together in general but were even in the same platoon. He wasn't aware of any protocol that prevented something like that from happening; however, he still felt like it was odd. He assumed siblings would be assigned to different units to avoid any potential complications of siblings serving together. He shrugged to himself, rationalizing that maybe SWORD did things differently in a lot of ways. Then again, maybe it was a good idea to have this. They were all building camaraderie as brothers, it was probably easy to do that when you were already someone's actual brother. Corbin didn't think that would work as well for him. Along with his two sisters, he had two brothers, and he didn't get along with them much as it was, he didn't think it would change much if they were all in Basic Training together.

Randy smirked a little, as if this was the first time anyone noticed at first glance, "Yeah, Jason is my little brother."

"You guys just that close to each other or did you just both have the same idea of getting into the military?" Alex questioned, a somewhat incredulous tone in his voice.

Randy and Jason paused, looking at each other for a moment. Neither one of them had been asked that before, and it seemed to start a bit of introspection in them both. There was a moment of silence as they appeared to look at each other, almost like they were communicating telepathically, before Jason tilted his head and shrugged as he looked back to Corbin and Alex.

"Guess we just both ended up having the same idea. One of our older brothers enlisted in the Navy and got in real deep with them, like the kind of stuff you can't even tell your family, and I think we both just admired his service and wanted to do something like that."

"Except not the Navy," Randy interjected. "Those uniforms are so lame."

The four of them shared a short laugh, stifling themselves quickly as a Drill Sergeant from 2nd Platoon walked within earshot and gave them a disapproving, sideways glance. They didn't want to sound like they were having any sort of fun or enjoying themselves; they may just end up getting smoked to break them of that. Once the Drill Sergeant had departed, they grinned at each other once more and then discussed their patrol route. Not much had been given to them by way of instructions, so they were left to draft up their own patrol route, as well as plans of response in the event of an attack on their FOB. Most of this was deliberated as they moved around the perimeter of the razor wire, beneath the guard towers at each corner, and weaved throughout the huts on their patrol. Corbin learned that Randy and Jason were only about eighteen months apart in age, Jason being just a touch younger than Corbin, and Randy being the oldest of the four of them. They were the last two sons in a family of five boys, and Corbin could only imagine how crazy of a house that had to have been. The two of them had to sort of band together because of the age difference between them and their older brothers, and it had always just kind of been that way.

Unfortunately, due to the unwillingness of the recruits who were supposed to be their relief, Alex, Corbin, Randy, and Jason ended up being on patrol all the third shift, and most of the way through the next. Corbin found it interesting how he didn't feel like he had been up for almost twenty-four hours straight, at least while he was moving. Any time that they paused for a moment, just standing still was enough for him to start to doze off. He wobbled a little on his feet before moving with the rest of his group to continue their patrol. He felt some resentment towards those who vehemently refused to accept their guard duties, but he felt more of a connection and brotherhood towards Alex, Randy, and Jason. He agreed with what their drill sergeants had told them on many occasions: "Through combined misery, you will grow closer."

It was about 0300 hours when the first signs of trouble emerged. While they were in the rear of the FOB, they could hear distant shouts from the guard tower at the front left. In the silence of the night, they could hear the challenge phrase being called out from the pair of privates stationed there.

"Joe!"

"JOE!"

For anyone within the FOB, whether guard or occupant, the response was supposed to be "Montana," which would indicate that the one answering was a friendly unit and that they should be admitted to the camp. However, no response, or an incorrect one would result in being fired upon. After several more attempts and silence as the answer, the rattle of blanks being fired from an M249 SAW broke out, followed by the frantic yelling of everyone trying to identify where the "enemy" troops were coming from.

"Southwest! Fifty meters! About twenty or more," echoed one voice in the darkness.

Corbin and the others sprinted towards the position, splitting into two pairs, Randy and Alex and Jason and Corbin, flanking away from each other to form a sort of 'V' field of fire toward the last position called from the tower. The guard tower flashed intermittently as the 249 continued to fire, joined by the "pop, pop, pop" of the second private unloading his M16. Corban scanned the tree line through his night vision monocle, only able to see the fuzzy outlines of a few bodies darting back and forth between tree trunks. He raised his rifle to his shoulder and Jason followed his lead. In unison, the two began to fire pairs of shots towards the movements that they could identify through their optics. Alex and Randy were quick to follow suit. It became easier to spot opposing units when they started to return fire, the flash of their muzzles giving away their positions.

Corbin was in the process of removing an empty magazine and loading a new one into his rifle when he heard more yelling coming from the entry gate, "Contact, twenty meters, coming fast," quickly followed by the sound of gunfire. He waved his arm towards Alex, who was about thirty feet away. He looked hurriedly at Corbin and shrugged as if to ask impatiently, "What do you want now?!"

"We've got contacts at the gate! You and Randy stay here, Jason and I will go support them!"

"Where's the QRF?!" bellowed Alex.

A good point. In the event of an attack, there was supposed to be a group assigned to be a Quick Reaction Force, which would deploy immediately to wherever additional support was needed. Corbin quickly glanced towards the TOC where they were supposed to be coming from, however, he didn't see any movement. What was that about? Were the four of them the only guys actually doing their job right now?! There wasn't any time to think about it further and he just shrugged as he looked back to Alex.

"No clue! Stay here and Jason and I will help the gate!"

"Well GREAT!" was Alex's sarcastic reply as he reloaded and continued to fire towards the tree line.

Corbin spun to his left and clapped Jason roughly on the shoulder. Jason looked up from his rifle and Corbin motioned toward the gate.

"Let's get to the gate! Move!"

Jason rapidly reloaded and sprung to his feet from his prone firing position. The two of them rushed in the direction of the gate, passing about twenty feet away from the TOC. Corbin looked quickly to see what looked like was supposed to be the QRF lying on the ground, scattered like twigs. There was no time to investigate right now; they'd have to figure out what happened once they repelled this attack. As they neared the gate, which was called the ECP, or Entry Control Point, he could see the sporadic twinkle of muzzle flashes in the dark beyond the gate and the small guard shed beside it. He could already see one of the guards laid out on the ground while his partner unloaded towards the dark figures closing in on their position.

"Hunt! Cover fire! I'll get the downed guy!"

Even though they were using blanks, everyone knew who got "hit" in a firefight as there was always a drill sergeant nearby to point out who became casualties. Jason ducked behind the barrier where the surviving private was and helped provide fire. Corbin baseball-slid next to the "injured" private and could make out the hulking shadow of a drill sergeant out of the corner of his eye. He paid no attention to the figure as he called out over the cacophony of gunfire and yelling all around them.

"You injured or dead?!"

"Dead," came the groan of the private.

"Screw it," Corbin grumbled to himself as he grabbed the downed soldier by his vest and dragged him to the side of the gate opposite of Jason and the other private. Once he had propped the casualty up against the barrier, he took a knee and started to open fire towards the approaching enemies, whose numbers seemed to be dwindling as he could hear "You're dead Private" being yelled out among the popping echoes of gunfire. He kept firing, reloading, and firing until he ran out of ammunition and started pulling magazines from the vest of the "dead" private next to him. He would steal a glance towards Jason during the firefight to make sure that he was still okay, as was the soldier he was helping. They were both still in the fight. Good. He looked back towards the approaching enemies to find only a handful remaining, and they had dropped their weapons and were kneeling with their hands raised.

"Hunt! You good?" Corbin asked, still aiming his rifle at the figures that appeared to be surrendering.

"All good! Martins here is okay too," came the response.

"Good! Martins, stay here and cover us, Hunt and I are gonna get those guys. Got it?"

"Yup, gotcha covered," was the private's determined answer.

"Nice! Hunt, let's go take a look."

"Right with you," Jason called back.

Corbin and Jason moved forward quickly, rifles trained on the troops kneeling about ten meters away. Corbin could see there were four privates kneeling, guys from 2nd Platoon, wearing their uniform blouses inside out and makeshift shemaghs wrapped around their faces. He noticed that their M16s were lying beside their legs, their arms stretched over their heads and looks of defeat in their eyes. He recognized the part of the face that he could see on the private second from the right, it was Private Rice. He moved diagonally to the right, Jason diagonally left, from their soon-to-be prisoners. There was a drill sergeant nearby, the female from 2nd Platoon, Drill Sergeant Rodriguez, who watched their every move intently. He didn't let that get in the way of what needed to happen now.

"You on them?" Corbin questioned, not looking away from the kneeling quartet.

"Yup," Jason replied, rifle pointed.

"Moving in."

"Keep your hands up," Jason ordered sternly.

Moving quickly towards the OPFOR, Corbin swiftly slung his rifle to his back and readied the thick zip cuffs they had been supplied when they began their patrols. The chilly morning air cooled the sweat that clung to him, giving him a bit of a shiver combined with the adrenaline that surged through him. One by one, he crossed the ankles of each of the privates, then cuffed their hands behind their backs and laid them onto their stomachs. In this position, there was no way any of them were going to be able to get up, and if they even moved, Jason was there to dispatch them in an instant. Once all four of them had been secured, Drill Sergeant Rodriguez called out, "ENDEX," in a volume he didn't know could come out of a person of such small stature, and the word echoed out of everyone else in a wave traveling back across the FOB. Corbin took his helmet off, wiping sweat from his brow as he helped each of the prisoners back to their feet. Drill Sergeant Rodriguez was quick to cut the zip cuffs off each of them before looking over her shoulder and saying abruptly, "Good work Kent and Hunt. We'll make soldiers out of you yet."

Jason and Corbin gave each other a fist bump after they shook off the initial shock of being complimented by a drill sergeant. Corbin patted Brent on the shoulder as he picked up his rifle and dusted it off. He was just as sweaty from the humidity and appeared to be shivering just a touch from the cool morning air. Poor guy probably didn't have a shred of fat to insulate him. Corbin chuckled to himself and shook his head a little.

"Almost had us there," he quipped at Brent.

"Apparently not; you guys had us pinned fast."

"Probably sooner if our QRF actually showed up," Jason added as he stepped up next to them.

"Yeah, about that," Brent said with a smirk, scratching the back of his neck. "Captain Moretti suicide-bombed your TOC."

"Aw, come on," Jason complained.

"That explains the body count," Corbin said with a groan.

Captain Moretti was the Company Commander for Echo Company, and it wasn't clear what his role was going to be, if any, during this FTX. Apparently, one of his roles was saboteur. Drill Sergeant Rodriguez rallied the members of 2nd Platoon and led them back into the trees where they soon disappeared. Jason and Corbin hustled back to the TOC to debrief the situation and, hopefully, receive relief from their seemingly endless guard duty. There was already a small gathering by the central hut in the FOB while other privates milled about the area. The debrief was quick, with a short tongue-lashing from the leadership towards those who were in the QRF, who apparently took their job seriously enough to doze off in and around the TOC. That was all that the Captain needed to practically waltz into the most important structure on the compound and disable it. Once the review had been completed, everyone was dismissed back to their previous positions.

As Corbin and his group moved back to where they had last been prior to the attack, Corbin let out a long sigh as he looked up at the night sky. Being out in the literal middle of nowhere made everything in the sky more vibrant. Without any assistance, he could see the Milky Way and the infinite number of stars that looked like they were clustered and organized together to make a huge, celestial roadway. Sure, he had seen stars at home, more when he was out camping, but he hadn't ever seen them like this. He paused, his steps slowing to a stop, as he was enraptured by the astronomical view above them. That was when he noticed something that he had never experienced in his young life. High in the heavens, he could see...well, movement. It was subtle at first, a star that looked like it was making slow progress across the sky from left to right. However, after a moment's pause to watch, Corbin could make out a handful of stars seeming to slide towards each other across the black sky. The progress was so sluggish that he had to concentrate very hard. That wasn't right, the stars didn't move.

Corbin wasn't a professional when it came to astronomy, but he was certain that stars were stationary, and that the light that he saw on earth was light that was most likely coming from millions of miles away, so, he was possibly looking at the light emitted from a star that very well could already be dead and dormant. If it took millions of years for the light to reach this planet, would it take just as long to see movement if...stars did move? What was more confusing was what he noticed next. There appeared to be smaller stars darting about between the larger stars that moved at a snail's pace. Intermittently, there looked like there were flashes that blinked around the smaller stars, and sometimes the bigger ones. All of this was really difficult to recognize unless he was very concentrated on the small spot in the sky where this was all happening. He squinted to try to improve his focus on the weird scene, but after a moment it just made his head hurt. He had forgotten what he was even doing; he was focused so hard on what he thought he was seeing that it took a rough nudge from Jason to bring him back to reality.

"Hey, Kent, you all good?"

Corbin shook his head as if to rattle his thoughts back into place before looking up at the stars again. "Yeah, good. But- hey, take a look up there. Do you see anything?" He pointed his hand up towards the spot in the sky he had been surveying.

Jason stood close to his arm to better align his focus with where Corbin was pointing. When he didn't see anything other than stars, he shook his head and looked back at Corbin.

"I just see stars, dude. What do you see?"

Corbin paused, eyeing the space where he had seen the strange sight. Now, it didn't look like there was anything other than stars. Had he imagined it? Were his eyes just playing tricks on him? Was fatigue finally setting in hard enough to make him hallucinate? He didn't like the thought of any of that, but one of those had to be the truth, right? He shrugged as he considered what he would sound like if he had relayed what he saw.

"Never mind. I think I'm just tired."

"I don't blame you. Let's finish off this patrol and check in to see if our relief is ready to go."

They made their way back to where they had left off their patrol when the base had been attacked. The occupants of the guard towers appeared to be settling back in, brushing empty shell casings aside with their feet as they positioned themselves behind the light machine gun and reviewed their hand-drawn cards showing their field of fire. The four of them gathered and resumed their patrol route, swinging by the TOC to see if the next quartet of privates was preparing to relieve them of guard duty. Unfortunately, they were not, and wouldn't ever show up, leaving them to keep patrolling out of fear of stopping, even though they felt like they would technically be in the right if they decided to just stop. However, they all agreed that the drill sergeants wouldn't see it the same way, and they decided it would be better to just keep going.

It was a long four days, especially because he hadn't slept for most of that time, and it felt like an even longer twelve-mile ruck march back to the barracks to finish off the FTX. However, after they dragged themselves into The Bubble, they were met with speakers blasting music and a display of flags including the American flag, the state flag of Georgia, the four flags of the four platoons, and one more that Corbin didn't recognize. Judging by the incorporation of an eagle holding a missile and an olive branch, he figured it was a flag for SWORD. The drill sergeants for the entire company, as well as Captain Moretti, filed up to the front of the structure, ordering everyone into formation. Chafed, sweating, blistered and fatigued, the company of recruits stumbled into formation, forming the ranks and files for four separate platoons, standing at parade rest as best as they could manage. Corbin was again so soaked with sweat that he appeared to have gone swimming in his uniform. He was grateful that he was farther back in the formation as his tired body found it difficult to keep the proper form of parade rest without a great deal of struggle.

"Echo Company," boomed Captain Moretti's voice over the speakers. "Congratulations. As of this moment, you have completed the Basic Combat Training portion of your journey. You are no longer recruits, but soldiers."

The word felt like it hit Corbin right in the chest with the force a twenty-pound sledgehammer. He could feel tears welling up behind his eyes. Never in a million years would he have ever guessed he would be doing this, seeing the beginnings of his military dreams becoming a reality. He was one step closer to making the bad guys of the world pay for what they did towards the vulnerable and helpless. He could imagine himself kicking down the door of Osama bin Laden's hideout and putting a bullet right between his damned eyes. Hearing the word "soldier" when applied to him gave him a sense of pride that he had never experienced before. It also made him think about his father and what a gigantic "F-you" it was to him and what he would think when he came home in his uniform.

His mind wasn't able to wander long as he noticed the drill sergeants making their way through the ranks, each pair of cadre moving through their respective platoons. Drill Sergeants Leonard and Melendez moved through 4th Platoon, Melendez holding a small wooden box and Leonard drawing something out of it, handing it to each soldier, and then shaking their hand before offering a salute. When they reached him, he could see that the box held large coins, thick and ornate. Drill Sergeant Leonard drew two from the box, and firmly placed them into his hand before grasping it and shaking it briefly.

"Thought you'd end up a little piece of crap, but you turned out all right," Leonard said curtly before saluting.

Corbin returned the salute and the two leaders moved on. He didn't hear Drill Sergeant Leonard say anything to the soldier standing next to him, so he took what was said as a deep compliment. His heart swelled and his eyes watered with emotion once again. Blinking back his joyful tears, he looked down into his palm to see what he had been given. Challenge coins. Medallions or tokens which are awarded to military members to commemorate a milestone, action, or some other noteworthy thing a soldier has done or accomplished. The first challenge coin, roughly larger in diameter than a fifty-cent piece, bore the crest of Echo Company, 2nd Battalion, 29th Infantry Regiment. On one side, it bore the image of a soldier, crossed rifles, and the words, "Home of the Infantry, Fort Benning" bordering the image. On the reverse side, there was a similar image of a soldier in front of an American flag, crossed rifles, and assorted images of infantry moments such as the Crossing of the Delaware, a Huey helicopter from Vietnam, and armored vehicles, Bradley fighting vehicles, if he could see the picture correctly.

The second coin was just a bit larger in diameter, almost two inches across. On one face, there was the image that was becoming familiar to him of the eagle grasping a missile and olive branches in its talons. On the other side, the words "Special Warfare Operations and Response Division" curled around the outside border, with another crest in the center. This crest was that of a gladius overlayed over a Roman centurion's helmet, and the words, "Defendere, Adiuvare, Liberare" beneath the crest. He furrowed his brow at the Latin, unaware of what it translated to. Regardless, his heart swelled with pride, and he stood a little taller as his tired frame held the position of parade rest. His feet throbbed and he could feel what used to be blisters on his heels, now probably tender, torn flesh. Hands down, it was all beyond worth it. This very moment would be locked into the core of his memories, as would the tidal wave of emotions that came with it.

Amongst all the emotions that swirled within him like a blizzard, he was reminded of the new brotherhood that he had begun amongst his fellow soldiers. Brent, Alex, Jason, and Randy were those who he valued most amongst the rest of the company. Though brief, so far, their time together had endeared him to them in a way only the rigors of Basic Training could introduce. He hoped that whatever happened after this point, he would be able to serve with them again, within the same unit, if not within the very same squad. He felt that whatever life could throw at them, they would be able to take it on together, and he almost *dared* fate to do so. In that moment, he felt invincible, and even more than that, whatever that word would be, when he thought about facing the future with his new friends. He even wondered if his dad would even dare look at him with a disapproving eye if he were to show up at home in uniform, flanked by his four friends and comrades. Whatever the world, fate, the future, or even his parents held in store for him, his challenge to it all would be the same: "Bring it on."

Chapter Five

I t's amazing how fast time flies when you are having fun, or when you become so concentrated on each day individually. Corbin thought that Basic Training had gone quickly, and that was only thirteen weeks of his life, but the following six years went by as if it were a fever dream. He could hardly remember what had happened after Basic, including the short interaction that he had with his parents, who had actually shown up to see his graduation from Basic Training. He could recall that his dad seemed pretty pissed off still, but also very proud that his belligerent, rebellious son had accomplished something like this at such a young age. There were some short hugs and congratulations offered, but then everything was a blur as Corbin and his friends were whisked off for Infantry Training, Airborne, Air Assault, Mountain, Jungle, SERE, and damn near every other training you could think of. Almost immediately after completing all the training, he, Alex, Randy, Jason, and Brent were assigned to a SWORD unit and deployed. They fought in Iraq, Afghanistan, Kosovo, Africa, the Philippines, South America, and plenty of other places that they weren't allowed to talk about with anyone else, not even their own families.

Due to their separation from anything familial, other than each other, the five of them grew closer, and became their own family, inseparable in almost every way. After years of being overseas, they were finally able to see some rest, as it were, by being assigned to an Army base in upstate New York. It was very nice to be on American soil, and even more enjoyable not to be constantly in combat zones or behind enemy lines on some mission. At first, what would be considered "normal" military life seemed a bit mundane, what with the absence of constant danger. However, as time passed, it became more and more pleasant to have what resembled more of a nine-to-five sort of job. Granted, it was mostly security patrols around the base, training, training, and more training to make sure that their fitness and combat skills stayed sharp, but knowing when work began and ended every day was a refreshing change from what they had become accustomed to.

When they weren't refreshing their abilities, Corbin, Alex, Jason, Randy, and Brent were assigned to a security patrol around the base. With international relations still in the toilet with many Middle Eastern countries, and al Qaeda and other terrorist cells doing their best to run amok globally, homeland security was a heavy focus, especially at military installations all around the U.S. With many of the Army units garrisoned at their base deployed to foreign conflicts, the Joint Chiefs had requested assistance from SWORD units to help fill the voids in positions across the country. At this installation, there was a battalion of three SWORD companies assigned and dispersed amongst the Army occupations. As far as the Army was concerned, these soldiers were displaced from other Army garrisons, organized under a parent Battalion called Eagle Battalion. It was a simple cover that allowed SWORD service members to be transferred nationwide to any military installation, regardless of the branch, and be accounted for on the military records of the base yet still maintain the anonymity of being members of their clandestine parent branch. Thankfully, when it came to the military, no one really asked questions if all the basic information was present. Also, thanks to the mandate of "need-to-know," even if someone had a security clearance high enough to know about an operation as black as SWORD, which was extremely rare in the first place, if they didn't possess the proper paperwork that granted them Need-To-Know, they weren't permitted to ask questions anyway. (Yes, need-to-know basis is a real thing). Hell, if the President of the United States wanted to ask about SWORD, if he didn't have the need-to-know access granted to him, he could be legally told to go piss up a rope.

The name of the Battalion also served another purpose, which was to explain the patch that SWORD members wore as their unit assignment patch on the left sleeve of their uniforms. Rather than conceal their patch containing the eagle with missile and olive branches or wear the garrison patch of the parent unit on the installation they served, it was as simple as saying, "I'm on assignment to Eagle Battalion," to deflect the curiosity of anyone who asked about their unit. As most everyone on this particular base wore the patch of the 10th Mountain Division, anyone who didn't bear that symbol stuck out like a sore thumb. It was the practice of SWORD to weave a cover story with the fewest number of threads, so it was easier for her members to keep their cover story straight and avoid detection or further investigation.

For every squad within the SWORD organization on a base, there was a call sign. This call sign was based on the company, platoon, and squad the soldier belonged to. Corbin and his friends had been assigned to Charlie Company, 3rd Platoon, 3rd Squad, which meant that they were, as a squad, referred to as "Charlie Three-Three." This identification was generally known throughout the administrative levels, even though call signs amongst Army units weren't commonplace, it was just a simple mention of Eagle Battalion that deflected any questions that could potentially follow. As such, on the rotation roster for security patrols, the Army was aware that Eagle Battalion, Charlie Three-Three, was assigned for mounted patrols on such and such dates.

Corbin had risen to the rank of Staff Sergeant and was the squad leader of Charlie Three-Three, and had become very close friends with Jason, who was a Sergeant and served as his team leader, or sort of second-in-command. Their squad shared neighboring rooms in their assigned barracks, each room a pair of bedrooms attached to a shared bathroom and kitchen area contained within a building that greatly resembled the sterile and uniform appearance of college dorms. Corbin and Jason were in one room, Alex and Brent having the next, and Randy was lucky enough to have one all to himself. Their three rooms in the barracks were next to each other consecutively, maintaining the ease of organization and communication within their squad.

It was late one Friday night, and Corbin was lying on his bed, dozing a bit from time to time as he lazily reflected on how he had gotten to where he was now. He could hear Jason playing a video game in his bedroom, making the occasional sound of struggle or frustration as the controller clicked with each command he input. Corbin smirked a little to himself, finding it amusing the mix of sounds coming from the next bedroom. He placed his hands behind his head and closed his eyes as he decided that he was going to try to get some rest before they needed to get up early to exercise and prepare for their patrol. He was a bit of a night owl, staying up late for whatever reason, and despite that, still being able to wake up early and function each day on little or, in some cases, no sleep. He always joked that the military had done that to him, always referring back to those four days straight that he stayed up in Basic, or the countless times they had executed missions that were twenty-four hours or more in length. With all that, sometimes sleep just seemed like a joke to him, seeing as he never really seemed to maintain a regular sleep schedule.

The video game playing had almost become a lullaby to him as he dozed, almost reaching a fully asleep state when he was startled awake. The room began to vibrate, at first, like the rumbling of a thunderstorm. Then, the vibrating intensified to a level that rivaled a significant earthquake. Articles on shelves danced and fell from their perches, dishes and flatware rattled in their drawers and some cupboard doors shook so much that they opened partially. There was a deafening roar that resembled jet engines and a bright light that flashed outside overhead, quickly illuminating the windows like the passing of a nearby aircraft. The rumbling subsided and was soon followed by another bright flash and a distant boom, which rattled the room once again; however not nearly as much as previously. Corbin jumped up from his bed and looked around, trying to make sense of what had just happened. He noticed that there was no sound coming from Jason's bedroom anymore, meaning he was also trying to make sense of what had just happened.

"Dude, what was that?" Jason said aloud from his bedroom.

"No idea. Maybe some dickhead was buzzing the barracks with his helicopter?"

It wasn't completely out of the realm of possibility, but he knew that wasn't the explanation. He was very familiar with the sounds of helicopter rotors and had gotten proficient enough to be able to identify what kind of helicopter it was, just from the sound of it. That sounded *nothing* like anything that he had ever heard. On top of that, what in the world was that flash of light and that boom sound? In the distance and direction that it had come from, it sounded like it was somewhere near or in where the impact area was for artillery fire. However, there weren't any night live-fire exercises scheduled for the base tonight, and there was absolutely no way artillery would be wantonly tossed over the barracks into the impact area unless a whole lot of people wanted to lose their jobs.

Before he could get too lost in mentally exploring possible scenarios, Corbin's cell phone rang. He hurried to pick it up off his nightstand and answer it.

"Staff Sergeant Kent," he answered sternly.

"Kent, it's Dickson."

Ah, Captain Dickson. He was the Platoon Leader assigned to Charlie Company, 3rd Platoon. Corbin stood up at attention, a subconscious response whenever he was addressing a commissioned officer.

"Yes sir?"

"We've got a developing situation near the main artillery impact area of the base. Apparently, something other than artillery fire has decided to hit there as well. What it is, we have no idea...yet. I need you and the rest of Three-Three to rally up and get to the armory," Dickson explained calmly.

"Yes sir, we will be there as soon as possible," Corbin responded quickly.

"I knew I could count on you guys. I'll look forward to briefing you once you are here. Also," there was a short pause from Dickson, "don't you ever sleep, Sergeant?"

Corbin chuckled quietly to himself. "On occasion, sir. I guess I just worry too much that I'll miss out on something fun."

"Well, just as long as you have your wits about you and shoot in the right direction, I guess I don't have much to say to that," Dickson responded, the sound of a smile in his voice. "I will see you soon."

"Yes sir, very soon."

The call ended with the sound of a click. Corbin hustled around his bedroom and started getting his uniform on. Jason had overheard some of the conversation and was now peeking into the doorway. Corbin bent to lace up his boots and spoke without looking up.

"Let's get everyone up and ready to move to the armory. We can take my car. Let's be ready in the hall in no more than ten minutes."

"A little late-night stroll for unit cohesion?" Jason joked, raising his eyebrow.

"Just do it, Sergeant," Corbin laughed, "Captain Dickson is waiting to brief us on something."

Jason didn't question any further and moved quickly to his bedroom to get dressed as well as to call the rest of the squad to get them moving. Corbin could hear from his bedroom through the wall as Jason called Brent, and then Randy, relaying the instructions and ending each call similarly: "Just do it, and meet in the hall in ten."

In all their experiences while deployed, it wasn't uncommon to receive orders at almost 2200 hours. Missions could happen at any moment, and they always had to maintain a state of readiness to respond whenever the call came in. However, since they had been stateside, it was very rare for them to receive a call after 1900 hours, and if they did, it was generally to let them know where they would be or what they would be doing for the next day. Never had they received a call regarding a potential mission at such an hour. Also, what exactly could this, "developing situation," be that Captain Dickson referenced? His curiosity was piqued, and his excitement swelled as he grabbed his keys and hurried out into the hallway, followed closely by Jason.

It wasn't any more than seven minutes before all five of them were in the hall, dressed in their multicam uniforms, checking their pockets for their accustomed personal items. Corbin let out a long sigh and twirled his keys on his fingertip.

"Okay, gents, lets load up in my car and we'll get ourselves to the armory."

There were no questions as they hurried down the stairwell at the end of the hallway, clearing three floors in no time at all. As they pushed out into the humid summer night, they were swift to locate Corbin's jeep and hop into it. Pulling out of the parking lot of the barracks, they sped off towards the armory. The armory was a somewhat antiquated cinder block building located at the almost geographic center of the base. It served as the main administrative building for the entire base a few decades ago when it was a lot smaller than it is now. When Eagle Battalion had moved on post, they needed somewhere to operate from, and they were so "graciously" given this old building, which would suffice for their needs. It even had an enclosed motor pool to house their small fleet of vehicles, mostly Humvees for those, like Charlie Three-Three, who conducted security operations on post.

As they drove, Corbin wondered how the word "Humvee" had even come about. It was common knowledge to anyone within the military that practically everything had an acronym, from vehicles to organizations to buildings and even equipment. However, he could never quite wrap his head around the one that originated Humvee. The vehicle was officially titled the High Mobility Multi-purpose Wheeled Vehicle, or HMMWV. If the 'W' wasn't in there, he could understand how it could be shortened to what it was, however, with it there, he wondered how that made any sense when it should really sound something more like, "Humwuv," or whatever. It wasn't important, to any degree, but it was a random tangent that his mind would wander down from time to time while he drove. It was a shorter tangent as well, considering that it only took them five minutes to get from their barracks to the admin building.

The building itself was very nondescript. It was two stories and a pale gray color from the faded cinder blocks that formed its walls. The windows were darkened for both sun protection as well as to keep private what was on the inside. As important of a building as it was, housing all the equipment, weapons, and other sensitive items for Charlie Company, it didn't even have a fence topped with razor wire encircling the perimeter. Captain Dickson had told them that was because they didn't want to draw any attention to the building because any person, whether military or not, understood that outward protections, such as walls, fences, or guards, meant that there was something important, and maybe even valuable within that building. SWORD needed their headquarters buildings to blend in as seamlessly as her soldiers did.

They pulled into the nearly empty parking lot, dismounting Corbin's jeep and hustling inside. Just beyond the tinted glass double doors was a large guard station manned by two SWORD guards, dressed in full armor, armed with both an M16 as well as sidearm. Rather than wearing Kevlar helmets, they wore their traditional uniform cap, referred to as a Patrol Cap, or PC. Normally, soldiers only wore their PC outdoors; however, in the case of security personnel, they wore their caps inside to indicate that they were armed personnel. The two guards looked a little more alert when Corbin and his squad came through the doors, one of the guards stepping forward.

"Identify yourselves," he demanded, more out of habit rather than as a legitimate challenge because, let's be honest, no one other than SWORD personnel ever came through that door.

"Staff-Sergeant Corbin Kent, Charlie Three-Three. We are here to be briefed by Captain Dickson of Charlie Company, 3rd Platoon."

The guard moved back to the guard station desk, referring to a clipboard with haphazard notes scribbled across a legal pad clipped to it. It took only a moment before he nodded and waved Corbin and his squad forward. "You'll be upstairs, briefing room seven."

Corbin nodded in return and led his squad up the stairs to the left of the guard station. The metal stairs vibrated with each step they took, the low hum of their footsteps reverberating off the concrete walls in the stairwell. It was a familiar and almost calming din, a noise he had become very accustomed to what with all the many times they had traversed these stairs on their way to a training, briefing, or meeting that usually contained a far beyond boring presentation. Anyone in the military would tell you those were lovingly called, "Death by PowerPoint." Cresting the stairs, Corbin opened the door from the stairwell that led into the hallway of the second floor. They swiftly moved through the doorway, Corbin stepping through last, and located the plain door marked with a fading number seven fastened to the center of it.

The room behind the door was a small, plain room with a few rows of folding chairs set up facing a table with a whiteboard behind it. Atop the table was a short podium with a microphone. Standing behind the podium was

Captain Dickson. He was a slender man, probably only about one hundred-ten pounds soaking wet and had a bit of a slouched posture even when he stood rigid, his hands clasped behind his back. A native of Arizona, his skin was more of an olive hue, though his facial features clearly showed that he was "as white as they come," as it were. In contrast with his tanned complexion, his blue eyes and seemingly perfect teeth stood out even more, which was easily noticeable as Dickson was a good-humored man and frequently smiled. Despite his seemingly diminutive stature, his authority and his confidence exuded an intimidating aura that commanded respect from anyone who met him.

Corbin respected Captain Dickson greatly, for many reasons. At the base of it all, it was because he was, as Corbin would say, "a true leader." Sadly, Dickson wasn't one of the few "prime" officers SWORD was able to commandeer from one of the other branches of service as was permitted at her founding, however, he very well could have been. He was a man who had started in SWORD as a lowly enlisted soldier. Beginning as a Private, he worked his way up to being an NCO, non-commissioned officer, a Sergeant First Class, to be exact. From there, he attended Marine OCS, Officer Candidates School. With the fluidity of SWORD, leadership ranks could be trained by the branch of the soldier's choosing. Dickson wanted to go with arguably the most grueling course offered, to ensure that his leadership skills would be taught and honed to the best potential possible. He was an officer who had seen it all, served everywhere, and experienced what it was like to be the lowest man on the totem pole and work his way to Platoon Leader. He knew what it was like to be in the position of the men whom he led, and how to best navigate the struggles and expectations of his subordinates. He was, in Corbin's opinion, the epitome of a good leader because he had literally "been there, done that."

In his time on deployments, Corbin had experienced the flip side of that coin as well. He held a particular disdain for officers who were from ROTC. In many cases, these officers were snot-nosed punks who simply took some college classes and carried themselves like they were God's gift to everyone around them. They also always seemed to love the sound of their own voice.

Generally speaking, they were aloof assholes. Corbin didn't think anyone should be leading combat units unless they had a few bullets whiz past their heads, and here were commissioned officers who, in some cases, hadn't even gone through Basic Training! Suffice it to say, there were very few, if any ROTC officers that he met that he didn't want to bury almost immediately. Thankfully, Captain Dickson was far from that, and he was grateful every time Charlie Three-Three interacted with him.

Corbin and his squad filed up to the front row of seats, standing at attention and saluting Captain Dickson, who promptly returned salute and a friendly grin. "Gentlemen, have a seat."

Everyone sat down, keeping their eyes trained on their leader. Corbin glanced at his friends and squad members, feeling proud of them as he had for years. Quickly, he turned and paid full attention to Dickson. When he caught his eye, he noticed the Captain had a knowing smile on his face. He had the distinct impression that Dickson knew exactly what he was doing, and what he felt at that moment, which only made him respect him more. Corbin sat up as straight as he could, arms folded across his chest habitually.

Captain Dickson cleared his throat and began to pace a short distance back and forth behind the table. "Gentlemen, we have a situation that occurred approximately at 2230 hours. An unidentified aircraft made a crash landing on the south side of the artillery Main Impact Area. Not a lot is known other than that. We are going to need you guys to go check it out."

Corbin swallowed a little. He was never a fan of any sort of situation with little to no intelligence gathered. It always felt more like a potential suicide mission. Naturally, the less you knew, the less you could prepare for and the more that could go wrong. In many cases, with SWORD's scope of missions and jurisdictions, the operations they went on were of an emergent nature and required more movement and questions and less answers. He'd be a liar if he said he had never been on a mission that was ill-informed or ill-equipped. Hell, there were a few times that the briefing they received before setting out was something to the effect of, "Well, the bad guys are somewhere in this area. Go get 'em boys." They were trained for everything, so even in these situations, they were able to conduct successful operations, though not without much difficulty. However, that was against objectives that were understood, to a degree at least. It's one thing to hear, "We know what crashed and we need you to do such-and-such," and a completely different thing to hear, "Hell if we know what is out there or what you're going to experience but go take a gander."

He didn't want to sound disrespectful, but Corbin spoke up. "Sir, are there any other details that you can tell us regarding the situation?"

"Thankfully, Sergent, I wasn't totally finished," Dickson answered with a smirk. He took a step around to the front side of the table and sat on the edge of it, leaning forward, his hands bracing on the tabletop on either side of him. "Naturally, something like this is going to draw a lot of attention, and as far as we know there could be pockets of rubbernecks out there trying to get a look at what is going on. To our luck, Charlie Three-One and Three-Four were on the night security patrols in that area, so they were able to cordon off the area to keep onlookers at bay."

"What does the Army brass have to say about this, sir," Jason questioned.

"Well, they have done what they do best and deferred to us, including turning over all responsibility to us as well, so 'Eagle Battalion' will be handling everything from the investigation to the cleanup. It was exceptionally easy for them to turn it over when they heard that we already had personnel on the scene. No worries, though, we will simply do what we do best and show them how to get the job done right. Hooah?"

Corbin and the others responded with a collective, "Hooah."

"That's my boys. Now, we are going to go with a normal loadout on this but toss in your promasks as well. We want to keep you guys safe, but we don't think you are going to need full MOPP gear or anything. A gas mask should cover your bases, considering we aren't sure what's even out there. Of course, if you analyze the situation to be more hazardous than what you are equipped for, get out of there and we can regroup and re-arm. I don't want you guys taking any unnecessary risks just to complete the mission."

"And what exactly is the mission, sir?" Alex inquired.

"Get in, gather whatever intelligence you can, then get out. Once we know what's out there, we can better prepare for cleanup operations, which will all be Bravo Company's responsibility. We have dispatched a couple of medics from Alpha Company to the scene, and they are holding there to provide any medical care that may be needed. Once you can confirm and report what we are dealing with, we will have you clear out for Three-One and Three-Four to cordon off the crash site. While those squads are carrying this out, we will be having squads from Charlie Two mustering to provide any additional support so you guys can RTB for debrief while the site is secured."

"What should we do with any physical intel we happen to gather?" Corbin asked, wondering what sort of things they were going to come across in this mystery crash site.

Dickson slid off the edge of the table and began to pace again, hands clasped behind his back as he moved. "If you can fit it in your pockets, pouches, or Humvee, bring it back with you. If it's more or bigger than that, consolidate it at a collection point of your choosing and we will gather it with the rest of the debris when Bravo rolls in for cleanup. Debrief back here in this room when you are finished. Seeing as this is all a bit impromptu, we don't have regular code words for mission start, end, et cetera, so just keep in constant radio contact so we are up to date with everything. I'll be here in the TOC monitoring your radio channel."

Corbin nodded, looking to the rest of his squad and seeing them nod as well. It wasn't much to work off, but it was enough for them. Sure, they could be facing something very ominous and dangerous, or they could be headed towards a routine civilian crash recovery where the poor idiot was dumb enough to crash on a military base rather than out in a corn field or something. Corbin's mind flashed to the morning of September 11th and how his thoughts were similar that day. Either way, it was extra comforting to know that Dickson was going to be personally listening in on everything as they worked.

Captain Dickson nodded to each member of Charlie Three-Three before saying, "If there are no more questions, go gear up and head out whenever you are ready. I want everyone with a radio on this op, understood?"

"Yes sir," Corbin responded on behalf of the squad.

"Excellent. Good luck out there and stay safe."

They all stood up and saluted, then turned an about-face and filed out of the room. They moved to the far end of the building on the second floor to a locker room with a door labeled, "Charlie Company." This room was filled with rows and rows of lockers that belonged to all the members of Charlie Company. The rows were organized according to each platoon and each squad, and their row of lockers was located near the wall opposite the door leading in. They moved to their lockers, which were solid steel and locked with a biometric and numeric pad, each one needing to enter in their own code and scan their handprint to unlock the door.

Corbin's locker was at the head of the row, and he quickly had it open and was strapping on his plate carrier, already weighted down with full magazines for his M4, magazines for his sidearm, dump pouch, flash grenades, and fragmentation grenades tucked tightly in their pouches. Next was a combat belt that had a drop leg holster attached to it for his sidearm, a Glock 22. As he put on his helmet, an Enhanced Combat Helmet outfitted with his radio headset, he positioned the wire to the radio around his back that ran from his headset to the radio handset which was positioned in a pouch on the back of his vest. He double-checked all his pouches and equipment before securing his sidearm in its holster and putting the sling to his rifle over his shoulder, letting his M4 hang securely across his chest. Lastly, he strapped on his protective mask, or promask as it was referred to, or gas mask by your run-of-the-mill layperson. This mask was contained in a pouch that attached to his belt and rested on his left hip. Being right-handed, this was a little bit awkward, however he trained to have it on that side of his body so his mask didn't impede his ability to draw his pistol from the holster on his leg. He had learned that the hard way early in training with the mask when he was able to don his mask in time for a simulated gas attack but then was unable to draw his sidearm and became a casualty in the exercise. He was pretty sure the cadre had done that to him on purpose to learn that valuable lesson on his own.

He was a creature of habit, and picked up on repetitive actions quickly, which meant that his established routine of gearing up was the fastest and most efficient of the squad. Corbin would always shrug and dismiss any comments about it as his "OCD." He felt like it was a good thing because, as the squad leader, he was prone to be the fastest to gear up, noticed little details that others didn't, and was always the first ready for the fight, which meant he was always ready to lead the group into the fray, rather than order them into the battle. He let out a sigh as he meticulously checked his gear and his weapons, securing a full magazine in both his rifle and pistol, chambering a round in each and then setting the safety on his rifle. He then waited for everyone else to be ready, signaling this by making eye contact with him and sternly stating, "Ready, up."

It was Jason next to be ready, followed by Alex, and lastly Randy. It was usually the same order, Randy being last as he was the one who carried the light machine gun, or LMG, for the squad. For this operation, he was going with the slightly smaller and lighter M249, rather than the M240. Alex was the grenadier, an M203 grenade launcher attached to the underside of his M4, as well as the support soldier for Randy. He carried the carry bag for the extra barrels to the 249, as well as a couple extra box magazines of ammunition for it. Brent was the designated marksman for the squad. His loadout included the M110 SASS, which stood for Semi-Automatic Sniper System. Brent was a qualified sniper; however, without the advent of a spotter to complete a full sniper team, he was designated in the squad as the marksman. From time to time, Corbin would be a stand-in spotter for Brent, but those instances were few and far between, unless the mission called for him to lead his team at a distance. Jason was the assigned breacher to the squad. With his primary weapon was the M4, his secondary was the Benelli M4 shotgun, equipped with a plethora of different shotgun shells spanning from less-lethal loads such as rubber bullets to more "spicy" ordnance such as incendiary shells. For this operation, he loaded and carried standard one ounce slug shells.

Once they were all ready, Corbin acknowledged them with a nod. "Jason, take the wheel. Alex and Randy take seats. Brent, take the turret. Let's go."

They hustled downstairs and outside into the motor pool, locating their Humvee quickly and taking their assigned positions inside it. Each vehicle had the standard markings on its front and rear bumpers, identifying what company and platoon the vehicle belonged to, with a little personalization added by the squad that used it. In their case, they had stenciled their radio callsigns under the window of the doors behind where they were usually seated. "Hobgoblin," or "Hobbie," for Corbin, which was just a nickname he had thought sounded cool when he was younger. The others had originally laughed at the idea, but then the name sort of stuck as a kind of endearing inside joke amongst the squad. Jason was "Rabbit," referencing his affinity for running. Of the members of the squad, he was the fastest when it came to running, and he always had been. Alex was, "Goober," and no one could exactly remember how that originated, but it had quickly secured itself as his callsign. Brent was "Spud," which was a slight variation to the nickname his family had given him, "Bud." Lastly, Randy was "Brutus," a name he always joked was one he would give to his firstborn son, should he ever have one. It also seemed fitting because Randy was the most bulky and brutish in build. This came in especially handy as the support gunner, having to carry the biggest and heaviest weapon in the group.

As they mounted up, Jason took the driver's seat, Corbin in the front passenger seat, known as the "assistant driver," or "A-Driver," seat. Alex and Randy took positions in the rear seats, and Brent climbed up into the turret, loading a belt of .50 caliber rounds into the mounted M2 Browning. As the A-Driver, Corbin was responsible for all radio communications while in transit. Everyone else in the vehicle who wasn't driving was responsible for being additional eyes and ears to the world around them, relaying any information through Corbin. Jason pressed the ignition switch to the Humvee toward the 'Start' position and the engine sputtered and rumbled to life, grumbling as it idled.

"This is Charlie Three-Three, radio check, over," Corbin reported.

"Charlie Three-Three, this is TOC, Lima Charlie," came the response through his headset.

'Loud and Clear.' A positive return over the radio meant that they could hear him, as well as a sort of unwritten protocol for 'continue.' Corbin smirked a little at the exchange. It was, in a sense, comforting to his regimented mind having these consistencies in their communications. He felt it important to be reliable, even in something as trivial as semantics in their radio transmissions. He would always joke that it, "did his OCD heart good." He gave the hand signal to Jason to move out, pointing forward with all his fingers extended in what was referred to in the military as the "knife hand." Jason shifted into gear and drove forward, steering toward the gate at the front of the motor pool which opened automatically as they approached. Accelerating with a sense of urgency, Jason directed the heavy vehicle toward their destination.

The drive was quiet and uneventful, but then again, what were they to expect? At this late hour, there were hardly any other vehicles on the road, apart from an occasional security patrol or late-night straggler tiredly driving back to their barracks. Even the skies were quiet, mostly because of a lack of operations needed for aircraft at night, but even then, there were scattered instances of nighttime aircraft patrols or exercises. Not now, however. Corbin figured that there was a high possibility that after this crash, SWORD was sure to ground any and all aircraft on the base and to make the entire installation a no-fly zone until they could discern what it was that had crashed. A part of him felt a little "naked" not having some kind of air support, even just on standby, in the off chance that something went wrong, and they needed an expedited way out of the area.

As they neared their destination, Corbin could see the high, razor wire-topped fences with large yellow warning signs bolted to them, informing them of the danger in the immediate area. Their approach to their destination was a bumpy drive through dirt and brush as there were no roads leading into this hazardous area save a maintenance road that was on the opposite side of the impact area from where they were headed. Corbin wondered for a moment how it was they were going to access their objective if they weren't going to enter by way of the road and gate that led into the desolate, crater-pocked area. Maybe Charlie Three-One or Three-Four had "fabricated" their own entrance through the fence on the south end where this crash was reported to be. He chuckled softly to himself, thinking of either squad ramming their Humvee through the fence and the assured hissy fit the Army would pitch when they found out.

As they approached, it became very evident how it was that they were going to be getting in. A massive scorch mark traced across the ground and the fence continuing until it ended in a crater approximately two hundred meters away. Where the scorch mark crossed the fence, Corbin could see that the chain link was melted and peeled away as if a giant, red-hot branding iron had been dragged across it and melted a car-sized opening in the metal linkage. Well, even if Three-One or Three-Four hadn't done the damage, he was sure that SWORD would still get a tongue-lashing from the base general when all was said and done.

They stopped their Humvee short of the fence by about thirty feet or so and Corbin opened his door and stepped out. He poked his head back in through the door. "Park it and position it to be ready to go in a moment's notice. Rally on me at the fence. I'll talk to our guys and get a feel for the situation."

Jason simply nodded and pulled away as Corbin shut the door with a metallic *thud.* He made his way up to the fence, being met halfway by two Sergeants, one a Sergeant and the other a Sergeant First Class. They each glistened slightly in the moonlight, a thin layer of sweat on both of their faces and necks. Even with the cooler temperature in the evening, it didn't do much, if anything, to combat the humidity. They each took turns shaking Corbin's hand before returning their grips to their weapons.

"Sergeant Mattis, Charlie Three-One," stated the NCO on the left.

"Sergeant First-Class Thompson, Charlie Three-Four," added the man to Corbin's right.

"Staff Sergeant Kent, Charlie Three-Three," Corbin returned.

"Are you our investigative team," questioned Sergeant Thompson.

"We are," Corbin answered flatly, "Is there anything you can tell us that could help us out?"

"Best that we have, Sergeant," started Mattis, "we've got a pretty big crater out there at about two hundred meters. Something looks like it's glowing in there. Haven't seen any movement or heard any voices, or any noises whatsoever. It's been kind of quiet, in an almost creepy way."

"Any guesses at what we are dealing with," Corbin questioned, looking towards the crater and raising an eyebrow.

"Not a clue," Thompson said with an abrupt laugh. "We were just out for a nice night drive and, next thing we know, they're calling us over here to keep out any curious passerby."

"Have we had any problems with that so far?"

SFC Thompson chuckled almost as if it were a stupid question. Corbin didn't pay it any mind.

"Something went 'boom' in the main location for stuff to go 'boom.' I highly doubt anyone else has paid it any attention, let alone care. But to answer your question, no, we haven't seen anyone else out here except you guys."

Corbin let out a quick sigh, glancing again towards the glowing abyss in the distance, "Okey dokey, we will go take a look. If it makes either of you feel any better, you're welcome to post one of your guys in the turret of our vehicle. Sergeant Mattis, set the radio in your Humvee to channel zero-nine-two-zero and monitor it. That's our channel. We have our TOC listening in as well, but I want to make sure we have someone closer in proximity listening as well, just in case. If you happen to hear one of us call 'FUBAR,' it has hit the fan, and we need everyone available to assist. Understood?"

"Yes Sergeant," was Mattis' reply.

"Excellent. I'll gather my guys and we'll get to it."

Corbin turned and moved towards his Humvee, his squad standing around it, weapons ready but standing in a more casual stance. Their body language became more alert as he approached. They all watched him unblinking, poised, and attentive. He let out a short huff as he stopped in front of them.

"Okay, take five to check comms and weapons. Everyone look over your gear and each other's. Make sure we are all on radio channel zero-nine-two-zero. Say again, zero-nine-two-zero. Once you are all good to go, give me a 'ready, up.' Sergeant, come check me."

Jason stepped forward and looked over Corbin's gear, patting down the connection points on his armor vest, pulling his radio and checking the channel programmed into it, and giving all his pouches on his vest a rough wiggle to ensure they were securely fastened. Corbin looked over his weapons again, ensuring that there were rounds in the chambers and safeties on. Once Jason gave him a hard pat on the shoulder to affirm that he was ready to go, he turned around and did the same checks on Jason's gear, also confirming his readiness by roughly rapping him on the shoulder. Keying the microphone on his radio, he started, "Hobbie, radio check, over."

"Rabbit, radio check, over."

"Goober, radio check, over."

"Spud, radio check, over."

"Brutus, radio check, over."

Good, comms were up, "All callsigns, Lima Charlie. I'll lead out. Let's move."

Corbin led his squad forward, single file, towards the melted opening in the fence. Once they had passed it, he gestured for them to spread out into a wedge formation, everyone following his command swiftly and silently. Once they had traveled fifty meters, he signaled for them to stop. Everyone dropped to one knee, aiming their weapons, watching for any potential threats and ready to eliminate them. Corbin keyed his radio mic.

"Spud, Goober, you two post up here. Keep a look out for anything and give us cover. Spud, if anything or anyone pokes their head up and looks like trouble, take it off their shoulders."

"Does that include you, Hobbie?"

"I'd prefer you not," Corbin laughed, "But do what you gotta do."

"Got it."

"Brutus, Rabbit, let's keep going."

Corbin, Jason, and Randy continued forward as Brent and Alex took prone positions next to each other. Alex took a spotting scope out of a pouch on his waist, deployed the small tripod and got set behind it. Brent extended the bipod on his rifle and flipped up the covers on each end of his scope. Peering through the optic, he adjusted the distance and windage knobs to account for their distance from the crater. It was all subconscious actions to Brent, who almost didn't notice what he was doing, the motions being second nature to him. Alex pressed a button on the top of the spotting scope, which activated a laser that measured the distance to the crash site, measurement flashing in small, green-lit numbers at the top of his viewfinder.

"One hundred and fifty-five meters," he said quietly to Brent, who adjusted his scope a few more clicks.

From where they were, the crater just looked like a glowing hole in the ground, appearing almost like a football stadium that had sunk into the ground. Alex reminisced on times he had been out with friends on Friday nights going to high school football games. He had always considered going out for the football team, but he hadn't ever gone through with it. Instead, he opted for choir, which was something his older sister had been heavily involved in. He wondered what, if anything, would be different if he had been on the football team, playing under the blinding Friday night lights, rather than cheering from the stands beneath those same lights. At this point, it didn't matter. He was doing something far more important than living the life of a high school jock.

"TOC, this is Charlie Three-Three, over."

"Three-Three, go ahead, over," came the reply through Corbin's headset.

"We are on site; I've dispatched Spud and Goober to provide long-range cover. Moving in with Brutus and Rabbit, over."

"Good copy, Hobbie, continue mission and keep us posted, over," was Dickson's response over the radio.

"Understood. Out."

Corbin, Jason, and Randy continued to move forward swiftly, making almost no noise as they hustled forward, moving around craters and brush and other obstacles while keeping their gaze fixed on the luminescent hole which was growing closer with every step. Once they had covered around one hundred meters, Corbin held up his fist, signaling for everyone to stop once again. They all took a knee, looking at their surroundings. Without taking his eyes off their objective, Corban keyed his radio again.

"Brutus, set up here. Cover us and keep an eye on things, all right?"

"You got it."

Randy assumed a prone position, pulling out the bipod at the end of his weapon and adjusting himself to be directly behind it. The holographic sight mounted to the top of his machine gun glowed a dull green in the night's darkness. Without taking his gaze off the crash in the distance, he actuated his own radio.

"You left my A-gunner with our marksman."

"I wouldn't think this was a situation you would need him or your extra barrels. That is, unless you plan on burning one out," Corbin replied.

"Well," Randy sighed, "you just never know."

Corbin suppressed a laugh. Sarcasm was just one of many services that Randy offered. For free, no less. He and Jason moved forward now, weapons aimed as they approached their objective. Their footfalls made hardly a sound in the noiseless night, a byproduct of their constant tactical training. Corbin could feel his heart thudding in his chest harder the closer they got to their destination. The more they closed the distance between themselves and the crater, the more details they were able to make out in the wreckage.

They followed along the scorch mark on the ground, the force and heat of the crashing object even creating a shallow scrape through the dirt as if something had been dragged through it. Corbin thought that was a bit strange. He had seen a few aircraft crashes over the years, and when they skidded across the ground, they left a much deeper crevice in the terrain, making it very evident where it had impacted and how far it slid through the dirt, or field, or wherever they had hit. However, the indentation in the ground here was very subtle, compared to what he had seen in times past. This almost looked like something that would result from holding a straw just above the sand and blowing a line along its length.

The hole at the end of the scarred earth still glowed eerily, pulsing softly as though the power source for the illumination was struggling to maintain a constant level. As he and Jason closed in on the target, he could make out a soft, very subtle thrumming noise, its cadence matching the pulsing of the light.

Stopping approximately twenty meters from their destination, he signaled a stop. Once he and Jason had taken a knee, he motioned to the promask on his side, nodding to indicate to Jason that he should don his as well. Their training with the equipment took over and they had each removed, donned, cleared, and sealed their masks to their faces in less than five seconds. After he had strapped his helmet back on, which fit a little tighter now, pressing against the edges of his mask, Corbin activated his radio.

"TOC, Three-Three, over."

"Go ahead Three-Three."

"Rabbit and I have donned promasks as a precaution. Within twenty meters, over."

"Copy, Hobbie. What is it?" Dickson inquired.

"Can't see yet. We will be in the wreck shortly, over."

"Understood. Be careful Three-Three, over," came Dickson's admonition.

"We will. Out."

Once Jason had confirmed to him that he was ready, the two of them moved onward, slowing down and carefully approaching the edge of the crater, which looked a lot deeper than Corbin had tentatively anticipated. It was probably around twenty feet deep, with steep, sloping edges of loose and charred dirt. The aircraft that lay in the middle of the pit was about the size of a private jet but had more of the appearance of a fighter. The hull was matte gray, with some kind of blue insignia near the cockpit and on the wings, what was left of them, which were swept backward. The first quarter of the craft was bent upward at a slight angle, indicating where the brunt of the impact from the crash had occurred. Towards the tail section of the craft, the tail missing, there was a doorway, which was missing a door. He could see there was a strange, blue glow emanating from the open doorway and spilling all over the hole.

"TOC, this is Hobbie, over."

"Hobbie, go."

"Crash is some kind of aircraft. No idea what sort of model, over."

"Any identifying features?"

"None," Corbin answered, "No idea what kind of aircraft it is. I don't recognize the hull. It also has markings I've not seen as well, over."

There was a long pause and Corbin could almost hear Captain Dickson letting out an audible, "Hmmm," as he considered his reply. It was one thing to find a crash site, but a completely different thing when what crashed is something you've never seen before. From his paradigm, this very well could be some kind of experimental aircraft from an enemy nation that was on a reconnaissance mission over this base that crash-landed and there was probably a pissed-off terrorist or something in the cockpit. Not even for a second did he consider it to be some kind of alien craft, because it didn't look like one. Then again, what in the world was he thinking? It wasn't like he was the resident expert on alien spacecraft and their identifying marks. Whatever it was, he made sure there was a round chambered in his weapons as they waited for a response from Captain Dickson.

"Hobbie, this is TOC, over."

Corbin's heart thumped in his ears as he actuated his radio. "This is Hobbie, go ahead."

"Good luck out there. Tread carefully and keep in touch. Out."

Well...okay. Corbin shook his head with a little smirk. It's not like he expected anything more, but considering the circumstances, it kind of felt like Dickson had just shoved them out in front of a rabid rottweiler and told them "Good luck." Of course, that wasn't really what had happened, but the irony of the situation felt summed up in such a way. He waved his hand to motion Jason onward and the two of them continued to the edge of the crater and surveyed the wreckage. Considering the concentric nature of the hole and its depth, there wasn't a better or worse side to descend, so Corbin figured where they were standing was as good as place as any to go down.

"Rabbit, give me some cover, and I'll get down there and give you cover once I'm set. Good?"

"Yup, I've got you covered," answered Jason, aiming his weapon down towards the craft, slowly moving the barrel up and down its length.

Corbin let out a short, sharp exhale and stepped down the embankment, the dirt very loose, like a pile of dirt just excavated from a trench. He mostly slid down the slope until he reached the bottom, righting himself and taking a knee, aiming his rifle and scanning the motionless craft. The thrumming noise he had noticed before was louder now, and he wondered if it was the engines. That seemed to be less of a possibility when he noticed that there weren't any outboard engines visible. How did this thing fly? Maybe that's the reason it was no longer flying; whatever engines it did have were no longer there, and even though he wasn't an aircraft expert, he understood an aircraft needed propulsion to maintain its namesake. He worried for a second that if the engines did leave the ship, where did they end up, and was this going to be just the first of multiple sites to investigate tonight?

"Rabbit, this is Hobgoblin, over."

"Go, Hobbie."

"I've got you covered down here. Be careful coming down, the ground is pretty loose."

"On my way."

Corbin kept his watch on the ship, which was as still as when they first saw it; however, the thrumming noise persisted. He could hear Jason making his way down the slope behind him, muttering an occasional curse word after the sound of his footing slipping. It was only a moment before he was next to him, panting a little and aiming his rifle. Corbin looked towards the door near the rear of the craft and nudged Jason. When he looked, Corbin nodded towards the door, aiming the muzzle of his weapon towards it and gesturing.

"What do you think?"

"Looks like a door to me, Staff Sergeant."

Corbin chuckled but also felt like he wanted to slap Jason for his sarcasm. At least the two of them could share some humor, considering the all-around ominous nature of what was going on. Back in the moment, however, he kept his gaze on the open doorway.

"We'll split it and go high-low. I'll go high, you go low, hooah?"

Jason replied in the affirmative and they stalked forward, Corbin going left and Jason to the right of the doorway. When they reached it, Jason took a knee and looked to Corbin for the signal. Corbin pressed himself to the side of the ship, which felt uncomfortably warm, making him start to sweat. He paused for a few seconds, listening for any changes in their environment, of which there were none. He moved his concentration back to the open doorway before glancing quickly to Jason and nodding. The two of them aimed their weapons into the cabin of the ship, Jason covering to the left, low, and Corbin to the right, high. The oscillating noise was considerably louder now, almost drowning out the sound of anything else. It was now at a decibel level that was almost physically uncomfortable for him, even with a radio headset on.

"TOC, this is Hobbie, over."

No reply, just radio static. Of course, there was a reason the military always joked about communications, or "commo" as they abbreviated it, being the first thing to fail in a mission; it was mostly true. Granted, SWORD operations usually had a couple of backup options if the main communication methods failed; however, this wasn't a normal mission that was set up with all the proper intel, gear, or contingencies. So, their main channel of commo was their *only* one. He wondered if their being so close to the aircraft was a contributing factor. Whatever it was, he couldn't waste too much time trying to analyze it. They had other objectives to get to. The cabin was an open space, resembling the interior of a private jet that had been stripped of almost all furniture save for a bed with a couple of glowing flickering control pads next to it and a strange looking glass cylinder with a blue orb glowing in it. The cylinder was tall, going from floor to ceiling, and the orb inside was about the size of a volleyball. There was a significant series of cracks stretching across the face of the tube, but it remained intact.

Considering the useless nature of their radio, as well as the near-deafening sound of, well, whatever it was making that noise, Corbin figured the only form of communication they could use was hand signals. He tapped Jason on the shoulder and motioned to move towards the front of the ship. Everything was brightly lit by strip lighting tracing the edges of the ceiling and floor at the top and base of what would be considered the walls. The interior of the cabin was the same matte gray as the exterior. It was all fairly minimalist, lacking any additional features past the bed, control consoles embedded in the wall, and the funky tube with the glowy ball thing. There was a door at the front of the cabin, no doubt leading to the cockpit. He gestured to Jason to move in that direction, which they did in tandem, weapons aimed and scanning every surface as they moved. He tried his radio again, but his voice was drowned out by the noise, and he could barely make out the sound of static in his ears once again.

Reaching the door, he was startled a little when it slid open automatically with an audible hiss. Jason looked at him with concern and a shrug. Corbin held up three fingers towards Jason and counted down from three. They rushed into the cockpit of the craft, which was barely big enough to fit the two of them amongst the mess that lay inside. Shattered glass and broken metallic pieces were strewn about the floor, probably the remains of the cluster of control panels that were in ruins at the front of the cockpit. Just in front of those was a single seat with a figure sitting in it. In the dim light, he could see that the figure, at least from behind, looked human in shape. The figure was slouched slightly in the seat and leaning a little to the right. He clicked on a torchlight towards the end of the handguard on his rifle and pointed it at the figure to get a better look. When the beam of light landed on it, he jumped back a little, taken off guard and quite confused.

The back of the figure's head was the blue of a clear summer sky and looked to have the texture of velvet. It was bald, save for the overall fuzzy texture. Sliding around the left side of the seat, back skimming against the wall, he came around almost to be in front of it, getting a full view of who, or rather what, was in this seat. There were no features on its face other than two glossy black eyes, about twice the size of human eyes with, no nose, no mouth, not even ears jutting out from the sides of its head. Its eyes were half open, a look in them that seemed to communicate pain. If that wasn't unnerving enough, this thing had four arms. Two arms came out from its shoulders the same way a human's would, and the next pair came out of the torso just beneath the first pair. It had only one pair of legs, like that was anything of note by comparison. It wore a high-collared, dark blue jumpsuit and what looked very similar to black combat boots. Its top pair of arms hung limply at its sides while the lower pair of arms were clutched around a large piece of metal jutting out of its right side. There was an almost neon yellow liquid, Corbin figured it was blood, dripping out from around the metal piece and the fingers closed around it. Each hand had three thick fingers, or two fingers and a thumb for those pickier to details.

In his trained habit of taking in as much information as he could in a short amount of time, Corbin didn't immediately analyze that they were looking at some sort of alien. He jumped back when his mind caught up with this analysis, his movement startling Jason, who had gotten a little lost in staring at the injured pilot. They both were startled again when the alien began to stir slightly, fingers gripping its injury and trying to wriggle free of the impaling object. Despite the loud droning noise, Corbin could swear that he could hear labored breathing. He focused again on the creature, feeling an intense sensation of unease as he looked upon something he could have never even imagined sitting in front of him. The being struggled to lift its upper left arm, pointing a meaty finger towards a control panel in front of it. There was a noticeable switch that had a blinking green light above it. Corbin looked towards the switch and was surprised to hear a struggling voice say something. He didn't catch it at first because he was surprised that he could hear anything, even though he didn't really hear it, not with his ears, but it was in his head.

"*Shut off...engines,*" struggled the voice, the alien again pointing to the switch.

Corbin didn't even think, he just reached forward and pressed the switch downward, the light now blinking red and the loud oscillating noise dying down to a quiet hum. His ears still rang a little in the absence of the noise, but he did his best to voice his question in a way that didn't sound like he was deaf.

"Who are you," Corbin challenged.

"*The...Marvel...*"

"The what?" It was difficult for him to comprehend that he was hearing this thing speak let alone that it was speaking exclusively in his head.

"*Touch it...save-,*" there was a long, shuddering breath, "*save us.*"

Corbin peered towards Jason with an expression as if to say, "Are you hearing this?" and gestured to his ear. Jason responded with a simple nod and had a confused look on his face. Corbin looked back to the alien that now sat motionless in its seat, all four arms hanging lifeless at its sides. What were they supposed to do now? What sort of information were they to glean from all of this to make any sort of worthwhile report to Captain Dickson? In reality, they had done what they were supposed to do by showing up and seeing what this thing was. At this point, all they needed to do was gather some evidence they could bring back with them, and then Bravo Company was the one to deal with cleanup. He met Jason's gaze again with a slight shrug and confused demeanor.

"What do you think? What can we bring back with us? For intel?"

Jason shrugged as well, scratching the back of his neck in a confused gesture, "No idea. You think we can bring this guy?" He motioned towards the now dead creature, grimacing in a way that communicated that he wasn't sure if they could, as well as being uncertain whether they should.

Corbin understood because he felt similar. Nevertheless, it was in their instructions to bring back whatever they could use for intelligence. Well, a dead alien was certainly a good start. However, there was that glowing thing in the cylinder just outside the cockpit. What was that thing anyway? Corbin looked at Jason and jerked his head towards the cabin of the craft.

"Come on, let's check out that glowing ball."

They moved back into the ship's cabin, staring wordlessly at the hovering, glowing ball contained in the cracked glass. Corbin had been motionless for what felt like ages when he finally came out of his trance, shaking his head and giving Jason a rough tap on the shoulder to get his attention. When he looked at him, appearing to have come out of his own sort of trance, Corbin nodded toward the cylinder.

"What do you think," he asked, hanging his rifle from the sling over his shoulder.

Jason could only shrug, glancing again towards the orb, "About what? Near as I can tell, that's a funky-looking light fixture, if you ask me."

"Didn't you hear what that thing said? It talked about touching something...he called it 'the Marvel.' You think that's what this thing is?"

Jason answered with a shake of his shoulders. "You're not seriously thinking about doing what that thing said and touching whatever the Marvel is, are you?"

Corbin stared off into the middle distance for a moment. *Was* he thinking of doing that? He hadn't thought about it to any great length. He was a little disappointed in himself for even considering doing what the thing, what the alien, told them to do. Despite all his training and experiences in hostile and unknown situations which constantly encouraged not jumping into anything before identifying all the hazards, he felt inexplicably drawn towards the idea of doing what the alien had asked. He felt almost like a chimp, just doing what he was told, no matter what, just because he was promised a treat. Except, he wasn't even promised a reward; he was just told to, "touch it," and "save us." Maybe that was what the reward was, saving who "us" was supposed to be. Whatever this Marvel thing was, it must have been important if, considering the circumstances, the last words of a dying alien referenced this thing, which apparently has some sort of ability to save...save what?

A soldier sometimes had certain, for lack of a better term, "trigger words," which could incite certain emotions that could, and usually would, overpower rational thought despite the potential for, or current state of, danger to himself. Give a rousing speech about being a patriot or defending the country against threats, it won't take much else to get military personnel or veterans worked up enough to just grab their weapons and prepare for battle, no matter the inherent danger. "Save" was one of those words for Corbin. He had always wanted to be a hero, to save those who were in need and who didn't have the means to save themselves. He had always liked the stories of a damsel in distress and the undaunted hero who rushed to her aid and saved her, riding off into the sunset to live happily ever after. He had always hoped he would find a girl he could be the hero for. Despite all of the times he had literally lived out this hero fantasy by saving helpless villages and peoples while deployed, the power of the word "save" never diminished to him, and the moment he heard it, he was ready to save the day.

Despite the flood of feelings the word activated within him, Corbin did take a moment's pause to consider the situation, even though his adrenaline was already pumping, urging him to go be the hero again. What was the Marvel and why was it needed to save who it was supposed to help rescue? Why did they need saving? From whom, or what, did they need saving? If this Marvel thing wasn't this glowing ball, what and where was it and what would it do to him if he touched it? Why was all this so important to him all of a sudden? Why was he even considering anything outside the parameters of their mission briefing?

"Hey, Sergeant, you still with us?" Jason questioned, breaking Corbin out of his inner struggle.

"Yeah, all good." Corbin sighed in response, taking a step closer to the glass cylinder and resting his hand against the cool surface, "I just have this feeling we should touch this thing."

"You're not serious, are you?" Jason raised an eyebrow.

"What would you think if I said that I was?"

It was Jason's turn to hesitate in a moment of introspection. Corbin could practically hear the gears turning in his head as he watched him. They had served together for so long and he had never steered his squad wrong or done something so reckless that it put them all in unnecessary danger. He trusted his gut, and so did the squad, and that had to be something of note in the present situation, right? Jason had to be thinking something along that line as well; he just knew it. His suspicions were confirmed when Jason finally spoke.

"This one of your gut feelings?"

Corbin took only a split second to re-visit the thought, double-checking himself to make sure it really was a gut feeling and not some errant bout of curiosity getting the better of him. He nodded resolutely to Jason, tapping the glass surrounding the orb.

"Yep, it is."

"Well, if that's the case, let's figure out how to get this thing opened and give this insanity a try," Jason replied with a smirk.

Corbin turned back towards the damaged glass, looking around to see if there was some sort of latch or switch or something that would allow them to open the container. He even took a moment to remove his helmet and promask in order to gain an uninhibited view around the cabin. At length, he couldn't see anything, so he resorted to the next option: brute force. He lifted his rifle and bashed the buttstock against the glass, which produced little to no effect. He heard Jason stifle a little laugh and he could almost hear him saying, *What, you can't even bust a little cracked glass? Put your purse down and hit it!* He reared back again and brought his rifle stock down against the glass as hard as he could. There was a dull 'thunk,' as the rifle came in contact with the glass again and bounced off. However, the sound of glass cracking followed and the already present cracks began to spider web outward in every direction as the cylinder's structural integrity began to compromise. Corbin glanced back at Jason with a look of satisfaction.

His small, internal victory was interrupted by the sound of shattering glass and a loud *BANG* that threw glass shards in every direction, including across the side of his face. He and Jason were thrown to the floor, the sensation feeling like getting tackled by some invisible force. Propping himself up on his elbow, he immediately looked over to Jason to make sure he wasn't injured, wincing as he felt the sting of several scratches across the side of his face where some glass shards had left their mark.

"You good?"

Jason simply replied with a thumbs-up. He appeared to have been spared the sting of airborne shrapnel thanks to him still wearing his protective mask. Corbin got back to his feet, brushing glass shards off him as he did. The orb was still floating in the exact same spot, the glass cylinder almost completely gone save for remnants of it near the ceiling and floor. He took a step forward, watching the glowing object with a bit more caution. With the encasement gone, how in the world was that thing still hovering? He ran his hand over and under it as if checking for some unseen support, such as wires, as if this were some sort of elaborate magic trick. After finding out for himself that it was, in fact, unsupported, he felt like his curiosity was satisfied enough to move on to the next step: touching it. He glanced over to Jason, who watched him with a slightly incredulous look.

"Well, you ready?" Corbin asked, nodding to his friend.

Jason shook his head and blew out a long breath, his cheeks puffing out slightly under his mask as he did, "I don't think I could be ready in any way, but let's do it."

Corbin shuffled to the side to allow Jason to step up next to him. The two paused for a moment, watching the orb as it bobbed softly in its suspended position. Then, without even looking at each other, they simultaneously reached forward and pressed their hands against it. It felt warm like the surface of a blanket that had spent all afternoon in a sunspot. It also felt like it was vibrating, ever so slightly, similar to the edge of a table when a phone buzzes on the opposite end. It was all very odd, but at the same time, it was a reassuring, if not comforting sensation. The brightness of the light in the room suddenly increased to a point where it hurt to have his eyes open. Corbin squinted, then clenched his eyes tightly shut before...

When he opened his eyes, he was looking at the ceiling from flat on his back on the floor. What had just happened? How long had he been there? He rolled to his right to check on Jason, who was in a similar position next to him and was wearing an identical expression of confusion. When Jason looked at him, he nodded to indicate that he was okay, and they both got to their feet. The glowing orb was no longer where it had been, and where there had been silence previously, his slowly recovering consciousness was noticing a noise coming through his headset. It was a voice.

"Hobgoblin, Rabbit, this is TOC. Come in Charlie Three-Three. Do you read me, over?"

Corbin took another second to gather his thoughts and solidify in his mind that this was, in fact, reality. He keyed the mic button for his radio. "This is Hobbie, go TOC."

"Hobbie, what happened?!" Captain Dickson sounded concerned rather than impatient or annoyed.

"Hard to say, TOC. Radio interference of some kind. Sounds like we caught a break in that regard, over."

"Very well. Wrap this up as soon as you can and head back for debrief. TOC, out."

"Understood. Goober, this is Hobbie."

"Go ahead," came the crackly, but audible return.

"Get the Humvee and bring it around to the edge of this crater. We have some," Corbin looked at Jason and gently bit the inside of his cheek in thought, "some evidence that we will want to load up to pack out of here."

"You got it. I'll be there soon."

"Let us know when you are in position. Spud, Brutus?"

"Go ahead."

"Get ready to mount up once we come back your way. I think we have everything that we can work with here."

"Got it."

Corbin picked up his helmet and gas mask and stowed the latter in its pouch. He then wiped sweat from his forehead before putting his helmet back on and snapping the chin strap in place. He did a quick, habitual check of his gear before letting out a long sigh and nodding his head towards the cockpit of the ship. "What do you say we wiggle our friend loose and get him ready to pack out?"

Jason turned without a word and headed back into the cockpit, Corbin close behind. The alien was still there, slumped limply in the pilot seat. The puddle of yellow blood had grown considerably since they had been in there before, and it looked like the pilot had bled all it could. Corbin stepped carefully around to the left side of the seat, attempting to gather his thoughts as he looked again over the dead body of the most foreign creature he had ever seen in his life. It elicited a strong mixture of fascination and feeling totally weirded out, much like a child would feel looking at roadkill and suppressing the urge to poke it. He positioned himself in front of the body and gestured to Jason to get behind its chair.

"I'll see if I can pull it up. Give him a little push as I do and let's see if we can't get it loose," Corbin instructed, taking hold of the wrists of the top pair of arms on the creature.

Jason shuffled behind the chair and placed his hands against the shoulders of the body, waiting for a signal. Corbin counted down from three and started to pull on the alien's arms while Jason pushed both hands against the shoulders of the body, feeling it start to move ever so slightly. Corbin could tell from the resistance he felt to his efforts that the object that impaled this thing was lodged in there pretty good and probably had lots of ragged edges that would embed further into the soft tissue and making it harder to remove. He let go of the arms and squared his feet and hips, bending his knees and preparing to put more force into his next attempt to pull the body free. Jason followed his lead, repositioning to get more leverage behind the alien. In unison, they put all their strength into their motions and the body pulled free slowly, emitting a sickening squelching noise as it came free of its chair and crumpled to the floor in a heap. The sound made Corbin gag a little and have to take a quick pause to steel his nerves before bending down and picking up the body, hanging it over his shoulder like a sack of potatoes.

Jason took point, leading out of the cockpit and heading out of the open doorway at the rear of the ship. The body on Corbin's shoulder felt a little hefty, but not nearly in direct competition with the heaviest thing he had ever carried. The tough part was trying to traverse the incline up the crater. He had to position himself just perfectly, so the weight of the body didn't pull him backwards down the hill, or make him fall flat on his face. All the jostling around had squeezed more blood from the corpse, which soaked into his uniform on his shoulder. With it so close to his face, Corbin could smell it now, and though the exact scent was difficult to describe, it had the same physical sensation of sniffing something extremely spicy. It was a sort of subtle burning feeling in his nostrils. Once again, he found himself betwixt feelings of disgust and curiosity.

"Hobbie, this is Goober."

"Go ahead, Goober."

"I've got the truck up here, backed up towards the crater. Where are you?"

"Coming up the slope now," Corbin grunted as he stumbled slightly. "Hang tight, we should be there soon."

"Will do."

"TOC, this is Hobbie, over."

"Send it, Hobbie."

"We've got some...evidence that we have gathered and will be loading it up shortly. I think we've seen everything that we can, might as well call in the cleanup crew, over."

"Good copy, Hobbie. We'll put in the call. Wrap up and head back for debrief."

"Understood, TOC. Out."

Corbin could hear the low rumble of the Humvee engine near the edge of the crater, letting out a heavy sigh as he crested the slope. He covered the last distance to the vehicle quickly, opening the back hatch and letting the body fall into the back storage area with a loud *thud!* Alex looked over his shoulder quickly, his view blocked slightly by the rear seats, but his eyes widened when he caught a glimpse of what Corbin had just loaded.

"Is that a body?"

"Yep," Corbin answered flatly.

In any other circumstance, with any other person, there would have been much more of a reaction to such a nonchalant response to loading a dead body into their Humvee; however, with as much as they had been exposed to over the years, all Alex did was give a little casual shrug and turn back around to face forward, waiting for his signal to drive over to pick up Brent and Randy. Corbin climbed into the front passenger seat, Jason taking the position in the gun turret. Corbin motioned for Alex to start driving, which he did, turning immediately towards the positions where Randy and Brent now waited.

"Brutus, Spud, be ready, we are headed back to you, over," Corbin ordered.

"You got it," answered Brent.

"Ready when you are," came Randy's response.

When they approached Randy, he was in a position on one knee, bipod on his weapon folded up and ready to move. He was quick to his feet and hustled to the vehicle, climbing into one of the back seats. As they neared Brent, he quickly jumped to his feet from a prone position and was in the vehicle in the blink of an eye. Neither bothered to look into the back where the alien's body lay, and no one else cared to update them as to the contents of the "evidence" they collected. As they neared the damaged opening in the fence, they slowed to a stop next to Sergeants Mattis and Thompson. Corbin stepped out, leaving his door open beside him.

"Well, we got what we needed here. TOC is going to send in the containment guys. Thanks for watching our backs," Corbin said, shaking both their hands.

"Find anything interesting out there?" Thomson questioned.

In a normal situation, or rather, any situation other than this, Corbin would have indulged Thompson's curiosity with even just a tiny bit of detail. However, this was something they had never dealt with before, and he figured it was best to keep information compartmentalized to maintain a tight circle of containment. Besides, he was pretty sure that even though they, as SWORD soldiers, shared the same security clearances, what they had stowed away in the back of their vehicle definitely fell under the scope of "need-to-know," and he was willing to bet these guys didn't need to know. Corbin just shook his head slightly and let out a little snort.

"Nah, and it's too bad too. I was hoping this evening would be even just a tiny bit of something exciting to see."

Corbin didn't wait around for either of them to answer, he simply climbed back into the Humvee and motioned for Alex to keep driving. He did this to keep from having to engage in any more small talk, and to avoid the possibility of either one of them noticing the yellowish stain on his shoulder. Both squad leaders appeared to understand his response, because neither of them tried to say anything else as they rolled away. As they rounded onto the main highway, headed back to the SWORD motor pool, everyone was still silent, until Corbin took the opportunity to speak on his radio.

"TOC, this is Hobbie, over."

"Go ahead, Hobbie, over."

"We've cleared the crash site and are RTB. Our ETA is ten minutes, over."

"Understood, Hobbie. What's your count, over?" came the request through the radio.

"Charlie Three-Three is green. Five for five, over."

'Technically plus one,' was what he thought next. He didn't really know how to report that; not only had they gathered some evidence, but it was also in the form of a dead alien. Sure, in a situation where there may have been a casualty in the event they didn't call in a nine-line, he would report that. However, this casualty wasn't a part of his squad or their platoon or...well, their planet. As far as he knew, there wasn't a SWORD procedure for a situation like this, so whatever course of action he took, he probably wasn't going to face any punitive charges should his actions not line up with unit expectations. Truthfully, his brain was still trying to catch up with everything that had happened so far tonight, and he doubted it was really going to sink in until he had a chance to sleep on it.

The trip back to the armory was silent and quick. As they pulled back into the motor pool area, Corbin could see that there was a group of medics waiting near their assigned parking stall. Alex backed the vehicle into its place and the five of them got out, immediately getting surrounded by the medics. There were four of them and two of them went directly to him when they noticed the lacerations along the side of his face. They looked him up and down, patting his joints, shining a flashlight in his eyes, and asking him a flurry of questions to figure out where the injuries had come from, and if he was cognizant enough to know what was going on. He waved a hand at them as if trying to swat away pesky flies, assuring them that he was okay. It didn't take them long to see that he was, in fact, just fine, and they moved away with the other two medics once everyone was confirmed to be unharmed.

They were next met by Captain Dickson. As the medics left, their quartet parted to go around him as they walked back inside the armory. Captain Dickson stood in his customary position, a bit slouched, hands behind his back. When it was just the six of them in the motor pool, he stepped forward, his hands never coming out from behind him. Corbin wondered how he had ever adopted such a gait, and if it happened to affect his balance at all, not having his arms swinging naturally at his sides. One of life's mysteries, he guessed, and put it from his mind. Captain Dickson slowed to a stop just a few paces in front of them, heaving out a long sigh.

"Well, that was…" He paused as if trying to find the right word. "Interesting. I'm sure you guys are pretty tired from being up past your bedtime, so we will make these debriefs as quick as possible. Judging by the activity on the radio, I believe Specialists Hunt and Rice and PFC McMann can be debriefed together as it seems that they didn't ever get that close to the wreck. As for Staff-Sergeant Kent and Sergeant Hunt, I'll need a little more time with them. Go drop your kits and head back to briefing room seven."

Alex, Brent, and Randy moved off without a word, making their way to their lockers to take off their equipment. Corbin and Jason stood rigid, the former waiting until he was sure the trio was out of earshot, glancing over Dickson's shoulder before looking back to his commander and clearing his throat as he removed his helmet, tucking it smartly under his left arm.

"Was there something else, Sergeant Kent?" Captain Dickson questioned, raising an eyebrow.

"Sir, I believe you will want to take a look at the," it seemed an odd word to use for what was in the back of the Humvee, "evidence that we collected from the site."

"Ah, yes," Dickson responded, sounding not even the least bit surprised. "Lead the way."

Corbin turned and moved to the back of the vehicle, opening the rear hatch and tailgate to reveal the body of the alien pilot lying there. A small puddle of yellow blood had started to form beneath it, filling the Humvee with a strange, tangy, spicy smell. When he looked at Captain Dickson, Corbin noticed that his eyes widened, and in an expression that lasted only a heartbeat, he looked genuinely surprised. Corbin didn't think there was anything that could have elicited a reaction like that from his commanding officer, but he also admired that the reaction was so brief that if he had blinked, he would even have missed it standing next to him. Corbin glanced at Jason, who looked a little grossed out, much like he did when they had first gone inside the alien aircraft. In that split second that elapsed, Dickson cleared his throat and closed the hatch.

"Well, we will have to have our investigative guys bag this thing and take it to the lab for further evaluation. We may even need to put in a call to our Air Force friends out in Nevada to send some specialists out." He said it all clinically, as if he had just looked at a dinner recipe and was vocalizing the ingredients he would need.

As if he hadn't already experienced a few of the biggest surprises he could ever remember, Corbin was yet again taken aback. He had always accepted the idea that Area 51 wasn't anything more than a military installation shrouded in secrets. Naturally, any military location in the world was going to have secrets, that was the nature of OPSEC, or Operational Security, but because of the knowledge it was out there plus the lack of knowledge of what was in there, people speculated, created conspiracies, and thus, a secret alien research center was born. However, he hadn't ever entertained the idea that there was any sort of truth to that, but his commander had just acknowledged that with an almost off-handed comment to himself. He remembered that he had made a joke about "guarding aliens" to General Easton years ago when they had first met, and that General Easton had casually commented back about it as if a joke. Guess he wasn't joking as much as he had originally let on.

"Go ahead and drop kit and meet me upstairs. We will need to speak more about this," Captain Dickson instructed, letting out a sigh and finally turning away from the Humvee to face Corbin.

"Yes sir, moving," Corbin answered with a salute. Captain Dickson returned the salute and Corbin and his team leader hustled inside to their lockers.

If putting on his gear and readying his armament was a simple, rehearsed task, it was far simpler and swifter to take it off and put it away. This was colloquially referred to as "dropping your kit." If anyone were to watch Corbin as he donned and doffed his equipment, they wouldn't be able to spot a difference in any instance that he did it, so ingrained in his muscle memory as it was. This proved to be very useful as he removed his gear now seeing as his mind was racing with everything that had happened and he wasn't even remotely focused on what he was doing. Nevertheless, his armor was removed and hung, his gas mask pouch stowed next to it, his drop leg holster housed on the shelf above, and his rifle and sidearm unloaded, safety actuated and locked securely in the fingerprint-programmed safe within his locker. When he closed his locker with a loud *'clank'* he suddenly realized what had happened, and the sensation was like someone waking up after passing out and realizing that the world did indeed keep going even while they were out. He noticed the same clanking noise as Jason closed his locker, and looked over to his team leader, who was running his hands down the front of his uniform blouse, smoothing the wrinkles that were an inevitable side effect of wearing armor.

A realization came over him as he mentally came back to the present: they were going to need to coordinate their story. He had a sneaking suspicion that Captain Dickson, as well as SWORD, wouldn't be too pleased to find out that they had broken into and touched some kind of alien technology, whatever it even did, other than make them pass out. They would also need to have some kind of explanation for the scratches on his face from the glass. He would have to be pretty creative with that one. In any sense, whatever the cover story was, they needed to be coordinated enough that they wouldn't arouse suspicion with any discrepancies between their accounts of the night's exploits. Corbin sat down on the bench in front of his locker and Jason followed suit.

"Okay, we gotta figure out what we are going to say in our debrief. Most of what happened is going to be fine, but the whole busting open and touching that orb thing are going to be something we need to have an alibi for."

"Well, that thing that was floating in there is gone, so we can just go with 'it was broken when we got there.' Not much they can prove different to that," Jason suggested with a shrug.

"True, but it doesn't really account for the glass I took to the face," Corbin reminded, pointing at his scratches.

His answer made Jason look to the floor in thought. His brow furrowed as he appeared to search for ideas that they could use. He looked up again a moment later. "You slipped?"

"Just what Dickson needs to think, that I'm a klutz who can't keep from slipping and slamming his face on the floor. Really speaks volumes for one of his squad sergeants."

Jason let out a soft chuckle as he considered the possibility. "Maybe it's all a ploy for me to take over the squad."

They both laughed, knowing it was a joke. Their time together in SWORD and a squad together, specifically in leadership roles of the squad had melded them together closer than brothers. Jason did feel and had told Corbin that he felt more like a brother in him than to his actual brother, Randy. Not to say there was anything wrong with his relationship with his brother; in fact, they were quite close, but their years of service so far had forged an even closer bond between him and Corbin. Sometimes, it felt even like they shared a brain, which proved to be very advantageous in combat situations where communication was limited, and they could trust that they were each thinking the same things. It was good to have a team leader who he could trust implicitly, no matter what.

After racking his brain for a minute or two, Corbin couldn't really think of another situation they could fabricate where he had sustained his cuts. "Well, I think if the question comes up, I did fall down, as stupid as it sounds."

"Well, going up and down that crater was a bit treacherous," Jason suggested.

Ah, there it was, the alibi and just another evidence of their mental connection. That could be convincing enough while absolving Corbin of sounding like he was an uncoordinated, clumsy oaf. He could even say it happened while trying to carry that alien out of the pit. It's easy and plausible to lose your balance while carrying a heavy body up a steep incline and lose your footing. Corbin nodded to himself as he accepted that as what had happened. Jason noticed the contemplative look on his face and his nod, understanding that was his acceptance of that idea. Then it was settled, and now all they had to do was get through the debrief, maybe even an AAR, (After Action Review), with the rest of the squad, and then go home.

Corbin stood up with a long sigh and looked around the empty locker area, "Okay, let's get up there and get this debrief done, we need to get back and get whatever sleep we can before morning PT."

Jason nodded in agreement and stood up, following his friend and squad leader upstairs to their assigned briefing room. As they stepped in, the room was empty, apart from the chairs and table setup that hadn't changed from when they were there for their briefing. The only difference to the arrangement was a solitary folding chair set up at the head of the room, in front of the table and facing the rows of chairs in the main part of the room. Captain Dickson sat in that chair quietly, his arms folded across his chest. As the two of them came in, he didn't stand, but his head quickly looked up in their direction as if he had been interrupted in thought.

"Sergeants, please, come in and have a seat," he said cordially, gesturing to the chairs in front of him.

A bit unorthodox, but not unheard of, to debrief two members of a squad at the same time. Corbin and Jason moved swiftly to the chairs and sat down. Captain Dickson turned and pressed the record button on a small, rectangular digital recording device that sat on the tabletop behind him. He turned back to face both of them, his face just as friendly and cordial as it always was. Corbin never really liked debriefs only because they always inherently made him feel like he was in trouble, or under investigation in some way, though he knew that not to be the case. It was just a uniform feeling to a uniform situation, which he had experienced hundreds of times, at least. Corbin passively noticed the small microphone, paired with the digital recorder, clipped neatly to the collar of Dickson's uniform.

Captain Dickson started by stating the date and time, and initial notations for the recording and then continued. "I am Captain Dickson, Charlie Company Commander, here with Staff Sergeant Kent and Sergeant Hunt, squad and team leaders, respectively, of Charlie Company, 3rd Platoon, 3rd Squad, callsign Charlie Three-Three. We are here to perform a debrief of the impromptu operation conducted this evening, starting roughly at 2300 hours. Intelligence reported the impact of a foreign object in the main impact area of the installation's artillery range. Charlie Three-Three was mustered and deployed to the area in question to investigate."

Captain Dickson had assumed a position sitting forward, elbows on his knees, both to be more comfortable as well as to get his microphone a little closer to Corbin and Jason. "Gentlemen, if you will please summarize your findings."

Corbin led out. "Yes sir. Upon arriving at the impact area, we discovered that what had fallen there was an aircraft of some kind. This wasn't immediately evident until Sergeant Hunt, and I entered the impact crater where it was. I had ordered Specialist Rice, PFC McMann and Specialist Hunt to cover positions outside of the crater while Sergeant Hunt and I went in to investigate."

"And it was just you and Sergeant Hunt who entered the impact crater?"

"Yes sir."

"Okay, and what happened next, Sergeant Hunt?" Dickson turned and faced Jason now.

"We went down the side of the crater, which was pretty steep, and prepared to enter the craft," Jason answered sternly.

"And when you say 'craft,' what do you mean by that?"

"It was…, "Jason paused for a split second, considering if there were any better word to describe it. "Like an aircraft, sir. Large, about the size of a Gulfstream private jet, sir. Staff-Sergeant Kent and I noticed that there was a door aft of the wings that was open, and we prepared to enter it."

Captain Dickson interjected for a moment. "Let the record note that at this point, radio communications with Sergeants Kent and Hunt became compromised. To clarify, their radio frequencies seemed to be interrupted in a way that prevented them from sending or receiving transmissions to the TOC. Continue, Sergeant Hunt."

Jason adjusted in his chair for the sake of comfort before continuing. "We entered the craft to find a large cabin area with no one in it. It was then that we moved to the cockpit area. That is where we found," he paused, trying to find the most accurate but innocuous word for it, "the pilot, sir."

"How would you describe the pilot, to the best of your ability?" Captain Dickson queried.

"It wasn't human, sir," Jason started. "Shaped a bit like one, but blue, kinda fuzzy, and had two pairs of arms."

Corbin jumped in now, continuing for Jason. "The pilot was evidence that we brought back from the operation." There was no need to get into too much detail about the alien as further descriptions and records would be made by the investigative team that would be assigned to analyze the body. Corbin also didn't want him or his friend to potentially sound crazy describing an alien on record. Jason appeared to understand the subdued cue, as did Dickson, it appeared.

"Please let the record note that further description of the craft, as well as the pilot, will be documented in the debriefs for squads Charlie Three-One and Charlie Three-Four and personnel from Bravo Company who are tasked with containment and clean-up of the crash area," Captain Dickson noted verbally.

"We found the pilot in the cockpit area, dead from an apparent wound from the flight controls being forced through its midsection. It was apparent that the force from the crash had caused that. We were able to recover the body and return it to the TOC." Corbin wanted to provide the information as succinctly as possible, also hoping to gloss over the potential for additional questions to be asked that could potentially shake loose what they weren't saying, such as talking to the alien, or the whole Marvel thing. He also hoped that his summary wasn't too rushed or making it seem like he was trying to hurry past potentially important details.

"There was a point where the communications seemed to re-establish themselves, was there anything down there that may have changed to allow that?" Captain Dickson asked the question in a neutral tone, not appearing to be asking it for any other reason than to record the details and ask their professional opinion.

"For most of the time that we were down there, it sounded like the engines to the craft were still idling. By the time we were preparing to leave with the pilot, the engine noise had died, and that was when we noticed that the radios came back," Jason explained.

"I agree. My observations were the same," Corbin added.

'*It was mostly the truth, just a little screwy on the timing,*' Corbin thought to himself. The engines had stopped, (he shut them off), before the radios started working again, but also after they had touched the Marvel and... passed out, or whatever. He did feel a pang of guilt for omitting information from his commander, whom he respected greatly, but he didn't think there was any need to include those items and potentially complicate the matter. Part of him also worried about what kind of test tube subject they would end up being if SWORD found out that they had meddled with some kind of extraterrestrial device. He imagined something like the scenes in the movie *E.T.* with all the plastic tunnels and biohazard suits and whatnot. No, no need to get into that kind of a mess, and as far as he was concerned, nothing happened anyway, probably nothing would, so no need to raise any kind of unnecessary concern. Right? As he was distracted by the internal monologue, he had failed to notice that the debrief had turned towards him in the form of a question.

"Staff-Sergeant Kent! Are you with us?"

"Yes sir," Corbin responded sternly, feeling somewhat embarrassed.

Captain Dickson didn't sound annoyed or impatient, however the fact that he had allowed himself to be distracted made Corbin feel sheepish.

"Would you mind explaining what happened to your face?"

Corbin let out a half-chuckle, as if recalling something stupid he had done when he was young. Well, younger than he was now. "Yes, sir. While carrying out the pilot, I lost my balance going up the side of the crater and caught most of my fall with my face."

Jason stifled a bit of a laugh, probably thinking about how comical that would have looked, if it had actually happened. Corbin shrugged a little, looking back at Captain Dickson. "I can't say I've scored outstanding marks in balance and grace, sir."

That comment made even Dickson chuckle a little. He smirked as he did, shaking his head and clearing his throat as if to get back on topic. "Had anything else happened while you were down there? Before you made your way back up out of the crater?"

Corbin had been interrogated by his parents enough times that this type of question always made him cringe on the inside. He was never sure if they formatted their questions like that to bait him into a confession because they didn't know exactly what he had done, or because they already knew what he had done and were testing to see if he would be honest without compulsion. He felt a similar sensation when Dickson asked that question. It took a moment, if just a heartbeat, for him to shake off that nagging sensation in his chest before he answered.

"No, sir. Nothing to report. After we pulled the pilot from the cockpit, we looked around to see if there were any other pieces of evidence we could bring out with us, found that there were none, and then made our way out. I had PFC McMann get the Humvee and come pick us up, and then we consolidated Specialists Rice and Hunt before returning to the armory."

"To your knowledge, was there anyone else who saw the pilot who you recovered?" Dickson asked, his tone the same level affect as the rest of the debrief.

"Not that I am aware of, sir," Jason answered.

"PFC McMann saw it as I was loading it, however, I don't believe anyone else in the squad did, sir," Corbin admitted. A part of him wondered if it was a mistake to reveal that information, however, he felt that it was probably more of a mistake than *not* doing so. Odds were Alex had already mentioned seeing it in his debrief.

There was a moment of silence among the three of them, Captain Dickson looking down in a contemplative manner. Jason regarded Corbin with a side glance and Corbin gave him a subtle and approving nod. Dickson looked up and drew in a long breath, the late hour of the night beginning to wear on him. Corbin felt the same way. It had been a long day, just the regular duty part of it, but then the mission, combined with all the tension that an operation brings with it, the fatigue was starting to set in now that they had had a few minutes of sitting still. It felt like his body suddenly had an opportunity to realize how tired it was. He clenched his jaw to suppress a yawn as he and Jason waited for their next prompt from their commander.

Captain Dickson smiled cordially at both of them and slapped his knees as he stood. "That should be all we need from you, gentlemen. Thank you."

Corbin and Jason stood a split second after him and simultaneously saluted him. He returned the salute, nodding and telling them, "Dismissed." They both made an about-face and began to head towards the door when Dickson called after them.

"Oh, Sergeant Hunt?"

"Yes sir?"

"Will you make sure Staff-Sergeant Kent actually gets some sleep?" Dickson jested.

Jason laughed knowingly, "Yes sir, I'll knock him out if I have to."

"Very good. Have a good night, gentlemen."

And with that, the two of them exited the briefing room, made their way down to the parking lot, and loaded into Corbin's jeep with the rest of the squad to drive home.

Chapter Six

Corbin woke early the next morning at his usual time of 0400 hours to send a group text to his squad to tell them they were going to skip their usual morning exercise, and then promptly go back to sleep. He hadn't paid attention to what time it had been when they got back to their barracks, but something told him it wasn't very long before his alarm went off. He was no stranger to poor amounts of sleep, so it wasn't the grogginess that was what convinced him to sleep in; it was the demotivation coupled with it that sealed the deal. He just wasn't feeling like a morning run and PT routine. Of course, skipping PT only meant that he would sleep in until 0500, but every extra minute felt like it was worth it. When his secondary alarm sounded, his brain was tricked enough into believing he had gotten all the sleep he needed, and it was no trouble getting up and getting ready for the day.

After his regimented morning routine of shaving, showering, and getting dressed in his duty uniform, he made his way into the kitchen area and started making himself something for breakfast. Jason came out of his room just a minute later, rubbing sleep from his eyes, and shuffling over to the refrigerator. As he milled about, there was an almost palpable sensation in the room, as if they were both thinking the same thing and those shared thoughts were somehow connecting in the air between them.

Corbin had sat down at the table and was helping himself to a fried egg sandwich he had made, opening the can of an energy drink he had gotten from the fridge. With how much his sleep had been muddled with over the years, he had developed the habit of drinking energy drinks almost as much as he drank water and joked that his blood type was "caffeine." He knew it wasn't the healthiest of habits and that he had better stop sometime but also justified that it wasn't smoking or drinking alcohol, so at least he had opted for the lesser of the habitual evils.

Despite the obvious elephant in the room and how much it nagged at the back of Corbin's mind; it was Jason who mentioned something first. "So, what do you think about last night?"

Corbin almost answered stupidly, "What about last night," as if to deflect the question of someone lacking security clearance but was quick to change his response. "I'm still not quite sure what to think. I mean, at face value, nothing happened other than we touched something an alien called 'the Marvel.' I don't feel any different, do you?"

Jason shook his head in reply, pouring himself a bowl of cereal. Corbin shrugged, taking a sip of his drink and continuing to eat his sandwich. They had about fifteen minutes until they needed to link up with the rest of the squad and head to their platoon office for their morning intelligence meeting and training assignment for the day. Corbin remembered that there was a possibility of a squad leader's meeting sometime today as well, which always amounted to a fat stack of nothing productive and him feeling like he was somehow dumber than he was before. They never really accomplished anything more than other squad leaders within the platoon pissing and moaning about something inconsequential and the platoon leadership giving the usual and noncommittal, "We'll look into that," as their response. Corbin chuckled to himself thinking about how much of military life was meetings, paperwork, and sitting around doing nothing waiting for further orders and wondered how many people would think the military was awesome if they knew how much of it was a whole lot of nothing.

"What do you think that thing even was supposed to do?" Jason queried.

"Your guess is as good as mine," Corbin answered with a shrug. "But it was apparently something important if that was on that alien's dying thoughts."

"What should we do about it? It obviously was supposed to do something."

"I don't know, man; I think just wait."

"Well, what if it is gonna make us sick, or kill us, or something like that? Like, what if it ends up giving us some kind of cancer or something crazy?"

"Dude, I don't know." Jason was starting to sound a little irrational, and it was getting to Corbin a little bit.

"What if more of those aliens start showing up because of that thing, and then we are going to have some kind of crazy invasion situation that we are responsible for starting and- "

"DUDE! Knock it OFF!" Corbin brought his fists down on the tabletop in frustration as he shouted, cutting Jason off. He expected Jason to fall silent; however, he didn't anticipate the legs of the table to explode out from underneath them as they did. There was the deafening sound of wood splintering and the two of them had a split second to jump back before the table fell right into their laps. They both stood at opposite ends of the kitchen, staring in disbelief at the wreckage that used to be their breakfast table. Corbin looked at his hands as if they were strange, foreign objects. Had he just done that? There was no way.

Jason let out a string of curse words in just about every language he could think of. "What just happened?!"

"I...I don't know," Corbin said, still just as shocked. "Piece of crap table, I guess. We did buy it from a thrift store."

Jason paused as if considering what to say in response, but Corbin interrupted whatever thoughts he was having. "We've got to get going, we will worry about this when we get back tonight."

Jason nodded his agreement and the two of them quickly grabbed their things and hurried out of the room, not even bothering to put away their dishes that now sat in a mess atop the floored tabletop. They both got into Corbin's jeep, driving off toward the SWORD building at the center of the installation. As they were the squad leadership and were usually together for most, if not all of any given day, they would carpool together while Randy, Brent, and Alex would either carpool together, or drive separately, depending on whether anyone was a few minutes behind the other. Today, it was difficult to tell as they were the first of the squad to leave and Corbin recognized all three of their vehicles still parked in their usual spots outside the barracks.

As they arrived, they parked as close to the headquarters building as they could and went inside, being met, as per usual, by the pair of guards at the front desk who challenged their identities and confirmed them using their military identification cards. Next, they made their way to their equipment lockers to don their sidearms. This wasn't common practice for any military personnel other than military police or assigned guard positions; however, with terrorism threat levels globally, as well as locally, being what they were, SWORD soldiers were given the option to wear their sidearm for duty outside of weapons training or security operations. Both Jason and Corbin agreed that they felt a little better having their pistols on them. Corbin strapped on his drop leg holster, loaded a full magazine into his Glock, holstered the weapon, and then clipped two spare magazines to his belt before securing the weapon safe in his locker and then locking the locker door with his thumbprint.

After arming themselves, they continued to their assigned platoon office on the first floor. The room itself was as large as an empty warehouse, divided into a section of desks for each of the squads of 3rd Platoon, an open weight room, a break area fashioned into a kitchen and sitting room area, and a general briefing area with rows of chairs and projection screen for platoon-wide training and deaths by PowerPoint. Corbin made his way over to his desk, sitting down into the swivel chair with a sigh, setting his replacement energy drink on the desktop, and signing into his encrypted laptop with his identity card. They had a few minutes to kill before they needed to be logged on to their virtual meeting with Intelligence, which was broadcast from SWORD intel members stationed somewhere in a cozy hotel in Dubai. Corbin was almost one hundred percent certain those guys were all Air Force personnel appropriated by SWORD. There was no way the government would spend that kind of money on Army or Marine operatives, nor would they have pitched a fit for something that posh. Hell, if you gave a soldier or a Marine a concrete floor with four walls, that was a veritable five-star hotel to them.

Corbin cracked open his energy drink and Jason gave him a reproving glance in jest. He just shrugged and smirked saying, "Hey, I gotta replace the one that I lost on the table."

"You could try sleeping more," Jason chuckled.

"I can sleep when I'm dead."

"What happened to your table?" came Randy's question as he sat down at his desk.

"Lousy piece of crap just collapsed on us this morning," Corbin answered quickly.

"Well, you did buy that thing second-hand, didn't you?" Randy said matter-of-factly.

Jason traded a knowing glance with Corbin. "Yeah, we sure did."

Brent and Alex sat down at their desks just in time to hear the telltale chime on their computers that their remote meeting was about to start. They quickly logged in and joined the video chatroom. After confirming that the video space was encrypted, they exchanged identities and pleasantries with a trio of intelligence officers, a gruff-looking Colonel, a softspoken Lieutenant, and a very pretty, green-eyed Captain who took the lead on narrating recent Intelligence reports from around the world. As per usual, this terrorist group still hated the United States and everyone else, and this new developing threat was threatening this and that...the usual stuff. Corbin had begun to daydream a little when he was pulled back to reality with a question from the Colonel, who cleared his throat roughly before speaking.

"What can you tell us regarding the investigation surrounding that crash on your installation last night, Staff-Sergeant?"

Corbin deflected, though his response was customary in this situation. "Nothing more than it was handled, Colonel, sir. Should you require more information, you are welcome to defer to my commander, Captain Dickson."

"Anything of note that the Intelligence community should be aware of?"

'It's none of your business,' Corbin thought. Of course, it was the business of SWORD Intelligence to know whether what had happened last night was of some sort of security concern to them as well as the general military community; however, even the chair jockeys at Intel had to go through the proper paperwork to get Need-to-Know on something like their operation.

Sometimes, and in the case of this Colonel at this moment, they just wanted to get whatever info they could "trick" out of the enlisted soldiers they outranked. Sometimes it worked, and their curiosity was appeased, however, Corbin wasn't one to let information leak, even to gratify an officer, and even for such an inconsequential question like this. However, this wasn't a power trip this Colonel was going to succeed in, no matter how hard he tried to flaunt his rank.

"With respect, sir, that is also a question best reserved for our commander, Captain Dickson. The events of the operation in question are classified and require the applicable Need-to-Know that can be obtained through proper paperwork which can be obtained by inquiry through Captain Dickson of Charlie Company, 3rd Platoon."

The Colonel seemed quite displeased and annoyed with his response. His lips were in a tight, flat line, and he cleared his throat again as if to exhibit his displeasure with Corbin keeping so tight to regulation. As if to take this as a cue, the pretty Captain continued her briefing to alleviate any uncomfortable silences. There wasn't much more to the briefing other than more of what they had already heard the time before, as well as the customary exhortation to treat every lead as legitimate, stay vigilant, and keep up the good work of maintaining the security of their assigned garrison, blah, blah, blah. Then they exchanged their parting pleasantries and signed off once the three officers had first. Corbin shook his head, still thinking about how the Colonel got bugged at his failure to "grease" him for information.

Alex leaned back in his seat and laughed. "You definitely ticked that Colonel off, Corbin."

"Well, if he wants the dirt on our operation, he's gotta fill out all the right forms. He's not gonna get it out of me like some high school locker room gossip. He can piss right off."

Everyone in the squad laughed. They all agreed, it was one thing to ask questions, but it was another thing completely to try to use one's rank to bypass regulation just for the sake of, well, gossip. If he really wanted to know more, he could, and probably already had filed what he needed to in order to get the full report regarding their mission the night before. Corbin was sure he would get a scathing remark from that Colonel to Captain Dickson and he was even more certain that Captain Dickson would let him know what he said as well as congratulate him on following protocol. It was too bad he couldn't do it on one of these virtual meetings so he could see the look on the Colonel's face when he suffered no reprimands for his actions. Oh well, just a personal victory he decided.

Corbin stood up and stretched, letting out an exaggerated groan as he did so. The Intelligence meeting had only been half an hour, and they had another hour before the platoon met together for their meeting. Though every squad in 3rd Platoon was supposed to be in the office at the same time, a lot of the others didn't bother to come in until just before the platoon meeting, opting to skip the intelligence meeting unless they suspected there was something of note or if Captain Dickson was planning on being there. If that happened, he was sure to let everyone know beforehand, so everyone knew to be there. Alex stood up, stretching as well, looking over to Corbin.

"Wanna grab some breakfast or something?" he offered. "I'll buy."

It wasn't the prospect of free breakfast, but the fact that most of his breakfast collapsed with the table that appealed to Corbin and he nodded. Randy tossed some cash to Alex, putting in his order for what he would like, and Brent declined, being the more stalwart of the group when it came to nutrition. Corbin always thought that ironic considering that Brent had a metabolism like an industrial laser that could vaporize anything he ate. He literally could eat an entire cow and not gain an ounce. Corbin motioned for Jason to come with them, figuring he could use a replacement breakfast as well, to which Jason accepted. They made their way outside to Alex's car and hopped in, making their way to the closest fast-food location.

"So, what happened with that body last night?" Alex asked casually.

"No clue," Corbin answered. "I guess it got cleaned up with the rest of the stuff. We just got debriefed like everyone else."

Alex just shrugged. If there was anyone in the squad who was unfazed and not curious about anything that had happened, it was Alex. He was the least prone to ask questions in general, and if he did, it was just out of superficial curiosity, or more so for conversation's sake, rather than trying to get more "dirt" on something. As unsatisfactory as Corbin's reply would have been to anyone else, it was all Alex needed to hear to just brush off the subject completely, probably never thinking about it ever again. Corbin admired Alex's simplicity in that way. He didn't want in on the drama or whatnot that was an inevitability in life, he just wanted to get up, do his job, and go home. They pulled into the drive through of Burger King nearby, placed their orders, and headed back to the HQ building with plenty of time to spare. They sat at their desks, eating their food and casually watching the rest of the platoon shuffle in and sit down at their desks, attempting to look like they had been there the entire morning.

The rest of the day was just a blur of routine and monotony. During their platoon meeting, Corbin and his squad were assigned to shooting and movement trainings for most of the week, with a twelve-hour guard shift on Tuesday and Thursday. They had spent the remainder of the day preparing for a day at the shooting range, shooting at the range, and cleaning and servicing their weapons at the close of the day. After his rifle and handgun were clean to his standard, Corbin locked them away in his locker safe, closing the door and letting out a long sigh. It was funny to him how a boring, routine day like today felt like it wore out his body more than one that involved more intense, physical activities. He looked around and saw that Randy and Jason were locking up their weapons as well, looking equally fatigued. That was when the thought came to his mind.

"Hey, guys, you want to go to Beck's tonight? I could use a little time off post," Corbin suggested.

"That sounds like a good idea to me," Randy answered.

"Count me in too," Jason responded.

"All right, Jason and I will meet you there. We drove together today. Let's just head straight there; I don't want to waste any time going home and changing."

"See you there," Randy said with a nod.

Beck's was a 1930's style candy shop and soda fountain that was located a ten-minute drive from the base. Corbin had stumbled upon it by accident when he had first arrived in the area, having gotten lost attempting to find the main entrance to the installation. It was fashioned to look like old diner on the outside, the kind that looked like a train car had been cut in half down its length and then fastened to the front of a building. The interior was a snapshot straight out of an era where Coca-Cola was all the rage and you were served ice cream, or soda, or a combination of the two, by someone referred to as a "soda jerk." There was a long bar with a white marble countertop and red-cushioned barstools down its length. The clean ice cream glasses, tall and flared outward like flowers, were stacked along the back of the bar area or right next to the soda fountain levers, which were long and polished chrome. Corbin was pretty sure he had seen this same place in about a dozen movies, but before finding it, he thought they were just a thing of the past, or a Hollywood production. He didn't believe there were any still in operation. That was one of the things that he enjoyed about Beck's; it felt familiar and comfortable to him, like somewhere he had always gone to as a little kid. The soda, ice cream, and candy selection couldn't be beat either. The shelves were a rainbow of colored packaging for candies, old and new, foreign and domestic. It was vintage enough to even have rolls of those colored candy buttons and jars full of lollipops and other candies you generally didn't see in stores.

As vintage as the store itself were the owners, Mr. and Mrs. Beck. They were older, at *least* in their seventies, but just as spry and lively as could be and they felt like adopted grandparents to anyone who went to their shop. Corbin felt so comfortable with them that he referred to them as "Ma" and "Pa," which was a habit of most of the regulars. Walter Beck was a balding man, wearing big square glasses and a traditional "soda jerk" uniform of white shirt, bowtie, slacks, a red apron and a paper hat. His teeth were a bit of a jagged mess, most likely from poor dental hygiene when he was younger, but his kind, jovial personality made his funky smile an endearing and unique feature to this kindly old gentleman. His wife, Nora, was short, hardly taller than five feet, with that big, old-lady hairdo and even bigger glasses. She had dentures, which gave her a perfectly white and straight smile, but they did cause her to slur her words a little due to a lack of sensitivity to actual teeth. She was just as jovial and welcoming as her husband, usually wearing a similar outfit of white blouse and slacks and red apron, minus a bowtie or paper hat. As near as he could tell, they were the only two who worked there, and it was very likely that they lived out of an apartment in the rear of the shop. Corbin had been there enough times that they could recognize him by sight, and it was no different as he stepped through the door this evening, the little brass bell jingling as he came in.

"Corbin! Good to see you again," Mr. Beck greeted happily.

"It feelsh like we haven't sheen you in a while," Mrs. Beck said with a cheery tone.

"Hey Ma and Pa. How are you this evening?" Corbin took a seat at the counter, motioning to Jason. "This is my friend Jason. He's my second-in-command if you will, for the squad. His brother Randy should be here soon too."

"Oh, that's sho nyshe," Mrs. Beck said excitedly.

"We've been just fine here," Mr. Beck answered. "Been busy up your way?"

"You know how it is, Pa," Corbin said with an exaggerated sigh. "The world has gone to hell and we are part of the cleanup crew."

Mr. Beck chuckled, handing a menu to Jason and Corbin each. "Well, we sure appreciate all the work you guys do. Just make sure you stay safe out there doing it."

"Anything to be sure I can come back here Pa. You sure know how to make a great ice cream soda," Corbin complimented, pointing out a combination of cream soda and vanilla ice cream on the menu.

"Well, we sure appreciate having regulars like yourself, Corbin," Mr. Beck mentioned, taking the menu from Corbin and getting to work on his order.

Just then, the bell on the door jingled and Randy came in slowly, looking a little distracted by all the colors and displays in the shop. His expression was almost a little surprised when he noticed that Jason and Corbin were already sitting at the counter. Corbin turned and waved him over, gesturing to a stool on the other side of him.

"Have a seat, buddy. Ma, Pa, this is Randy. He's my heavy gunner, and he's Jason's older brother," Corbin introduced as Randy sat down.

"Randy, nyshe to shee you." Mrs. Beck smiled.

"I- uh, hi," Randy said, almost absentmindedly.

"You all right, man? You seem a little off," Corbin pointed out, patting him on the shoulder in a brotherly manner.

"I'm..." Randy shook his head as if trying to reset his thoughts. "Yeah, I'm good. I was just a bit surprised by this place. I didn't know what to expect. I know Corbin talks about this place quite a bit, I just didn't know how ornate it would all be."

"Isn't it cool? I never thought a place like this was real, let alone so close to us. Here," he handed Randy a menu, "take a look at what they have. My treat."

"Thanks, man," Randy said with a grin.

Jason was next to order, also an ice cream soda, and Randy ordered a sundae that looked as if it had enough ice cream and toppings to bury a horse. Mr. Beck commented on his confidence in Randy's ability to finish it, considering his muscular size. Corbin agreed, pointing out how he made an excellent heavy gunner for the squad. Mr. Beck pointed out that very few, if any visitors to the shop who had ordered that sundae were able to finish it in one sitting and offered the challenge that if Randy could do it, he wouldn't charge for it. Randy smirked slyly as if already sure he was going to get a free dessert this evening. Corbin casually sipped at his drink and admired the surroundings, thinking to himself how he would never get used to the nostalgia and comfort of this place, and how that was a good thing.

He was in this contemplative state when the bell at the front door jingled once again. Corbin didn't bother to look up as he was used to people coming and going. He could passively recognize the sound of footsteps and several female voices moving from the door to the counter, several seats down from where he and his friends sat. He hadn't even noticed who had sat down even when Mrs. Beck pulled him out of his trance when she asked him a question.

"Sho, Corbin...do you have a girlfriend?"

Corbin furrowed his brow. It seemed a bit random of a question, however, they hadn't been engaged in any conversation, so it could have been more just a question for the sake of starting a conversation. He looked up from his glass and smiled at her a little in bewilderment. Randy and Jason each chuckled a little at the question.

"I'm sure he'd date that intelligence officer," Jason jested.

"Bro, *I* would date her if I could," Randy said with a smirk.

"Good luck with that," Corbin scoffed, "both with the long-distance thing, and with the 'frat' charges you'd have to try to dodge."

"We practically have the long-distance thing down to an art already. We meet at least weekly over our video calls," Randy laughed.

"What is, how'd you say it, frat?' Is that some sort of Army slang for something?" Mr. Beck asked.

"Fraternization," Corbin specified, "it's a rule in the military where enlisted soldiers, and commissioned officers can't be in relationships unless they were already married or in that relationship before they enlisted. I'm not well-versed on the reasons why that is other than I think it's the Army's way of making sure no one is trying to sleep their way to the top, or at least to a better assignment or something."

Mr. Beck nodded his understanding. Mrs. Beck shook her head with a smile in a way that only a grandmother could. "But you never anshwered my question, Corbin."

Corbin smiled, looking back down at his ice cream soda and taking a sip. "No, Ma, I don't have a girlfriend. I guess I haven't found the right girl, or the time to go looking for her." He shrugged, realizing it seemed a bit strange in his mind that he hadn't thought about a girlfriend or his feelings towards having one for...well, years. The last time he could remember thinking about girls in that way was when he was about to leave his high school with General Easton all those years ago. He was very interested in having a girlfriend back then, though he wasn't very confident in trying to get one, but that subject hadn't seemed to cross his mind from that point until this moment. Truthfully, he felt a little bashful at himself, as if he had somehow forgotten who he was over the years he had been with SWORD. At the same time, however, he wasn't too worried because, as he saw it, he had grown, changed, and matured in a way that adjusted his priorities from chasing tail to keeping the world safe. That was a noble change in perspective, right?

He must have been caught in this train of thought for some time when he realized Mrs. Beck was waving her little, wrinkled hand in front of his eyes as if to try to break him out of a trance. "Corbin, you shtill with uhsh?"

"Huh? Oh, yeah. Still here." Corbin cleared his throat to conceal some embarrassment he felt. "I really don't know why I don't have a girlfriend. Maybe I just don't have the time?"

Mr. Beck chuckled and shook his head, "Come on now, a handsome guy like you has time to come hang out with a couple of old bats at an ice cream shop but not go out and find a pretty girl to be with?"

Corbin was feeling pretty confused now. This subject had never come up before when he had been here, what prompted it now, of all times? He tried to backtrack through their conversations since they had gotten here, trying to locate a point where girlfriends or relationships or something of the like had come up and he had missed a cue. He couldn't think of anything, and again tried to decide whether something had prompted Mrs. Beck to ask and he was just a little behind in the flow of conversation, or if it was just an innocent question brought up on the fly. He looked around as if to search for some sort of clue to the mystery when he found what had to have been the source of the inquiry.

There was a quartet of women who had come in and sat down a few stools away from them at the bar. Corbin then made the connection between what he had heard moments ago to the reality of these women being the source of the entrance and the voices he heard. He also noticed that they looked to be around the same age as himself and his friends. Aha, that's what it was. Ma Beck was looking to potentially do some matchmaking. He smiled to himself as her motivations became clear to him. He looked over to Mrs. Beck, who gave him a knowing smile and a little nod. All he could do was chuckle softly and slowly shake his head with a grin. He looked back over to the quartet and immediately noticed one of them. When he did, his smile faded to a sort of look of being dumbfounded.

Sitting closest to him and his friends was a gorgeous brunette wearing pink scrubs and matching pink sneakers. Her long hair was pulled back in a thick ponytail that cascaded down to the middle of her back. Mixed in with the dark brown were highlights of subtle blonde. Her bangs swooped gracefully across her forehead and accented her hazel eyes, which appeared to change from a deep, warm brown to an electrifying green at the simple change in angle that the light hit them. Her lips were full and her smile was bright and infectious. Just seeing her smile made him smile and feel a little drunk. As she talked with her friends, she laughed, the sound making him feel elated, almost addicted, as if he needed to hear her laugh and see her smile more. She was...intoxicating. Forget that pretty Intelligence officer; this girl was breathtaking. Was she a regular? If so, why had he never noticed her before? Why hadn't Ma or Pa ever pointed her out before? How had this been the only time he had ever seen or noticed her? His mind was a veritable collision of thoughts and feelings that left him looking, rather stupidly, in her direction.

* * *

She had seen soldiers around before, and plenty of them had tried to hit on her, even here at Beck's, but this guy seemed a little different. At this point, it wasn't uncommon to already have been hit on by someone in uniform and she and her friends taking their usual defensive personas to shoot the cocky SOB down before he could even begin to think he had a chance with any of them. Heck, when she noticed the trio as she and her friends came in, she was admittedly surprised that at least one of them didn't immediately jump to their feet and tried to shoot their shot at them before they could even sit down at the counter. Instead, they stayed where they were, conversing with Ma and Pa almost as if they hadn't even noticed that they had come in. They weren't married, her friend had already determined that by looking for wedding bands or the smooth skin indicative of a ring that had been removed, and she quietly pointed that out. Okay, they were all cute, but she and her friends weren't going to point that out to them and risk "activating" the arrogant braggart in them that seemed to be so prominent among soldiers.

She noticed that after Ma had asked the guy in the middle something, he looked over to her and her friends and was now kind of stupidly staring at her. What had Ma told him? Darn it, she better not have mentioned that she was single. If she had, it wouldn't be the first time that Ma Beck had tried to set her up with someone else who came into the shop. Of course, evidenced by her still being single, each of those attempts had failed. Now, not only had Ma said something to hone interest in on her, but she had also done it with another soldier. Another potentially arrogant dickwad that was going to flaunt his muscles and his tiny IQ at her like he was *exactly* what she was looking for in a partner. Well, if she was going to shoot him down, she might as well get it over with now. It looked like he was most of the way finished with his dessert, so he at least wouldn't have to finish the bulk of his ice cream in embarrassed silence.

"You keep staring like that for too long, you'll go blind, soldier," she said with a slight edge to her tone.

'Crap, she saw me,' was the only thought Corbin could manage when he heard her. He quickly looked down, blushing. If he didn't feel like a complete idiot before, he sure felt it now. How long had he been staring at her like a moron? Obviously long enough that she noticed, but how long was that? He could have been gawking at her for minutes on end before she decided to call him out on it. He could feel panic setting in, his heartbeat speeding up and sweat beginning to form a thin layer on his forehead. He felt like such an idiot now, and it was only going to get worse unless he could figure out some way to apologize and try his best to not make himself look and sound like a total goon.

"I apologize, ma'am. I didn't mean anything by it." He nervously stirred the remains of his ice cream soda, which had melted enough to resemble more of a soup.

Well, that was new. She hadn't ever experienced someone who was apologetic for having admired her. This was refreshingly different. She looked to her friends who each exchanged a glance that she couldn't decipher. She shook her head at them and looked back to the embarrassed Staff-Sergeant. She was intrigued to see someone of his age at such a rank, which was a difficult feat at best, and not exuding an annoying level of confidence and swagger. How in the world had he gotten to where he was in, what, maybe two years, three at best? He couldn't have been more than twenty-one years old, and enlistment age being eighteen, seventeen if his parents were crazy enough to sign off on him enlisting, and he had badges for Combat Infantry, Airborne, Air Assault, Special Forces, and Mountain tabs on his uniform, and his shoulder patches showed that he had deployed with the 10th Mountain Division and...Ah, yes, there it was. The garrison patch on his left shoulder. He and his buddies had it. That patch with the eagle with the missile and olive branch. He was part of Eagle Battalion.

She was familiar with a lot of the military lingo and units on base as she worked there as a civilian nurse, and she had seen handfuls of soldiers wearing that patch. Not a lot was known about them other than they were a filler unit to help cover jobs on post while the other units garrisoned here were deployed. She had made some observations on her own whenever she noticed them. They always had a lot of skill badges and, in a lot of situations including him, looked a bit young to have their ranks and decorations. Maybe Eagle Battalion just recruited baby-faced soldiers? Well, whatever it was, they obviously had very skilled men in their unit, and some very cocky ones. Except this one. He was skilled, based on just his rank and badges alone, but he seemed to lack the tenacity others in his position had. He was handsome and built enough to catch the eye of any girl even if he were a civilian, and the uniform just added to his allure, but it was almost like he didn't know any of that. His silver-blue eyes were captivating, serious, focused, but somehow insecure at the same time. His eyes alone suggested he had the knowledge and experience to kill a man in an abundance of ways, but at the same time would be nervous to strike up a conversation with someone of the opposite sex. That intrigued her even more, and she rested her chin in her hand as she leaned against the counter and studied him, eyes narrowed slightly in a studious manner.

* * *

"Dude, she's still looking at you," Jason informed Corbin under his breath before taking a sip of his soda.

If he hadn't been panicking before, he was now. What was wrong with him? He had stared down the literal barrel of rifles pointed at his face and not even blinked but any time a girl looked at him, or tried to talk to him, he was a nervous wreck, feeling like a stage actor who had forgotten to wear clothes and remember his lines. He was certain he had somehow alienated her by staring at her like an idiot, and now he was facing the consequences of it. He had apologized to her; what else did she need? He hesitated for a moment before looking towards her, clearing his throat politely.

"Is there- is there something I can do for you, ma'am?"

"Well, you can stop calling me 'ma'am;' it makes me feel old," she quipped.

"I- uh, I apologize. Force of habit I guess," Corbin offered bashfully.

Her friends were listening now and giggled at his response, which only made him feel more sheepish. She, however, seemed unfazed by it as she continued to eye him, almost as if she were trying to figure him out. "What's your name?" she asked.

"Kent. Uh, sorry, Corbin. Corbin Kent." He was so used to hearing his last name used as if it were his first name that he sometimes got confused for a split second if someone happened to call him by his actual first name.

"Why don't you come over here, Corbin, and let's discuss your behavior," she said in a tone that mimicked a teacher disappointed in a student's misconduct.

Randy had finished his sundae a minute or so before and Jason swallowed the last of his dessert and the two of them stood, patting Corbin on the shoulder. They wished him luck and told him they would ride together back to the barracks in Randy's car. In his panic and embarrassment, Corbin only barely processed what had happened until he looked around him to find himself now alone on one end of the bar. He could feel his cheeks flush and his heart thudding in his ears. He slipped off his stool and moved towards her, her friends moving aside and taking seats at the opposite end of the bar where he and his friends had been previously. Sitting down next to her, Corbin swallowed hard, he was sure hard enough for her to hear. She only smiled slightly at him as he took a seat. He didn't wait before he tried to apologize once again.

"Look, I'm sorry for staring, I just- I don't know. I- well, I-" He sounded like a complete moron. He knew what he wanted to say but felt like that would just make him sound stupid, too. Well, he figured he already sounded dumb, so it's not like telling the truth would make him sound any more stupid than he already did, trying to speak and decide what to say at the same time. He took a deep breath and gathered his nerves as best as he could.

"I apologize. I just– I think you're beautiful, and I'm not very good at this kind of thing," he admitted, feeling himself blush again.

"That is very apparent," she said with a short laugh. "But you're doing great, keep it up."

Corbin laughed at himself nervously, "Uh, thanks. I just couldn't help noticing you when you came in and, well, when Ma pointed you out."

It was her turn to laugh nervously now, Corbin noticing a little red showing in her cheeks. "Ah yes. Ma Beck doing what Ma Beck does best."

He was a bit surprised to hear her say that. He hadn't ever noticed her here before; however, it was usually only more regular customers who referred to the Becks as Ma and Pa. How had he ever missed her? None of that seemed to matter now that he was talking to her, feeling more and more comfortable with her as the seconds passed.

"Not the first time she has tried to get you hooked up?" Corbin raised an eyebrow.

"Oh, heavens no! Sadly, she has only ever had the opportunity to make those attempts based on looks and I've been unfortunate to find out that the personalities haven't matched the pretty faces. Of course, I can't just shoot down her matchmaking offers; I don't think her sweet old heart could take that. So, for the sake of diplomacy, I accept her offers, speak with whomever she has chosen for me, and then discontinue once I'm no longer around."

Corbin could feel himself getting a little nervous. Was he going to end up like all the others? Was this simply a diplomatic conversation on behalf of the feelings of a nice old lady before she ghosted him after they left the shop? He hoped not, but he didn't think that he would be able to focus if that question lingered at the back of his mind. He had to ask, and he hoped it didn't sound too forward or arrogant.

"Uh-oh," he started, smiling slightly, "where does that leave me once we leave here?"

She smiled, looking down and brushing some of her hair behind her ear. "Well, we will just have to cross that bridge when we get there, won't we?"

It wasn't a complete rejection, so he could roll with that for now. He brushed the anxiety of uncertainty from his mind as they continued to talk. He bought her an order of cookie dough ice cream with a warm snickerdoodle cookie on top as they got to know each other more. He learned that she was a civilian nurse on base and noticed quickly that she was familiar with military jargon, so he didn't have to translate his speech into something a regular civilian could understand. He was also becoming very aware of how easy it was to talk to her, about anything, and how comfortable he felt with her. There was no sense of urgency to talk about anything particular to try to impress her. As far as he was aware, it was just them, talking, completely unaware of what or who was around them. In fact, he had no idea what time it was until Pa Beck informed them that the shop was closing. Corbin let out a long, content sigh, standing up and waiting for her to do the same.

"I'll walk you to your car," he offered, lifting his arm for her to take it.

"Thank you, kind sir," she said with a smile, taking his arm.

He led her outside and she gestured to her white sedan parked only a few stalls away from his jeep. He led her there, stepping back to give her room to unlock and open her door. She was about to climb into her car before he realized something.

"Hey, I never got your name," he said, trying not to sound too desperate, though he felt fairly panicked on the inside.

She smiled slightly, making his heart flutter in his chest. She ducked into her car for a moment before handing him a folded sticky note that she held between her fingers.

"My name is Brianne. My friends just call me 'Bree.' You can call me that the next time I see you."

She got into her car and drove away, leaving Corbin standing on the curb, smiling like a lovestruck teenager. To him, her name was just as beautiful as the rest of her, and he didn't want to do anything in that moment other than to stand there and bask in the elation he felt, thinking back to their short time together. A little part of him wondered how he had managed to pull off any of what had just occurred when he had made a complete fool of himself upon first meeting her. He wasn't a professional in the dating game, by any means, but he was pretty sure that picking up girls was based more on being cool, debonair, or anything opposite of the bumbling idiot he had been. However, here he was holding, (he unfolded the note), yes it was her phone number, and her name written above it. He half-stumbled over to his jeep and climbed in, mind swirling with thoughts of her and how she looked, how she sounded, how she smelled. On one or two occasions, he had to refocus on the road before he rolled through a stop sign or completely off the road.

When he got home, he shuffled into his room, completely ignoring the fact that the kitchen table was still in a heap in the middle of the floor as he passed it. Flopping down on the bed, he let out another content sigh as his mind still lingered on her and as he dozed off, the image of her smile was still burned into his memory as sleep overtook him and the last word to leave his lips was, "Brianne."

Chapter Seven

C orbin woke up with a start at the sound of his alarm the next morning. The last thought on his mind was the same as the first after recovering from the initial shock of waking up: Brianne. He had a feeling she would now be the primary inhabitant of his thoughts throughout the day, and he took no issue with that. He wasn't surprised that would most likely be the case, but he was surprised that he was still fully dressed in his uniform, right down to his boots, still bloused and laced as if already prepared for the day. He hated it when he fell asleep in his clothes. He always felt so grimy and stinky as if he had failed to shower for several days, even if that wasn't the case. He wanted to take a shower, but he knew that would be useless considering he was going to conduct PT, (physical training), with his squad. He chided himself internally at the thought of taking a shower only to sweat and take another shower as he changed into the PT uniform of an Army-labeled shirt and shorts, taking the patches off of his OCP camouflage uniform before tossing the uniform into his laundry hamper.

Jason tapped on his door and opened it slightly. "Hey, how'd it go last night?"

Corbin smiled again, thinking once more about Brianne, well, Bree. "Good. We talked for a good, long time. I even got her number."

"What?! After such an *amazing* first impression you gave her," Jason teased.

Corbin laughed and shook his head, "Yeah, I'm still reeling at the fact that she didn't smack me and run away screaming after that 'impressive' introduction."

"Maybe you're onto something," Jason joked. "Success through totally bombing the pickup."

Corbin laughed, tying his sneakers, and standing up straight. "All right let's get the others and get the PT hashed out for today. We still need to make up for not doing anything the morning after that op."

PT that morning was a "leisurely" four-mile run which included running up and down the stairs in the football stadium of the high school. Once they had finished, it was high-intensity rotations of push-ups, sit-ups, burpees, and pull-ups. Everyone was panting and soaked in a satisfying amount of sweat. Corbin felt that he and his squad had done well. He had intentionally pushed them a little harder today, wanting to make sure they compensated for a missed morning of exercise. He was confident in his ability to keep up and even out-exercise everyone in the squad, except when it came to running. Jason had them all beat. He could easily run two miles in twelve minutes and look as if he had simply walked around the block. Corbin did his best to keep everyone at a constant pace while running, but Jason had to hold back so he didn't leave them all in the dust. Several times during each run, Corbin would let Jason speed ahead at his own pace, if he waited further ahead for the rest of them to catch up.

Once they had all cleaned up and got dressed in their uniforms, they gathered outside the barracks building to make sure everyone was ready and to make arrangements for driving to work. Jason and Corbin habitually drove together in Corbin's vehicle, and Brent, Randy, and Alex opted to all drive together in Brent's car. This allowed the rest of the squad to go home unhindered if there happened to be a surprise leadership meeting at the end of each duty day, which was becoming more frequent. Corbin drove to the nearest gas station to pick up a couple of energy drinks to get him through the day. At this point, he considered that it was the habit of it all that kept him going, rather than the actual caffeine. He had found that he could drink an entire can of Monster before bed and still be out like a light within minutes. It wasn't anything that the drink lacked; it was the fact that Corbin was sure he was caffeine resistant and would probably need enough to power a small city to feel any actual effects.

Arriving at the HQ building, Corbin and Jason were inside and at their desks just moments before the rest of the squad. They had gone straight to checking their training and operation schedule for the rest of the week. Brent read through an e-mail from the armory regarding an updated optics system for one of his rifles. Randy was researching lighter and faster internal parts for his LMGs, hoping to requisition some to improve their overall weights and rates of fire. Alex lazily scrolled through an online training he still needed to finish, paying nearly no attention to the presentation. Corbin noticed that there had been a conflict in the patrol schedule with Charlie Three-One and another guard obligation to which they had been assigned. According to their schedule today, they were supposed to be at the firing range in an hour for marksmanship practice for most of the day. They were all solid shooters, and marksmanship nowadays felt more like a formality rather than a legitimate need. SWORD required a specific amount of "trigger time" for all her soldiers to maintain their edge over other branches and Corbin felt like all they were doing nowadays was putting a check in the proverbial box on that subject. Additionally, he took opportunities to cover or assist other squads for two reasons: first, because he felt the engrained obligation to help his fellow brothers and second, he always used those opportunities to secure the benefit of reciprocity in the future.

He looked up from his computer. "Hey guys, any objections to covering for Charlie Three-One today for their security patrol? They were double-booked and are supposed to be providing guard support at the airfield today."

"You buying lunch?" Randy proposed, not bothering to look up from the requisition form he had begun.

Corbin rolled his eyes, laughing in Randy's direction. "Always about food for you, huh?"

"Hey, a guy's gotta eat, man. I can't keep this girlish figure by starving myself during the day," Randy answered matter-of-factly with a musing smile.

"Gotta fuel the tank," Brent said with a brotherly slap to Randy's shoulder.

"I'm glad I don't have to pay for your caloric intake on the regular. I'm pretty sure you could eat the DFAC out of its budget if you set your mind to it," Corbin quipped. "But sure, if it means you'll agree to the patrol and not whine about it, yeah, I've got lunch for us this afternoon."

There was a chorus of consent from everyone. Corbin nodded resolutely and replied to the platoon-wide e-mail, stating that Charlie Three-Three would pick up the patrol for the day. Once he had clicked 'send,' he leaned back in his chair and looked around the office area. It was mostly empty as most of the other squads were already out on their various assignments. They would need to get to their lockers soon and start inspecting and preparing their equipment and Humvee for their patrol. On the opposite end of the office area, Captain Dickson stood up from his desk and stood in the doorway of his office.

"Thank you, Charlie Three-Three, for your willingness to take over for Three-One. I'll make sure they buy you a round or something at the NCO club to show their appreciation."

"I'll be happy with a reimbursement for whatever its gonna cost me to buy Specialist Hunt's lunch today," Corbin called back. "I have a sneaking suspicion it isn't going to be cheap."

"Duly noted," Dickson responded in a businesslike tone. "Hunt, just try not to eat your poor squad leader out of house and home, will you?"

"I make no guarantees, sir," was Randy's answer.

Everyone chuckled. Captain Dickson turned and returned to his desk, shaking his head with a grin. Corbin looked back to his computer screen and noticed that there was a new e-mail message that had arrived in his inbox. He habitually hovered the cursor over the message and double-clicked to open it. There was no subject line to preface the content of the message, nor was there an e-mail address that showed in the column identifying the sender. Corbin had a somewhat poor habit of simply opening any electronic correspondence he received, putting his trust solely in the encryption software that protected their communications. His eyes widened and his heart raced as he read.

Staff-Sergeant Kent,

It is imperative that we speak concerning the events of two nights ago. It has come to our understanding that you and Sergeant Hunt were responsible for deploying Codename: Marvel to yourselves. It would be within all our best interests that we meet and discuss the potential effects it may have on you. Is there a location where we may meet to gather further information? This is of the utmost importance, and we exhort you to take swift and decisive action in organizing a rendezvous. We await your response with great urgency.

-A Friend

What in the flying fart in space was this? This had to be some kind of joke. There was no other explanation for it. Someone was messing with him. Who was this and how did they know information about that operation, including things that only he and Jason knew? He could feel his heart thudding in his head out of slight panic and much more anger. There was no excuse for leaked information, and if he ever found out who was dicking with him, he was going to have some choice words, at the very least, to share with that guy. His brow furrowed as he read through the message again, trying to make sense of how any of this had come about. As far as he knew, the only people who knew any details about what had happened on that operation were his squad and Captain Dickson. Even then, there were also details that even *they* didn't know, including what kept getting called the Marvel, or "Codename: Marvel" in this message. That was a specific detail that only he and Jason knew of, and they didn't know much more about it other than that is what the alien pilot called that glowing ball thing in its ship. It was all so far-fetched that he could only rationalize that this message was some sort of lousy hoax someone was trying to concoct, and the logical side of his mind couldn't even accept that because there were so many holes in that logic.

He looked around as if afraid he was going to get caught looking at something he wasn't supposed to. When he established that no one was concerned with what he was doing, he forwarded the message to Jason. He was still in awe that a message like this had bypassed all the encryption protections while also lacking a sender's address. He watched Jason and knew exactly when he saw the message by his expression of confusion and panic and him shooting a glance to Corbin across their desks. Corbin simply nodded and gave him a look as if to say, "We'll talk about this later."

Out in the motor pool, after having donned his weapons and armor, Corbin sat in the front passenger seat of their Humvee, locking in the radio frequencies into the transmitter mounted to the dash between the two front seats. His helmet was set on the bare console between him and the driver seat, sweat beginning to show slightly in the rising humidity of the day. Jason climbed into the driver's seat and closed the door behind him to help seal their conversation in the cab of the vehicle. Corbin had been working with the radio with one leg hanging out his door. When he noticed Jason, he pulled the door closed with his toe as he pulled his leg into the vehicle. The heavy armored door banged shut with a heavy '*thunk.*'

"What do you make of that e-mail?" Jason asked in a hushed tone, still leery of anyone hearing them.

Corbin shrugged, still looking at the radio as he finalized the settings on it. "Well, I've got a lot of questions about how they found me and how they managed to get an e-mail to me through security settings, but I don't think that's the most pertinent thing at the moment."

"What is?" asked Jason, looking over his shoulder.

"Who or what we are dealing with. It's apparent that top-of-the-line security and encryption doesn't mean anything to them and they have some way of knowing what happened that night. On top of that, however it is that they know about that operation, we were, well are, oblivious to how they know."

"You think that ship had security cameras on it?"

It wasn't a possibility that he had considered previously, but in lieu of the message he had received, it suddenly became a very real possibility. He also scolded himself in his head, feeling stupid and amateurish for not considering before now that there was a real chance that was the situation. He did have to give himself a little bit of grace, though, seeing as neither he, nor his squad was given any intensive training on counter-surveillance. He also had to think that if SWORD considered that even a slight risk, they would have been told about it in their briefing, as haphazard as it had been. No, Corbin considered, there had to be something bigger at play here. As outlandish and borderline supernatural as it seemed, whoever sent that message had found out what had happened and found a way to contact him. How any of that was even possible, he couldn't even begin to fathom, but it had happened, and now they needed to figure out what they were going to do about it. If they did happen to decide to meet up with their mystery person, how would they set that up? The message didn't have a sender's address, so he determined that simply pressing the 'reply' button wasn't going to amount to anything.

"I have no idea. I mean, I guess we can't rule that out as a possibility," Corbin finally answered. "However, at this point, I think what we do about it is nothing. We have a security patrol to conduct, and trying to speculate about things we have no information about is nothing but a waste of time. I've got a feeling that whoever sent that message is going to try to get in touch with us again. Maybe then, we will have a chance to speak with them and really get some answers as to what is going on."

Jason nodded silently, showing his agreement. Corbin finished preparing the vehicle radio, making sure his personal radio handset was synced to the same frequencies. He performed a radio check for both systems, getting a positive return from the vehicle dispatch personnel. Jason did the same for his radio, adjusting his microphone as he did so. Corbin used a dry-erase marker to write the radio frequencies on the upper corner of the windshield panel in front of himself as a reminder as well as for the rest of the squad to set their personal radios once they mounted up. Jason climbed up into the turret and positioned himself behind the .50 cal mounted there, then loaded a belt of ammunition, pulling the charging handles roughly two times to ensure the lead round was properly seated. Randy had opted to drive first, placing his M249 in the back of the Humvee before climbing into the driver's seat, Brent and Alex getting into the rear seats. Once they had all settled in, Corbin called in to the dispatch that they were ready to move and signaled for Randy to drive out of the motor pool.

The first part of the morning felt like it took about a week to pass. The heat and the humidity were especially oppressive today, giving Corbin the sensation of breathing through a hot, damp washcloth. They had stopped at a gas station to stock up on some snacks and water as they all were feeling hungry and had consumed the contents of their hydration packs. They took turns going into the convenience store, making sure that their vehicle wasn't left unattended. Jason, Alex, and Brent went in first, leaving Corbin and Randy to guard the vehicle and man the turret. Corbin thought it somewhat comical that anyone in a convenience store on base wouldn't even bat an eye at fully armed and armored soldiers walking in and buying themselves some chips and soda, but if they were anywhere on "the civvie side" as they referred to it, people would panic thinking they were in some dystopian nightmare or something.

Once the trio had returned and switched him and Randy out in the rotation, the two of them made their way inside. Randy made a beeline for the snack shelves, looking to relieve his hunger with an armful of salty snacks. Corbin was feeling extra parched, so he made his way to the refrigerated section at the rear of the small store, glancing at the wall of water bottles of varying sizes and manufacturers. He had gotten somewhat lost in his search for the largest water bottle to refill his hydration pack, so he didn't even notice that someone had stepped up next to him. When he sensed someone nearby, he didn't bother to look their way, figuring they were just a fellow patron browsing the beverage selection. He didn't even think to pay attention when he saw in his periphery that the figure turned to face him and heard him clear his throat. It wasn't until the second or third time the person did so that Corbin realized that they were trying to get his attention. As he looked up, he noticed a man standing next to him, facing him and offering a congenial smile. He was about a head taller than Corbin, with a bald, perfectly shaped head, no facial hair, and in plain, rather unnoticeable attire. In passing, this man wouldn't have struck anyone as memorable and would have been just another simple face to forget in a crowd. What stuck out to Corbin was the man's eyes. They were dark, most likely a really dark brown, but to him, they looked almost black. It was like looking into the eyes of someone wearing those dark-tinted Halloween contacts or something. It was a stark contrast to the man's overall bright and cheery appearance but didn't seem to change the man's look from friendly.

Corbin raised an eyebrow at him as the man simply looked at him for a silent moment. "Is there something I can help you with, sir?"

"Staff-Sergeant Kent, I believe we are still in need of establishing a meeting."

Corbin furrowed his brow at the man, unaware of who he was or what he was even talking about. It didn't even faze him that he knew his name, his rank and last name were displayed in patches on his body armor. As for a meeting, he didn't even know this guy; why would he want to meet with him? The dots didn't start connecting until the man made his next statement. He leaned forward slightly and lowered his voice so only Corbin could hear him.

"This is regarding," he looked back and forth, "Codename: Marvel."

Corbin felt like his eyes almost bugged out of his head as they widened at his response. He repeated the man's actions and looked around to see if anyone was in earshot. "Did you send that message this morning?"

The man disregarded his question. "It is extremely important that I meet with you and Sergeant Hunt. We will need to go somewhere that can accommodate our speaking without the possibility of interruption. Ideally, this would need to be somewhere that is not located on your military installation here. Are you aware of anywhere we may go that meets those parameters?"

Corbin frowned slightly but tried not to give this man too incredulous of a look. Who was this guy? His more cautious, or as he joked, his more paranoid side considered this man as some kind of impostor here to mess with him. For all he knew, this was all some intricate hoax, and at any moment someone would pop out of a hidden space laughing and pointing out hidden cameras here in the convenience store. Sure, this guy had mentioned the Marvel by name, whatever it was, but he still couldn't get over his apprehension that this could all be a joke, or a trap, or something else that would leave him feeling like a fool if he just jumped into it without a second thought.

He figured he could give the guy a little bit of a benefit of the doubt by not immediately telling him to go pound sand. "How am I supposed to trust you? I have no idea who you are."

The man didn't appear to be offended at all. In fact, he looked more amused, giving Corbin a small smile. The next words he said didn't come from his mouth, Corbin noticed that his lips didn't move at all. Instead, these words resonated in his mind, exactly like the few words that had been spoken by that alien pilot.

"My deepest apologies, Staff-Sergeant Kent. I have neglected to offer a traditional introduction of myself. My name is Uniz. That pilot you spoke to was one of mine. He was transporting a very important piece of technology. You and your friend Sergeant Hunt now hold its power. As I stated previously, it is of the utmost importance that we meet somewhere to discuss it further."

Corbin's doubtful look changed to one of absolute surprise as Uniz spoke to him in his mind. He immediately changed his attitude, realizing that this guy was not only real, but have some discussing to do with him. His mind was flooded with questions that he wanted, no, **needed** to ask, but he knew that now wasn't exactly the best time to do it. He needed to get back to his squad. Looking around again to make sure no one else was watching them or near enough to hear them, he grabbed a gallon-sized container of spring water and turned towards Uniz again.

"There's an old farm and field just a few miles off post. North of here. If you can find me like this, I have a feeling you can find the place I'm talking about. Jason and I will be there once we are off duty for the day. Got it?"

Uniz looked slightly perplexed at first, as if something that Corbin had said didn't quite make sense to him. However, after a short pause, he appeared to understand and nodded his head. "I will meet you there," he said audibly.

Corbin only nodded and then moved to the counter to pay for his water and then headed back out to the Humvee. As he approached the vehicle, Randy held out both of his arms as if to welcome a long- lost relative.

"It's about time you showed up. You making friends in there? I mean, a bald head and the fact that he's a dude doesn't really make him my type, but I'm sure you two make a lovely couple, "Randy joked.

Crap. So, he had seen him talking to Uniz. If he didn't hear anything, there was no harm in seeing him talk to someone who was just a random civilian as far as he knew. Corbin did his best to look as detached as possible as he shrugged, handing his water jug to Jason, and gestured to the hydration pack fastened to the back of his armor vest. Jason understood his assignment, twisting off the cap to the pouch and filling it with the water jug.

"Just some random dude who thought he recognized me," Corbin said with an uninterested tone. "You know, one of those, 'don't I know you?' sort of situations."

"Did you tell him that if he did, you'd have to kill him?" Alex chuckled, returning his rifle to the mount on the inside of the door where he sat.

Corbin snorted, trying to stifle a laugh so he didn't make Jason spill water all over him as he filled his hydration pack. "No, but that would have been a lot better. I'll have to try to remember that one if that ever happens again."

Everyone shared a laugh as they took their places in the Humvee. Jason finished filling up Corbin's pouch and screwed the lid back on, rapping him twice on the shoulder roughly to signal he was done. Corbin turned to face him, taking the bottle from him and taking a swig of the water that remained in it. When he was sure that the others were in the vehicle where they couldn't hear the two of them, he spoke quietly.

"We've got a meeting this evening, off base, off the record, as it were."

Jason looked a little surprised. "Any other details you want to divulge at the moment?"

Corbin shook his head. "You'll understand when we get there, but it's just you and me. No one else needs to know."

That was what changed Jason's demeanor to one of understanding. If it was something that needed to happen off duty and off base *and* with only the two of them, that could mean only one thing: the Marvel. He nodded to Corbin, clearing his throat to signal the end of the conversation and pointing out that they should get going. The two of them climbed into their designated seats, Jason now driving and Corbin still in the front passenger seat. As they pulled out of the gas station, he looked to see if he could catch another glimpse of the man who called himself "Uniz." No sign of him that he could see. It was odd; it was almost like he appeared out of nowhere in the convenience store and apparently left in the same manner, just vanishing into the ether. Admittedly, it was unnerving to him, and he hoped that after this gathering tonight, things would feel a lot less ominous and cryptic.

The rest of the day seemed to pass just as sluggishly as the first, leaving Corbin feeling beyond spent by the time they rolled into the motor pool and began to offload their weapons and gear. After returning all their equipment to their lockers, they were quick to turn in paperwork outlining the patrol and any fuel stops, as well as a written AAR that the squad quickly signed and which usually said something to the effect of, "Everything was fine, nothing to improve." In an effort to surreptitiously separate from the rest of the squad, he had told everyone else that they could just go home and that he and Jason would take care of the "red tape." As they all looked as spent as they felt, there was no complaint and Brent, Randy, and Alex were quick to depart, happy to leave the tedium to their leadership.

After turning in all the necessary documentation, Corbin and Jason went back to the barracks where they cleaned up a little and changed into civilian clothes. He wanted to look as civilian as possible but remembered that a military-style haircut and clean-shaven face gave him away no matter what he was wearing, so he just settled for what was comfortable to him, which was a pair of jeans, a T-shirt, and western boots. Wearing boots was a hard habit for him to break. However, he didn't want to look like some of the goofballs they saw on base who would *still* wear their military boots with their regular clothes, so he had found a Western supply store in the next town over and purchased a pair of cowboy boots that, once broken in, were as comfortable to him as sneakers. Once they were both ready, they climbed into Jason's car and headed to their predetermined spot just outside of town.

When they had first been assigned to this base, Corbin had made it a habit to go out on the weekends and wander around, learning the surroundings as well as giving him something to do when he wasn't familiar with the area. On one of his many weekend drives, he had passed this farm that had been abandoned for a substantial amount of time, as far as he could tell. There were two large fields with a gravel road dividing them that led to a dilapidated old farmhouse and run-down barn about a quarter mile after turning off the highway. The fields were unkempt and overgrown, suggesting that no farmer or farming work had been done for quite some time. He had taken a couple of occasions to drive to the far end of the gravel road to investigate the farmhouse and barn, never having run into anyone or any sign that anyone lived or worked there. He concluded that this would be the best spot to meet up as it would be far enough off the main highway that they wouldn't have to worry about being seen as they met with Uniz and anyone else who may show up with him.

As they neared the end of the gravel road, Corbin had Jason park his car around the back of the barn, keeping it concealed from anyone who might approach by way of the driveway. They both sat silently, the only sound in the cab being the air conditioning and the rhythm of their breathing. Corbin looked back and forth slowly, scanning everything that he could see like a detective on a stakeout. Jason lazily leaned back in his seat, placing his hands behind his head and letting out a long sigh. He obviously didn't feel quite the sense of urgency that Corbin did, having not seen or communicated with the bald man from this morning. Corbin felt anxious, like he was on the threshold of a groundbreaking discovery. He didn't know what to expect and didn't want to speculate as to how this meeting would go. He had a laundry list of questions and wanted, well needed, to get answers to them all. It was the least that he felt they owed to them. Maybe they will give them all the answers they sought and more, really putting to rest what that crashed ship was about, as well as the glowing object the pilot had called "the Marvel."

He wasn't sure how long it had been since they had parked, but it felt like it was forever, and no one had shown up. He was starting to feel impatient and decided to take a look around. Maybe he could see Uniz coming. Stepping out of the car, he glanced around again, seeing nothing and no one. Shutting the door, he took a few steps towards the old farmhouse, head on a swivel to reduce the likelihood of being surprised by an unseen approach. Still nothing. Well, he hadn't really set a specific time to meet up, had he? He had just said they would be here after they got off duty. It was a time but lacked specificity. He continued forward, eyeing the farmhouse as if concerned that something was going to jump out at him. Everything was quiet and still, aside from the creaking and settling noises of an old structure. He had ascended the stairs to the porch when another noise made him spin around in surprise.

"Staff-Sergeant Kent, good to see you once again."

It was the same bald man who had called himself Uniz, (up until now, Corbin hadn't considered how strange a name that was), as well as two other men who looked almost identical to each other with the same height, build, short and cropped hair, and unimpressive attire. They too had strangely dark eyes that somehow didn't make them appear sinister or foreboding. They also had the same kindly, inviting demeanor that Uniz had; even now, after somehow materializing out of thin air, it still didn't take Corbin off guard as much as he thought it would have. He shook his head to himself, feeling a bit sheepish that someone was able to "sneak" up on him. He felt like he was losing his soldierly edge, but then again, how can you properly prepare for someone who seems to just pop out of nowhere?

"It's...Uniz, is that right?" he said as he stepped down from the porch.

"It is indeed, Staff-Sergeant," Uniz replied with a smile.

"No, you can just call me Corbin." He motioned towards Jason, who shut off his car and cautiously stepped out of it. The look on his face said it all; he was trying to figure out where this trio had come from. "Over there is Sergeant Hunt. You can call him Jason. We aren't too stringent on formalities when we are off duty."

Uniz looked in Jason's direction and appeared to be making a mental note. He turned back to Corbin and stood straight, hands clasped behind his back. His stance made Corbin think of Captain Dickson. "Please forgive our intrusion into your lives. It was never our intention to interfere with life on this planet; however, it appears that the stars had different plans for our prototype weapon."

"I'm sorry, you mean to tell me that ball thing was a *weapon?* What's going to happen to us now?" Corbin asked, trying not to sound as worried as he felt. Jason had stepped up next to him now and caught the last part of what he had said.

"Weapon?! What?!"

"If you will both please have a seat, I would like to instruct you further on the parameters of what we have codenamed, 'Marvel.' We have much to discuss and, I fear, far less time."

Considering all the strange details surrounding this guy, including his ability to find and contact them with seemingly no effort, how he seemed to be able to appear and disappear like a wizard, and how his speech was always so formal, it was his last statement that made Corbin feel uneasy. He glanced at Jason before focusing his attention again on Uniz. Still watching him, he sat down on the porch steps, Jason following his lead.

"Okay, Uniz, what did we get ourselves into?"

Uniz paused, appearing to process how he was going to begin. His eyes moved back and forth as if he were reading an invisible script and trying to find the best place to start his monologue. Corbin figured the two others with Uniz must have been his guards, and they stood just as still and stoic as they had when they first appeared. Corbin wondered if they were even real because they looked more like wax figures rather than actual living beings. Uniz let out a quiet "Ah," moving his hands from behind his back and clasping them in front of him now.

"We are a species known as the Nazecs. For years now, we have been embattled in a civil war that has spanned a great deal of your galaxy. Unfortunately for us, our enemy, known as the Brotherhood of the Claw, is formidable and has caused great loss to both our military and civilian populations. The tide of this war has turned greatly in their favor, and we needed something to aid our ability to take control of the conflict and eventually end it."

For whatever reason, Corbin remembered the "moving stars" that he saw that night in Basic Training. Could that have been them? Was he really watching a space battle that night? Have they really been fighting *that* long? He refocused and looked back to Uniz, who appeared to have noticed his mental tangent and had paused until he was paying attention again.

"Recruitment of new soldiers did not satisfy our defensive needs, so our next option to consider was increasing the quality of the soldiers we already have. Upgrades to equipment and weapons could only go so far as it consumed valuable resources and time and had risk of being destroyed or captured by the enemy. So, how could we improve our military without addressing the obvious avenues of warfare? Instead of advancements in the items the soldiers used, why not discover enhancements to the soldiers themselves? These were the seeds planted in the cultivation and completion of the codename: Marvel project.

"After countless experiments and tests, we finally perfected what was to be our crowning achievement towards eventual peace. We had a working prototype and all we needed now was to replicate it on a large scale and disseminate it to our armies stretched all across the galaxy. Much to our chagrin, the ship transporting codename: Marvel was ambushed on the way to our development facilities and eventually crashed on your planet. You, Corbin, and your team were assigned to investigate the crash and you, and Jason deployed the prototype to your bodies at the behest of our pilot. It is now our desire to see how the Marvel pairs with your human anatomies and is utilized in combat situations. The prototype itself had not yet been combat tested in a real-world situation."

"Wait a minute," Corbin interjected. "You mean to tell me that Jason and I used your only working prototype of this thing on ourselves, and now you want to use us like test dummies to see if the thing works in combat?"

Uniz looked slightly perplexed at what Corbin had said. "Your terminology seems somewhat colloquial; however, I believe you do understand the significance of the situation."

"Can't you just, I don't know, take it out of us?" Jason questioned.

Uniz sounded almost apologetic, "Please understand, this prototype was proven to be successful in the pairing and enhancing of military personnel; however, we had not yet developed a method of extracting the weapon once it had been paired with its hosts. It had not been a priority at the time we were developing it. In fact, it had not even been an idea that had crossed our minds, that is, until you two took hold of our only working prototype. Additional development details were going to be considered and applied as codename: Marvel was being mass-produced and delivered to our soldiers."

"So, not only do you have no other copies of this thing, but you don't even have a way to get it out of us?!" It was all sounding worse and worse each time Uniz answered their questions.

Again, Uniz's demeanor was remorseful. "Corbin, please accept my sincerest apology. Our main concern was creating something that could give us a tactical advantage in this war. It is of the utmost importance that we stop Claw from defeating us."

"Why? You that afraid to die?" Corbin had added a bit of venom to that question. He wasn't sure if it was on purpose or the natural reaction to how betrayed he felt at that moment. Part of him didn't think that they had been tricked into doing what they had done with the Marvel, but with all this new information coming to light, it almost felt like a last-ditch effort on the part of the Nazecs to keep their precious weapon from getting captured and turned against them. It felt selfish, as if they would rather see it in the hands of a couple of unsuspecting humans than in the hands of Claw, or the Brotherhood of the Claw, or whatever.

There was a long, awkward silence before Uniz spoke again. "Our fears as a civilization do not lie solely on our well-being, the effects of this war have the potential to spread much farther than just the Nazecs. Staff-Sergeant, if we lose this war, we fear that Earth will be the next target for the Brotherhood."

Now he felt like an ass. If Uniz was telling the truth, his civilization was not only looking out for their safety, but his safety. His safety as well as the safety of the billions of people on the planet. "Why would they want to come here?" he asked, wondering if he even wanted to know the answer.

"Claw has a secondary goal, next only to our annihilation, and it is to assimilate or subjugate other planets and create an empire that encompasses the entire cosmos. Our intelligence began to notice that the movements of Claw fleets and armies were trending in the direction of Earth. Through their engagements with our forces, they were driving us towards your planet. Once we had ascertained that Earth was a target of their future tactics, it became clear that their leader, Fizer, was targeting Earth in hopes of taking advantage of her vulnerability as a whole planet. With many of your major nations in conflict across the globe, he could strike more effectively without the concern of those nations being able to consolidate and mount a counter offensive. Once he had weakened the population of Earth enough, he would take control of the entire human race, using your armies and technologies and peoples to bolster his campaign of universal conquest."

Suddenly, the gravity of the situation began to unfold to Corbin. They weren't just fighting to win their civil war; they were fighting to prevent the enslavement of Earth, and later the universe. They had been forced into fighting the war of two civilizations, a veritable war on two fronts. He had excelled at history, particularly war history, and he knew the eventual outcome any time an army tried to stretch itself across two warfronts. It never ended well for them. As his paradigm shifted, he realized how fortunate it was that this Marvel weapon had ended up in their hands rather than some random civilians who found it in the middle of a cornfield or something. If its purpose was to pair with and enhance soldiers, it was one insanely lucky coincidence that it was two soldiers who found it and paired with it. He wondered if Uniz was aware of the serendipitous details.

Jason spoke next, breaking another short silence. "So, what is this Marvel supposed to do? I know you said that it is supposed to enhance your soldiers, but enhance them how?"

Uniz turned his gaze from Corbin to Jason, smiling slightly as if pleased with the question. "The objective of codename: Marvel is to enhance the abilities of a soldier based on their personality traits. In our trials, some subjects were found to have enhanced vision, strength, or even precognitive or telekinetic capabilities."

"So, you're saying that the Marvel gives someone superpowers," Jason said with an air of incredulity.

Uniz gave him a look of bewilderment. Jason had assumed the reason they had named their weapon what they had was because it gave soldiers superpowers and that they were somehow aware of a certain comic book company that dealt almost exclusively in superhuman beings. As if he were somehow aware of what Jason was thinking, Uniz shook his head with a slight chuckle.

"No, Jason, we are not aware of these... 'comic books' as you call them. Our purpose in code naming our creation Marvel was because it was simply a marvel of ingenuity and technology. However, for sake of my own curiosity, I will research these comics you are thinking of and determine if there is any coincidental similarity to them and codename: Marvel."

Corbin looked at Jason as if he had just been intentionally excluded from an important conversation. Jason could only shrug, unsure of how Uniz was aware of what he was thinking. Again, Uniz appeared to be bemused by it all, letting out a sigh similar to a parent entertained by the naivety of their children. He crouched now, lowering himself to match their eye levels.

"We, the Nazecs, communicate telepathically. Do you not remember how it was that our pilot communicated with you? Was it not, as you say, 'a voice in your head?' Our telepathic abilities also enable us to hear the thoughts of other species, such as humans."

That fact brought Corbin's mind back to the night of the mission. He had noticed the pilot didn't have ears or a mouth, and he remembered distinctly how his voice sounded in his head. He raised an eyebrow, "We spoke to your pilot verbally, so how did he hear it?"

"Ah, but when you speak, do you not also have to think the words you are saying? Though we may not hear your voice speaking the words you are communicating, our telepathy hears those same words as you think them," Uniz explained with a knowing look.

Corbin shrugged. "Fair enough. If the Marvel is supposed to enhance us, how has it done that to us? What sort of powers are we supposed to have?"

"In our tests, we found that the enhancements were as unique as the individual who had paired with codename: Marvel. However, there was a similarity in the manifestation of their enhancements which was that they first became evident in a moment of high emotional response. It is our understanding that you, Corbin, recently experienced such a response during your morning meal."

He immediately remembered that they still had a busted kitchen table that they needed to replace. Did that really happen because of some superpower? He didn't have a habit of splintering table legs simply by pounding on the tabletop, but that explanation seemed too simple to him, as outlandish as it was. So did he have some kind of super strength that showed up when he got agitated? It was sounding more and more like a comic character, one of a particular green color and perturbed disposition.

"I'm not going to end up turning green and going on a raging rampage if I get too mad or something, am I?" The question was only part joking.

Once again, Uniz's reaction was one confusion. He furrowed his brow, considering Corbin's words before answering. "I suppose there is some amount of sarcasm in your question; however, the context bewilders me. I suppose there is a reason for your query? If you are concerned about physical changes, such as changing color, no results from our volunteers showed alterations in dermal pigmentation. Granted, all tests were done on Nazecs and our knowledge of codename: Marvel's effects on human anatomy is completely undiscovered. Would a change in your color be an adverse effect to you?"

Oh yeah, he didn't know about comics. He apparently wasn't too familiar with the concept of sarcasm either. "Well, we humans come in many colors, but green isn't one that is, how shall I put it, normal to us. I'm sure if I were to turn green, I would be the subject of a lot of unwanted attention."

"Our anatomies are not excessively different; therefore, I would not suspect that such a side effect would be a potential; however, I will not dismiss it as a possibility at this time. For the present, I would like to work with you two in attempting to manifest your powers and begin to control them."

Uniz gestured for both Jason and Corbin to stand up, which they did, exchanging wary glances. Uniz looked around them for a moment, as if looking for something. He stopped, pointing to the old barn close to where Jason had parked his car. "Ah, it appears there are some items we may use to our advantage in there."

The five of them moved into the barn, which leaned to the right in an unnerving manner. Inside was an old tractor that looked like it hadn't been used in decades, as well as several old, rusted farm tools and a pile of dry, rotten hay in the back of the barn. The scent of decaying hay, dust, rust, and age assailed Corbin's sense of smell and it took a few minutes to acclimate to the aroma. The two attendants with Uniz stepped over to either side of the door to the barn, leaving Uniz, Jason, and Corbin standing just in front of the old tractor, parked in the center of the old structure. Uniz turned and looked at the old tractor, running his fingers over the engine cover and leaving trails in the dust with his fingertips.

"Corbin, do you think you can lift this vehicle?" Uniz asked, not turning to look at him.

"Uh, nope. I'm one hundred percent sure that I can't lift that thing."

Uniz seemed completely unaffected by his answer. "Why not give it a try? Perhaps you will surprise yourself."

'Not friggin' likely,' Corbin thought to himself as he stepped up alongside the tractor. He eyed the length of the vehicle and tried to find a decent spot to try to lift it from. He was sure that just touching the old junker would require him to get a tetanus shot. He grimaced a little as he surveyed his objective, feeling hesitant to try to lift it. If it wasn't the threat of infection from a cut or something from the oxidized metal, he was concerned he'd just wreck his back or injure himself in some other way *trying* to lift something so heavy with no guarantee that any sort of superpower was going to kick in. He stood there for a moment longer, weighing his options and deciding that he may as well give it a try.

Squaring up to the tractor, he crouched down, placing his hands under the engine area and pulling up to attempt to lift the front end. His arm and leg muscles strained against the immovable object, but he kept trying to lift until his lower back began to protest, which he knew wasn't a good sign. He let go of the tractor and exhaled a breath he didn't notice he had been holding as he exerted his body in the futile act. Jason stood nearby, looking a bit confused and concerned. Uniz looked as unaffected as he had so far, and those two dudes who came with him looked just as stoic as when they had appeared. He felt stupid trying to lift something he knew he couldn't lift at the behest of someone he didn't know and had barely met. If it wasn't for the fact that Uniz looked so impassive, he would have suspected that he was doing this all just to get a good laugh at him. He shrugged his shoulders in exasperation, unsure of what to think or even feel at this point.

"What was it that caused you to break your table?" Uniz asked calmly.

"I don't know. I didn't mean to. I just got frustrated at Jason for asking a bunch of questions I didn't have any answers to. He was getting kind of annoying. I just slammed my hands down on the table and the thing crumpled like a cheap pile of crap."

"Why not try to replicate those feelings you were experiencing then? One could speculate that those feelings are instrumental in unlocking your enhancement."

Corbin let out a somewhat unbelieving grumble. How was he supposed to repeat something he had done out of spontaneity? He couldn't even remember what it was that Jason was saying or asking that had annoyed him so much. It wasn't even that important; it was over, and the only thing that was left was a wrecked table. He let out a long sigh and turned back towards the tractor. He readied himself and leaned forward, placing his hands on it and trying to replay his feelings from the other morning in his head. He tried to concentrate, seeing if he could stir up any of those emotions again, but he was interrupted.

"You gonna put your purse down this time and actually try to move that thing?"

Corbin shot Jason an "Are you serious?" look, standing up from his ready stance. Jason didn't alter his challenging demeanor, his arms folded across his chest.

"You gonna let a hundred-year-old pile of junk kick your butt? WEAK!" Jason taunted him in a way he had never heard him taunt him before. Sure, there was plenty of ball-busting in the military, and it was all in good fun, but everyone knew it was just joking around. What Jason was doing felt personal, filled with venom and spite, like he was really trying to get to him. He hadn't ever felt it before, but Jason was getting under his skin. He had never experienced such malicious behavior from his longtime friend and squad mate. He narrowed his eyes, not quite sure how to take this curveball Jason was throwing him.

"Dude, I haven't even tried to do anything yet. Can you back off?"

Jason shook his head in a disappointed way. "C'mon, man, you really think you can do that? Freaking meathead, why don't you try to smack it with your club, half-wit caveman."

Corbin usually did well when it came to taunts or personal insults. He had siblings and he had years of experience knowing that if you just ignored the insults, they usually stopped. He was a big brother; he knew from experience as well that it was only fun to taunt a younger sibling if it got a reaction out of them. This, however, was getting to him far more than he had anticipated. He looked back to Jason again, feeling his blood boil a little.

"Why don't you give it a try, you little punk?" He knew that if he were ever pitted in a fight against Jason, he'd obliterate him. He had speed, sure, but all he needed to do was get one good shot in and he'd flatten the little twerp. He rolled his shoulders back, clenching his fists at his sides.

"With how you keep pussyfooting your way around that thing, I bet I could actually lift it before you," Jason barked back.

"Listen here, dickhead! I'm *TRYING!*" He threw a punch into the side of the tractor's engine cover. With a deafening sound, the engine portion of the tractor buckled, and the entire farm tool slid eight feet sideways, leaving deep cuts in the dirt floor where the tires had carved into the earth. Jason and Uniz were barely able to get out of the way before getting sideswiped by the tractor. Corbin looked up from where he stood, panting from surprise as well as an effort to keep a somewhat cool head. When he looked at Jason, he was smiling in a satisfied way. That punk knew what he was doing the whole time. He knew how to push his buttons, and he utilized that to get him to successfully use his powers, or enhancement, or whatever. Straightening his posture, he cleared his throat and looked at his stinging, gouged, knuckles, which were throbbing and bleeding steadily

"As you can see," Uniz started, "heightened emotional response is a key factor to the manifestation of your enhancement. Corbin, it appears that codename: Marvel has enhanced your physical strength, as well as provided you with rapid regenerative abilities."

"What do you mean by that? How can you tell—" Corbin stopped when he noticed that his injured hand no longer throbbed or stung. He looked down to see that his knuckles were unharmed; the only evidence that they had ever been injured was the drying blood that had run down between his fingers. He glanced back up at Uniz, who simply nodded to him. Jason also looked taken aback by the sudden healing of his damaged knuckles. Corbin stepped away from where he had punched the tractor and took a few steps towards Uniz.

"So, what about Jason? Do we need to make him angry enough to get him to show what he's capable of?" He rubbed the knuckles on his right hand, feeling the crusted, dried blood but nothing else. He was still trying to process everything that had just happened, and even feeling the evidence of his apparent healing abilities wasn't doing much to help his mind wrap around the concept.

"Heightened emotional response can be any of the range of capable human emotion. The key to manifestation is finding the emotion that he feels the deepest, with the most conviction, and then exploiting it," Uniz explained.

Corbin considered his friend for a moment, wondering if he could be of help the same way Jason had been for him. Jason was pretty cool-headed; he didn't have a temper like Corbin did even when he kept it in check. He wasn't a "cryer," at least not that he had ever seen; then again, how would he even try to test that? He was the youngest of five brothers, that had to account for something. Corbin thought about what sort of emotions being the youngest sibling could be. He thought for a moment before changing his point of view. He was an older brother; what sort of emotions did he enjoy eliciting from his younger siblings? The first thing he thought about was how much he enjoyed scaring the daylights out of them at any given moment. Whether it was jumping out at them from around a corner or just taking them completely off guard by shouting as loud as he could at any moment without any warning or context. He laughed to himself thinking about how he would do it multiple times in a day, leaving his siblings constantly on edge, afraid that he'd startle them again when they least expected.

Corbin smirked to himself at the thought. He turned to Uniz, brow furrowed as if considering something. "Uniz, once we have figured out our powers, how do we, I don't know how you would say it, but how would we practice using them? I mean, it doesn't seem like a sustainable tactic to keep me in a state of anger constantly so I can smash stuff."

"Utilizing your emotional response is simply the first step towards mastery of your enhancements. It is just the trigger to reveal what they are, and then we train you to use your abilities on command through mental discipline and focus," Uniz answered, looking almost deadpan as he had the entire time.

"So are you going to teach us some meditation or something like that—JASON!" Corbin shouted as loud and as bestial as he could as he turned quickly towards Jason, raising a fist as if he was going to punch him squarely in the face. Jason first reacted just as he would have expected. His eyes widened, looking like they were going to bug out of his head, and he jumped back, putting his fists up in front of him in a defensive manner. What happened next was, but also wasn't what he had expected.

In the blink of an eye, a fireball materialized out of thin air between Jason's fists. It was about the size of a basketball and burned blue-hot. Corbin saw what it was, but before he could react, the fireball burst forward, hitting him squarely in the chest and igniting his shirt. He yelped in surprise and pain as he jumped back and started patting his shirt down as fast as he could to extinguish the flame. When the flame had died out, he was left with a scorched hole in his shirt and very burned, very painful skin on his chest and palms. He winced as he moved to analyze the extent of the damage his skin had sustained. His hands looked pretty bad; deep red and already forming blisters. His chest was even more red, showing patches of bloody subdermal layers as well as sections of his skin where his shirt had actually melted to it. His first thought after how much it hurt was wondering how he was going to explain injuries like this to the platoon medic. After Jason had taken a second to look at his fists in awe, he looked up and, noticing the burns on Corbin, immediately looked apologetic.

"Oh man, I'm sorry. I had no idea. You scared the crap out of me," he rationalized.

"No, no it's totally okay," Corbin assured. "I figured I could get the jump on you, but neither of us could have known how that was going to turn out." He groaned as he gingerly touched his burned chest.

"You're going to have to see the doc about that," Jason said, a sound of regret in his voice.

"Yeah, I was thinking the same thing. I guess we've got to figure out a somewhat believable cover story for this. I can't think of a single thing that doesn't end up making me sound like I was doing something stupid or reckless. I'm sure Captain Dickson will be thrilled that I'm going to be out of action for however long this is going to take to heal..."

Corbin trailed off when he suddenly noticed that the stinging pain in his skin was gone. His eyes snapped down to inspect his injuries and saw that they were gone. On his palms and his chest was the soft pink flesh of newly healed skin. It was still a little sensitive and warm to the touch, but what was just a mangled bunch of burnt flesh was now mended, scar-free skin. Sadly, his shirt was still a melted mess which, in contrast to his healed skin, looked pretty silly. Oh well, if it were between his skin and his shirt, he was glad it was only his shirt that he couldn't fix.

Uniz silently stepped between both Corbin and Jason. "These results are very pleasing to see. It appears that your human anatomy and composition have not hindered the ability of codename: Marvel to pair with you and manifest enhancements. I can only hope that your training will prove just as promising. Until we can secure a location that can facilitate your training, I ask that you keep these proceedings, as well as your abilities, a secret. I would speculate that not everyone would share an open mind regarding your enhancements."

"You mean, we shouldn't even tell the rest of the guys in our squad?" Corbin asked, already feeling guilty for keeping secrets from Alex, Brent, and Randy.

"In my personal opinion, I would advise against telling your friends. However, that is at your discretion. You obviously know them better than I," Uniz advised.

In his mind, it was difficult to justify not telling his friends everything, feeling like it would undermine the level of trust that they had between them. On the other hand, he did have to also consider how they would handle learning that there was much more to the mission they conducted in searching the remains of an alien crash site. Would they be angry at them for not keeping them in the loop? Would they think that they were a couple of weirdos making everything up? He and Jason would have to discuss that more and decide together what they thought the best course of action would be. In the meantime, it wouldn't hurt to keep quiet about things a little longer, right?

"We will take our leave for now, gentlemen, but we will be in contact again when it is time to develop your skills with your enhancements. In the interim, might I suggest that you try not to get too angry or startled?"

"We'll do our best, I guess," Corbin answered. "When can we expect to hear from you again?"

"That is uncertain at this time. We will, once affairs are ready, make contact with you again to make arrangements for our next meeting. Contacting you through your electronic mail seems to be an effective method. Would you be opposed to my utilizing that again?"

"No, I don't think that will be a problem. How did you manage that in the first place, by the way?"

Uniz simply smiled a knowing smile. "Corbin, do you really think your technologies can keep us from contacting you?"

It seemed a simple and straightforward answer but almost felt somewhat ominous. If Uniz and these Nazecs had the ability to bypass government encryption technology as easily as opening an unlocked door, what other sorts of advanced science did they have, and how dangerous was it? As near as he could tell, the Nazecs were the good guys, so that kind of worry wasn't really an issue, right? The questions began to stir in his mind, but he put them aside for now, knowing that he would end up keeping himself awake for days pondering on all the possibilities and outcomes that could come to pass. '*Suffice it to say,* he thought to himself, '*if they had the tech or weapons to wipe us off the face of the earth, they've been nice enough not to use it.*'

Uniz chuckled, breaking the silence. "Staff-Sergeant Kent, if we had planet-killing capabilities, do you think we would need to create codename: Marvel?"

Truthfully, he felt a little violated knowing that Uniz had just listened to his thoughts without his consent. He wondered if it was all thoughts that they could hear. That could prove very awkward in an instance if an intrusive thought or other random thought happened to hit him while in Uniz's presence. He didn't seem to understand sarcasm, or comics, how would Corbin explain to him any number of things that occurred in a human's mind at any given moment?

The two attendants to Uniz silently stepped forward and flanked him on either side. Uniz nodded to them wordlessly before returning his gaze to Corbin. "Please, take care of yourselves and your abilities. The fate of the Nazecs, as well as your planet, rests with your ability to master and use the enhancements you have." He and his pair of guards moved towards the open barn door, which is where he stopped and turned to face them. "We will see you again. Until then, be safe."

Corbin looked at Jason and gave him an assuring nod. When he turned to say words of farewell to Uniz, he saw that he and his attendants were already gone. How did they do that? Well, it was just another of about a billion questions he was going to have to ask Uniz if he ever got the chance. Until then, they just had to wait. Well, wait and try not to light anything on fire or rage smash anyone or anything into oblivion. Not a problem at all, right? Probably not as much of a problem now that they knew what it was that could set off their powers unintentionally. In any case, he felt a little unfulfilled by this first encounter with Uniz and what their "enhancements" were, as he called them. It was about as lackluster as testing a light switch, seeing that it worked, and then leaving without much further explanation.

As he and Jason made their way to Jason's car, he gave his friend a pat on the shoulder. "Well, what do you think?"

"I think we better get back home before anyone sees your poor shirt, or we better have a solid story to try to explain it," Jason said with a smirk. "Because I don't really see that as a fashion trend that will catch on."

He slugged his friend jokingly in the arm as he laughed. "Well dang, there go my dreams of making millions on fashion crazes and leaving my cozy life as a soldier behind."

They both laughed as they climbed into the car and made their way back towards the base. Thankfully for them, the only person they encountered and the only one to ask a question about Corbin's shirt was the guard at the gate. He gave Corbin a funny look when he noticed his shirt and, thinking on the fly, Corbin fabricated a tale of checking something under the hood of the car and melting his shirt on one of the hot pipes. It seemed sufficient enough for the guard who simply shook his shoulders in an indifferent gesture and waved them through the checkpoint after checking their military ID cards.

Chapter Eight

SWORD carries many burdens in the world of national security. Naturally, one of the primary responsibilities is that of counter-terrorism operations anywhere from intelligence and reconnaissance to direct action against terrorist leaders and their cells. Her soldiers were also used within garrisons such as was the case with "Eagle Battalion," covering the many security and other military operations on post. Depending on local requests for assistance, SWORD can be utilized in law enforcement capabilities where normal police forces might be underwhelmed or undertrained for particular situations. Rather than send overwhelmed officers into a situation better suited for a SWAT team, local jurisdictions could request assistance which, unbeknownst to said jurisdiction, would be forwarded to a nearby SWORD command, if one was available. This meant that for the state of New York, there was a highly trained military force at their disposal that they would never even know about, other than they were to be assisted by the Army. Such was the case for a developing occasion downstate from Corbin and his squad in Albany.

"Staff-Sergeant Kent, will you please see me in my office?" Captain Dickson requested, turning and going back to his desk once he had asked.

"Yes sir, moving," was Corbin's response. He stood up from his desk and signaled for Jason to follow him. Unless specifically told not to, Corbin always had his number two come with him, mostly out of habit.

The two of them stepped into Captain Dickson's office and shut the door softly behind them, "You requested to see me, sir."

"Yes, please have a seat you two." Captain Dickson didn't look up from his computer monitor as he extended his invitation.

Corbin and Jason sat down without a word, exchanging slightly confused glances. It wasn't uncommon to be called into Dickson's office as squad leadership; however, there wasn't any context to it in this case. They weren't in trouble, that they knew of, and there weren't any emergent needs for coverage by one of the other squads, or even Alpha or Bravo Companies. Captain Dickson didn't appear to be distressed, or surprised, or anything other than indifferent as if there was nothing outside of "business as usual" to attend to. He seemed to be reading over something on his computer for a few moments longer before he cleared his throat and looked towards them.

"Gentlemen, we have an assist opportunity that has come our way. How well do you guys clean up?"

An odd question. Granted, he was pretty sure that Dickson hadn't seen him or any of his squad in anything other than uniforms, but it didn't seem to explain anything. He gave Dickson a befuddled look, raising an eyebrow.

"Sir?"

Dickson smiled and leaned back in his seat, gesturing towards his computer monitor. "With national security as it is, Washington has been playing the 'shell game' with her gatherings of world leaders and diplomats. What would normally be a dinner or gala or whatever at the White House, Pentagon, or what have you, these gatherings have been taking place in stately but less iconic locations in order to make it more difficult for terrorists to try to crash the party."

None of that made it any easier to understand his original question. Corbin still gave him a blank look. What in the world was he getting at with this? He shrugged, showing Dickson he still wasn't following. Captain Dickson smiled and continued.

"There's a little shindig going on down in Albany at the State Capitol soon. Some kind of international peace summit. Lots of senators, ambassadors, dignitaries, blah, blah, blah. Well, Albany PD and the Sheriff's Department have voiced concerns that they won't be able to spare enough officers to cover the entire event. As the President will not be attending this event,

Secret Service has only offered consultation and intelligence services. Each attendee will be allowed a small detail of personal security, but they aren't going to be a part of the overall site security."

"So, they asked for help, we got the call...the usual story? What does that have to do with us cleaning up?" Corbin inquired, still a bit confused. He and his squad had been assigned to task forces that assisted in security or policing matters before, and they were always dressed and armed in the uniform and equipment of the department they were assisting. Generally, the police, soldiers, SWAT, et cetera. had a similar overall appearance; they just had different uniforms.

"To an extent, Sergeant," Dickson answered, bobbing his head from side to side contemplatively. "This is a black-tie event, so the security within the facility is going to need to dress the part. Albany Police and Sherriff's departments will be covering the site security and entrance and exit checkpoints. You and your squad and Charlie Three-Two will oversee keeping the peace inside, which means you'll be dressed to match the rest of the visitors. Apparently, uniformed guards are just such a faux pas in a fancy event like this. So, we will need to get your men packed and transported down to Albany to get you fitted for tuxedos and learn the lay of the land of the venue. The event is in three days. You think Charlie Three-Three can be packed and ready to go within ninety minutes?"

"What do we need to bring with us, sir?"

"Just some civvies, toiletries, whatever you need for a four-day hotel stay. Clothing and equipment for the event will be handled by the local authorities. I'll get the information forwarded to you in a file and leave it on your desk. We will have a couple of vans waiting for you in the motor pool when you get back."

"Yes sir. We will go pack and be ready to go."

"Very good. Dismissed."

Corbin and Jason stood and turned in unison, exiting Dickson's office and going back to their desks. Brent looked up from an instruction manual he was reviewing for a new bolt carrier system for his M110, "Uh oh, you guys in trouble?"

Corbin shook his head as he sat down, smirking a little at Brent's joke. "No, we are getting loaned out to Albany PD to help with security for some fancy-schmancy gig going on at the Capitol. Three-Two is being sent out with us. We all need to pack and be ready back here in an hour and a half at most."

"What's our loadout?" Randy asked, closing his laptop on his desk.

"Civvies. Just pack civilian clothing, four days' worth, and whatever else you need. The local PD is going to supply our equipment, including getting us fitted for tuxes," Corbin explained.

"Tuxedos," Alex said, sounding interested.

"Yeah, apparently it's so fancy that they want their security teams to match the aesthetic," Corbin answered. "So, let's all go back and get ourselves packed and be back here so we can catch the vans they are going to have waiting for us here in the motor pool."

Everyone stood up and filed out to their cars, driving back to the barracks to start packing. Corbin had ridden with Jason, as per usual, and the two of them were silent on the ride home and most of the time that they packed. He carefully packed his clothes and toiletries into a military-issued green duffle bag. The bag was large enough to pack practically all his clothes, boots, and personal effects, so four days' worth of civilian clothes and a toiletry bag would barely fill the bottom quarter of it. As he made a final account of everything he packed, he remembered a book he had that he wanted to start reading, finding it in the drawer of his nightstand and tossing it in his bag. As he closed and secured the duffle with its metal clasp, he remembered something else. Taking his phone out of his pocket, he opened a text thread and wrote to Brianne.

Hey, this is Corbin, we met the other night at Beck's. Sorry I haven't called or texted earlier. I wanted to say I am going to be in out of town for a few days, maybe we can get together when I get back? Maybe I can take you out for dinner. Just let me know.

Putting his phone back in his pocket, he slung the strap for his bag over his shoulder and stepped out of his room, shaking his head at the now-empty kitchen. They had taken some time one evening to clean up and throw away the broken kitchen table, however they hadn't had a chance to shop for a new one. It was a little weird to him to eat standing in the middle of the kitchen or even sitting at the small desk in his room, but it wasn't something that put their meals out of commission. A minor detail, to be honest, but it always made itself evident any time they were home.

Back at the headquarters, they parked their cars on the side of the building closest to the motor pool, taking a side door that required a keycard that led through the locker room and into the motor pool area. It felt strange to him to be where he worked in civilian clothes. Charlie Three-Two showed up just minutes after Corbin and his squad had started loading their bags into one of the two black, fifteen-passenger vans that were parked in the center of the vehicle courtyard. They filed towards the other van, opening the back and loading their bags as well. The squad leader for Charlie Three-Two, a Sergeant-First Class Muniz, came over and shook hands with Corbin.

"Sergeant Muniz, how have you been," Corbin asked the short, Hispanic, muscular squad leader.

"Not bad, man. How's Three-Three?"

"As good as ever. Looking forward to something a little different, though. We can really only take so much of being in our Humvee all day."

SFC Muniz laughed. "Yeah, I know how that can be. You ever had an assignment like this before?"

"We've been 'rented' out to some law enforcement operations before, but nothing fancy like this. What about you guys?" Corbin nodded towards the rest of Three-Two, who were now loading into the cab of their van.

Muniz shook his head, "We haven't been out on loan ever, let alone on an assignment like this. My guys are excited for a change of scenery, even if it is just for a little bit."

"I agree. You happen to know where they are setting us up for a hotel?" In his experience, it wasn't in the interest of the government to pay for anything more expensive than a greasy motel that no one in their right mind would voluntarily stay at.

"The only thing I know is that we are going to be pretty close to the Capitol. However, you and I both know that 'pretty close' is a subjective term," Muniz answered with a laugh.

Corbin laughed as well, knowing all too well that "close" was in the eye of whomever was using the term. He had been on ruck marches and dismounted patrols where "close" was fifteen miles. That far on foot isn't all that troublesome, unless you are in full kit, full ruck, and have already been hoofing it for at least that long. His thoughts were interrupted by his phone vibrating in his pocket. It was a text message from Brianne. It read:

Corbin! How could I forget you? I am out on business for a couple of days as well, but let me know when you are back and hopefully I will be in back too. Dinner sounds great. Keep in touch.

Seeing her text made him smile to himself. He had already saved her number in his phone as "Bree," just as she said her friends called her, and had permitted him to call her as well. He hoped that meant that she intended him as a friend as well, hopefully more than that. He spun/flipped his phone in his habitual way before returning it to his pocket. The rest of his squad had loaded their things into the back of their van and were now waiting for him to join them. He hopped into the first bench row next to Jason and got situated, mentally preparing himself for the ride ahead. Alex had already fallen asleep on the third-row bench, Brent next to him dozing as well. Randy was sitting on the second-row bench, listening to music on an MP3 player clutched in his hand. He looked absentmindedly out of the window and gently bobbed his head to the beat of whatever song he was listening to. Jason looked over at Corbin as he climbed in.

"Everything good?" he asked.

"Yeah, yeah, just small talk. We were wondering where they were going to set us up for quarters when we got there. Muniz said somewhere near the Capitol. I guess we will see how much the government is willing to spend on us when we get there, huh?"

Jason just chuckled and shook his head. He was thinking the same thing that Corbin had been thinking, and he could tell he was already mentally preparing himself for a dingy room and mattress with springs that you could feel poking your ribs. Sure, they had slept in worse conditions, but it always felt a bit like a slight towards them when an organization asking for their help "repaid" them with lousy accommodations. Oh well, he figured if he really wanted comfy pillows and five-star hotels, he would have enlisted in the Air Force.

The ride was long and uneventful. Corbin had spent almost the entire drive gazing out of the window. When he had first heard that they were being ordered to their duty station in New York State, he had imagined their destination to be somewhere in a crowded city, something akin to Manhattan, as if the entire state was just one massive metropolis. He had never realized that the larger part of the state was farmland and forests. It was fascinating to him to see how wherever there weren't buildings, roads, or anything else manmade, there were trees, and lots of them growing in an almost unstoppable abundance as weeds. Even driving down the freeway was like driving down a long trench that had been cut through the endless expanses of trees. The off-ramps looked as though they had just branched off from the main thoroughfare and disappeared into the foliage. In a lot of ways, it reminded him of the bus ride from the airport to Fort Benning on the way to Basic.

As they approached Albany, it was a completely different view from what they had endured for the past three hours. A tall cityscape stood towering above the highway. There was what looked like a large plaza area with four identical buildings in a row, another skyscraper about twice the height of the quartet of towers, and some goofy-looking semicircular building that their driver referred to as "The Egg." It did indeed look like half of an egg suspended on a concrete base and it was the strangest bit of architecture he had ever seen. As they traveled through a tunnel that went under this massive plaza area, they emerged on the other side facing a massive building that looked to him almost like a European castle. The behemoth building was a central square-shaped structure flanked by two towering wings with tall, pointed roofs and lots and lots of arched windows. The staircase that led up the front of the building was wide, gigantic, and made of the same gray stone as the rest of the building. The first flight of stairs was wider than the second flight, which appeared to taper upward to the front doors. Turning right, they traversed the downtown area until they reached the hotel.

It wasn't the government accommodation he was used to. It was a "brand name" hotel, about fifteen stories tall, and looked far out of the normal parameters for what the Army, or SWORD would even think to pay for. As they pulled up to the front doors and offloaded from their vans, the two squads were met by a pair of uniformed Albany police officers who greeted them and escorted them inside to get checked in. Corbin still expected the cheapest of rooms even within this beautifully contemporary and modern hotel but was surprised to hear that they had all been checked into the executive level of the hotel, which was on the top floor. Stepping off the elevator on the executive level, the squads were split into pairs and divided amongst the rooms. He and SFC Muniz were the last to be shown their rooms, and they were separated and led to their own accommodations. One of the officers handed Corbin his room key, letting him know there would be a meeting with the chief of police in the executive lounge in an hour and promptly left.

Opening the door to the room, he was flabbergasted by what lay behind it. It was massive, containing a large living room with a couch, coffee table, television and desk on the first level. He moved through the spacious area trying to remember if he had ever stayed in a hotel room in his life that had this much space. At the rear of the sitting room was a spiral staircase which led upward to a loft where there was a king-size bed with another large flat screen television. He was amazed at the lavish scope of the room, thinking to himself that he and his squad could have fit in this room comfortably, but here he was, in a hotel room that was bigger than even his barracks' living space and it was all for him. For a moment, he felt so out of place that he almost called the front desk to let them know that there must have been a mistake in his room assignment.

Tossing his bag onto the bed, he went back downstairs to see that there was a cardboard tube on the coffee table with a note tucked under it. Picking up the note, he read that the tube contained the floor plans for the Capitol Building, and stapled to the note was an itinerary of the meetings, trainings, and fitting appointments he and his squad had for the next two days before the event began. Opening the tube, he poured out the rolled-up plans and laid them out flat on the coffee table. This place was massive, to say the least.

The building and grounds covered three acres according to the specifications! He sat back on the couch with a sigh, contemplating how the property would be divided up between the police and Charlie Three-Two and Three-Three. Glancing at his watch, he decided that he would rest for a while before what would be the first of their many meetings over the next two days. Kicking his feet up and lying back on the couch, he set a timer on his watch, put his hands behind his head, and promptly fell asleep.

Waking up with a start at the sound of his watch beeping, he hopped up and straightened his clothes. He checked his reflection to make sure he looked more awake than he currently felt, eh close enough. Deciding he needed a little pick-me-up, he grabbed a soda from the mini-fridge next to the desk and made his way out into the hallway, seeing a handful of police officers and plain-clothed members of Three-Two making their way up the hall away from him. He hustled to catch up, following them around a corner and into a large, narrow dining area with a television on the wall at each end. The tables, which were normally square and looked only big enough to have two or three chairs for each of them had been pushed together to form one long table that stretched nearly the entire length of the room. He was the first of his squad to arrive and, after noticing that there were no assigned seating arrangements, took a seat near the head of the table. He had wanted to make sure that he had woken up early enough to still make it to this meeting earlier than most if not all his squad and others who would be attending.

A few minutes later, Jason stepped into view, taking a seat next to him. Brent was next, followed by Alex and then Randy, who all took seats next to or across from Corbin. Hotel staff approached them and filled water glasses that had been set out in front of them, followed by others who placed small plates of fruit next to their water glasses. Corbin asked one of the staff if it was possible to get an energy drink, to which they nodded and moved swiftly from the room. He sipped at his water as he watched the other attendees shuffle into the room and take their seats. There were many uniformed Albany police officers, wearing their black uniforms complete with their tactical vests laden with their duty equipment. Then there were state troopers in their gray uniforms, not encumbered with tactical vests but carrying their hats which he thought looked a little silly. The light-colored hat had tops that looked like cowboy hats, but had a round, flat brim like that of a campaign cover worn by a drill sergeant, though not as broad in circumference. He thought to himself that he hoped whoever oversaw designing those hats didn't get paid a lot for it. Charlie Three-Two was seated across from and a few seats down from where Corbin and his squad sat; he and Muniz exchanged quiet nods as they noticed each other.

The low buzz of conversations quieted as a man in a white police uniform shirt stepped into the room. He looked to be in his mid-fifties, gray hair combed back and oval glasses sitting atop his nose. He was a bit soft around the midsection, Corbin noticed, probably the result of a lot of time behind a desk. Nevertheless, the crisp crease to his shirt sleeves and the sparkling gold stars pinned to his collar gave him a very sharp, professional appearance. This was definitely the Chief of Police. He took a seat at the head of the long table with a sigh, sitting forward in his chair and resting his forearms on the tabletop.

"Good afternoon, everyone, and welcome to what we are calling 'Operation: Embassy.' Now, I know that we aren't using an embassy as our venue; however, the dignitaries and ambassadors who will be in attendance would normally be seen within an embassy, so it might as well be one," the Chief started.

Corbin thought it amusing that the Chief felt the need to explain the name of the operation. For all he or any soldier was concerned, the name of the operation wasn't useful other than for record purposes. There just had to be a name on file for the events that happened on such and such a date, blah, blah, blah. For all they cared, the whole thing could be called, "Operation: Dog Dookie" or something completely ridiculous or unrelated and they wouldn't even bat an eye. Maybe police forces did things differently in that regard or didn't know how to do it in general. Whatever the case, he smiled to himself and shook his head a little.

"For those of you who don't know, I'm Police Chief Tuttle, and I'll oversee all security operations during this international summit. If you'll notice, we have the assistance of the Albany Police Department, the New York State

Troopers, as well as two squads of soldiers from 'Eagle Battalion' from upstate."

There was a short pause where many of the officers and troopers glanced towards Corbin and the other plain-clothed members of the SWORD squads sitting amongst them. He didn't exactly know how to acknowledge their stares, so he simply nodded and smiled at anyone looking in his general direction. Chief Tuttle went on as if he had permitted the proper amount of time for people to gawk at them.

"Now, I don't think we as law enforcement can't handle this event; however, I didn't want to stretch our forces so thin that we couldn't adequately look after our respective jurisdictions while we handled this security. That's why I reached out for military help as well. Unfortunately, our National Guard units are out of state on an Annual Training, which is why we couldn't use them. Now, for the sake of simplicity, considering we all have way more meetings coming up in the next couple of days, I wanted to just get us together as an introduction as well as a general overview of our objectives.

"First of all, our State Troopers will be handling the security on-site and the outdoors, specifically our entrance points, roving patrols on the grounds and perimeter, as well as in our 'backstage' areas such as the staff-only areas. Albany PD will oversee close-street patrols, specifically patrols spanning a ten-block radius around the Capitol. These guys know our streets the best, so they will cover any potential ingress or egress routes for anyone trying to cause trouble. That leaves the interior common areas to our Army boys here. They are going to be the ones in the middle of it all covering all five floors of the Capitol wherever any of the guests or their personal security can go. I've left a set of floor plans with each of you to familiarize yourself with the building so our walk-through exercises can be brief," Tuttle explained, nodding to Corbin and Muniz.

"I have also made sure to include an itinerary of the meetings you are expected to attend so you should all know where you should be and when to be ready for this summit. For now, let's use this time to introduce ourselves and get to know each other a bit."

The hotel staff stepped forward and began serving food, the one Corbin had spoken to returning with an energy drink for him. He thanked her cordially as she set down his drink and his food. As he began to eat, Chief Tuttle came over to where he and Jason were sitting, leaning down in between the two of them.

"Thanks for your assistance, gentlemen. If there is anything you need, please let me know, and we can make sure to get you taken care of."

"Thank you, sir," Corbin responded. "This is already far more than we could have expected. We appreciate the high-class treatment."

Tuttle nodded with a smile, standing up straight and moving down the table to speak with a group of officers who had congregated around the water cooler. Corbin leaned forward, getting the attention of the rest of his squad, "Hey, let's meet up in my room after this and we can start going over the details of the building." Everyone nodded their assent before continuing to eat their meal. During the short meal and meeting, Corbin spoke with the State Trooper who had seated himself next to him, finding out that he had once been in the Army himself, stationed out of Fort Jackson, serving a four-year term before deciding to get out and serve in law enforcement. He told Corbin that he vaguely remembered soldiers from an "Eagle Battalion" out at his duty station as well, asking if there were any correlation between them. Corbin confirmed that there was, stating the traditional cover story regarding them being filler units for ones deployed.

Back in his room, he, Jason, Brent, and Randy pored over the floor plan printout of the first floor of the Capitol while Alex wandered around, marveling at the size of the hotel room. He made some comments about thinking the rooms that he and the others were given were huge and how they paled in comparison. Corbin, however, wasn't paying much attention as he was engrossed with the absolute eyesore that was the floor plan. The black-and-white-printed page looked more akin to a grid rather than a building layout. There were so many meeting rooms, offices, closets, kitchens and restaurant areas that it divided the first floor into a mess of squares and rectangles across the page. Jason and Brent both shook their heads slowly in disbelief, counting at least fifty or more rooms, and this was just the first floor. Alex finally finished his self-guided tour of the room and took a seat on a chair he pulled up to the coffee table.

"This is nuts," Randy started. "All these rooms, and there are four more floors! Are all of them this crowded?"

Corbin flipped through the other pages of prints, "Pretty much. We have fewer individual offices on the upper floors because there are meeting halls and art hallways, but the architecture itself is a challenge on its own. Lots of columns, hidden corners, nooks and crannies, stuff like that. I mean, if I was someone who was up to no good and wanted to hide out somewhere to ambush some ambassador or something, this would be the building to do it."

"How are we splitting this place up with Three-Two?" Brent asked.

"Muniz and I haven't gotten too much into details yet, but I'm thinking we split the floors with his squad with one overlapping level. Maybe we take floors three through five and they cover one through three. Something like that. That is, unless Chief Tuttle has some other plan in mind that he'll fill us in on in one of our next meetings."

Alex began looking over the plans as well, displaying the same look of surprise and disbelief as the others the more he reviewed the images. Corbin looked down the itinerary and internalized the times and locations of all the listed meetings. For the rest of today, they were practically free, other than a tuxedo fitting at a local tailor shop in the evening. He stood up, still glancing at the itinerary and pacing back and forth in front of the coffee table. The others were gathered around the floorplans, pointing out potential points of concern and cross-referencing the plans with images they were able to look up on the internet on Corbin's laptop. Their discussions had become a din in the background as he now absentmindedly paced, his mind wandering to Bree for a moment. He wondered where she was, thinking about her text and how she said she was out of town as well. Without thinking about it, he pulled out his cell phone and texted her:

Hey, just thinking about you. Hope all is well. Just wondering what you thought of Italian food?

He slipped his phone back into his pocket, looking over at his squad still gathered studiously around the coffee table. He appreciated how dependable they were without his having to keep on them. It was refreshing to know that he could trust them to stay on task in a mundane situation, though no less important, such as now. Sure, they could be anywhere in the city right now, taking in the sights and experiences that Albany had to offer, but they were here, holed up in a hotel room studying building plans and making notes on the pages, seriously discussing an operation that was still three days away with two full days of training and planning. He made a mental note to make sure to give them some downtime before they didn't have any, as a show of appreciation for their dependability. There would be plenty of time to let them loose this evening after their fitting, and he knew a little free time would help them be ready for the rigors of their schedule ahead.

A few hours later, they were gathered in a formal wear shop a couple of miles away from their hotel, having been dropped off by a black SUV driven by a plain-clothes police officer. They had told him not to worry about a return ride as they wanted to wander the city after their appointment. The shop itself was a quaint little brick building that sat across the street from a vacant, overgrown lot and flanked by two small businesses whose buildings looked more like houses than places of commerce. Most of the squad had already been measured for their tuxedos and dress shoes and now sat in large leather chairs, half-watching Randy be measured for his attire. The seamstress had mentioned that his muscular build would prove to be somewhat challenging to fit a tuxedo without having to special order a jacket. "I'm sure I can get you cared for, honey," was the seamstress's response in her honey-sweet southern accent. Corbin's phone buzzed in his pocket, and he quickly pulled it out and looked at the message that had just arrived. It was Bree:

Sorry! It has been busy here! You're super sweet! Italian sounds amazing, I look forward to meeting up!

He smiled to himself, sending a short response before putting his phone back in his pocket. He looked up to see Randy appearing a little sheepish as the kindly, elderly shop owner measured his inseam. Poor guy probably never had that happen to him before.

"Was that your girl?" Alex asked with a smirk.

"Well, nothing's official, but yes, that was her," Corbin responded with a slight blush. "What gave it away?"

"You don't smile quite as stupidly when Captain Dickson texts you." Alex chuckled.

"If he took me out to dinner or dessert or something, I bet I would," Corbin joked back.

Everyone laughed, which appeared to ease Randy's tensions a little bit. The seamstress, whose name appeared to be "Erna," according to her name tag, considered them all for a moment before speaking.

"Y'all Army boys from up north? There was 'nother group of y'all in here just before you boys. Said they was in town to help out at the Capitol."

"Yes ma'am," Jason answered. "We are with those guys. We are in the same Company up on base."

"Now, what they got a buncha soldiers gettin' all dressed up fo'? Not any kinda trouble we need to be worryin' about?"

"None whatsoever, ma'am," Corbin answered. "Just providing some help with security at the Capitol."

"Well, I'll be sure to have you boys lookin' sharp as a tack, I promise y'all that," Erna said with a smile.

"Thank you, ma'am. I could use all the help I can get." Corbin chuckled, and everyone shared a laugh.

After their fittings, they started their walk back toward the hotel, which ended up being a leisurely four-mile trip. It was of no consequence to them, they ran that distance practically every day, so walking it was something they all could do in their sleep. As they neared their hotel, Corbin hung back at the door, eyeing Jason, giving him the non-verbal cue to do the same. Everyone exchanged a nighttime farewell and dispersed. Randy opted to go straight to his room while Brent and Alex took a look around the lobby for a potential bar to lounge in before heading upstairs. Corbin and Jason waited for their squad mates to disappear from view before walking back out into the city.

It was only several blocks from their hotel, but they found themselves in the large plaza across the street from the Capitol, a sign indicating that it was called Empire State Plaza. The open walking area was divided down its center by a long, shallow pool, punctuated by fountains at even intervals, which glowed with underwater lights. They walked in silence for a time, watching others taking advantage of the warm night and going for a stroll in the impressive plaza. Corbin's mind flashed between thoughts of Bree and the Marvel, the former being a far more pleasant thought. He worried, mostly, about what the next step was after training to use their powers. First of all, how were they going to master them? Secondly, what was going to happen once they had? His imagination trailed off into scenarios of global invasion, spaceships and landing crafts burning through the atmosphere and wreaking havoc all over Earth, and somehow, he and Jason were the ones who were supposed to stop it all. What if they did? Worse, what if they *didn't?* His thoughts then began to mix, his mind conjuring up scenarios where his failure to save the world ended up also being his failure to save Bree, and she was captured or killed in the conflict for the fate of Earth. For a moment, he felt like the entire weight of the planet was resting squarely on his shoulders.

His worrying thoughts were interrupted by Jason. "So, what is that thing supposed to be anyway," he asked, pointing at "The Egg."

"I looked it up online, and it's some sort of concert hall, I think is what it is," Corbin answered, admiring the strange building that was so much more massive up close.

"I wonder what the architect was smoking when he thought that thing up," Jason laughed. "It must have been pretty strong stuff."

Corbin shared a laugh, looking again at the peculiar building before continuing his casual saunter down the plaza. He took a moment to consider his and Jason's abilities, wondering that if something were to go amiss at this summit then it would prove to be a useful opportunity to try using their enhancements. Was that something that they wanted? He couldn't imagine it being too easy to explain away superhuman powers to a bunch of foreign dignitaries and news crews, which were sure to be in attendance. That's all they would really need; a news feed broadcasting him bashing inhumanly through the building and Jason shooting fireballs like some video game character. Then again, maybe if they were able to develop even a slight mastery of their powers, then could use them in some subtle way that would be useful to them, but unseen by outside parties.

He turned to face Jason. "What do you think about maybe trying out our powers while we are out here? Maybe get a little self-guided practice in?"

Jason looked a little surprised. "What do you think we should practice on? It's not like there is an overabundance of old tractors around here."

Corbin laughed at Jason's reference. "I know that, but maybe there's and old trash can or park bench or something we can try our skills out on. I don't think it would hurt to try, especially if it means that we have something we could use if all hell breaks loose at this summit."

Jason looked at his friend with skepticism. "Why, you get the feeling something bad is going to happen?"

"Well, no, but I don't know, I just feel like it would be a good idea to try to get a head start on getting a grasp on our powers, rather than just sitting around wondering how Uniz is going to train us to use them."

Jason tilted his head a little with a shrug as if to say, "Yeah, you do have a point there." He looked around slowly, attempting to catch a glimpse of something that they could use to practice on. The two of them walked slowly, taking in their surroundings and mentally checking things around them to determine if they would make for a good practice target. It was all a very public area anyway, so if they were to find something they could use, they hoped to find it somewhere that wasn't quite so out in the open. Practically in unison, they spotted a park bench that was positioned against a planter box that sat off to one side of the plaza, mostly obscured by shadows. They both moved over to the bench, sitting down and looking around casually. There wasn't anyone in the immediate area, so Corbin relaxed, looking over the bench they were sitting on. It was a combination of wrought iron and wood slats, sturdy enough to withstand some punishment which meant they weren't going to damage this thing unless it was with their powers.

"What do you think? Can you hit it with some fire?" Corbin nodded downwards at the bench.

"I can give it a try if you want to be my lookout," Jason countered.

"Easy peasy."

Corbin stood up and took a few steps away from the bench, looking outward to the main area of the plaza, watching for any passerby. It was getting late, and foot traffic was becoming sparse, at most. He glanced back toward Jason, who was staring at the empty spot on the bench beside him, looking very concentrated. He placed his hands flat against the surface and closed his eyes, the expression on his face appearing to show a little struggle. He didn't want to interrupt Jason and mess up any progress he was making, so he went back to scanning the area for other people. Still no one. He looked back to Jason, who was in the same position and still appeared to be struggling. He took a few quiet steps backwards towards him, still eyeing their surroundings and finding nothing and no one. When he was right next to Jason, he turned to him, leaning down to whisper to him.

"How's it coming?"

Jason must not have heard his approach because when he asked the question, Jason jumped in his seat with a string of curse words. Simultaneous with his startled reaction, there was the sound of a *'fwoosh'* and flames erupted from beneath his palms, charring the wood and warping the metal of the bench. They both jumped back from the bench now, watching the wood smolder and the metal frame crackle and creak under the stress of the heat. They regarded each other quietly, then turned their gaze back to the bench, which was now aflame. They had to find some way to put that out before it got out of hand. Too bad his power didn't have something to do with manipulating water or something like that.

Corbin hurried up to the bench, the flames getting a little bigger and smoke starting to billow from it. He looked down to find that the feet of the bench were bolted to the stone walkway it sat upon. Well, that wasn't good. Well, if there were a moment that he would need his strength abilities, it was now. He looked over the burning wreckage, considering where he was going to grab it and receive the least amount of burn damage from it. As the flames grew, he decided that it wasn't an idea he could waste time on anymore and lunged forward, grabbing the bench and immediately regretting it. The metal frame had become so hot that he could hear the skin on his hands sizzle when he grabbed it and was sure that his skin had now melted to the surface. The pain was indescribable as he pulled on the bench with all his might, gritting his teeth to keep from shouting out in pain. He could feel his adrenaline pump into his muscles, making them feel swollen, coiled like a spring.

In one last-ditch effort of fear, anger, and desperation, he lifted as hard as he could, feeling the ground buckle under his feet as the stone around the bottom of the bench cracked and then gave way. Wrenching the flaming bench free, he stumbled towards the fountain nearby, tossing it into the water while he was still ten feet away from the edge. The bench separated from his hands with a sickening peeling sound and cleared the remaining distance easily, plunging into the water with the sound of hissing steam and bubbling water. Allowing his momentum from the throw to carry him forward, Corbin fell onto his hands and knees, clamoring towards the water in desperate need of relief for his burning hands. However, before he could reach the cool water of the fountain, his hands were already as good as new, and the skin on his face and arms didn't sting from the burns they had received only seconds before. He swore under his breath, not from pain, but from the surprise of the regeneration. He wasn't sure he'd ever get used to that. Hopefully he wouldn't be injuring himself frequently enough to have to get used to it.

He walked back over to Jason, who stood staring at where the bench used to be. There were evident cracks that webbed out from where Corbin's feet had been when he had lifted the seat and four large chunks of the stone were missing where the bottom of the bench had ripped them up. They stood silently for a time, looking at the wrecked stone in disbelief. Corbin twisted around to look at the wreckage still steaming in the fountain and felt bad. That was a decent amount of damage they, mostly he, had dealt to this place, and part of him felt responsible for finding someone he could report this to in order to make amends for their vandalism. Of course, the more logical part of him decided that probably wasn't the best idea, and he gave Jason one quick rap on his shoulder and jerked his head to the side to say, "We should go." Jason agreed silently and they both walked hurriedly from the plaza and back to the hotel.

Chapter Nine

Two days and an innumerable number of meetings and run-throughs later, Corbin stood in the main foyer of the Capitol with his squad, Charlie Three-Two, and the leadership of each of the groups of law enforcement officers involved in Operation: Embassy. In stark contrast to the police and state trooper uniforms surrounding them, the SWORD soldiers were dressed in tuxedos. Their slacks, vests, and bowties were black with crisp white jackets. This was to make sure that they could spot each other easily in the crowd, being assured that everyone else in attendance would be wearing black tuxedo jackets. Beneath his tuxedo jacket, Corbin made a mental note of the Glock 17 holstered on his belt, along with two extra magazines and a pair of handcuffs. He also considered the thin, soft Kevlar vest strapped to his torso beneath his tuxedo shirt. Compared to his normal loadout of weapon systems and armor, he felt almost naked and was sure that the rest of his squad and Charlie Three-Two felt the same with their identical equipment. Randy had already mentioned on their way from the hotel that he felt like he was just carrying toys rather than the bulky machine guns he was used to slinging around. Corbin adjusted the radio earpiece in his ear, making sure it was seated properly. Police Chief Tuttle stepped forward, wearing a black tuxedo. He wore an identical radio earpiece, adjusting his glasses so they would sit properly over his ears along with the radio piece. He cleared his throat before speaking.

"Gentlemen, Operation: Embassy is a go. Remember, our radios are linked by channels assigned to each basic group. Albany Police, channel fifteen,

State Troopers, channel sixteen, and Army personnel, channel seventeen. You have full discretion for radio disciplines within your respective channel but know that I'll be listening in on everyone. If things go south, remember to switch to channel zero, which is a master channel that will broadcast to every group. Unless it's an emergency, stay off that channel. Understood?"

There were scattered nods of understanding. Corbin looked around at his squad, seeing them all nod as well. The threat level for this event was declared low; however, Corbin never took threat assessments for granted. In his experience, it always seemed that the lowest-threat situations were the ones that went sideways hard and fast. His mind wandered momentarily to some of those particular memories as Chief Tuttle droned on in the background of his attention. He refocused on the briefing a moment later, catching the last bits of it including code words for different emergencies, medical staff is on hand, blah blah blah, all pretty standard for a detail like this. He mentally reviewed the different code words, making sure he understood the significance of each and cross-checking them with the laminated reference card he had in the inner pocket of his tuxedo jacket. When he was satisfied with his recollection of the essentials, he glanced at the other tuxedo-clad members of his group. SFC Muniz brushed down and straightened his jacket as he stepped up next to Corbin.

"Okay, like we discussed yesterday, we are going to split the floors. You guys take one and two, we will take four and five, and then share three, hooah?"

"Hooah," Corbin responded with a nod. "Keep in touch and don't get too bored up there."

"Oh, trust me, with all the people who are going to be here and all the little hidey-holes someone could go, we are going to be plenty busy," Muniz scoffed. He offered his fist for a fist bump, which Corbin returned, before they parted ways, their squads following them.

Moving over to the massive, ornate staircase, Corbin turned to face his squad. "Okay, we have the first three floors, level three being shared territory with Three-Two. Pair off, spread out, and keep an eye out for anything suspicious. We'll rotate partners and floors from time to time to make sure we don't get too complacent. Feel free to call in a switch when you feel you need one. Any questions?"

No one said anything. They were all looking sharp, both fashionably as well as tactically. Corbin nodded his head. "Good, get set up on your floor and do a radio check. We'll use our call signs for simplicity's sake. Let's go."

Charlie Three-Three split up, Randy and Jason paired off and headed to the second floor, Brent and Alex went to the third and left Corbin to meander about the first floor by himself. As he passed the front doors, he looked at the guarded entry points with their metal detectors and X-ray machines. There were already expensively dressed dignitaries and well-dressed press personnel making their way through the security checkpoints. Corbin pressed the talk button for his radio, which was situated just inside the cuff of his left sleeve.

"Charlie Three-Three, this is Hobgoblin. Radio check, over?"

"Hobbie, this is Rabbit, Lima Charlie," Jason replied.

"This is Goober, loud and clear," Alex answered.

"Brutus, all good," was Randy's short reply.

"Spud, Lima Charlie," Brent answered.

"Good copy everyone. Keep your eyes peeled, and try not to have too much fun," Corbin advised to which he heard sarcastic chuckles in response.

Corbin made his way around the entire main floor, watching faces and movements as he walked, watching for any subtle signs that would suggest ill intent. As he scanned the event guests, he noticed a medic station in one of the far corners of the large foyer at the rear of the building, a mirror image of the one at the front of the Capitol. The sign above the table was a simple red cross, a universal sign for medical personnel. Behind the table, rather than nurses or doctors clad in traditional scrubs or white coats, everyone wore formal wear, the men in tuxedos and the women in black gowns. Each one of them also wore a red cross pin, easily visible on their person, designating their role. He looked over each of them in turn, making sure to consider them as much of a potential threat as any other individual in attendance. He had seen on deployment too many instances where the enemy posed as neutral medical staff, obtaining access to places even normal civilians couldn't, and then wreaking havoc on the population soon after.

While making a mental note of each face, wanting to make sure he would recognize each one of them later, he noticed a nurse who was all too familiar to him. Her hair was pulled back in a simple ponytail, her bangs swooping across her forehead. Her hazel eyes glimmered in the light as she smiled at another nurse she was speaking to. Her black gown held beautifully to her body, a vent in the left side extending up to her mid-thigh. His heart raced as he recognized her and admired how gorgeous she looked. Moving quickly over to the medical station, he stepped up behind her and cleared his throat.

"Pardon me, you wouldn't happen to know of any good Italian restaurants around here, would you?"

Bree's eyes widened as she turned and recognized Corbin immediately. She threw her arms around his neck and embraced him excitedly, which made his heart race even more. After a moment, she released him, straightening out her gown and the red cross pin clipped to the single strap on her gown that extended diagonally over her right shoulder.

"Corbin! I had no idea that you were going to be *here*! It's good to see you!"

His voice caught in his throat for a moment, feeling almost as nervous and flustered as the first time he met her. "Bree, it's good to see you too. I had no idea that your being out of town was the same out of town as me. How'd you get roped into this?"

She chuckled and nervously brushed a lock of hair behind her ear, which Corbin found to be immensely adorable and attractive. "Oh, just on loan for this summit. Apparently, they didn't want to stretch their own medical staff too thin, so they sent out a request for volunteers across the state to come help. What about you?"

"Pretty much the same, except for the volunteer part. We were, as we would put it, 'voluntold' for this assignment," Corbin answered with a laugh.

Bree chuckled. It sounded like music to Corbin and all he could do was smile as she did. As his heart thudded in his chest, he felt energized, like a tingling just beneath the surface of his skin and his muscles tightened, like a coiled spring ready to release. It was almost like he felt stronger when he was near her. It was addicting, as was the sweet scent of her skin, beautifully evident standing close to her. He wanted to just wrap his arms around her and kiss her but knew that would be just a bit too forward, especially in this setting.

"How about dinner tonight," he asked. "There has got to be a good Italian place here somewhere."

Bree smiled, looking into Corbin's eyes and gently biting her bottom lip. "Sounds great. What time are you off?"

Corbin shrugged and looked around passively. "Well, I'm sure that all depends on if anything 'eventful' happens around here. If it stays as boring as it seems to be already, then I'm sure I'll be off sooner than later."

"Perfect, I'll call you later, then," Bree said with a sweet smile, leaning up and giving Corbin a quick peck on the cheek. She then turned back to the group of nurses who had suddenly taken interest in their conversation.

Her kiss had taken him off guard, but pleasantly so. He felt like he could fly at that moment, his heart thundering in his chest and his spirit soaring. He smiled somewhat stupidly to himself as he walked away, continuing his patrol physically, but mentally lingering on her and her kiss. He was distracted just enough that he almost bumped into a couple who looked to be representatives from a country in the Middle East, judging by their olive complexion. Corbin begged their pardon stopping short as he noticed the man trailing behind the couple, most likely their personal security. He shared similar physical characteristics as the couple, but with a distinct difference in his eyes. His eyes looked a bit darker, which wouldn't normally be something he noticed, especially for someone of his nationality, but the way he glared at him as they passed made his demeanor just a touch more concerning. He seemed to be far more upset about the near miss than the couple was, they having graciously excused Corbin when he had apologized. He was tempted to call out the guard, to ask him what his problem was, but he quickly turned and followed the couple up the stone stairs to the second floor. Something wasn't sitting right in his gut.

Corbin keyed his radio, "Brutus, Rabbit, this is Hobbie."

"Go ahead," Jason replied.

"Hey, there's a couple headed to level two up the rear staircase. They look Middle Eastern, maybe Iranian. The female is in a silver gown; the male has a green sash. They've got a guard with them, let me know when you have a visual."

"Standby, we are headed to the rear stairs." There was a short pause, "Got 'em. What's up?"

"What's your take on the guard?" Corbin asked, eyeing his surroundings.

"Looks a little grouchy if you ask me," Randy answered.

"Yeah, I agree," Jason added.

"Should we be concerned?" Randy asked.

"Well," Corbin thought for a moment. Should they really be concerned? Maybe this guy had a grumpy demeanor as his general appearance. Maybe he was bugged that he was roped into being personal security for such an uneventful assignment. Maybe he was just overtly a jerk. Were any of those real reasons to consider him a threat in some way? Probably not, but something in the back of his mind told him to keep a mental note.

"Probably not someone we need to worry about," he radioed back, "but something rubbed me wrong a little about him."

"Maybe he just has a sunny disposition," Randy joked.

"Possibly. I'll let you guys make a call on him. Hobbie, out."

The next couple hours were very uneventful; the only "excitement" Corbin and his squad experienced was when they swapped pairings and floors to patrol. Corbin was now paired with Randy, the two of them casually strolling around the third floor, occasionally passing a couple of guys from the other squad, exchanging subtle waves or nods of acknowledgement. The third floor itself was hardly interesting as very few, if any guests of the international summit made their way up that far. So, the only things to give their attention to were the archaic-looking paintings on the wall in the viewing halls or the occasional glance over the stone banister to the floors below where the guests mingled and discussed whatever it was that people in their positions discussed. The occasional flash of a camera could be seen among the masses of gowns and tuxedos as the press took full advantage of all the glitz and glam of the event.

Corbin could hear the murmur of the crowd lessen and a single voice stand out among the rest. The sound echoed repeatedly off the stone walls and stairs, making the words almost indiscernible; however, he knew what was happening now. According to the schedule for this summit, the people were gathering to meet in the Senate chamber for a presentation by representatives of the State and foreign governments in attendance. As far as he knew, it was something in the way of, "Let's all have peace and kumbaya," stuff to align goals with other nations towards world peace, or whatever. It was all very cliché in his mind, though he was sure the actual presentations would be far more articulate. All he knew was he would never make it as a diplomat. This was all way too much pomp and circumstance for a simple peace talk when they could all just sit down over coffee at a local Denny's and hash out how they could all just get along. Or, even better, just have a video call and save everyone and every country time and money by not wasting it on the venue, the travel, the guests, the food, the clothes, et cetera, et cetera. Then again, maybe he would be a good diplomat. He shrugged to himself at his internal monologue.

"Charlie Three-Three, heads up, they are gathering everyone into the Senate chamber," Jason's voice said over the radio.

"Copy that, Rabbit. Goober, Spud, stay out here and keep an eye on levels one through three. Rabbit, Brutus, and I will go into the chamber and look after the proceedings," Corbin instructed.

"You got it," Brent answered.

"Good copy," Alex replied.

"This is Charlie Three-Two, Cheecho. Come in Hobbie."

It was Muniz. Corbin keyed his talk button, "Cheecho, this is Hobbie, go."

"It's really quiet up here above level three. I'm gonna roll up half of my guys and have them help out on levels one and two. You think one guy per floor on four and five will be enough?"

"Yeah, that sounds good. We appreciate the assist."

"Happy to help. Cheecho, out."

Corbin gestured to Randy and the two of them made their way down to the second floor and into one of the viewing areas overlooking the senate floor below them. They stepped up to the banister, Corbin leaning forward against the cold, stone barrier, looking all around the massive, open room. The large desks for the senate were gathered into two large semicircles facing a raised dais. Many of the attending delegates had taken seats at the desks, their names displayed on large placards placed on the front of the desk facing the dais. The press attendees lined the walls, snapping photographs and taking notes on notepads as everyone took their places. Corbin could see Jason shoulder his way into the senate chamber on the ground level, standing quietly between two reporters who busied themselves with notepads. He looked across the chamber to the viewing balcony opposite him and noticed another pair of white tuxedo jackets in similar positions, two of Muniz's guys, for sure.

Scanning over the area below them once again, Corbin soon found the couple he had almost run into earlier in the day. They were seated at desks in the rear semicircle, and according to their placard, they were from the United Arab Emirates. Their guard was standing straight and still behind them. His arms were folded across his chest, and he looked just as surly as he did when Corbin had first encountered him. As unsurprising as that was, something about that guy still didn't sit right with him. He concentrated on the man, squinting his eyes a little to help his vision focus. What was so off about this guy? Why did he give him such an off vibe? While Randy remained standing upright, Corbin leaned further forward on the barrier in front of him, trying to make sense of his gut feeling. He must have been concentrating a little too hard because in an instant, the guard looked up in Corbin's direction. His face went from one of disgruntled indifference to one of surprised recognition. Crap, he caught him staring. The guard stared back for a moment before his appearance returned to grouchy and he folded his arms across his chest once again. Now, at least to Corbin, he looked a bit more annoyed, maybe even determined. Jeez, had he pissed the guy off *that* much by staring at him? He considered approaching the man after this meeting and apologizing for whatever perceived offense he had caused.

One of the New York State Senators stood at the center of the dais and welcomed everyone to the summit, thanking them for their attendance and outlining the intent and structure of their meeting. There were to be several speakers including ambassadors to several countries such as Iran, Iraq, Israel, and even a dignitary from Afghanistan. They were to speak on the impacts of the conflict in the Middle East before allegedly proclaiming their resolve to help end the bloodshed with the assistance of allied countries. They were to be followed up by delegates from allied nations such as Great Britain, America, Canada, and Russia. These speeches were to outline promises and resolutions to provide aid and withdraw forces from war-stricken areas to let those places stabilize and rebuild. It all sounded good, in theory, but he had seen enough on his deployments to know that the only thing keeping some of those countries from devolving into complete anarchy was the presence of foreign militaries. They didn't have any way to police their own populations, let alone fight terrorist groups who were growing in number and force each and every day. However, those fanatical rats were slippery, and it was about as easy as nailing Jell-O to a tree as it was to catch and stop them, which meant that time, money, and lives were being wasted every day chasing what they couldn't capture. He pursed his lips as he thought about it. Maybe it was in the best interest of America and her allies to withdraw and just let these struggling countries flounder by themselves. At least, outlined in speeches like these, it sounded like they were doing it for their benefit, whether that was the truth or not. Maybe that was the essence of diplomacy, he considered, doing things within your best interest but making it sound like it is in the best interests of whoever you may be screwing over.

Lost in his train of thought for a time, Corbin hadn't noticed right away that the guard had moved. Instead of standing directly behind his assigned wards, he had shifted several desks to the left. Despite his having moved, he stood in his usual, unapproachable stance, looking as if there was nothing amiss. Corbin narrowed his eyes, watching him intently. He pressed the talk button on his radio.

"Rabbit, you got eyes on the guard who was standing behind the UAE reps?"

Corbin could see Jason across the chambers subtly pressing his radio earpiece into his ear before responding. "You mean, the angry guy you had mentioned earlier?"

"Yeah, you see where the couple for the UAE is sitting? Back row, near center?"

"Yep, I see them. Where's their guard?"

"Look a few desks to their left. Standing and looking just as pissed as ever." Corbin pointed out, nodding his head as if Jason could see him do it.

"Standby," Jason cautioned.

"This is Tank and Griff, Charlie Three-Two. We are on the balcony opposite of you. We can see him. What's the word on this guy?"

"Not sure," Corbin answered, shifting a few steps to his right to get a better view. "Something doesn't seem right. He looks like he's drifting away from those who he's supposed to be guarding."

"Maybe he's just getting a better view," call sign "Tank" suggested.

"Why would he want to do that? He's personal security, not press," Corbin stated. He had crossed his arms over his chest, casually concealing him pressing his radio talk button to anyone who may have glanced his way.

"Maybe getting in a better position to take a shot?" Jason said what Corbin was thinking but didn't want to consider.

"Let's not jump to any crazy conclusions yet, but keep an eye on him, everyone."

There were several clicks from the others pressing and releasing their radio talk buttons, a silent way to confirm their received order. Corbin looked towards Randy, who was now sitting casually in one of the seats, feet stretched out in front of him as he leaned back comfortably. Corbin shot him a stern look, and when he saw it, he sat forward, looking more intently as he leaned forward, putting his elbows on his knees. Corbin shook his head and huffed a short laugh. Sure, it wasn't very eventful, but it was no time to get sloppy, especially with this mystery dude looking more and more suspicious. He caught Randy's eye and signaled for him to stay sharp.

"Hobbie, this is Rabbit. He's moving again."

Sure enough, this guy had started to shuffle to his left again, stepping between a pair of guards attending to a woman in a sparkly blue gown. The man's gaze never broke from the dais even as he moved. He was locked on to an objective, Corbin could tell, but who this dude was looking at was still a mystery. It could have been anyone on the two-tiered platform at the head of the senate chambers and at the angle he was, it was impossible to determine who the man was focused on. Corbin shifted to his right a little more, getting a better vantage point as well as shifting into a position that was outside of the guard's periphery.

"I see him, I see him. Tank, Griff, can you guys get better positions over there?"

"We'll try, but not much we can do if we need to act. Lots of collateral down there."

"I can reposition," Jason offered.

"No, stay put. You're the closest, I don't want you to tip him off if you move." Corbin leaned forward, seeing that the man had moved into a position that was diagonal to the rostrum. Where he was standing now was in an opening where there were no standing security personnel between himself and everyone sitting at the head of the chambers. He had stopped moving now and Corbin had a very bad feeling about him.

"Rabbit, Brutus, and Griff, hold position. Tank, head downstairs and cover the door to the chamber. I'm going to move to the stage area and see if I can't get up there. Everybody play it cool, we don't want to rile him up."

"Hobbie, this is Cheecho. Where do you need us?"

Corbin gave Randy a rough tap on the shoulder as he passed behind him, headed towards the stairs leading down into the front foyer. "Hold positions on levels one and two. Watch any of the exits that you can, just in case this guy tries to make a break for it."

"Got it, moving now," came Muniz's reply.

Corbin hustled down the stairs, doing his best not to look as though he were in a hurry. As he rounded the corner, he glanced over to see the several of the medical staff grouped together chatting. Bree was with them. The sound of his hard leather-soled shoes echoed in the gigantic marble foyer, drawing the attention of the nurses. Bree smiled and waved to Corbin, and he did his best to smile and wave back, but how he looked when he did it must have been less convincing than he thought because her smile faded, and her brow furrowed with concern. She hurried forward, intercepting him as he reached the door leading to the rostrum of the chamber.

"Everything okay?" she asked in a worried tone.

"Not sure, but we are going to make sure that it is," Corbin answered quietly, hoping his voice didn't carry too far. "Stay out here with the others. Do you guys have a radio?"

"All the med stations do, yes."

"Good, keep yours on channel seventeen, that's my squad's channel."

"What are we listening for?"

"Well, if all goes well, nothing that will need to involve you or the other nurses," Corbin said with a shrug before giving her a short kiss on the cheek. "I owed you one." Opening the door quietly, he slipped in, closing it silently behind him.

* * *

That wasn't what she was hoping to hear. She could tell the moment she saw him coming down the stairs that something was off. She didn't know how she knew, but she did, and now she found herself praying that he didn't get himself hurt or killed before they could have their first official date. Moving swiftly to her friends, she confirmed where the nurse's station radio was and went to get it, not offering any other explanation to her coworkers. Once she had gotten it, she quickly turned the channel dial to the number seventeen and held it close to her ear.

"This is Hobbie. I'm heading up to the platform now. What's our guy doing?"

Bree recognized Corbin's voice as Hobbie. Her grip tightened on the radio in anticipation as her friends gathered around her, moving in close to listen to the radio chatter as well.

* * *

Corbin crept up the short, dark hallway that ramped up towards another door, which was cracked slightly open. Pressing his face near the door, he tried to get a decent view through the thin opening in the door frame but couldn't make out anything of use.

"All call signs, what's he doing? Over," he whispered into his radio.

"Well, he's stopped moving for a sec, but he's too close to my side for me to see him below me," Randy answered. "Want me to move?"

"No, hold there. Rabbit, Griff, you see anything?"

"Yeah, he's directly beneath Brutus, clear line of sight to the platform. He's just watching. What's the call?" Griff reported.

"Hold position. Rabbit, what's your view?"

"Messy. Too many guards and other personnel between me and him. If he does go live, we are gonna have to rely on a long shot from Brutus or Griff."

"Let's make sure it doesn't come to that. I'll see if there is any way for me to get up on the stage area without arousing suspicion."

Corbin could hear the indistinct hum of someone speaking on the other side of the door, then there was a short moment of silence, applause, and then another voice speaking. Concentrating on the voice, he could tell that it was a female voice with a Russian accent. He pushed the door open a little more, not being able to see much, but now he could spot the speaker at the topmost section of the platform. He could see the dais area to his left, opposite the direction of where their person of interest was standing.

"Talk to me guys. I can't see him from where I am," Corbin insisted.

"He's still watching. Standby," Griff answered.

Several minutes passed with the only sound being the woman speaker's voice echoing around the chambers. Soon, her speech came to a close, and applause began to build and, with no other prompting, so did his unease. The chorus of applause and cheers rose in a crescendo of clamor, reaching an almost thunderous magnitude. That's when Corbin heard the shout over the radio.

"Gun! GUN! Down! EVERYONE DOWN!"

Reacting on instinct, he flung open the door to the dais. He vaulted the table in front of him and rushed towards the podium where the Russian delegate still stood, waving cordially to the applauding crowd. At that very moment, it felt like everything went into slow motion as he took two lunging steps towards the woman and leapt forward. His arms wrapped around her waist as he fell to the floor, turning his body to shield her from the direction of the gunman. He heard the echoing report of gunfire followed by the distinct hiss and "zip" of several rounds barely missing him as he and the woman fell to the floor. Time seemed to return to normal as he hit the floor, the woman landing on top of him, shouting what were most likely curses and colorful refrains in Russian, swinging at him to get him to let her go. He lurched into a crouching position, shouting over the screams for her to stay down.

"Get everyone out of here! Rabbit, cover the door! Cheecho, we need your help at the senate chambers!"

"Copy, on our way Hobbie," came the reply through the radio.

Corbin drew his handgun, aiming it in the general direction of where the gunman had last been seen to find that he was still there, weapon aimed upward at Griff on the opposite end of the room. Jason was posted next to the single door leading out of the chambers, weapon drawn in one hand and the other hand ushering and pushing people through the doorway. Corbin looked quickly up towards Randy who had his weapon drawn but was not in a good position to have a bead on the gunman. Aiming his gun at the assailant, Corbin flipped his radio switch to lock the talk button down. He didn't need to waste effort pressing the talk button to use his radio. Gripping his weapon in both hands, he aimed at the gunman who stood calmly, aiming his handgun at Jason now.

"Brutus, get on channel zero and call this in. Get this place locked down," Corbin ordered.

"On it," Randy called back.

Corbin could hear a click of static as Randy switched radio channels and could hear his voice from the balcony. "All channels, break, break, break! We have shots fired in the senate chamber. Say again, shots fired. Go Code Black. I say again, Code Black!" Corbin moved to his right and forward, getting in a better position for both cover and aim. The gunman didn't move, other than to rotate his weapon from Jason, to Griff, to Corbin. Any time he was aiming at someone else, Corbin would move in a little closer, stopping whenever he was the target once again. Out of his periphery, he could see that Jason was doing the same.

"Drop the gun and put your hands on your head," Corbin shouted.

The man didn't respond. Rather, he continued to aim his weapon, a Beretta .45, between Corbin and the others in the chambers. Corbin repeated the command, again receiving no response or compliance from the man. He wondered if this guy was being belligerent or didn't speak enough English to know what he was being told. That seemed a stupid thought, however, seeing as having a handful of men aiming guns at you was the universal sign for "Put your gun down and surrender." Nevertheless, he tried shouting the words "gun" and "down" in his limited skill at Arabic, which only seemed to amuse the man who smirked at him and shook his head in a disapproving manner. Corbin could hear Randy giving a play-by-play over the master radio channel and even the muffled sounds of footsteps running and orders being shouted in the foyer beyond the chamber doors.

"Listen, dickwad, you wanna get shot?! PUT THE GUN DOWN!" Griff demanded, his voice echoing from where he stood.

Corbin had had enough of this and readied himself to take a shot. With the room now empty, he could venture a non-lethal shot to this guy to disarm him or at least distract him long enough that they could move in and take him. Sure, he could take the bullet, fall, and empty his magazine in a Hail Mary attempt to take them out, but with no civilians in danger of errant rounds, it was a risk he was willing to take. Besides, they all had armor vests on, and though they felt far too thin to stop a .45 slug he knew the Level IIIA soft plates could stop it with no problem. What he would have given to have his full armor and weapon loadout right now; he still felt so naked.

"Hobbie, this is Cheecho," came Muniz's voice in his ear.

"Go ahead."

"The police have the place locked down and everyone sheltered in one of the restaurants on the northeast corner of the first floor. We have the door covered here, want us to move in?"

"Negative, stand your ground. We are going to move in for the takedown—
"

He was cut off by the staccato of gunfire and the sensation of being kicked in the shoulder. The force spun him around and threw him to the floor. He felt a warm pressure in his right shoulder as if something had been stuck in there and his arm went slack. Sitting up, he saw that he had been shot. There was a hole in his tuxedo jacket that was progressively getting red with his blood. Of **course** he would get shot outside the cover of his vest. Erna was definitely going to be disappointed when they returned his tuxedo. As he struggled to his feet, he heard several more gunshots ring out around the room and a door slam, followed by muffled gunfire on the other side of the door.

"Shots fired! Two down! He's out of the chambers now," Randy called in.

Two down? Who else did he hit? Corbin clutched the edge of the table in front of him and pulled himself to his feet, looking towards the door to see Jason slowly climbing to his feet as well. Mantling the table, he sprinted towards his friend, grasping his gun in his left hand. When he reached Jason, he pulled him up to his feet, noticing him clutching his midsection and grumbling a string of curse words.

"You good?!"

"Yeah," Jason groaned. "Hit me in the vest, but I'm good."

"Good," he looked up towards Randy. "Brutus! Griff! Get out there and provide cover from level two!"

Randy and the soldier he only knew as "Griff" shouted their confirmation and sprinted from the chambers. Corbin looked over Jason, making sure he didn't see any blood. He could see a large hole in Jason's tuxedo vest and shirt on his left side, the back of the bullet glimmering in its place embedded in his armor vest. Poor guy, he was going to have some wicked bruising, if not possibly a cracked rib with that hit. Jason looked over Corbin at the same time, noticing almost immediately the bloody hole in his shoulder.

"Corbin! You're hit. Are you all right?!"

Corbin shrugged with a grunt. When he did, he noticed that his shoulder didn't ache, nor did it feel like he had something lodged in there. He looked down to see the skin beneath the blood-soaked hole in his jacket was perfectly untouched. Well, that was convenient, but it was going to need some sort of explanation once this was over. He switched his handgun back to his right hand and rotated his arm to check his shoulder's efficacy. Nothing amiss—well, other than the fact that he had one hundred percent healed in seconds from a gunshot wound.

"More than all right, it seems," he said with a laugh of disbelief.

"Hobbie, this is Cheecho! Gunman has gotten out and barricaded himself in an office."

Corbin pressed his radio earpiece into his ear. "We are on our way, hold there and don't let him out."

"Copy that, we are on the south side, the office is interior to the building."

"Good copy. Hold fire on the senate door, we are coming out now."

Corbin and Jason rushed through the door to be met by a cluster of State Troopers, guns drawn and held at a low-ready position. Just behind them was a quartet of nurses, one of them was Bree. The moment she saw him, her eyes went wide, and she rushed forward, clutching a medical satchel in her hand. Another nurse hurried forward assessing Jason at the same time. Bree's hands brushed over Corbin's shoulder, her other hand resting on his cheek.

"You're hit! Are you okay?! Put some pressure on it— "

"Bree! I'm okay, we've got a bad guy to catch. I'll be back," he interrupted.

Jason waved off the other nurse, confirming to her that he was fine and showing her that there was no blood on his clothing. Bree and her colleague stepped back as Corbin and Jason rushed towards the south side of the building. SFC Muniz and two of his men took cover behind stone columns near the closed door of an office, their weapons trained on the door. Muniz looked just as surprised and somewhat panicked when he noticed the blood on Corbin's shoulder, but Corbin just waved his hand to dismiss him and signal that he was okay. He and Jason moved to opposite sides of the doorway, listening closely while keeping themselves out of the potential line of fire. Corbin tried the doorknob which was locked. He could tell by the feel of the door that it was at least a couple of inches thick of solid wood. There wasn't a window in the door that they could break to try to access the lock from the office side. They'd have to try to breach the door, but how? A door this robust wasn't something you could just kick in, despite all the Hollywood portrayals. They would need something much more effective, either a battering ram, or maybe even a directional explosive.

"Brutus, this is Hobbie. Ask Chief Tuttle if they have any breaching tools; we've got a beast of a door to try to get through."

"Standby, I'll ask," came the response. There was a moment of silence before Randy's voice came back over the master channel. "None on site, but they can have one here in ten minutes."

Judging by where the office was in this building, there was no way that there was a window or any other secondary way to get out of it, so this guy was going to be stuck camped out in that room for the next ten minutes. However, he didn't seem the type to just wait around to get captured. If he had the balls to try to assassinate someone in such a public and well-guarded venue, he probably had the fanaticism to just kill himself rather than end up a prisoner. No, they couldn't wait around; they needed to get in there now if they wanted to get this guy alive. Corbin had an idea; he could use his strength...hopefully. Uniz did say that they were looking for real-world applications to their powers. At this point, it was evident that his regenerative powers were working just fine. That, as it stood, was going to be a difficult story he'd have to make up once this was all over now that Bree and Muniz had seen his injury from afar, but that would have to wait. He needed to find a way to get rid of their audience of fellow soldiers in a believable way.

"Brutus, call in the breacher. Cheecho, take your guys and wait outside to receive it," Corbin ordered.

"Copy, calling it in now," Randy complied.

"On our way," Muniz answered, gesturing for his men to follow and hurrying away.

When they were out of sight, he leaned down to Jason who was getting a closer look at the doorknob and deadbolt on the thick door. "Think you can do something to melt those?"

Jason shook his head, not looking up from the lock. "Not sure. I can give it a try, but you know I can't guarantee anything."

"You aren't talking to Yoda here," Corbin joked. "There is a 'try' in this scenario. I figure, you try to weaken the lock and the knob, and I'll see if I can't kick it in."

"Well, it's an idea..." Jason sighed as he cocked his head to the side. "Keep a lookout, I'll see what I can do."

Corbin straightened up and looked around, finding the area they were in deserted. He could hear sirens wailing in the distance and the occasional shout from a police officer checking the status of other officers nearby. He glanced back at Jason, who was now gripping the doorknob with both hands, a determined look on his face. He could see what looked like smoke starting to rise from the door, and if he wasn't mistaken, it looked like the doorknob was starting to glow red as if being superheated. He patted Jason encouragingly on the shoulder as he looked up again and checked their surroundings. As he did, he could hear Jason grunting with some effort behind him before letting out a sigh.

"Well, that's about all I could manage, maybe it'll help?"

Corbin turned to see that the doorknob did look warped as if it had been melted just enough to deform it. The keyhole for the deadbolt looked relatively unfazed, but he could tell Jason had tried to melt it as well. He pulled Jason to his feet and ushered him aside out of the way of the door. He concentrated, trying to remember how it was that he had managed to smash the tractor at the old barn. What was he feeling? He was pretty mad at Jason, definitely. How was he going to replicate that without trying to have Jason goad him again? It probably wouldn't work anyway because he would know what he was trying to do. He cursed quietly under his breath, wondering how he could conjure up his powers on his own, rather than have them manifest by sheer reaction. He wouldn't get long to think about that as there was the sudden eruption of gunfire on the opposite side of the door and three rounds burst from the door at about chest height. Due to the thickness of the door, the rounds fragmented and exited as small chunks of shrapnel that peppered Corbin across his shirt but lacked the force to even tear the fabric.

"Oh you're dead, you sonofa—" he reared back and kicked the doorknob as hard as he could. Expecting his foot to land solidly against the hardened metal and door, he was surprised when it splintered and his foot traveled forward as the door swung inward, breaking the door jamb and crunching the knob inward into the door itself. Jason recovered quickly from his surprise and pushed the door further inward and Corbin, gun drawn, rushed forward.

"Put the gun down and get your hands up—" He stopped just inside the doorway. Inside the small office was a desk, two filing cabinets, and a corkboard on the wall behind the desk; however, there was no one inside. Stepping around the desk, Corbin saw several empty bullet casings and a discarded Beretta, its slide locked back due to an empty magazine. Next to it was a man, dressed in a black tuxedo and red shirt, his hands at his sides and a blank, indifferent look on his face. Corbin stepped to the side to allow Jason into the room; his weapon trained on the gunman.

"Get your hands up where I can see them," Jason shouted, and the man complied.

"You got him?" Corbin asked.

"I'm on him," Jason answered.

Corbin holstered his gun and stepped forward, removing the handcuffs from their pouch positioned at the small of his back. All arrest formalities aside, he landed a kick to the man's back, knocking him forward, his face striking the edge of the desk. While he was stunned by the impact, Corbin wrenched his arms behind his back and latched the cuffs around his wrists. Shoving him forward onto his face on the floor, he stepped down on his back, putting a little extra pressure down on his foot. He switched his radio to channel zero, the mic still locked in vox.

"This is Staff-Sergeant Kent, all clear. We have the perp in custody. I say again, all clear, one in custody."

"This is Chief Tuttle, bring him out, we have a ride waiting for him out front."

"Copy that, on our way," Corbin responded, hauling the man to his feet. He got a good look at the man now, specifically his eyes. He recognized how dark they were. They looked nearly identical to Uniz, except their darkness extended to a deeper level, an evil level. Whoever this guy was, he wasn't human, and he wasn't good. Blood trickled from a gash across his cheek from where his face had hit the table when Corbin had kicked him. He gritted his teeth angrily and let out a hostile sort of hissing noise. Jason smacked him across the back of his head, jolting it forward.

"Enough of that, who are you? Who are you with?"

The man spat at Jason's question, shooting him a furious look before turning to look at Corbin with an equally venomous glare. Corbin pulled him roughly around the desk, pausing by the doorway before exiting the office.

"Who are you?!" he demanded.

The man's eyes narrowed, and Corbin heard in his mind, *"In time, you will learn my name. As for now, know that I am your end."*

Corbin looked at Jason to confirm that he had heard the same thing in his head, which Jason confirmed with a nod. Corbin looked back to the man, gritting his teeth in an attempt to keep his fury at bay. "Is that so? Doesn't look like you're headed anywhere other than a paddy wagon."

The man looked somewhat confused by his statement but still glared at Corbin as he dragged him from the office, Jason following with his empty Beretta in his hand. As they rounded the corner to the main foyer, they were met by a gaggle of police officers, guns still drawn, including Chief Tuttle. They returned their weapons to their holsters at the sight of the detained man and Tuttle released a short sigh while another officer took the handcuffed assassin and dragged him towards the front doors. Corbin switched off the microphone lock on his radio and Jason handed the empty Beretta and magazine to another officer as Chief Tuttle slung his arms over their shoulders.

"We're forever in your debt for this, Staff-Sergeant. Excellent work. No casualties, no injuries—" he stopped himself when he noticed Corbin's shoulder. Corbin looked at his "injury" and shrugged the Chief's arm off him.

"I guess I better go get this checked out. We'll be sure to link up with you for a debrief once all the excitement has cleared," Corbin said as he moved away quickly, gesturing for Jason to follow.

The two of them made their way over to the nurse station where some of the medical staff were checking on guests who were feeling a bit faint from all the excitement. Bree saw Corbin coming and rushed to him, satchel in hand once again. Corbin held up his hand to slow her down as she approached, accepting her hug when she reached him. Pulling away, he made sure to look into her eyes to keep her from seeing his shoulder.

"Hey, is there somewhere you can look me over that isn't around everyone else?"

She looked confused, stepping back half a step and looking at Jason, who only nodded and shrugged. She looked back to Corbin, her concerned eyes glittering green, "I— I guess so. Follow me."

They followed her across the foyer to a sizeable coat closet tucked in a corner beneath the main staircase. Corbin grabbed a chair and dragged it with them into the closet, Jason shutting the door behind them and standing against it as if to guard it from any unwanted entry. Corbin sat down in the chair and Bree quickly went to work removing his tuxedo jacket, vest, and shirt, leaving him wearing just his armor vest. She paused, gasping, running her fingers over the undamaged skin of his shoulder where a bullet should have been. Corbin pulled the Velcro straps to his Kevlar vest, letting it plop on the floor. Bree was still dumbfounded, staring at his shoulder.

"Corbin...what—?"

"It's...it's uh...." He struggled for an explanation. What could he say that didn't sound crazy? He wasn't grazed, that would have still left a mark. Why would he fake an injury in the middle of a gunfight? He could either tell her the truth and sound insane, probably leading to her never speaking to him again, or he could lie, nothing he could fabricate would be a good lie, and possibly have her not speak to him ever again anyway. He paused, letting out a long sigh and taking her hands in his.

"Do you trust me?" An odd question, but it was the one that came to mind.

She paused, her eyes darting between Jason and Corbin. "I – uh, yes."

"This has a reasonable explanation, but we definitely don't have time for it now. Is there any way you can just patch me up like I'm hurt, and we can talk about this later?"

"Also, I could use a little checkup." Jason groaned, motioning towards his side, the soreness of the injury starting to fill in where the adrenaline was ebbing away.

Bree nodded and promptly got to work. She had Jason remove his shirt, vest, and armor to reveal a large, deep purple bruise forming across his ribs. She cautiously pressed the skin, feeling for fractures and finding none. Poor Jason was going to be keeping the painkiller business running for the next little while. After she had determined that Jason was otherwise okay, she turned back to Corbin and let out a long sigh. She took out gauze, a bottle of iodine, and some medical tape and went to work on his shoulder as if he was in fact injured. Dousing his shoulder in the iodine, she removed the sterile gauze and folded it to size before pressing it to his skin, putting his hand over it.

"Hold this, please."

Corbin complied, watching her work and admiring her beauty. The lines on her forehead were barely visible as her face mirrored her concentration, her eyes the concern he had seen when she first spotted him injured. She thoughtfully bit the inside of her cheek as she unfurled the medical tape and pressed it against the gauze, securing it to his skin. The stain of the iodine extended beyond the borders of the gauze and soaked into it, giving the illusion that he had been treated for a wound in a hurried, emergency situation. As Corbin put his tuxedo back on, Bree stopped him from putting on his jacket. "Here, this will help," she said as she folded the jacket into a makeshift sling, tying it over his shoulder and immobilizing his right arm. Corbin stood up, grabbing his armor vest in his left hand.

"Thank you, and I promise, I'll explain everything. How about over dinner?"

"If we ever get out of here," Jason scoffed. "There's going to be mountains of paperwork and reports and probably news interviews we are going to have to do."

"We can keep off the radar of the news if we just avoid the reporters. However, you're right. The paperwork is probably going to bury us. In any case," he turned to Bree, his eyes meeting hers, "dinner tonight, even if it's in the middle of the night?"

Bree paused for a moment as if considering her answer. She looked down to the floor, then back up, meeting Corbin's gaze. "It's a date."

Corbin chuckled excitedly, giving her a hug. "Thank you! I'll let you know when I'm out of here."

"What am I supposed to put on my report for your injuries, Staff-Sergeant?" Bree asked with a wink.

Corbin thought for only a second. "Ah, just tell them it was a 'through-and-through,' no need for anything more than a bandage for my boo-boo."

She laughed, nodding her head and moving to the door. "Deal. Stay safe, Corbin." She patted him on the chest affectionately and then left, Corbin opening the door for her.

Before he stepped out, Jason stopped him and pushed the door shut. "So, we are just going to read her into our secret before we even tell our own friends?"

"We can break the news to them sometime soon as well. We might just have to, this has already gotten us into some trouble," Corbin answered, lifting his "injured" shoulder.

"Better sooner than later," Jason said in an almost cautionary manner.

"I'll take care of it. No worries," Corbin assured, opening the door and stepping back out into the foyer.

Thankfully, most of the media attention was focused on the attendees of the party than the law enforcement personnel, so it wasn't too difficult to slip out of the coat closet and make their way unnoticed to the foyer on the opposite side of the building. This area was far less crowded, having only a couple of nurses and a handful of police officers milling about. Corbin keyed his radio microphone as they stopped in the middle of the open area.

"Charlie Three-Three, where are you guys?"

"Second level. Where do you want us," came the return from Brent.

"Level one, rear foyer."

"On our way to you now."

Corbin did his best to stand somewhere that wasn't quite out in the open, just in case any of the news reporters happened to make it to where they were. He wasn't in the mood to answer media questions. It was also a policy of SWORD to avoid media attention as much as possible. Sure, they had cover stories to keep their true identity off the record, but it was a lot easier not to use them at all. Thankfully, in a situation like this, there were plenty of high-profile individuals to distract the cameras and reporters, keeping the attention off him and the rest of his squad. As he considered this, the rest of his squad came into the foyer, each man looking over his shoulder every so often to make sure that they weren't being followed by newscasters. Brent and Alex looked surprised to see Corbin's arm in a sling, his shoulder bandaged.

"How bad is it?" Alex asked.

"Just a flesh wound. Straight through. Nothing a bandage and some ibuprofen won't fix," Corbin answered with a nonchalant look.

"You get one of those cute nurses to patch you up?" Randy joked.

"As a matter of fact, yes. That nurse I met at Beck's the other night. It just so happens she was working this event too."

"Ha! Did she give you a little kiss for your boo-boo, too?" Randy chuckled.

Corbin felt himself get a little flush. "Yep."

Randy looked a little surprised at his response, as well as slightly jealous. He laughed and shook his head with a smile, "Lucky SOB. And how about you, Bro, you make it out okay?" He gave Jason a playful jab in the shoulder.

Jason winced a little. "Just some gnarly bruises. Nothing a *lot* of ibuprofen can't fix."

"Yeah, it's surprising to me how these vests can catch a .45 like that," Brent said with a chuckle. "It feels like I'm wearing paper mâché rather than actual armor."

"Thank goodness they work so well. Otherwise, I might have to be putting out applications for a new team leader," Corbin said with a nod towards Jason.

"Yes, thank you for not dying," quipped Randy. "We are already going to have a bunch of paperwork. I would have hated to have to add funerary paperwork and detail to the list. Plus, it would have been made for one lousy trip home to our parents."

Everyone laughed, their voices echoing in the massive, open space. As Corbin looked around, he noticed a new group of figures making their way towards them. There was a cluster of black tuxedoed men walking almost in step, surrounding a figure in their midst that appeared to be wearing a blue, sparkly gown with a silver sash. As the men parted, he could see that it was the Russian woman he had pulled out of the line of fire. She stepped forward, seeing him, a look of concern showing on her face as she noticed his arm in a sling. Taking his face in her hands, she said something in Russian before kissing him on both cheeks. Corbin felt beyond sheepish at the gesture, feeling the familiar heat of embarrassment in his cheeks, looking towards her guards to see if there was anyone who could translate what she had said. They simply parted to allow her to return to her position within their midst, and then they all turned and left just as swiftly as they came.

"Well, at least we know that if things didn't happen to work out with Brianne, you've got an admirer in Russia," Jason said with a smirk.

Chapter Ten

As much as they joked about paperwork, it was the grim reality of any operation, and that reality became far more tedious if something "exciting" happened to go down during the mission. That was no different in this case. Corbin and his squad were bogged down for several hours just filling out what would have been the normal amount of reports and red tape, but then they had to also fill out witness statements, incident reports, and a plethora of other forms. Add getting injured in the event and Jason and Corbin felt like they had filled out enough papers to kill the rainforest. Thankfully, during it all, they were sequestered from all other personnel, including the media. To their relief, they had avoided having their faces plastered all over news reports. The most any media outlet had was statements from Chief Tuttle that, thanks to a joint police and Army security force, they had one suspect in custody and there were no fatalities.

By the time Charlie Three-Three had finished their reports and were dismissed, it was late in the evening, and the entire Capitol was almost empty, save for a handful of police officers who were responsible for emptying and securing the building. As they passed the officers, they exchanged quiet glances and nods as Corbin and his squad made their way out of the building and into the cool evening. As the doors closed behind them, Corbin removed his phone from his pocket and texted Bree.

Didn't think they'd ever let us go, but I'm a free man. How about that dinner? We've got some stuff to talk about. Italian food still sound good?

He turned to the rest of his squad and let out a long sigh. "Okay, you guys are free to get out of here and make whatever you can of the rest of the night. We'll link up tomorrow morning for the trip back home. I'll hit you up with more details as I get them."

Randy, Alex, and Brent wasted no time turning in an about-face and walking off hurriedly. Corbin was sure that they were all starving, especially Randy, and wanted to let off some steam after a hectic day. He thought about the word, "hectic." Most people would use that to describe maybe a busy or haphazard workday, or a lousy commute home. Both he and Jason had gotten shot and they both just shrugged it off in their minds as if it had just gotten a little busier than normal at the office. Part of him wondered, if he hadn't joined SWORD, what would he be doing now, and what would be his definition of "hectic"? He smirked to himself, finding it all pretty amusing.

Now, he wanted to go back to the hotel, clean up, and get out of his monkey suit. He liked getting dressed all fancy from time to time, but for how long he had been wearing this tuxedo, it had started to feel suffocating. He made a mental note to himself to write an apology to Erna for wrecking one of her jackets. Now that he was beyond the inquiring and curious eyes of other officers and all the news vans had gone home, he felt that it was safe enough to take his arm out of his sling and wear his jacket normally. The blood stain was a stark contrast to the white material, and he cringed a little. Yeah, that didn't look good. He settled with just draping the jacket over his shoulder to hide the stain and his "injured" shoulder. He lost himself for a moment, trying to decide whether he wanted to get a ride back to the hotel, or just walk and enjoy the calm evening weather. Considering the day he had, he opted to just get a ride.

"You going to hitch a ride back to the hotel?" he asked Jason.

"I hadn't decided, what do you think?"

"Yeah, I'm going to get a ride. I want to get out of this tux as soon as I can and try to decompress. Wanna just ride back with me?" he offered.

"Sure," Jason accepted.

Several police officers stood next to their squad cars in the front driveway, all waiting to provide transportation to any of the stragglers in the building. Corbin and Jason moved over to one and asked for a ride back to their hotel, to which he obliged. The ride back was short, and mostly quiet, apart from a short conversation where the officer congratulated them on their success in getting the bad guy as well as his hopes that they both recover quickly. By that time, they were pulling up to the front doors of their hotel. They exchanged pleasantries and thanked the officer for the ride.

Inside his room, Corbin changed out of his tuxedo into a simple t-shirt and jeans and militantly arranged the tuxedo back on its hanger. Sadly, no matter how organized it was, the bloody bullet hole made everything look awful. He still felt bad about it and remembered that he was going to write an apology to Erna. Glancing around the room, he spotted the customary pad of paper and pen that came with any hotel room. Sitting down at the desk, he started to write a note explaining how sorry he was that he ruined some of her merchandise and promising that if the Police Department didn't compensate her for it, he would be glad to do so. He was in the process of writing his contact information down when his cell phone buzzed. Pulling it out, he saw that Bree had responded to him.

I'm glad you're free, and yes, I'm starving! Where should we meet?

Corbin scrambled to grab his laptop and look up Italian restaurants nearby. He found one that was only several blocks away from the hotel. He texted her the name and address of the restaurant, asking if she could meet him there, to which she happily agreed. He got up excitedly, checking himself in the mirror to make sure he looked presentable. When he had changed into civvies, he had removed the gauze and scrubbed off as much of the iodine that had stained his skin. He paused, staring for a moment at his shoulder, still in a bit of shock about it. He wondered for a moment if these regenerative powers made him, in essence, invincible. He also wondered what that meant for aging. Would his body just continue to regenerate aging cells and keep him in his prime forever? The thought scared him a little. What would that even be like, living forever? Pulling himself out of his reverie, he found his cowboy boots and slipped them on, checking his computer screen one last time to quickly memorize the directions to the restaurant before stepping out the door.

The restaurant was a short walk away and he arrived before Bree, giving himself time to put them on the seating list. He stood outside the brick building, breathing in the cool night air, enjoying the feel of it in his lungs and trying to calm his nerves a little. He really liked her, to say the very least, and he hoped that what he was going to tell her wasn't going to muck anything up between them. He didn't want to dwell on that too much, he was nervous enough already. He closed his eyes and re-routed his train of thought to Bree, picturing her smile, her eyes. He could feel his pulse speed up and his muscles felt taut and rejuvenated. He recalled the same feeling after she had kissed his cheek earlier today. He had liked girls before, but they never made him feel this way, almost like she gave him life. It was strange, but so invigorating at the same time. Already, he almost ached for it. He was half-distracted by what he was feeling and he almost didn't notice Bree step up to him.

"Don't tell me you've been waiting so long that you have started to fall asleep," he heard her say.

Smiling, he opened his eyes to see Bree standing in front of him, arms folded across her chest and smirking playfully. She was wearing jeans and a white T-shirt with a band name on it, what band he couldn't tell with her arms covering most of it. He smiled as he admired her, not realizing that he hadn't answered her yet. She smiled, raising an eyebrow, and leaning a little towards him, letting him know that she was still waiting for a reply.

"Wha-? No, NO! Definitely not. I was just thinking, that's all."

"What's on your mind?"

The hostess at the front door called out his name to indicate that their table was ready. He offered his arm to Bree, who took it with a smile.

"I'll tell you when we're inside."

Escorting her inside and following the hostess, they were seated at a booth in the corner of the restaurant. Gesturing for her to sit down first, he positioned himself in the booth directly across the table from her, admiring her in the low light. It didn't seem to matter where they were, she always looked incredible, no matter the lighting or the situation. He lost himself in her again, not realizing that she was giving him the same expectant smirk, awaiting his response.

He sat up and cleared his throat when it became evident what was happening. "Ahem, sorry. I just, well..." He paused for a moment, trying to say what he was thinking without sounding too forward. "I think you are absolutely gorgeous."

Bree smiled and looked down, trying to conceal her blushing cheeks. She chuckled to herself before looking up. "Thank you."

Corbin worried for a second that he had been a little forward. "I apologize, as you already know, I'm not very good at this. Toss me in a combat situation, no problem. Put a beautiful girl in front of me, and I'm a wreck."

"No, you don't need to be sorry. I guess I'm not used to someone so genuine, so when you say that I'm gorgeous, I feel like you are saying it genuinely, rather than trying to butter me up for the sake of getting some action."

Corbin gave her a concerned look. "Oh no, I mean it, one hundred percent."

Bree smiled, her eyes glimmering the color of honey. "Again, thank you."

Their server arrived and took their drink orders as he handed them each a menu before stepping away, giving them time to look over the dinner selection. Corbin looked over the edge of the leather-bound paper, admiring Bree quietly as she decided what she would order, not noticing his gaze. All he could do was smile; he was just so enamored by her. He had almost forgotten to decide on what he wanted to eat before their server came back. He quickly decided and ordered after Bree had done so. As their server took their menus from them, Corbin sat forward, resting his elbows on the table.

"So, what got you into nursing?" he asked, still admiring her beauty.

Bree smiled, looking a little bashful, tucking a lock of hair behind her ear. "I had an older sister who had a lifelong illness. She was always in and out of the hospital and I just admired how much of a positive influence the nurses had on the time she spent there. I wanted to be someone who could do the same thing for people like my sister. Being in the hospital sucks, and sometimes the only thing that can make it any better is the nursing staff. I love to take care of people and show them the love and appreciation they may not always get when they are stuck in a medical facility."

As if he wasn't already so infatuated with her, listening to her reveal how caring and compassionate she is just upped the ante. His heart was abuzz for her, as well as ached for her. She spoke of her sister in the past tense which, he suspected, meant that she was no longer alive. He didn't want to ask for fear of touching on a potentially sensitive subject. Instead, he just rested his chin in his hand and watched her, listening to her every word. He had gotten lost in her for a moment before he realized that she had stopped speaking and was looking down at her water glass as she turned it with her fingertips.

"I really admire that. How caring you are. Plus, it can't be easy at all to be a nurse," he said in awe.

"It's nothing, really," Bree said with a blush.

"It definitely isn't *nothing* to the people you are helping," Corbin said, surprised at her humility. "It means *everything* to them, I'm sure. Like you said, sometimes the only thing that can make a hospital visit better is the nursing staff."

Bree blushed, smiling slightly to herself before speaking again, her forehead wrinkling as she spoke. "So, what's the story of your shoulder?" she asked somewhat hesitantly.

Corbin swallowed. He knew he had promised to explain everything when they got here; however, part of him sort of hoped that she wouldn't ask. Then again, he was stupid to think that she would just brush aside being a witness to a miraculous healing of a gunshot wound in seconds. Anyone would be beyond interested in learning how he managed that, but he had to imagine that someone with a medical background like herself would be even more curious to know how it happened. He shifted, feeling somewhat uncomfortable in his seat. He pondered for a second where he would even begin. Would he need to include being a part of SWORD? Probably not. Was he lying to her by not telling her absolutely everything, or was need-to-know something that could appease his conscience?

Bree could see that he was struggling internally. "Or is this the kind of thing that if you told me, you'd have to kill me?" She laughed a little, giving him a smile.

"Wha—? oh, NO, no it's not anything like that. It's just," he wasn't quite sure how to word it other than truthfully, "I'm not quite sure how to explain it and not sound like a total psycho."

"Try me," she responded, giving him an assuring and playful smirk.

Corbin took a deep breath and let it out slowly. "Okay, well, some of this is of a classified nature, just as a heads up, but did you happen to hear anything or see anything on the news about a crash on the military post a little while ago?"

"I don't think there was anything on the news that said something about a crash specifically, but there was a lot of talk around base regarding something in the artillery area."

"Well, it was a crash. An..." He paused, "It was an alien aircraft."

He was surprised to see that Bree's expression didn't change. He wondered why that was. Did she believe in aliens? Had she ever had an experience with them or UFO's or anything like that? Was she simply being polite and waiting until she got home to dump him and spread the word of his insanity? There was no time to dwell too much on that now.

"So, my squad and I were assigned to investigate the crash, and my team leader, Jason, and I were the ones to actually go *inside* the craft. Well, what we found was a dead alien pilot and a piece of technology. It was..." He shook his head. "I'm sorry, this all sounds insane."

Bree reached forward and rested her hand on his. "No, keep going."

Her touch sent shivers down his spine and made his heart leap. He felt a surge of confidence and assurance that he hadn't expected. He took another deep breath and went on, explaining the Marvel, meeting Uniz, and finding out about his and Jason's powers. He chronicled their attempts at using their powers, including their destruction of a bench in the Empire State Plaza just a few nights ago. He finished everything off by connecting it all to their using their powers to breach the door to get to the attempted assassin today, and how those same powers healed his shoulder. By the time he had finished, he was sure that something in what he had said would leave her wanting to run for the hills, but when he had finished speaking, there she sat, just as sanguine as she had been when they first sat down. Corbin looked around the restaurant, suddenly hoping that the wood paneling along the walls wasn't enough to make his entire confession echo around the whole building.

Everyone around them appeared to be happily engaged in their own meals and conversations, making him feel better about the situation. He looked back to Bree and shrugged.

"I apologize, that was a lot to take in. I hope you don't think I'm too crazy or anything. Honestly, hearing myself say all of it makes **me** think that I've lost my mind."

Bree just shook her head and smiled. "No, don't be sorry. Sure, that is a lot to digest, but the thing is; I don't know if there would be any other explanation that could even come close to explaining what I saw in a satisfying way. Corbin, you had a gunshot wound heal better in seconds than one would normally heal over several months. Think about it for a second; do you think you could have **made up** a story that could have made any amount of sense? If so, I'd suggest you start writing books."

Corbin chuckled, feeling better now. She did have a point. With something as outlandish as what had happened, the more logical the explanation, the crazier it sounded. However, his fantastical healing had an equally fantastical explanation, and it all just made sense together. Somehow, matching crazy with crazy just seemed... less crazy. If he had tried to explain his healing abilities as some scientific breakthrough of proper diet and exercise accelerating healing, it would sound ludicrous. However, alien technology giving him superhero powers? Of course that makes sense, right? Well, it all made sense in his mind, and it appeared that it made the same kind of sense in Bree's mind too. That was all well and good, but now he felt like he just made her an accessory in a crime. Now she was burdened with the truth that he hadn't even put upon the rest of his squad. Again, he felt like he needed to apologize.

"What do you think this all means for everyone on Earth?" Bree asked before he could offer yet another apology.

"Well, hopefully nothing," Corbin started. "I think the whole idea is to make sure this Marvel works and then figure out some way to take it back so they can go fight their fight and keep it from getting to Earth."

"What if they can't? Keep it from getting to us, that is." She looked slightly concerned.

Corbin squeezed her hand. "Then my squad and I will have a little more work to do. In the end, I'll do whatever I have to do to keep you safe."

Her demeanor softened a little. Corbin gave her a reassuring smile. Just then, their food was brought to them by their server. It all looked and smelled amazing. As he started to eat, his mind wandered to the assassination attempt. Where had that come from? The threat level had been identified as low, sure, but there was no mention of even the slightest potential for something like that. Even in instances where attacks happened in the past on him and his squad while on deployments and other operations and the threat level was considered low, there was almost always mention of talk, or even just passing rumor of ill intent, because terrorist groups never really stopped terrorizing; they just lay in waiting, plotting their next move. So, even something like Operation: Embassy would have had some sort of report about terrorist groups even passively saying they'd like to take a shot at someone at the gala, whether it was an empty threat or something more.

Maybe their intelligence wasn't as adequate as SWORD intel was? No, that couldn't be it. Captain Dickson had mentioned to him that the Secret Service had offered consultation and intelligence resources. They used a lot of the same sources, if not *all* the same intelligence that SWORD did, and those services were top-of-the-line, including Top Secret resources used by the guys in Langley. Even something as insignificant as an off-handed comment from some low-level hadji like, "Wouldn't it be nice to hit that gala?" would have received mention in intelligence reports because every single tidbit was considered a legitimate threat. That was because no one wanted to see another 9/11. When it came to terrorists and their intelligence, they had *almost* as efficient a means of knowing who was doing what and where. So, there was little chance they didn't know the peace summit was happening today and even less possibility that someone didn't say something, even in passing, regarding the event. There were leaders of every single country that they hated all in one place. It would have certainly raised a lot of interest amongst terror cells.

So, what was he to make of that? Even though there were so many high-profile delegates gathered together, this particular meeting was of no consequence to *any* enemy group? In his mind, the only other explanation for that was that the threat they stopped today wasn't from the "usual suspects." Did that mean there was a new or developing terror cell that hadn't yet popped up on the radar and that made a big move on world leaders without arousing any suspicion on the world intelligence front? No, no, that couldn't be it. Even if there wasn't solid evidence leading up to an attack, there was always something, even breadcrumbs of signs foreshadowing terror events, especially high-profile ones like the one today.

Where did that leave them? Surely every law enforcement group in the state as well as national enforcement teams were already deep into their own investigations regarding this attack, but what were they going to find? If there wasn't anything that had already come to light, especially from high-end intelligence groups, *would* there be anything? If there wasn't anything that was discovered, what would that mean? This guy wasn't some lone wolf unless he was some jilted ex-lover of the Russian woman he tried to kill but that didn't seem to make sense either. There was a connection somewhere Corbin was sure he was missing. However, whatever that connection was, he couldn't even begin to know.

"What's on your mind?" Bree asked. She had been watching him long enough to see the gears turning in his mind.

"The attack today. It doesn't add up," Corbin looked up from his food. "I'm sorry, I don't mean to bring work to dinner, as it were, but I can't shake the thought that something isn't fitting right with it all."

"What do you mean?"

Corbin explained his reasoning to her, taking her down the long train of thought he had already reviewed. He explained why he thought there was some sort of missing link and not quite being able to figure it out, and how it was now consuming his thoughts and frustrations. Bree smiled, giving him a little shrug and going back to eating her dinner.

"Maybe it has just as crazy an explanation as your powers," she said with an air of bemusement.

The idea hit him with the sensation of a bat to the back of his head. How had he not thought about that possibility until that moment? Uniz had already told him and Jason that the leader of Claw, Fizer, if he remembered the name correctly, had his eyes on taking over Earth, and part of that goal was aided by the global unrest the world was currently in. So, what better way to keep the world in turmoil, if not throw it into further chaos, than have an assassination of a world delegate during a peace summit? As far as anyone knew, a security guard from the UAE went off the rails and tried to kill a representative from Russia. If he had succeeded, that would just stoke the fire of strife with the Middle East. Additionally, it would strain the already troubled relationship between Russia and the United States because, "How dare the US let such an atrocity happen under their watch?" It was a perfect starting point for a proverbial domino effect that could potentially result in a world war. What better way to take over a planet than to swoop in and dominate it after it had taken some time to kill itself? The reason they hadn't seen any intel pop up was because they didn't have intelligence on combat forces that didn't exist to them!

"Bree, I could kiss you right now," Corbin said happily.

"Can I at least finish dinner first?" she quipped.

Corbin laughed, setting his fork down and withdrawing his phone from his pocket. He quickly dialed Jason, who answered after only two rings.

"What's up, Corbin?"

"We need to get in and interrogate that shooter as soon as possible!"

"Why? You don't think the police aren't already on that?"

"I'm sure they are, but *we* need to get some information off this guy. You and me."

"I don't think I get it. What are you trying to say?"

Corbin looked around to see if anyone appeared to be interested in what he was saying. No, thank goodness there wasn't. He cupped his hand around the microphone area of his phone, hoping to funnel his next words into his phone so only Jason could hear them.

"I think that our shooter is from Claw."

"From wha—" There was an abrupt pause. Corbin could tell that the pieces were starting to come together in Jason's mind, "I'll get in touch with Chief Tuttle and have us in there as soon as possible."

"Good idea. Send me a message when you have it all arranged. We'll bring the squad. I think it'll help in bringing them up to speed about everything."

"You got it. I'll get back to you."

The line went dead immediately afterward. Corbin slipped his phone back into his pocket, looking apologetically at Bree. "I'm sorry, I had to make sure I took care of that thought as soon as possible. Things might be a lot more serious than we thought."

Bree shook her head, smiling. "Don't be sorry. I get it, and with everything that you've told me, I understand that this could be a lot bigger than just a random assassination attempt. Do you need to leave? I totally get it if you do."

Corbin shook his head emphatically. "Oh no, definitely not. I don't want to leave, and I've got Jason looking into things, so we're good. I really appreciate your understanding and apologize that it is kind of a lousy first date."

"Well, thankfully it is the first of many dates," Bree said with a playful wink.

Corbin's heart felt like it skipped a few beats. "Do you mean..."

"You can't get rid of me that easily, especially after everything that you've told me," Bree said with a smile.

"Oh, believe me, I never had any intention of getting rid of you," Corbin started to explain. "In fact, I was hoping to ask you tonight—"

"Yes," Bree said with a grin. "Definitely yes, and not because of everything that I know now, but because of you."

He felt like he was going to hyperventilate. His breathing quickened and his heart felt like it was buzzing, rather than beating. He smiled because it was about the only thing that he could think of doing at that moment. She smiled back, her eyes resembling the color of warm amber. He felt like he could melt right then and there. She was absolutely stunning. Once again, he could feel his muscles feeling taught and ready, like he had before. Whatever she was doing to him, he welcomed it. He hadn't ever experienced anything like it. He wanted to be close to her any chance he could, even if it was as simple as sitting across from her at dinner, like he was doing now. He also wanted to hold her, to kiss her, to just feel her close to him.

After they had finished dinner, Corbin and Bree stepped outside, Bree immediately taking his hand in hers and standing close to him. He smiled at her and then looked up, surveying their surroundings. It was nearing eleven o'clock at night and most traffic, both pedestrian and automotive, had become sparse. He took advantage of the quiet moment to wrap his arms around her and hug her closely, feeling liberated now that he had gotten everything off his chest, and that she hadn't made a mad dash out the front door the moment he had. He gently kissed her forehead, breathing in the scent of her hair.

"Hey, mister, you missed," Bree said, pulling him close to kiss his lips.

It took him somewhat by surprise, but he took no issue with it. Until his lips touched hers, he never realized how much he ached for it. The feel of her soft lips, the taste of her breath, it was heavenly. He wished he could stay there, kissing her, holding her close, for eternity, but his thoughts were interrupted by the chime of his phone. He lingered, not wanting to break the kiss, but the second chiming of his phone told him he had better check it. He gently pulled back, resting his forehead on hers.

"I'm sorry, I better at least check that," he apologized, still holding her with one arm while fishing his phone out of his pocket with his other hand.

It was Jason. He had messaged him to say that they had access any time to the jail where the assassin was being detained, all they had to do was show up and they would be allowed in, no matter what the time of day. That was useful considering they would need to go in tonight seeing as they were going to be headed back home in the morning. The rest of the squad was going to be a little surly, he was sure, but he wanted them up and with him and Jason when they interrogated this guy. He sent out a group text message to the squad, telling them to get themselves ready and together so they could meet at the jail. He figured there was a good possibility that some of them would be asleep by now, so he planned to call each one of them a few minutes after he sent the message.

"I'm sorry, Bree, I've still got work to do tonight. Can I take you back to your hotel?"

"I'm staying with a friend from nursing school, but yes, I would love to have you walk me back."

"Gladly," Corbin answered, offering his arm to her, which she took with a smile.

It was only a ten-minute walk down the quiet neighborhood streets until they reached a set of stone steps leading up to a tall, brownstone home sandwiched between two identical homes. It was a stereotype of what he imagined homes looked like in Manhattan. Escorting her up the steps, they stopped just in front of the door, exchanging quiet glances. He hugged her, squeezing her affectionately and kissing her cheek.

"Have a good night, Bree. Thank you, for everything."

He felt her squeeze him in return. "Thank you, Corbin, and please, be safe. You may have superpowers, but I feel like they may also come with a weakness. Don't go finding out the hard way what that is."

He lifted his head, and she cupped his cheek in her hand. The look in her warm eyes told him that she was genuinely concerned, if not worried about him. He smiled reassuringly and kissed her softly.

"I'll be careful. I promise."

"Let me know when you get back to your hotel. I don't think I'll be able to sleep much until I know you are back safe," Bree instructed.

"Yes ma'am," Corbin answered with a smile.

Bree gave him one last kiss before opening the door and stepping inside the house. As the door closed quietly behind her, Corbin turned and gazed at the sky, which was clear and speckled with stars. As he stared at the pinpricks of light in the dark, velvety background, he noticed something he had seen before, many years ago. He was reminded of that night during Basic when he looked skyward and saw...moving stars. There they were again, but somehow, they looked closer than when he had seen them before. He didn't have to focus hard on the blips of light to see that they were moving as well as the smaller "stars" darting around and between them. He still wondered what those were but also considered the possibility that those were starships. It was an awe-inspiring thought, but also an ominous one. If they were, in fact, spaceships, that meant that they could be enemy ones closing in on

Earth in preparation to take over. He didn't want to think about it too much, because it made him feel a little nervous, but also because he needed to focus on this guy they had in jail.

Chapter Eleven

After hurrying back to the hotel, Corbin called his squad and got them mustered in his hotel room. It was after midnight now, and they each looked a little bleary-eyed, but determined and ready to work. Once he had outlined his intent to question the shooter at the local jail where he was being held, they all went downstairs to pile into a pair of taxis Corbin had called for earlier. The ride to the jail was just a twenty-minute drive from there, which drive was done in silence amongst Corbin and his squad. He was sure most, if not all of his squad was napping during the drive, a useful habit they learned in their time in the military; napping whenever possible because it may be the last time to rest for a long time. He would have gotten some shut eye himself; however, he felt too amped up, his mind darting between planning his interrogative questions and Bree. He was still floating on cloud nine after their date, realizing that he was smiling absentmindedly to himself each time he thought about her.

Arriving at their destination, they filed out of the taxis after paying their fares. They made their way up to the front gate, which was tall and topped with rows of razor wire and led into a small motor pool area with two police cruisers parked inside. Opposite the gate was the front door leading into the building itself. Corbin pressed the call button on the small box beside the gate, listening to the speaker buzz to signal the guard housed somewhere inside the building. There was a minute's pause before a voice came over the speaker, sounding gravelly and tired.

"What can I help you gentlemen with?"

"We are here to see an inmate you have here. He was involved in a shooting at the Capitol earlier today," Corbin answered.

"Right, and who are you guys?"

"We are the guys who detained him. My name is Staff-Sergeant Corbin Kent, United States Army. The men who are with me are my squad." Corbin named off the name and rank of everyone with him, looking up towards the security camera he could see that was aimed directly at them.

There was another short pause before the speaker crackled and the gravelly voice answered, "Stand back from the gate, please. I'll send some guards out."

Corbin and his squad stepped back a few steps and watched as a trio of guards came out of the building and made their way to the gate. Once they stopped at the gate, one guard called through his radio to have it open, which it did with a loud click and whirring of gears. The guards stepped out and the gate shut behind them. Once it had locked with another loud click, the guards searched each one of them, making sure they didn't have anything that was or could be used as a weapon. Once they had been cleared, the gate was opened once again and they were escorted into the motor pool area, and then inside the building once the gate had closed and secured behind them. Corbin thought about how tedious it must have been to have to have every action segmented by waiting for a door to open and then close before moving on to the next task, but he understood the necessity for the security.

Once they had been checked over a second time by another set of guards, they were led into a large atrium area amid two levels of closed and locked cells. There was a quartet of circular tables in the center of the open room, each encircled by four steel stools permanently attached to the tables. The cavernous, concrete structure echoed quietly with each step, each movement they and the correctional officers took, but it didn't seem to disturb any of the inmates as the darkened cells remained quiet and still. There was the occasional sound of snoring as Corbin and his squad stood silently in the atrium. One of the officers approached them and, judging by the Lieutenant pins on his collar and the lofty way he carried himself, must have been the guy in charge. He stepped up to Corbin, thumbs tucked in the front of his duty belt.

"You here to see Arab Andy?" he asked with a nod of his head.

"Who?" Corbin furrowed his brow, obviously not following.

"The Capitol shooter from earlier today. Lousy scrub wouldn't ever tell us his name, or anything for that matter. So, not knowing what to call him, we just call him 'Arab Andy.' He is Arabic, isn't he?"

Corbin shrugged, "All we know is he was posing as a guard for a couple of delegates from the United Arab Emirates. So, he's being tight-lipped about everything?"

"That's putting it lightly," the Lieutenant chortled. "Doesn't even tell us if he's hungry, thirsty, or if he needs to take a dump or anything. He's just been silent, sitting in his cell and staring off into the distance."

"Is it all right if we try to talk to him?"

"By all means." The Lieutenant huffed. "But don't get all bent out of shape when he doesn't say squat." He keyed the radio handset clipped to his shoulder. "Roll Arab Andy out here, will you?"

"With respect, Lieutenant," Corbin started, "is there anywhere we may be able to speak to him that is a little more private?" He looked around the atrium to acknowledge all the cells.

The Lieutenant gave Corbin a knowing look and keyed his radio again. "Scratch that, go put him in the Quiet Room."

There was an acknowledgement over the radio, and the Lieutenant jerked his head over his shoulder towards the wall behind him. There was a single door that swung open, and another correctional officer gestured towards them. They followed that officer through the door, down a long and empty hallway, and into a dead-end area that had a single door. On the door was painted "QR-1" in big block font. Peering through the small window on the door, Corbin could see that their guy was already sitting in a single chair to which he was shackled, and the chair was bolted securely to the floor. He sat silently and stared at the floor, hands resting in his lap.

"Try not to make too much of a mess," the correctional officer joked. "Otherwise, we'll have to send the cleaning bill to the Army."

Corbin didn't find it all that funny, but he smiled politely and nodded, waiting for the officer to open the door for them. As he did, he let them know that he would be just outside the door to let them out whenever they were finished. Everyone filed into the room, one by one, until the door shut behind the last of them, which happened to be Alex. As the door locked with a loud, metallic *'snap,'* the man they knew only as "Arab Andy" looked up and smirked a little when he regarded Corbin and Jason; however, he didn't say anything. Corbin stepped up to him, arms folded across his chest.

"Who are you?" he demanded.

The man shook his head slightly and scoffed. "Have you not heard? My name is Arab Andy." His dark eyes glinted with malice.

"Don't play with me, dillweed," Corbin said, slapping him on the back of the head. The man let out a quiet grunt and a sort of growl noise when he did.

"If you aren't going to tell us who you are, why don't you tell us where you are from?" Jason tried.

The man looked a little confused at first, as if he didn't seem to understand the question. Corbin had seen the look before and got the distinct feeling it was due to this guy not mentally preparing a deflection to that question. Good, if they could keep him a bit off balance, they just might be able to get some truth out of him. Corbin took a step back, Jason took a step forward, repeating his question. The man shook his head mockingly.

"Do you really think that you will get any information out of me? What makes you think that I am of any disposition to talk?"

Corbin narrowed his eyes, watching the man quietly. He sure had a formal way of speaking and, though he was no profiler, he had spoken with enough criminals and terrorists like him to know that they typically didn't speak so well. Maybe security guards from the oil-wealthy UAE were different, or maybe his suspicions were already being confirmed. The guy's dark eyes had caught his attention when he first saw him, but coupled with his speech pattern, he appeared to have a lot of similarities with Uniz. He didn't want to jump to any conclusions just yet.

"Well, it would make our job easier," Jason started, "but if you're looking to make things more difficult, my friend Corbin here doesn't mind doing things the hard way. Or even better, you see that big guy there?" Jason pointed to his brother. "He *really* likes it when you guys want to do things the hard way. You ever been knocked around by a guy his size?"

Randy flashed an evil grin and pounded his fist into his palm in the same manner a baseball player softens his glove with his fist. The man clenched his jaw, looking at Randy and then back at Jason.

"Threats of physical violence are hardly a motivating force to me," he said through his gritted teeth.

"That's fine by us," Corbin said with a shrug. "Except we don't threaten physical violence, we **promise** it."

As if on cue, Randy stepped forward, squaring up with the man in the chair. He reared back and landed a heavy punch directly to the man's torso, right in the soft spot beneath his ribs where his diaphragm would be. The punch landed with a soft but strong 'thump' and the man doubled over, wheezing, and struggling to breathe. Randy stepped back, looking satisfied. It had been quite a long time since he had been able to have a little fun in an interrogation. Corbin stepped forward, holding the man by the shoulder so he was sitting upright, still struggling to catch his breath.

"Now, as big as he is and as easy as it is for him to beat the ever-living daylights out of you, I can assure you that we can do this a lot longer than you'll be able to outlast it. Being so, I would suggest that you be a little more cooperative," Corbin explained coolly.

The man released a few more wheezing gasps before looking up at Corbin with the same venomous glare. "What makes you think that I will be more communicable after you assault me?"

"I haven't run across a man that hasn't," Corbin answered with a shrug. "It's only a matter of time until we find out. Either you start talking, or we beat you to death. Either way, it doesn't matter to me and my team, not really anyway. We stopped you from killing someone today, no one was hurt, and you're now in a box and will continue to be in one until we decide otherwise or until you die."

"And what makes you think death is an ending that frightens me?"

"I don't think it's so much the death that is the scary part; it's the way in which it comes about that can be motivating," Corbin threatened. "Once you're dead, no big deal, but we can make sure that it happens quickly or over a very, VERY long period of time."

The man swallowed. Something about what Corbin had just said didn't seem all that appealing to him. Good. He straightened up and circled the chair, taking exaggerated, heavy steps as he did so. His footsteps echoed dully against the cinderblock walls. Jason watched him with a demeanor as if he couldn't trust Corbin to maintain his composure. It was a ploy they had used countless times, their spin on the "good cop, bad cop" approach. If their prisoner was under the impression that even Jason couldn't trust what Corbin was going to do next, and was afraid of whatever it may be, then it could help motivate him to act in favor of self-preservation. The unfortunate thing about the age of information that they lived in was that even the enemy could perform a quick internet search and learn the rules that the United States military operated by in terms of the treatment of their captives. Once they knew what they could and couldn't do, it was easy to exploit it, knowing that their captors would be held responsible for their actions. However, once you broke down that protective barrier, just about everyone sang like a canary.

"So, let's try this again, shall we?" Corbin continued to circle the man. "Who are you?"

"Even if I were to tell you, it would mean nothing to you."

"And why is that? You that insignificant of a puke? Your boss doesn't even know who you are?"

"I am of a power you have never heard of, nor will you ever have the ability to repel. I lead the greatest force this planet will ever see. You may feel assured in your victory now, but saving the life of one person is hardly a victory to the retribution soon to come."

Corbin was almost completely sure of his initial suspicions now. There was no way this guy *wasn't* what he thought he was. He was annoyed at his pomposity and his being so convinced that he was going to be the victor. It really made him want to beat this guy to death just to shut him up. He closed his eyes for a split second and took a deep breath, attempting to calm his nerves, which had been riled up to a point that felt almost unbearable. When he opened them again, the man was looking right at him, the cut under his eye having reopened and now bleeding a single line of blood down his face. He was glaring at Corbin, seething and his dark eyes gleamed under the fluorescent lighting.

Just then, Corbin had an idea, "You wouldn't happen to be from the Brotherhood of the Claw now, would you?"

The man immediately went from menacing confidence to unexpected shock and surprise. His mouth slightly fell open in disbelief and the color seemed to drain from his face. He sat silently, a surprised look still on his face.

"Aha, now that I have your attention..." Corbin began to pace in front of the man, a devilish grin on his face. "Didn't think you'd run into anyone who knew who that was, did you?"

The man still didn't reply. He continued to watch Corbin, flabbergasted. In fact, everyone else in the room, except for Jason, was looking at Corbin with mixed levels of confusion. He ignored their glances at the moment, keeping his attention solely on their prisoner.

"You see, we aren't just any Joe Schmo humans here. In fact, we are aware of your intentions to take over this planet and make us fight in your war. So, what was your play at attempting to assassinate that Russian delegate? Were you looking to stir the pot and make things even worse for us before swooping in and assimilating us into your galaxy-domination plan?"

"Corbin, what are you even talking — "

"I'll explain in a second, Randy," Corbin interrupted, still watching the shackled man.

The man simply curled his lip in a silent snarl, glaring at Corbin. Corbin circled him, watching his squad members as he did. Brent and Alex looked bewildered but determined not to let it show to their captive. Randy looked a bit offended, maybe because he had been interrupted so abruptly. Corbin turned to face their prisoner, a smirk on his face.

"So, let me ask this again. Who. Are. You?" He punctuated each word with a step towards the man shackled in place. Once again, the man didn't answer, clenching his jaw and letting out a long breath through his nose.

Corbin pulled up a chair and spun it around, sitting astride it backwards, resting his arms on the chair back as he leaned forward. "Hey Jason, what would you bet this is ol', what's his name, Fizer? Yeah, that's it. What do you think?"

"I don't know, man. You think the leader of Claw would get himself captured like a useless rookie?" Jason responded, arms folded.

Again, the man's curdled look softened with surprise. He narrowed his eyes as if he were trying to size Corbin up or consider if he was bluffing. Corbin kept solid eye contact with him, letting him know that he was serious. There was a long, awkward silence as everyone just looked at each other. Brent, Randy, and Alex still looked like they didn't know what to think, Jason looked stoic, almost impassive and Corbin looked determined, fixing his gaze for most of the silence on the prisoner.

Breaking the silence, the man smiled slyly and asked, "Do you really think you can hold me here?"

"That was the general idea, until you died, or at least until we could turn you over to Uniz," Corbin answered with a tilt of his head. "I'm sure he would be really interested in having you in his possession. Why? Do you have other plans?"

"Oh, a great many," the man said with a vicious grin. "And to waste my time in this meager place is nothing more than an annoyance. I find your confidence that I am a captive here, laughable and naïve."

Corbin maintained an unaffected appearance, though his mind had begun to race. What did he mean by that? Was he already plotting something, or had he already figured out some sort of miraculous escape plan? What confidence he had in the situation was now starting to waver. Had he played his cards too soon? Did he even have the upper hand at all? Why did he suddenly feel like this whole encounter was suddenly turning against him?

"Ah, not so confident in yourself now, are you? Or did you forget that we can hear your thoughts?"

Corbin silently used every last swear word his mind could think of, including a whole bunch he made up on the fly. Part of him hoped that this guy had heard every one of them, for whatever that would have accomplished. He felt so exposed now, which wasn't good because most of the guys in this room weren't even close to aware of what was being exposed. This was absolutely **not** how he wanted this to play out. So, what was the next move?

"Can someone please explain what in the he- "

"It appears your friend has not been completely candid with you," the man cut off Randy before he could speak. "Such a shame from the squad leader as well." He shook his head reprovingly.

"Feel free to shut up," Corbin warned, pointing at the man and shooting him a hostile look.

"*You know that does nothing for someone with telepathic abilities,*" the man said to him in his mind. "*Whether you like it or not.*"

"I told you to shut up!" Corbin barked.

"Dude, he didn't even say anything," Alex pointed out.

"*It is not looking good for you, Corbin,*" he goaded.

Corbin could feel his blood boiling now. His muscles were tensed, poised to strike at any moment. Jason could see the anger building in his friend and took a step forward, raising his hand in a cautionary pose.

"Corbin, take a breath, brother. You know you don't want to get all worked up," he warned.

"*And why is that? Is our fearless leader one with a penchant for tantrums?*" the man mocked.

"*Believe me when I say that you wouldn't like what happens if you get me mad,*" Corbin thought back, making eye contact with his antagonist.

"*Hardly a threat from someone who reacts so childish,*" came the derisive telepathic response.

Corbin had had enough of this guy. He was going to shut him up any way he could. The first thought to come to his mind was the chair that he was sitting on. Standing up, he grabbed the chair back and wielded it over his head, preparing to bring it down on the man in the hopes of caving in his skull and ridding him of the smug look on his face. In a flash, he reared back and brought the chair down with blinding speed.

"Corbin, NO!" Jason bellowed.

He was going to enjoy this, the feeling of the man's head crumbling under the blow of the chair. Nothing was going to bring him more joy in that moment than to feel this guy's head smash like a watermelon under his attack. However, as the chair came down in its downward swing, there was a flash of light and something hot wrenched the chair sideways and out of Corbin's grip, sending it clattering across the floor. When he paused to look at the chair, he found that the synthetic fabrics were scorched and the aluminum frame melted and bent where something obviously superheated had struck it, causing it to come out of his hands. He looked to his right to see Jason still lunging forward, his hand outstretched and emitting a small string of smoke. The room was silent, save for the quiet sizzling of the scorched chair on the floor.

The surprise of the deflection had dispelled most of the rage that Corbin felt, but not all. Part of him felt angry that Jason had prevented him from offing their captive who now sat silently, wide-eyed. It was probably for the better that he hadn't killed this guy; that would have required quite the explanation to the authorities, but he didn't feel totally satisfied to the point that he wasn't angry. To offload the frustration he was still feeling, Corbin stepped over to the wall and punched it several times. The cinderblock cracked and then shattered from the blows, collapsing into powder and fragments on the floor, revealing the soundproof paneling behind it. The punches had split and fractured his knuckles, he could feel it, but he could also feel the bones and skin beginning to right itself. Walking back over to "Arab Andy," Corbin held up his battered knuckles to him and let him see the damage heal itself in a matter of seconds.

"Again, not something you were expecting, was it?" Corbin asked coldly.

Alex, Brent, and Randy stood silently, their expressions reflecting the surprise and confusion they collectively felt. Corbin shook his head, scolding himself for letting his emotions get the better of him and blowing everything out into the open in such a violent manner. He had hoped that he could somehow use the interrogation to bring everything to light in a more prudent manner. Well, it was definitely past that point and now he had to figure out the best way to do damage control. To be optimistic, there wasn't any beating around the bush to get to the point of their powers or the Nazecs, or any of that.

"Marvel..." was all that the man said.

"I wondered if you knew something about it. Probably the last place you figured you would find it, huh?"

"Another proverbial target you have so graciously painted upon your back," the man said in an arrogant tone.

"Or just another problem in your way of taking over this planet," Corbin returned.

The man just sneered in reply. Corbin stood up straight and flexed his hands, his knuckles fully healed. He walked over to the door and pounded loudly on it several times to signal to the guard in the hallway that they were finished. There were several loud clicks to indicate the door being unlocked before it swung open slowly, being guided by a correctional officer.

"We're done here. Thank you for letting us question this guy," Corbin said to the guard as he stepped out, followed by Jason and slowly by Randy, Alex, and Brent. The guard locked the door behind them, escorting them back the way they came, all the way to the front door. From there, the trio of guards who had escorted them in checked them one last time before taking them outside and finally through the perimeter gate. They exchanged courteous farewells before the guards disappeared back inside the building.

"Somebody want to explain what exactly happened in there?!" Randy sounded borderline irate.

Corbin looked at Jason with an expression that said, "You want to start, or do you want me to?" Jason gestured to him to go ahead. Starting with the night of the crash investigation, he relayed everything that had happened, sparing no detail. As he spoke, he could see that Brent and Alex were connecting a few dots in their minds, probably to things they had noticed that may have seemed a bit off. Randy stood quietly, arms folded and looking...well, Corbin couldn't really tell. If he had to guess, he would have said that Randy looked kind of annoyed. If that were the case, he understood. This was a **lot** of information that he and Jason had withheld from him over a considerable amount of time. He wondered if Randy felt betrayed, and if he did, he understood. They had served together for years and had been candid with each other all that time, so something like this, as good of intentions as he and Jason had in keeping it secret, could feel like a betrayal.

After he had finished, Corbin looked at his friends and shrugged. "And that's it. You're all read into the situation now. I'm sorry we didn't tell you guys about this sooner. I just didn't really know how to."

"That...is a lot to take in," Brent said, letting out a long sigh. Brent was always pretty level-headed. Most people just referred to him as, "chill." It was a quality that Corbin envied. Brent could be in the middle of a firefight, or lazily watching a trivia show in his room, and his affect was the same.

"To say the least," Corbin said apologetically. "What do you guys think of it all?"

"Well, that's about the best that I have, at the moment," Brent answered. "I'm sure a couple of nights' sleep will stir up some more questions."

Corbin laughed, "Keep me posted. Jason and I will be happy to answer anything that comes up." He turned to Alex next, who looked surprised, but also intrigued.

"So, you mean to tell me that you have been pretty much superheroes all this time and you haven't been running some, like, side gigs or something to make some extra cash? I mean, dude, you smashed a cement wall like it was nothing, and don't even get me started on Jason doing some straight-up Street Fighter stuff!"

Everyone chuckled. Corbin shook his head with a grin. Good ol' Alex. He never had to worry about him. He was a good friend, a great soldier, and down for anything. He had always been the same goof Corbin remembered from the bus ride to Basic, sharing a box of Teddy Grahams he had smuggled along for the trip, so he knew that comment about a "side gig" was both a joke and a semi-serious suggestion.

Lastly, Corbin regarded Randy. He still stood, arms folded across his chest, looking a little...well, he still wasn't sure. The shadows from the dim street lighting around the parking lot concealed his expression, and his stance was rigid and impassive, but he couldn't tell what emotion that reflected. He took a step closer to him, and he didn't move. He could feel his gaze on him and his gut told him that Randy didn't seem too pleased.

"Randy...what's on your mind?" Corbin questioned cautiously.

There was a long silence, each passing second making Corbin feel progressively insecure. Randy could be a tough nut to crack sometimes. His hardened build and stature reflected his sometimes-harder disposition. Corbin had nearly grown accustomed to the quiet to the point when Randy responded, it almost startled him.

"You couldn't have let us in on your little secret before now? Did you plan on telling us at all, or did your little demonstration in there force your hand?" He sounded sarcastic but also a bit resentful.

"Come on, Randy," Corbin started, "it's not like that. I just...didn't know how to tell you guys. And don't hold anything against your brother; he was just acting under my orders. I was planning on explaining all this to you tonight, but I just hadn't worked out all the details on how I was going to do it. Sure, what happened in there did kind of force a confession, so to speak, but it didn't force something that wasn't already going to happen.

"I worried about how we were going to tell you all about this, especially the more everything seemed to get more complicated. I didn't want you guys to think we were a couple of crazies, but each time something new happened, I worried more about you guys feeling like we lied to you or betrayed you or something like that."

Randy's shadowy expression appeared to soften a little. His rigid stance slackened slightly, and his arms dropped to his sides. "You do realize that even with what happened in there, everything you told us still sounds pretty crazy, right?" Corbin could hear the hint of a smile in that question.

"Oh, believe me, I've spent every moment since the crash trying to convince myself that I'm *not* losing my mind."

Randy chuckled and he and Corbin embraced in a brotherly hug. Corbin was relieved; his friends hadn't immediately assumed he and Jason were nuts, and they all seemed to forgive them for keeping them in the dark for as long as they had. He felt lighter, almost physically, now that the weight of their secret had been off-loaded. As they made their way to the curb along the main road in front of the jail, Corbin phoned for a couple of taxis to come get them. Within minutes, they had been dispatched and arrived, the five friends piling into the vehicles, laughing and joking as if nothing out of the ordinary had happened.

Back in his hotel room, Corbin didn't even bother to change into anything comfortable, he just kicked off his boots and flopped onto the bed. Turning over, he emptied the items in his pockets onto the bedside table, pausing for a moment to send a message to Bree to let her know that he was back safe in his room and wishing her a good night. He didn't expect a response, considering the ungodly hour that he was texting her. He figured she would see the message when she woke up and know that he was okay. Much to his surprise, he received a text back within a minute or two, telling him she was glad he was back safe, and to sleep well, with a heart symbol at the end. He didn't know exactly why, but the heart especially made him smile just before he dozed off.

Chapter Twelve

"You haven't told Captain Dickson about any of this?" Brent queried, picking up a case of ammunition with a grunt.

"No, noooooooooo," Corbin answered, drawing out the second "no" with an exaggerated shake of his head. "Nothing against Dickson, but I know both Jason and I didn't want to become some Area 51 lab experiment or something."

He secured six magazines filled with rounds into the pouches on the front of his vest and stepped away from the ammunition booth positioned at the head of more than twenty outdoor shooting lanes. It was a "range day," for Charlie Three-Three, and they were to spend most, if not the entire day honing their shooting skills on the assorted shooting lanes ranging from long range, rifle, pistol, and even machine gun.

Randy was putting miles on his M240B while Jason and Alex were having a friendly competition with each other on a pistol lane. Brent and Corbin had decided that they would practice as a sniper team, with Corbin spotting and taking opportunities sporadically to fire his M4 in simulated cover and support situations. The plan was to have Randy come over after he had finished with some solo practice and fire his weapon right next to Brent while he engaged targets in order to practice his composure and marksmanship in a firefight.

"What do you think ever happened to that alien body you guys pulled from the wreck?" Brent wondered aloud, setting his ammo box down next to his massive CheyTac M200 sniper rifle. This weapon system was for situations where Brent didn't go anywhere for a while. With his M110, he had the mobility of an assault rifle but the accuracy of a sniper system. However, the M200 was a big rifle firing a big bullet, meant for camping out in a hide for extended periods of time. It fired the .408 CheyTac, which was essentially a .50 BMG round that had been souped up and trimmed so it would fly further and hit harder. Brent, with the help of the armory staff, had developed a specific powder load based on the countless hours he had spent on the rifle. Corbin was fairly certain these rounds could practically vaporize an elephant from two miles away.

"If what Dickson said was anything to go off of, SWORD probably sent it off to Area 51," Corbin answered as he looked over his M4.

Brent's eyes nearly bugged out of his head. "Are you serious?!"

Corbin lifted his shoulders in a guessing gesture. "He had mentioned something about having Air Force guys from Nevada come take a look at it."

Brent gave him a surprised look. Corbin just nodded. Brent rolled out his shooter's mat on the ground in front of the weathered wood table and set himself down behind his rifle. Corbin loaded his M4, placing it on the ground beside him as he lay prone to the right of Brent, setting up a spotting scope and making sure his rifle was propped on some sandbags. He opened the ammunition box and handed Brent a fistful of the behemoth rounds, which was only about five. Brent pulled back the bolt on his rifle, dropped the box magazine, and began to load the rounds Corbin had given him into the magazine.

"You think they'd tell us anything about that alien or what happened to it, or its ship?" Brent pushed the rifle bolt back into place, seating the first round into the chamber. He then flipped open the covers on his optic and peered through it.

"Probably not," Corbin answered, looking down the range with his spotting scope, lasering the distance of the first target. "I'm sure there are people far smarter than me and getting paid more than all of us poking and prodding that thing. Let's start with the target at eight hundred meters."

Brent acquired the target, adjusting his scope a click or two. Corbin drew a little sketch of the target, noting its distance, in a little notebook where he had begun to draw a diagram of the range to map out the targets. Once he had made the note, he re-acquired the target in his spotting scope. It was a life-size mannequin-type figure, made of hard plastic and filled with sand to give it the approximate weight of a real human. There was a short pause before Brent spoke again.

"On target."

"Send it," Corbin said, keeping his eye on the mannequin.

Shortly after giving the word, there was an earth-shaking *"BOOM,"* and dust was kicked up all around them. Corbin was always startled by the first shot, never fully accustomed to how loud and concussive Brent's weapon was. He watched the round in his spotting scope, seeing the telltale vapor trail marking the bullet's flight path, which was a long arc that mimicked the arch of a ball being thrown. The round impacted the chest of the target on a downward angle, blasting a massive hole in the front of it and spilling sand like dusty-colored blood. Once the sand and dust cleared, there was a volleyball-sized hole in the target's chest.

"Hit, center mass," Corbin reported.

Brent racked the bolt back, cycling the next round into the chamber. "So, when is the next time you are meeting up with that Uniz guy?"

Corbin righted himself and shifted behind the spotting scope, finding the next target for Brent to engage. "I'm not entirely sure. We hadn't set up anything in advance. It was sort of a 'We'll see you later,' sort of a thing. I would venture a guess that he has gotten word of the guy we tagged at the Capitol, so I bet it's only a matter of time until he shows up again. Mortar nest, twelve hundred meters, three men."

There was a pause, and then, "On target."

"Fire at will," Corbin uttered, his eyes on the mannequin targets huddled behind sandbags around a 160 mm mortar tube.

Another quiet moment, Corbin knew Brent was acquiring his first target and adjusting his aim to compensate for bullet drop, wind, et cetera. He knew the moment Brent was about to fire when he heard him let out a long, quiet breath before squeezing the trigger. There was another ground-rattling report from his rifle, the vapor trail, and the inevitable impact on the first mannequin, the one in the center, and the telltale explosion of dust and plastic debris. Corbin called the hit, and Brent was already racking the next round into place and aiming at the next target. He dispatched this one with another perfectly placed shot to the chest, blasting a gigantic hole in it and knocking it completely to the ground. The final target was nearly blown entirely in half as the round struck it just below the navel, ripping a hole big enough to only leave a narrow strip of plastic. The torso of the target wobbled and then slumped downward, hanging by the scrap of material still left intact.

"Yank the trigger a bit on that one?" Corbin asked, eyebrows raised.

"Nah, he was just looking at me funny," Brent jested, pulling back on his rifle's bolt, leaving it in an open position.

Corbin laughed, shaking his head slightly. At that distance, an enemy combatant wouldn't even know they were there, let alone be able to look at them. He recalled several occasions where he had been spotting for Brent while on deployment and seeing the looks of panicked surprise on the faces of other enemies when they saw their buddy suddenly burst into a cloud of red mist as if he had spontaneously detonated. It was morbidly satisfying to him to remember how it felt knowing that they had destroyed one enemy physically and obliterated his friends psychologically with one well-placed bullet.

"Speaking of which, we've got a pair of guys in a car about a hundred meters out. Care to give me some cover while I reload?" Brent suggested.

"I'm on it," Corbin said as he grabbed his rifle, propping himself up on his elbows and taking aim through his ACOG sight.

The targets were mannequin torsos positioned in the front seats of an old, shot-out sedan. The car was facing toward them as if driving directly at them with a vehicle-borne IED inside. They had seen this situation plenty of times overseas. Taking a moment to assess the targets, Corbin then chose to start with the passenger, firing a pair of shots that impacted in the chest and neck of the target. Quickly acquiring the driver, he fired another controlled pair of rounds that struck the driver just below the left eye and in the mouth. He could see sand trickling from the holes left by the bullet impacts, a macabre confirmation that his shots were effective hits.

"Got 'em," Corbin stated as he switched his M4 to "safe" and placed it back down beside him.

"Thank you," Brent said with a smile as he seated his freshly reloaded magazine back into his rifle and slid the bolt forward, loading his next round.

As Corbin repositioned himself behind his spotting scope, his cell phone buzzed in his pocket. He gestured to Brent to give him a second as he pulled out his phone and saw that he had a new text message from...it didn't have a sender's phone number listed. Normally, this would have been a point of concern, however, he immediately thought of the similar situation with an email he had received. The text read:

Corbin,

Recent developments have accelerated our need to train you and Jason more aggressively. If you will kindly meet at our previous location of rendezvous this evening when your daily duties have been completed?

-Uniz

Corbin took a short moment to forward the message to Jason before returning his phone to his pocket. Brent eyed him for a moment as if waiting for an explanation the way a teacher would if they were to catch one of their students doing the same thing. Corbin got behind the spotting scope again, scanning for the next target to call out for Brent.

"Uniz," he started, not looking away from his optic. "He wants to meet up with Jason and me tonight to train."

"Kind of makes you wonder if he can hear us or something," Brent said with a short laugh.

"Truthfully, I don't think that would surprise me if they could." Corbin looked skyward as if to check for some airborne surveillance device or something like that. Granted, if it wasn't for the "good guys" keeping in contact with him in such an enigmatic way, he would probably feel a bit more uneasy, but he felt like he could trust Uniz and the Nazecs. Nevertheless, there was that natural feeling of unease, not being one hundred percent aware of how his alien counterparts managed to communicate with him in such a conventional, but not-so-conventional way.

"In any case," Corbin said, looking back at Brent, "we are going to meet up tonight and work on our abilities. You want to tag along? Could be fun."

Brent gave a little shrug while still looking down his scope. "Maybe. I might have a few questions for Uniz myself."

"Just let me know. We are headed out after we are released today."

"Will do."

That evening, Corbin stood next to his jeep and waited. He had extended an invitation to everyone in his squad to come to this meeting. Now that they were all in the loop, it seemed only fair to offer them a chance to join him and Jason whenever it involved the Marvel, Nazecs, et cetera. Randy had declined the invitation, saying he had slept poorly the night before and wanted to get to bed at an earlier hour to try to recoup the lost sleep. Brent and Alex had been somewhat noncommittal when he had originally asked them, but neither of them had given him a resolute "no," so he still waited to see if they would tag along. Jason came out of the barracks building, followed by Alex and Brent. He could hear part of their conversation as they approached.

"You don't think Corbin is invincible or something like that, do you? I mean, so far, he has healed from everything including getting shot."

"I'm not in any hurry to put that theory to any extensive tests," Corbin called out to Alex as they got closer. "So don't get any wild ideas about shooting me in the face or something and seeing if it grows back."

"Aw, well go ahead and take away all my fun," Alex joked.

They chuckled together as they piled into Corbin's jeep and headed off to their meeting place at the old farm. Alex and Brent were surprised at the existence of it, having never noticed it in their travels outside the base. Corbin parked on the far side of the barn just like before, shutting off the engine and sitting back in his seat, letting out a short sigh.

"So, what do we do now, blow a whistle or something?" Alex asked with a slight tone of jest in his voice.

"Ha, no, we just wait. Uniz will be here at any moment," Corbin answered, keeping his eyes forward.

"What's he going to do, just pop out of thin air or something?"

"Yeah, that's pretty much how it happens, right, Jason?"

Jason nodded in agreement. "We don't know how it works, and we haven't bothered to ask, but yeah, he just kind of appears out of nowhere."

"And...you guys are just okay with that?"

"Well, it's not the craziest thing we've seen, as of late," Corbin said matter-of-factly.

Alex looked like he was about to say something else, but he nodded with an accepting expression on his face. Never mind something that could be replicated as a magician's parlor trick; he had seen his friends pull off some straight comic-book-type-stuff like healing instantly from gunshot wounds and shooting fireballs like a freaking wizard or something. As he thought about his question, he realized how silly it sounded compared to what he had already witnessed firsthand.

"When you mention 'crazy,' it would denote an idea of abnormal mental status whereas all you have witnessed would better characterize as extraordinary. My grasp on your language still appears to require additional learning," Uniz said from beside the jeep, startling Alex and Brent so badly that they both physically jumped in their seats.

Corbin let out a soft chuckle at their reaction. "It's a lot of slang, Uniz, that's for sure. We use a lot of words that way rather than their original meaning. I'd say it's more an understanding of context." He climbed out of the driver's seat and moved over to Uniz to shake his hand.

"I see...A concept I will need to acquire additional knowledge of."

"Just spend enough time around us, and I bet you'll understand it in no time," Jason assured, having exited the jeep as well.

"That is something that I wish to discuss with you as part of our training this evening. As a matter of fact, there is a great deal I wish to speak with you about." Uniz glanced quickly at Brent and Alex. "It appears you have spoken with the rest of your friends regarding Codename: Marvel?"

Corbin nodded. "It was only a matter of time until they found out anyway, so Jason and I explained everything to the rest of our squad. That is Alex, and that's Brent. Our last squad mate, Randy, is at home resting. Oh, and I also told my girlfriend, Bree."

Uniz considered the newcomers for a short moment before looking back to Corbin. "You do realize that their knowledge of this situation would mean that they are now involved?"

He had considered that whoever knew was bound to be involved, but he suddenly worried about Bree. How involved would she be? Was it a bad idea to have confided in her? Regardless, he would do everything he could to keep her safe.

"I wouldn't have it any other way. These guys are my brothers, and I trust them, and you can, too."

Uniz looked befuddled for a moment, but quickly appeared to understand, "Considering there is no familial relation between any of you within the squad outside of Jason and his brother, I believe this is another of your 'slang,' as you explained."

"See, you're catching on already," Corbin said with a smile, patting Uniz on the shoulder roughly. "Now, what was it that you wanted to talk to us about? It sounds like you have quite a bit to tell us. Oh, Alex, Brent, you can get out of the car if you want."

The two of them slowly slid out of the back of the jeep, watching Uniz with an air of caution as they did. Uniz extended his hand to them for a handshake.

"I am Uniz, General of the Nazec Unified Military."

"This guy looks pretty human to me," Alex said, tentatively shaking Uniz's hand.

"Yes, well a disguise is necessary to keep this situation covert. Additionally, my assumptions have led me to believe that showing my true appearance to the general public could result in hostility towards me. Humans in general seem to have difficulty with beings that do not look like them."

Brent shook Uniz's hand in turn after Alex. It felt like a little bit of a dig at humans; however, he wasn't wrong. Humanity historically had issues with integrating and getting along with others who didn't look the same as them, and that was with other humans. Sure, humankind had come a very long way from the times of colonization, segregation, and stuff like that, but there was a lot of inexperience with alien species, and Brent felt sure that inexperience would help history repeat itself towards the Nazecs.

"Your thoughts are correlative to my concerns regarding the subject.

As such, we endeavor to take precautions to blend in with the human population."

Brent looked surprised. "Did he just read my mind?"

"Oh, yeah, they are telepathic, that's how they communicate. It's just kind of a byproduct of speaking that way," Corbin said, sounding completely unbothered by it.

"So, what keeps them from just reading our minds all the time?"

"Human communication is primarily a verbal exchange. Your communication can be regulated to intended recipients by means of adjusting your volume, physical proximity to others, and other such controls. Nazec communication, which is telepathic, has similar controls to designate the recipient of our communication. They simply require practice and acclamation much like yours. At the basest level, there is nothing that can keep me from hearing your thoughts, that is, until you are able to master the methodology of Nazec communication. However, I do respect the perceived privacy of your thoughts, and I endeavor not to listen unless it pertains to what we are conversing about. My apologies if this unnerves you."

Brent didn't immediately look placated. He shifted his stance a little as if still somewhat uncomfortable with the idea of being in the presence of a telepath. Alex, much like himself, looked intrigued. As strange as the thought may be that he was in the presence of not only an alien, but one who could change his appearance and read minds, it didn't seem to deter him. Corbin could practically hear him in his mind saying, "Cool, man!"

Uniz cleared his throat, and Corbin shifted his focus to him, "What was it that you wanted to talk to us about?"

Uniz seemed to hesitate for a moment as if to formulate where to begin. He straightened his posture and clasped his hands behind his back as he spoke, "The individual you captured during your assignment at the State Capitol."

"What about him?" Corbin asked cautiously.

"He was who you suspected he was. Fizer had attempted to do just as we had forecasted. His attempt on the delegate's life was an attempt to create further unrest and war on Earth in hopes of weakening mankind's defenses against extraplanetary invasion."

Corbin's heart felt like it jumped into his throat hard enough to puke it up. He could feel the color drain from his face as he swallowed in an attempt to push the sensation down into his chest. His mind rattled off every curse he knew, to which Uniz gave a concerned and puzzled look.

"Judging by your reaction, I would conclude that this revelation has invoked mixed feelings in your mind. Please accept my apology as I continue to bear undesired news. In addition to that, our resources have discovered that he has escaped his custody."

Corbin felt almost like reality was beginning to distort around him. Despite everything he and his friends had experienced so far, there was still a skeptical part of his mind that held onto the hope that this was all somehow a joke, a dream, or something that made it all fake. Somehow, this piece of his mind considered, there was a perfectly reasonable explanation for everything that would make it all not real. His rational thoughts knew there was no way that was possible, but somehow his mind was surprised all the same. The gravity of the situation, a situation he had willingly included his friends and Bree in, felt like it had just begun to weigh on him, almost as if an invisible anchor around his neck had finally started to lower. He suddenly thought about what Fizer had said to him that night at the prison. He had indeed painted a target on his back, which target also now hung on each person he loved and cared for the most.

"Your concerns are valid, Corbin," Uniz stated, interrupting his thoughts. "Following your revealing that you and Jason possess the powers of code-name: Marvel, Fizer has refocused his efforts towards capturing or even killing you in order to find a way to make the technology his own. It has now become a race to see who can develop a means of extraction first."

"Is killing us a legitimate way they could get the powers from us?" Jason asked, looking somewhat concerned.

Uniz simply offered a shrug. "As our knowledge of the possibility of extraction is in its infancy, the only answer I may offer is that it *could* be a legitimate means of extraction. As you and Corbin are the sole holders of the only fully functional prototype, our capabilities of testing extraction theories are very limited. Additionally, we are still monitoring your use of the powers to see their efficacy in combat."

"Well, we've used them a few times successfully," Corbin offered. "Haven't those been good enough?"

Uniz shook his head, looking apologetic. "Unfortunately, those instances were not in true combat situations. Our endeavor is to test the efficacy of codename: Marvel in combat, after the recipients have been properly trained to utilize their powers on command, not simply in times of heightened emotion. We wish to test its ability to be *controlled* as well as utilized."

Corbin was starting to feel like he was trapped. He regretted having forced Jason to use his powers to stop him from using his own against Fizer. He wondered what would have happened if he had been allowed to kill him. Would that have just ended this whole war between the Nazecs and Claw, or would someone just replace him? He was feeling more convinced that what he had done at the prison was a terrible idea. Well, there wasn't anything he could do to go back on it now, so it was time to get trained up and prepare to face the music.

"Are there any suspicions on how Fizer plans to try to get a hold of us?" Corbin asked.

"We do not know, nor can we be specifically sure what his plans are at this time, apart from the fact that you and Jason are now a high priority to him."

Corbin let out a sigh that displayed his feelings of concern. "Well, we better train up so we can stand a chance against Fizer and whatever he is planning."

Uniz gestured to the barn where they had practiced previously. Everyone followed him into the dusty structure, Alex and Brent twisting their faces a bit when they first smelled the old, dilapidated barn. The vintage tractor was still where they had left it, buckled and shifted from the impact of Corbin's strike. Alex looked at the vehicle and pointed at it, giving Corbin a look as if to say, "Was that you?" Corbin just nodded, feeling a little bashful as he recalled the situation that accomplished that feat. Uniz stood in front of the four of them, hardly even regarding the damaged tractor behind him.

"As I am sure you recall, you were able to make considerable progress in actuating your powers here, and I hope to expand on that progress to the level where you can use your abilities on command. Naturally, we do not wish these powers to be solely dependent on whether you can get angry or startled enough to use them, especially in the case of a combat environment."

Alex raised his hand. "So, any chance the rest of us can end up with powers?"

Corbin shot him a reproving look. "Dude, are you serious?"

Brent and Jason also looked at Alex in similar fashion and Alex just shrugged. "What? You don't think Brent, Randy and I don't want a piece of that? I'd kill for the ability to shoot lasers out of my eyes or something like that."

Uniz looked thoroughly perplexed at Alex's comment. "Would it be safe to assume that this is another one of those instances where the context of your statement is more indicative of your intent rather than the literal meaning of your words? 'Slang,' as Corbin termed it?"

"What? Oh, yeah, totally. I wouldn't actually kill anyone for the chance to have powers like Corbin and Jason." Alex chuckled.

Uniz's gaze lingered on Alex for a moment, one eyebrow raised, as if he were still trying to figure something out in his mind. He smirked, shook his head subtly, and said, "Unfortunately, the only fully operational prototype of Codename: Marvel has been assimilated into your friends."

"Selfish jerks," Alex joked. "Didn't want to share the fun."

Corbin laughed and slugged his friend in the shoulder in a playful manner. Uniz again appeared to not quite understand Alex's comment and Corbin's gesture but took less time to smile a little and appear to understand the context. Corbin wondered if being able to hear their thoughts made it a little easier to comprehend the intent of their conversations. Part of him wondered what a conversation would be like between Nazecs. With the apparent absence of slang and sarcasm in their communication, how would they even keep a conversation interesting?

"Jason, I would like to begin with you this time," Uniz started. "Your apparent ability to manipulate flame could prove to be immensely effective in combat."

"It could also cook us all real quick in *this* place," Brent observed, looking around the barn.

"Ah, yes, the combustible nature of this structure does appear to be an apparent hazard. Perhaps you and Alex can find some means of countermeasure should the flames get uncontrollable?"

Brent and Alex looked at each other and immediately set out to find whatever they could get their hands on to fight an unintentional fire. They were able to rustle up a few old, dented metal buckets and a hose hooked up to a spigot that still had water running to it. They set the buckets down and filled them with the hose before tossing the hose aside, leaving the water running. They were probably thinking the same thing that Corbin was that the barn would be even harder to burn down if it were soggy. They would just have to make sure to watch their footing as the puddle grew larger.

"Jason, if you will," Uniz said, gesturing for Jason to stand a few feet in front of him. Jason stepped forward, glancing around as if he were still a little nervous about burning the barn down on top of them.

Corbin took position next to Alex and Brent, near the buckets of water and the running hose. He looked around the barn as well, analyzing possible alternative escape routes just in case something bad happened and they couldn't get out via the main door. He then thought to himself that if worse came to worse, he could use his powers to just smash through a wall to get everyone out. He was certain he'd be feeling heightened emotions enough to use them if the whole barn was aflame. Even thinking of the possibility made him feel a little tense and he clenched his fists as he turned his attention back to Jason and Uniz. Uniz stood with his hands clasped in front of him as he addressed Jason.

"Jason, are you able to remember the emotions you have felt each time you have used your powers?"

Jason shrugged a little. "Yeah, I can remember kind of how I felt each time. I mean, just about every time was a bit of a surprise when it happened, so I can't remember *exactly* what I was feeling at the moment."

"That is understandable. In moments of surprise, it is difficult to consciously catalog what your emotions are as your defensive reactions and adrenaline are dominating your senses. Our thoughts and emotions require a bridge, as it were, between their mental state to their being translated into actions. In cases of surprise or danger, this bridge is created subconsciously as your body initiates what you refer to as your 'fight-or-flight response.' It is the way your body preserves your safety in a split-second reaction when the time it would take to analyze the situation and act consciously could result in your injury or death.

"It is my endeavor to assist you in creating a voluntary bridge between your emotions, and inevitably your abilities, and your physical capability to use them. You have experienced this ability in limited capacity while you were in Albany. Is this correct?".

Jason glanced back at Corbin before answering, "Yeah, a couple of times. I lit a bench on fire after Corbin scared the crap out of me, and I tried to melt a doorknob and lock too. I don't think I did all that great on the doorknob though, and that was the time I was trying to use my abilities voluntarily."

Uniz nodded silently, "The fact that you were able to use your powers in any degree voluntarily despite having little to no formal training is a feat you should be proud of. What was it that you did to call upon your abilities?"

"I don't know, I just— I just tried to focus hard on what I wanted my powers to do, which was to melt a doorknob in order to gain access to the office Fizer was hiding in. It seemed to help, but not a whole lot. I guess I wasn't feeling much emotion while I was doing it?"

"Nevertheless, your efforts produced some positive effects. You were able to damage the doorknob with your abilities, were you not?"

"He was. There was no way he did what he did to that doorknob other than with his powers," Corbin assured, for Jason's sake. Jason glanced back at Corbin with a grateful expression. Corbin nodded silently with a grin. Uniz seemed to notice their inaudible exchange and appeared pleased.

"The connection you two share is quite fascinating. It is as strong as a familial bond, but there is a factor that appears to make it deeper, more meaningful. Is it customary for humans to share bonds of this caliber in situations where they are not of family relation?"

"I think that it is when we, as humans, have gone through as much crap together as we have. If you ask me, Jason and everyone in my squad are more brothers to me than my actual siblings," Corbin answered, looking to his friends.

Uniz, again, looked somewhat confused by what Corbin had said, his brow furrowed. It was probably in connection to him using slang again. His expression changed shortly to one of understanding as if he had found the answer he was looking for in the silence.

"The connection you have developed with your friends is borne from the struggles you have endured during your time together," Uniz suggested in a tone that sounded more like a question.

"It's a pretty simple way to put it, but yes. There isn't anyone I feel like I can trust more than these guys."

"Aw, stop, you're gonna make me cry," Alex joked.

"I'll give you something to cry about," Corbin kidded in return, giving him a slug in the shoulder in jest.

Jason looked back towards Uniz, smiling now and looking a little more confident in himself. If he could read his mind, Corbin was sure that he was thinking almost the exact same thing that he was. This was all feeling far more daunting now that the need to learn their powers was an urgent one. It had gone from a feeling of "Learn at your own pace" to being thrown into the ocean and told "Sink or swim, buddy, and you better hurry up because a real big wave is coming!"

"Now, Jason, if you will indulge me. Concentrate on what you can remember feeling each time you have been able to successfully use your powers."

Jason closed his eyes and drew in a long breath. His forehead wrinkled a little as he concentrated, his breathing deep and controlled and his eyes darting back and forth behind his eyelids. Uniz watched him intently, silent, his face a neutral expression. Corbin peeked over at Brent and Alex, noticing how silent they were, out of respect for Jason or out of curiosity, he wasn't sure. Inwardly, he prayed that Jason would find the connection he needed to make this all work. He felt like time was a precious commodity that they now had even less of and he yearned for Jason to find success, for his sake, as well as everyone else.

That was when he noticed what looked like a red-orange glow emitting from within Jason's clenched fists. At first, he wasn't sure if he was actually seeing it, or if his mind was somehow playing tricks on him, but as he focused more on it, he could see that he wasn't imagining things. He smiled to himself as he kept silent; he didn't want to throw Jason off in any way.

"Good, very good, Jason," Uniz said calmly and quietly, sounding like a hypnotist. "Hold onto what you have, those thoughts, those feelings, and now see if you can connect them to your powers. Think of how you want to use them, what you want to do with them."

With his head bowed and his eyes still closed, Jason lifted his right hand and flexed his fingers in a half-fist. A fireball the size of a baseball suddenly ignited with a startlingly loud *"fwoosh"* sound, the blaze hovering just an inch above his palm. Alex stepped back, clearly a little nervous, and Brent took a half-step towards one of the water buckets. Corbin stood his ground, fascinated by what he was seeing and excited for the success of his friend. Uniz held up one hand towards Alex and Brent while still watching Jason.

"Remain calm. Your friend is in complete control of his actions. I can sense it," he assured them.

Everyone stood still, watching Jason as his hand slowly rotated, the ball of flame staying suspended above his palm as if it were being held in place. To Corbin, it was oddly hypnotizing to watch Jason manipulate it, almost like watching a fire dancer. He knew it was all thanks to the powers of the Marvel, but part of his mind still couldn't fathom what he was seeing. Sure, he had seen Jason use his powers before, but never in such a controlled, almost flawless manner.

"Jason, try to use what you are holding. Throw it. Use it as an attack toward something," Uniz instructed.

In a single motion, Jason spun around and threw the fireball, giving Brent and Corbin a split second to dive out of the way. As the fireball flew past him, Corbin could feel the heat radiating off it as it missed him by no more than a foot and burst into an inferno in an old pile of hay behind him. He took a quick moment to look at his friend and saw that not only did his fists glow as if they were ablaze, but his eyes glowed a red-orange of embers. Unnerving to say the least, but exciting to see. At the same moment, Alex and Brent sprang into action, extinguishing the flames that were quickly spreading.

Jason let out a chuckle, looking at his glowing hands. "No freaking way. This is awesome!" He maneuvered his hands in a manner that resembled an interpretive dance as he stared at his palms and admired how they appeared to flicker like torches being spun.

Uniz looked pleased, standing silently, hands customarily clasped in front of him. "This is very pleasing to see, Jason. You appear to have been able to harness the sensation of your emotions in such a way that you can call upon them when you desire."

Jason chuckled excitedly as he conjured another fireball and tossed it between his hands like a boy with a ball he was about to throw to his father. He glanced towards one of the buckets that Brent and Alex hadn't used to put out the hay pile, still full of tepid, murky water. He smirked slightly before tossing the fireball into it, a loud hissing sound and a pillar of steam coming from the bucket as the water vaporized as it cooled the blazing projectile. When the steam had finally fizzled out, there was only a thin layer of water at the bottom of the pail, still bubbling from the remaining heat.

"Whoa, those things pack some heat," Alex admired.

"I can't imagine what it would be like if it hit an enemy," Brent said, blowing out a breath of air as he wiped sweat from his forehead.

Corbin made a sort of grimaced look as he smiled. "Heaven help anyone who ends up on the receiving end of one of those."

When he looked back towards Jason, he saw that he was already trying something different. Both of his hands were held out in front of him, forming a larger ball of flame, this time about the size of a basketball. Brent was already looking more nervous as he watched the fiery orb grow, taking a hold of the worn rubber hose that still burbled water. Jason laughed as he held the large flaming ball in both hands, his eyes flickering like candles in a breeze.

"Relax Brent, it's not like I'm going to try to play catch with you or anything."

"Well, I'm not worried about that, but that is quite a lot of fire in probably the biggest pile of kindling I've ever been standing inside," Brent said as he looked around the old barn. "We'd probably have less than a split second to get out of here if you hit the wrong thing in here."

Jason simply shrugged, giving a devilish grin that looked especially true to the word since he looked like he was holding fire while on fire internally. Uniz stepped forward, clearing his throat and holding up his hand in a cautionary manner.

"Your friend does have a point, Jason. While encouraging as it is to see your skill of your powers progress so well, this may not be the ideal venue to test the intensity of flame manipulation you can reach. As good-intentioned as your efforts may be, I feel it wise to use heightened caution."

Jason huffed a dramatic sigh like a child who was just told, "no," pressing his hands together, which made it appear as if he were crushing the fireball into a smaller size. He did this until his palms pressed together and the fire was gone, his hands and eyes returning to normal, and the only evidence of his abilities was a thin trail of smoke emanating from between his hands. Corbin heard Brent let out a quiet sigh of relief and could see the same amount of relief on Alex's face. He just laughed to himself, finding humor in his friends' discomfort but then wondering why it was that he didn't seem to be as worried. Did he trust Jason more than Brent and Alex did? He did know him better than the two of them by the grace of their living and working situation. Maybe he wasn't quite as concerned because part of him was aware that his powers made him, as far as he knew, impervious to physical harm. Well, not necessarily impervious; he did get hurt, but he just healed from it.

"On that thought, Corbin," Uniz started, "Will you please replace your friend up here and demonstrate what you are capable of? If you do not object, perhaps it would be a good idea to replicate what you were able to do last time with this... tractor, you call it?"

Corbin cleared his throat and stepped forward, Jason stepping back to where Corbin had been standing next to Alex and Brent. Uniz smiled in a kindly, fatherly manner as he stepped aside and gestured towards the tractor a few feet behind him. Taking a few more steps forward, Corbin rubbed his palms together, blowing out air in a long sigh, cheeks bulging out slightly as he did so. He started to think about his powers, and what he felt whenever he was able to use them.

'*Okay, buddy, you can do this,*' he thought to himself as he stepped closer to the tractor, within arm's reach of it. How did he usually feel when he was able to use his strength? He thought about when Jason had ticked him off, when Fizer had nearly shot him through the door, and then again when he goaded him on at the jail. '*Great, so I'm just an angry rage monster inside,*' he said in his mind, feeling a little embarrassed that his powers seemed to be associated with the grownup version of him throwing a tantrum. Pressing his fist against the side of the tractor, he tried to concentrate on the same feelings of anger that he felt in all the instances he had considered, already feeling his muscles tightening, poised to strike.

Chapter Thirteen

Corbin wasn't sure what he noticed first; the searing hot yellow bolts blasting through the barn doors and barely missing him and his friends or the strange sound they made. His first thought was it sounded like something out of Star Wars. Instinctively, he leapt to the ground, covering his head and stealing glances towards Jason, Alex, Brent, and Uniz. Luckily, they all had the wherewithal to dive to the floor as well. Alex was ducked behind a metal workbench, Jason had Uniz pulled behind the bulk of the tractor, and Brent had managed to tuck himself behind one of the support columns for the barn. When the firing had stopped, Corbin noticed that there were scorch marks in the barn doors and all around the barn where these bolts had impacted, some of them smoking and some even smoldering with small flames.

"Unfortunately for you, class is dismissed," a voice called from outside.

The voice sounded vaguely familiar. There was a slight air of arrogance and mocking in his tone. Corbin shot Uniz a look and he simply nodded.

"*Fizer,*" Uniz told him telepathically.

Corbin uttered a continuous chain of curse words under his breath as he kept low and made his way over to where Jason and Uniz crouched at the rear of the tractor behind the seat and between the large back wheels. They shuffled over as he approached, making room for him in their already cramped little spot of cover between them and the barn doors. He crouched low and waved his hand toward Brent and Alex, getting their attention. He signaled to them to see if they were okay, to which they both responded with a silent acknowledgement that they were unharmed. Thankfully for Brent, he was slender enough that he was almost completely covered by the width of the column he hid behind.

"What? No welcoming embraces for your dear friend? I do have to say, your accommodations in your prison facility were far better than anything we offer those weaklings you have chosen to side with."

Corbin was starting to feel completely sure that he should have ended that guy when he had the chance. Maybe this would be the chance he hoped for. He could prove to Uniz that the power of the Marvel was effective in combat and off this pompous jerk all in one go. The idea greatly appealed to him.

"I advise caution, Corbin," Uniz stated telepathically. *"Overconfidence is a danger that even wielders of codename: Marvel have fallen victim to."*

"What do you want?!" Corbin shouted toward the barn doors. He considered the number of holes in them and decided that Fizer was definitely not alone. Okay, fine, that may complicate things a bit, but maybe he and Jason could make quick work of this if they were able to utilize the element of surprise. He didn't think they could know how many of them were inside, which was a blessing for Alex and Brent, seeing as they were even more unarmed than he and Jason were. Well, maybe. He got both of their attention and held up his hand as if he were holding an invisible pistol, gesturing with his pointer finger as if he were pulling the imaginary trigger. They both gave him an apologetic shrug. Damn.

"I have come to negotiate the terms of your surrender, the surrender of Uniz, and the surrender and dissolution of the Nazec Unified Military. Once these traitors have been apprehended and assimilated back into one, unified civilization, we can end this conflict between them and the Brotherhood of the Claw."

None of what Fizer said sounded right, especially based off what Uniz had already explained to him. Sure, every story had at least two sides to it; however, when Fizer's apparent paradigm was almost identical, but reversed, to the Nazecs, that is that the **Nazecs** were the traitors and Claw were the good guys, it threw up a few red flags in his mind. Furthermore, based on the evidence that had presented itself so far, such as Fizer trying to kill a

285

Russian diplomat, as well as himself and Jason, to say the least, and how it matched up to Uniz's explanation of attempts at global domination, it was pretty clear who was telling the truth and who was full of...well, yeah. Corbin felt somewhat disappointed in himself that he even had to take a moment to consider any of that.

"Surrender, my eye! How about you just turn yourself in? You, and whoever you have out there?!" Corbin shouted from behind the tractor wheel.

"Corbin, do you honestly think there is any possibility that I would surrender to you and your unarmed friends? What could you, Uniz, and your friend Jason do to us?" Fizer sounded almost mocking, and it really made Corbin's blood boil.

"Okay, so three of us, but how many do you have? Maybe this is more of an even fight than you think."

"Why not come out here, nice and slow, and we can discuss things face-to-face?"

"Why do I feel like that's a terrible idea?" Corbin challenged. "You don't honestly think we are going to just waltz on out there and trust you and your cronies won't pump us full of holes the moment you see us? I mean, you already tried to, lousy jerk."

There was a long pause, and Corbin had a distinct feeling Fizer was caught off guard by being called out on his lie; however, Uniz smiled amusedly and whispered to him, "Evidently, your colloquial turn of phrase confuses him as well."

Corbin stifled a laugh. Maybe he could use that to their advantage. If he could confuse Fizer with his slang long enough, he might be able to get a bit more information on what they were up against and formulate a game plan. He leaned close to Jason and whispered, "What do you think? If I can distract him long enough, do you think we could recon what they've got out there to know what kind of fighting chance we have?"

"Whatever will give me a chance to light this guy up," Jason answered with a hushed laugh.

"Cool, try to get up there and see through whatever opening you can get to while still being in cover and relay what you can see."

"You got it," Jason said with a nod, getting up into a crouched position.

"So, what is your definition of 'discuss,' Fizer? Considering the fact you assume like a dough-head that we are unarmed, and the fact that you are aliens, I'd guess that you'd like to beam us up back to your mothership and do some classic '50's-era probing and prodding and 'Take me to your leader,' stuff, huh?"

The long, heavy pause continued and Uniz continued to smile while Jason slowly made his way down the far side of the tractor, creeping towards the front wall where the doors were. The thought of thoroughly confusing Fizer with simple slang amused Corbin to the point that he almost snickered out loud as he watched his friend sneak forward.

"Gotta say, I hope you use lube with your probes and such. It would be my first time, and I don't want any hard feelings between us. However, I at least would have hoped that you'd take me out to dinner first."

The silence lingered and Jason managed to shuffle quietly up to one of the holes in the barn wall. He carefully peeked through it, holding up his hand behind him as he continued to glance out. He signaled the number five, then made a gesture like a gun, then pantomimed what looked like a vest on his torso before carefully ducking back and making his way back towards the tractor. Okay, so five of them, armed, wearing armor vests. This was going to be tricky. They had been in tricky situations before, but not without weapons. Well, they didn't have any *human* weapons, anyway. Guess this was as good a time as any to put the power of Codename: Marvel through its combat tests.

"Your stalling will do nothing to prolong your life if you do not wish to comply," Fizer threatened, sounding very impatient. "You give me what I want, and perhaps I will let you live."

"What kind of lousy negotiation offer is that? You can't offer me some donuts or something more appealing than the classic 'Maybe I'll let you live,' villain crap? You may need to watch a few more movies and brush up on all the stereotypical bad-guy garbage you're spewing here. Perhaps you could get some better ideas," Corbin called out mockingly.

He could almost *feel* the tension rise in the air, as if he could sense Fizer growing more and more impatient with his sarcasm. He remembered the level of arrogance he had displayed even as a prisoner in a jail cell, and he only wanted to poke the proverbial bear even more. Whatever Fizer was trying to accomplish, Corbin wasn't going to make it easy, and he was going to have a few laughs at his expense in the process. He struggled not to laugh currently, imagining Fizer struggling to comprehend what it was that he had just heard. He glanced over at Uniz, who wore an expression of confusion that Corbin would have expected.

Another pause, shorter this time. Corbin could hear Fizer draw in a long breath as if trying to remain calm. "Very well, perhaps there are some additional bargaining chips that can be introduced to the situation. I understand that not only were you foolish enough to bring the rest of your friends into this... shall we say, unfortunate situation, but to involve your significant other? A 'girlfriend' is the term you use?"

Corbin felt his heart sink into his stomach. The guilt of bringing Bree into this whole soon to be mess was churning in his gut. He knew better than what he had done, but it just felt right to tell her. He knew she was going to find out somehow anyway, because this entire scenario seemed to be spreading faster than he could have anticipated. He thought of her, how she looked, how she smelled, how she felt in his arms. He felt his muscles tighten, poised like a predator getting ready to strike its prey. He had felt this before, that primed feeling in his muscles as if they were ready to attack. It was one way when he was angry, but whenever he thought of Bree, it was almost as if those sensations were intensified. He remembered the same feeling in the Capitol when she had kissed him. Maybe he was onto something.

"Ah, I seem to have struck a sensitive subject, have I not?" Fizer mocked.

Corbin didn't reply. He looked around the barn, searching for something he could weaponize against their attackers. It was slim pickings, to say the least. Why couldn't whoever had owned or still owned this shack have kept some sharp objects in here? Jason appeared to be doing the same thing while Brent and Alex did their best to remain in cover. He peeked around the edge of the tractor towards the barn door, beams of sunlight streaming through the scorched holes in it. He couldn't make sense of anything outside the barn, so he couldn't even begin to guess where Fizer and his men were positioned other than somewhere on the other side of those holes.

"No quick-witted response for that, Mr. Kent?" Fizer's voice had recovered some of its arrogant tone.

'*Oh, I've got plenty of responses...*' Corbin thought to himself, looking in Alex's direction, trying to think of a way that he could ask if there was anything near him worth using as a weapon. Waving his hand at him to get his attention, it took several attempts before Alex noticed his motions in his periphery. He shrugged his shoulders to acknowledge he was watching, and Corbin gesticulated in a way to mimic a knife, and a bat, and even punched his fist into his palm in an effort to get Alex to look around for some kind of weapon. Alex, who looked completely befuddled at first, suddenly lit up and nodded silently, beginning to look around him, pantomiming a similar message to Brent, who appeared to understand faster than Alex had and started quietly surveying the area around him. Corbin looked back towards the barn doors, noticing that the sun had started to set, backlighting Fizer and his men, casting vague shadows against the barn. Corbin could now make out the approximate location of them, seeing that they stood shoulder to shoulder, Fizer no doubt in the center of the group. He looked back towards Alex and Brent, both of whom shrugged and looked apologetic.

"If you are finished with your futile stalling attempts, I would like to offer you a bargain: surrender yourselves and I will leave your precious *Breanne* unharmed," Fizer said, emphasizing Bree's name in a mocking tone.

"You better leave her alone, no matter what," Corbin warned through gritted teeth.

"Or what? Are you going to get angry? Well, I assure you that after I am finished with her, you are going to be far beyond anger, or any other useful human emotion you think could be helpful to you. In fact, I promise that you will do nothing but weep at her fate as I gladly slit your throat."

Corbin couldn't quite comprehend what happened next. Everything seemed to go into slow motion as the coiled, poised, ready-to-strike feeling in his muscles surged to such an intense level that he felt like he was on fire.

Jumping to his feet, he reared back and delivered a front kick to the tractor as if he were kicking down a door. There was a deafening crashing noise as the tractor buckled where he kicked it and slid forward with a force as if it had been launched from a catapult. Jason and Uniz scampered back as it hurtled forward, smashing through the front of the barn and rolling sideways when the tires caught in the thick gravel outside.

There were screams mixed with surprise, terror, and pain and a mushy sort of squishing and crunching noise that made Corbin's stomach churn a little. When the dust cleared, he could see a massive hole where the tractor had carried through the barn, a pair of rut marks where the tires had dragged through the soft dirt and gravel, and then a large yellow spatter mark on the ground. Fizer and his two remaining guards were getting up off the ground, having been able to jump out of the way of the flying farm equipment before it struck them. Two guards were obviously not as lucky, judging from that spatter mark, and what appeared to be pieces of them strewn about in the distance. The tractor had rolled for another hundred yards or so before tangling in a barbed wire fence and coming to a stop. Fizer dusted himself off, his expression one of alarm and anger mixed. Jason and Uniz struggled to their feet, brushing dirt and hay off their clothes as they did.

As if everything was still in slow motion, Corbin sprinted forward, his muscles carrying him faster than he could ever remember moving. He could hear Jason shouting something behind him, but everything sounded like it was far away and underwater. As he ran forward, he focused on the remaining pair of guards. They looked identical, wearing black coveralls and boots and wearing vests that looked like they were made of something that resembled thick plastic. As they saw him approaching, they scrambled to pick up and ready their weapons that looked like some kind of space-age version of an assault rifle.

Shifting to his left to avoid being shot, Corbin closed the distance between himself and the guard on the left, swinging a punch towards him with all his might. In this slowed-down state, everything looked like it blurred as it moved, and his arm was no different as it swung forward, his fist connecting with the center of the guard's chest. The vest he was wearing caved in under his fist and Corbin heard and felt a muffled crunching noise behind the armor. The guard let out an abbreviated grunt and crumpled to the ground, lifeless. His eyes remained open, and a stream of yellow blood leaked from the corner of his mouth.

The second guard had just enough time to react and swung his rifle, connecting solidly with the side of Corbin's face. The blow made him see a bright flash and his ears rang as his body was spun around and he landed hard on his face on the ground. As he tried to gain his composure, he struggled to his feet, a sense of foreboding growing in his mind, and he tried his best to turn around and face his attacker. His head was pounding, and he felt like he was trying to move his body through thick mud. He could feel his heartbeat behind his eyes as he saw the second guard seat his rifle into his shoulder and take aim at him. Corbin struggled to his feet and clenched his fists as he lunged forward to strike at the other guard. If he was going to die at this moment, he was going to make sure that Fizer and his surviving crony were going to have nightmares about him forever afterwards. If he had to, he was going to tear this guy limb from limb with his bare hands in his final moments.

The look on the guard's face showcased his fear as he raised his rifle and fired a shot, which went wide and struck Corbin in his left side. There was an excruciating, searing-hot pain in his ribs and the rest of his torso as the laser bolt struck him and made him stagger back a few steps. In his rage, Corbin hardly realized what had happened as he clutched his side with one hand, feeling the heat from the wound under his palm, and staggered forward, his other hand ready to land a blow against his attacker. His punch landed just forward of the guard's hand grasping the front of the rifle, and there was a startling scream as his fist broke the rifle into two pieces and shattered the guard's hand.

At that moment, there was another agonizing pain, white hot, emanating from his right shoulder now. Fizer had recovered the rifle of one of the guards who had been dispatched by the tractor and managed to take a shot at Corbin as he attacked the remaining guard. The shot had missed his head during his attack on the guard and hit him squarely in his shoulder, causing him to stagger back, tripping over the other guard and landing roughly on the ground on his back. His vision blurred slightly from the pain he felt from his wounds, and he struggled to focus on Fizer, who stepped past his injured comrade and aimed his rifle at Corbin's face.

"A noble effort, for sure, but not enough to save yourself, nor your friends," Fizer shamed.

Another scream and a flash of light interrupted what would have been Corbin's end as the guard he had injured suddenly burst into flames, running frantically around trying to extinguish himself. Fizer spun around to see what had happened and Corbin struggled away, his body already having healed, but the pain from the wounds still lingered and slowed his movement. He looked towards the barn and saw Jason stepping forward, cradling a basketball-sized sphere of fire between his palms. His eyes glowed the same fiery red-orange as the fireball and his expression was menacing. Uniz stood a short distance behind him, looking quite confident, flanked by Brent and Alex who had managed to find some lengths of what looked like pipe and were handling them like makeshift bats. The screaming from the burning guard had stopped and his lifeless body had dropped, smoldering and smoking on the ground several yards beyond where Fizer stood.

"It appears that the abilities of my friends were greatly underestimated," Uniz said with an air of smugness Corbin hadn't heard before.

"Evidently," Fizer sneered. "So where do we go from here?"

Corbin hurried to his feet, his body not aching quite as badly now. While Fizer's attention was on Jason and Uniz, he swung his leg as hard as he could, landing a powerful kick to the back of Fizer's leg just below his knee. There was a sickening crack and Fizer bellowed in pain as he fell to the ground, dropping the rifle he had. Corbin was quick to get it out of Fizer's reach and break it over his knee like a dry twig. Fizer lay sprawled on the ground, panting heavily from the pain of what looked to be an obviously shattered leg. Corbin *almost* felt bad, having only intended to sweep Fizer's leg out from under him. A large portion of his thoughts were gravitating towards stomping his head to a pulp like an old pumpkin; however, those thoughts were interrupted by Uniz's voice in his head.

"Calm yourself, Corbin. We have him subdued, perhaps there is a chance he will decide to negotiate."

"I highly doubt that" Corbin said aloud. "I can't imagine what use there would be in letting him live."

"Perhaps," Uniz responded telepathically as he tilted his head thoughtfully. *"However, we cannot guarantee that his death will force the Brotherhood of the Claw into surrender. With every organization there is succession, and I am confident that Claw is no different. Who is to say that whoever is Fizer's successor will not continue to try to carry out their cause?"*

As much as Corbin hated to admit it, Uniz was right. He would have given anything to end Fizer in the most brutal way possible, but there was no guarantee that ripping Fizer to pieces and sending his parts back to the rest of Claw would do anything other than really piss them off. And who could say whether the next guy to take his place wasn't going to be equally, if not more zealous towards getting rid of Corbin and his friends, as well as the rest of the planet? Unfortunately, for his vengeance-fueled mind at this moment, diplomacy was their best option. Letting out an aggravated sigh, Corbin straightened his stance, relaxing somewhat but still keeping his eye on the injured Fizer.

Uniz stepped forward, his hands characteristically clasped behind his back and speaking aloud. "Fizer, in exchange for your personal surrender, as well as that of those who are members of the Brotherhood of the Claw, I offer you and them the opportunity for a proper trial before a Nazec tribunal and sentencing according to personal crimes. Additionally, I offer you my word that the trials will be conducted fairly, devoid of any bias or prejudice," he paused for a moment, glancing at Corbin, who rolled his shoulders and flexed his arms, "which is far more than I am inclined to believe Corbin has to offer you."

Fizer looked from Uniz to Corbin and back to Uniz again. His expression was painful, obviously from his leg, but also defiant and unwavering, as if neither option were good enough for him to even consider. Corbin hoped he would choose to decline surrender. He clenched his fists, his knuckles cracking quietly, muffled under the cover of his biceps as he continued to fold his arms across his chest. Alex and Brent quietly padded the pipe they held into their open palms, showcasing their resolve to use them. Fizer looked towards them with a disgusted sneer before looking back to Uniz.

"I am so sure you are willing to extend the hand of friendship and forgiveness after all this time at war," Fizer grumbled sarcastically.

"Oh no, never did I say anything regarding friendship, or forgiveness," Uniz said with a slight chuckle. "You and your followers will be tried and **punished** for your crimes against the Nazec civilization, and for someone such as yourself, the outcome of that trial does not look hopeful."

"Pathetic," Fizer insulted. "Rather than waste your time getting to my inevitable end, why not just prove your resolve by just killing me now?"

"Unlike you and those whom you misled into following you, I endeavor to be the better individual. However, I could just leave you to those who obviously do not share my sentiment."

Corbin, Jason, Alex, and Brent all took a step forward, looking even more eager to put an end to Fizer, who looked around, appearing just as belligerent, but also displaying what appeared to be a bit of fear behind his eyes. Sure, it was one thing to be a defiant pile of crap towards Uniz; they had history. How much history that was, Corbin didn't know, but odds were that Fizer knew or was at least confident about what Uniz would really do, and what was all talk. Near as he could tell, Corbin and his friends were still essentially wild cards. They didn't have any real history, and what they did have, for all Fizer knew, was a moment when Jason had to keep his friend from going completely feral and punching his face through the back of his skull. Was he really willing to gamble the promise of safety and a fair trial against the potential to be brutalized by a handful of humans he had practically just met?

"Ah, but you assume that whatever choice I accept is one that I do peacefully?"

Corbin furrowed his brow. What was he talking about? He was alone, very injured, and very much outnumbered. He wasn't even armed, so what was his play here? Did he really think he stood a chance at anything other than being a prisoner of war, or a mangled piece of mincemeat? Corbin peered over at Uniz, who also looked somewhat puzzled, but was obviously doing a better job concealing it. Uniz stood still, the same position he always held, watching Fizer with unblinking eyes.

"Do you suppose that you have some other means to resist?" Uniz questioned.

Fizer laughed mockingly. "Resist? You apparently believe that I stand no possibility of escaping."

"Escape," Alex chuckled. "What, is he going to sprout wings out of his—"

"Probably not," Corbin interrupted, "but seriously, what upper hand do you possibly think you have?"

"Sometimes, it is not a matter of having an upper hand," Fizer grunted as he shifted on the ground, grasping at his injured leg. "It is simply having the element of surprise."

'Well, that doesn't sound good,' Corbin thought to himself. He quickly looked up to survey his friends and the surrounding area, finding only the abandoned farm and the carnage he helped scatter about. Nothing seemed out of the ordinary upon first inspection, but that didn't seem to put him at ease. Something was afoot, and he wanted to get to the bottom of it before anything bad...well, anything worse happened.

As he turned his attention back to Fizer, he was startled by a sudden, blinding flash of yellow light and a deafening "boom!" Blinded in that moment, Corbin felt himself being thrown backward as if he had been violently shoved in the chest. In his blindness and confusion, all he could do was brace himself as he hit the ground, the force of it knocking the wind out of him. In the seconds that followed, what could manage to think of doing was lie still and try to get his lungs to start breathing again. It was a difficult task, to say the least. He couldn't see, his ears were ringing loud enough that he couldn't hear anything else, and his lungs were still struggling to draw in air. On top of it all, his military instincts were in overdrive as his senses scrambled to gain a grasp of his surroundings and prepare to defend against another attack. It was no use, and Corbin had to resign himself to waiting for his sight and his hearing to return once his lungs started to function normally.

As his hearing began to recover, he noticed how silent it was around him, save for the soft sound of an evening breeze rustling the tall grass in the distance. As he sat up, his vision was still pretty blurry, but he could vaguely make out the dark outlines of four other figures spread out from each other about twenty feet away from where he sat. Shaking his head, hoping to rattle his eyesight back into focus, Corbin slowly moved from a seated position to one on his knees. Carefully, cautiously, he put one foot underneath himself, then the other, and slowly stood up, his eyesight still obscured. He could see the other figures stirring in his hazy view. Clearing his throat, which felt dry and atrophied, he called out hoarsely.

"Jason? Alex? Brent? What's your status?"

"Ugh, green," Jason groaned.

"Green," Brent answered with a gravelly voice.

"By definition, green," Alex started, "but I'm definitely feeling more like I should be dead."

"If," started Uniz, "green means that you are alive, I would voice the same status, Sergeant."

Corbin's eyes had recovered enough that he felt safe to start walking, even though his head felt like it was spinning, and his eyes were watering incessantly and felt like they were on fire. He got to Jason first, reaching down and grasping him by the wrist, pulling him to his feet. His eyes looked just as red and watery as Corbin's felt. They exchanged an affirming nod, wordlessly assuring each other that they were each okay. Corbin struggled over to Uniz, pulling him up by his elbow and helping steady himself on his feet.

"What just happened?" Corbin questioned, looking around for Fizer and finding no sign of him, "Where's Fizer?!"

Uniz looked around, appearing to be equally concerned. Apart from the five of them, they were alone. Only the damage from the fight, the yellow splatter on the ground, the wreckage of the tractor, and the old barn with a massive opening smashed through it, were signs that anyone else besides them had been here. Corbin started to get a little concerned that the noise from their fight might have alerted someone who may have contacted the police and wondered if it was even a good idea that they were still there, not like they had any kind of a choice up to that moment. Corbin couldn't hear any sirens in the distance, so maybe they had a little more time to recover and then get out of there.

"It appears that Fizer has deployed some sort of incapacitating device that allowed himself time to escape from us," Uniz said, tapping on something on his wrist that looked like a wristwatch with a glowing blue screen.

"Well, that seems pretty obvious, but what do we do now?" Brent asked.

"At this time, I must get back to my fleet and attempt to locate Fizer and his forces. Despite the fact that you have foiled his initial plan to ambush and destroy us, there is no telling what his next course of action may be. The Nazecs must be ready to respond," Uniz explained quickly.

"That's all well and good, but what are we supposed to do—" Jason stopped short when he saw that Uniz was now gone. "Aw, come on, what the hell?"

The sun had set between the time Fizer had done...well whatever he had done to them and now, and Corbin wasn't sure how long it had been that they had all been incapacitated. He took mental note of how he was feeling, and how each of his senses seemed to be functioning, and made a silent assessment of himself regarding his physical ability to drive everyone home. Aside from a growing headache, which was the least of his worries, he felt fit to get everyone out of there. He turned when he heard Jason's complaint, seeing immediately why he said it. Well, among the many things that Uniz could learn when it came to "human communication," it would be to give a proper farewell before he vanished into the ether.

"Come on, guys," Corbin said with a sigh. "Let's get out of here before we get caught in the middle of this mess."

The four of them swiftly made their way to Corbin's jeep and piled inside, Corbin quickly starting the engine and steering away from the farm as fast as he could. Thankfully, as they made their way back to base, they didn't run into any law enforcement en route to the farm and the guard at the gate to base wasn't paying enough attention to question the suspicious-looking holes melted through Corbin's shirt. He simply checked their military identification cards and waved them through as if they were the millionth vehicle he had dealt with while on duty, which may or may not have been the reality. Once they had parked at their barracks and before everyone climbed out of the vehicle, Corbin turned to his friends.

"I don't know what to think about all this, but I think it's safe to assume that things are going to be a lot more interesting from this point onward. Whatever happens, let's make sure we do everything we can to keep it contained to just our squad."

Jason, Alex, and Brent all nodded in the affirmative. They all exited Corbin's jeep and made their way inside, wearily returning to their rooms. On their way upstairs, Corbin sent a text message to Bree, letting her know that he was okay, and to call him first thing in the morning. He intended on keeping her in the loop as well. At this point, he felt like it was probably a good idea to keep her as close as possible as well. With Fizer knowing about her and what she knew meant that he would use her as leverage at any chance he could. He had already made it clear that he would in order to get to him. He didn't want to take any chances.

He and Jason trudged through the door of their barracks unit and shuffled through their empty kitchen area, (they had cleaned up their damaged table and gotten rid of it but were yet to find a replacement for it). Jason silently went into his bedroom and Corbin heard him flopping down onto his bed with a long sigh. Corbin did the same, not even bothering to kick off his boots. His head was still throbbing, both from the events of the evening and all the questions that were now swirling in his mind. Before he slipped into a deep but fitful sleep, he remembered considering how this all felt like the beginning of an escalation and wondering just what the future held in store for him, for Bree, and the rest of Charlie Three-Three and how they would stay ready for whatever unexpected things which were sure to come.

Chapter Fourteen

"It is a curious effect," Uniz stated thoughtfully as he, Corbin, Jason, and Bree walked casually through a public park in the center of the town just outside base. Corbin held Bree's hand tightly, as if he were afraid something bad would happen to her if he let go.

"What is?" Corbin asked, watching him with an eyebrow raised.

Uniz was silent for a moment, as if considering his explanation. "When we had originally tested the reaction of the powers of the Marvel in you, Corbin, it appeared that your emotional trigger was one of either anger or surprise."

"Yeah, getting angry always seemed to get the job done the best," Corbin agreed, feeling a little bashful at admitting that fact in front of Bree, once again thinking of himself as nothing more than someone who couldn't control their temper.

"Indeed. However, in retrospect to situations where your powers were made manifest, or leading up to those moments, it appears that there was a more powerful catalyst at play."

"And that is?"

Uniz stopped and everyone stopped along with him. The early evening heat and humidity stuck to them as they stood in what felt like stagnant, muggy air. At least while they were walking there was some semblance of a breeze that helped them feel a little cooler. Corbin's palm was sweaty against Bree's, their fingers still interlocked, but he refused to entertain the idea of letting go, even if it were to wipe his wet palm against his pant leg.

"You," Uniz responded, looking directly at Bree.

"Me? What do you mean? Do I make him more angry than normal?" Bree asked, somewhat in jest, but more for concern about her effect on Corbin.

"Quite the contrary, Breanne. It appears that his affections towards you augment the power of his abilities compared to any instance where he was simply angry or surprised. His innate protective instinct, especially for you, fuels his Marvel abilities to a greater level than I have previously witnessed."

Bree looked to Corbin with an affectionate expression, and he could make out the subtle sign of tears forming in her eyes. He smiled back at her and gently kissed her forehead, that being the only reaction he could think of in that moment. This revelation was a bit of a surprise to him, but at the same time, it wasn't. He did feel very strongly for her and had practically from the very moment they had met, but he had never thought that those feelings would positively affect the powers of alien technology. It all sounded outlandish to him, but then again, he had been feeling quite the bouts of "imposter syndrome" ever since they had investigated the Nazec crash site two months ago. Nevertheless, it had all happened, and he was still one of two human-holders of an alien weapon that gave him the ability of a superhero.

"In fact, the effects of the emotion of love are now a priority for the Nazec researchers who are responsible for the Marvel," Uniz announced.

"What about getting this thing out of us?" Jason asked, sounding a little tentative.

"Not to worry, we have been and continue to research a safe and effective way to remove the weapon in a way that will neither harm you, nor the Marvel itself."

"That's good to hear," Jason said with a sigh and an air of relief in his voice.

Corbin perked up, noticing a small but seemingly significant detail. "Wait a sec, you have been referring to it as just 'the Marvel.' What happened to the 'codename' part of it?"

Uniz shrugged a little and gave them a little smirk. "We have adjusted naming regarding the Marvel. Seeing that their abilities have been successful in combat, the culmination of the Marvel's development has been realized, and it is no longer a codename for a research campaign, but the name of a completed project. Our focus is now upon the next commissioned codename."

"And that is?" Corbin asked.

"Codename: Extraction."

About the Author

Christopher Kenner is a blue-collar worker who has dreamed of writing for over two decades. He is also a veteran of the Army National Guard and lifelong lover of science fiction, most especially Star Wars, Star Trek, and the Warhammer 40K universes. Before choosing a career as a pipefitter and plumber, he pursued studies in English with the hopes of making a living of writing. Despite the setbacks and redirections that life sent his way, he always maintained his desire to publish the books he had been writing since the ripe, old age of fourteen. Codename: Marvel is the first of a series of four he plans to publish. He, his wife, and their five children reside in Spanish Fork, Utah.

You can connect with me on:

🔗 https://www.instagram.com/bluecollar__author